Good Taste

Good Taste

CAROLINE SCOTT

A Novel in Search of Great Food

WILLIAM MORROW

An Imprint of HarperCollins*Publishers*

GOOD TASTE. Copyright © 2022 by Caroline Scott. All rights reserved.
Printed in the United States of America. No part of this book may be used
or reproduced in any manner whatsoever without written permission
except in the case of brief quotations embodied in critical articles
and reviews. For information, address HarperCollins Publishers,
195 Broadway, New York, NY 10007.

HarperCollins books may be purchased for educational, business,
or sales promotional use. For information, please email
the Special Markets Department at SPsales@harpercollins.com.

Published in Great Britain by Simon & Schuster UK Ltd. in 2022.

FIRST U.S. EDITION

Library of Congress Cataloging-in-Publication Data has been applied for.

ISBN 978-0-06-332581-4

23 24 25 26 27 LBC 5 4 3 2 1

HB 08 23 2023 0208

This one is for you, Mum.

With respectful apologies to Florence White
and Elizabeth Raffald.

"Of course it was French. What passes for cookery in England is an abomination (they agreed). It is putting cabbages in water. It is roasting meat till it is like leather. It is cutting off the delicious skins of vegetables."

VIRGINIA WOOLF,
To the Lighthouse (1927)

"We had the finest cookery in the world, but it had been nearly lost by neglect; a whole lifetime would not be sufficient for one person to rediscover it."

FLORENCE WHITE,
A Fire in the Kitchen (1938)

(Letter to the Editor, published in a number of newspapers, 1932)

TRADITIONAL ENGLISH RECIPES

Sir, Would any housewife in your region be kind enough to share a traditional recipe with which she may be acquainted? Many lines of verse have been devoted to the roast beef and plum pudding of olde England, but are you aware of other foods that are in peril of being forgotten? Is there a favorite pie made by your grandmother? A cake that you fondly recall from childhood? A dish that's particular to your village? Perhaps a great-aunt left you a handwritten book of her recipes? This knowledge and these flavors have been passed down to us through the generations. They are our inheritance, but in recent decades our food has been ravaged by war, the factory production line and the can opener. Our ancient know-how is in danger of being crushed out of existence by the steamroller of modern uniformity. Are we to let our old recipes die of neglect? Are we to turn our backs on our inheritance? Surely not! But an urgent effort is required to collect and catalog these dishes. If you are able to assist with this task, you would be doing a great service.

Please correspond with the address below. I will gratefully acknowledge all contributions.

STELLA DOUGLAS
(Author of *The Marvelous Mrs. Raffald*)

Celandine Cottage,
Bethesda Row, Hatherstall, Yorkshire

Chapter One

Hatherstall, West Riding of Yorkshire
November 1931

Josephine Baker had made him cry. Only, it wasn't really Josephine's fault. It was Stella who had made her father cry.

She had looked through the box of records and deliberately picked out a song that might lift the mood. As Josephine rhymed blue skies and bluebirds and the band played with brassy exuberance, Stella had found herself smiling. It brought back a memory of Paris, of dancing barefoot on a warm pavement, colliding with laughing strangers, and of the amusement in Michael's eyes. But when Stella turned away from the gramophone, she saw her father with his head in his hands.

"Daddy? What is it?"

She went to him and put her arms around him. Oh Lord, what had she done? This music made Stella think of stage lights in crowded cellar clubs and Rhum Saint-James cocktails in Montparnasse, but she was suddenly conscious of the minor key, and the lyrics were about being in love, weren't they? The song's sunny optimism now seemed garish—and interminable—as she felt her father's shoulders shake. It was too much, too soon, wasn't it? Should she be standing here, saying soothing words, or leaping to still the gramophone needle?

"I should stop it, shouldn't I?"

But then the trumpets had their last flare, the drummer hit his final beat, and the song was abruptly over. A door closed on Stella's memory of Paris, an over-bright light blinked out, and she felt both regret and relief at that. The record crackled as the turntable continued to rotate, a noise which seemed to emphasize the improbability of blue skies and underline the stillness of this room.

Stella squeezed her father's shoulder, walked to the gramophone and lifted the needle from the record. She looked out of the kitchen window at gray skies, at clouds heavy with rain slanting down on the horizon now (she imagined making the mark with a wet brush in watercolor), and the winter colors of the fields. She would paint this day in umber, sap green and Payne's gray. Hatherstall was blackthorn and hawthorn, bramble and bog-cotton, sooted brick and millstone grit. It was the Liberal Club and the Mechanics' Institute, chapel voices singing "Jerusalem," and the wrong kind of brass bands. At this moment, Paris felt so distant that it might just have been an image projected onto a wall by a magic lantern.

When she turned back to him, her father had sat himself up and taken out his handkerchief. "I'm sorry," he said. "What a bloody fool. What must you think of me?"

Stella returned to her chair at his side. There were tears on his cheeks as his eyes met hers and she wanted to stretch her fingertips out and gently wipe them away. There were new lines and shadows on his face too, she saw now, as she looked at him closely.

"No, it's my fault. I should have thought. Was it that you remembered her playing that record?"

Her mother would often have her father carry the gramophone into the kitchen and she'd put on Al Bowlly or Paul Whiteman as she worked here at this table. She liked the big sound of the American bands and knew the lyrics to Cole Porter and Irving Berlin songs. Stella couldn't recall that she'd ever heard her mother playing Josephine Baker, but did that record have a particular significance for her father?

He seemed to be making an effort to compose himself now. She heard him take a deep breath. He straightened his knife and fork, reminding Stella that their dinner would probably be burning in the oven, but it didn't matter. She put a hand over his.

"It just reminded me of what she was like," he said, looking down at the table. His fingers traced the grain of the wood and he shrugged his shoulders before he looked up. "Of how we were, of how it used to be."

Stella laced her fingers through her father's. She knew what he meant. They used to be a family who had music in the background, who practiced their Charleston steps in the kitchen, checking their reflections in the window, and who laughed a lot. In her mother's day, this room had always been full of music and laughter. Now, in the spaces between their words, it was silent and the atmosphere was heavy with her mother's absence.

"I understand. I'm sorry," Stella said.

Would they ever be a family who danced around the kitchen table again? At this moment, it seemed unlikely.

"I made my father cry today," Stella said. She was glad that she'd caught Michael before he left for the restaurant, but his voice on the telephone seemed dreadfully far away. "I thought it might be cheerful to have some music in the background, but it reminded him of my mother."

"Your poor father," his said. "He must miss her terribly still. And poor you too! How upsetting for you."

"I'm trying so hard—honestly, I am, Michael—but some days I can't seem to get anything right."

Stella wished that she could put her head on Michael's shoulder and tell him how the slightest thing upset her father now, how fragile he seemed to have become, and how sometimes they sat in long silences because she was frightened of saying the wrong words. There were days when they were irritable with each other and she felt tension knotting in her stomach. She longed to have a conversation that wasn't threaded with tripwires and, just briefly, to be able to tell someone how she was feeling. She wished she could have a face-to-face conversation with Michael, like they used to, both of them pulling their feet up onto his sofa, a direct, candid conversation that didn't have to be curtailed by him running off to his next shift at the restaurant.

"It's still early days, I suppose, isn't it?" he said. "How long has it been now—nearly twelve months? Is he looking after himself?"

"He puts a clean shirt on every day and he's keeping the house tidy, but he seems to be shrinking." Stella tried to juggle the telephone receiver as she poured herself a brandy. "When I walked in today it struck me that he looks like he's wearing someone else's clothes now. It's not just that he's lost weight, I'm sure that a couple of inches have disappeared from his height, and there's a gloss that's gone off him too."

Her mother had given him that, Stella realized, with her top-of-the-head kisses, her rich fruit cakes and her special smiles. Stella supposed that gloss was love. She wished that she could find a way to restore it, but all her well-intentioned gestures had seemed to misfire recently.

"Are you regretting moving out?" Michael asked. "Are you having second thoughts about taking on the cottage?"

Stella could hear the concern in his voice and was grateful for his understanding. Michael always understood. But with the crackle on the telephone line, her image of him seemed to slip out of focus.

"I had to get back to work and I thought it might do him good to try to establish a new routine. I don't know if it was the right thing to do, though. Every time I walk out of the door I ask myself that and I'm not sure of the answer. I'm only five minutes away, but perhaps it's five minutes too far?"

Did her father sit crying at the kitchen table when he was on his own? Did he often feel hollowed-out, as he'd told her he did today? Left on his own, might he do something foolish?

"I wish I was closer," said Michael. "I wish I could come up. I would, if I could."

"I know how busy you are."

"If I can get away before Christmas, I will."

"You'll be working around the clock. I remember what December is like."

She wasn't looking forward to Christmas, in truth, and wasn't sure that she ever would again. It would be the first Christmas without her mother. She'd been so frail on the last Christmas Day they'd had together. She'd hardly eaten anything, but had sat there in her new blouse with a brave smile on her face. Like a ghost at the table, that memory would always be there at Christmas now, wouldn't it? Stella did understand why her father had cried. On days like today, she found it difficult to come up with words that might make it better. But she had to keep on trying, didn't she?

"If I can, I'll come down to London for a few days in the new year. I'll have to see how my father is doing, but I'd so love to see you."

"Do. Please. I miss you, darling," Michael said.

"Let's speak again soon. I miss you too."

Stella caught her own reflection in the kitchen window as she put the telephone back on its cradle. She saw herself mirrored against the November colors of the garden.

Lucien's voice had been there in the background as Michael had rung off and she thought of them stepping out into the early-evening London streets now. She could picture the glimmer of the lights in the shop windows and the bustle of the crowds in their winter coats, all winding their way to theater seats and cinema screens and restaurant reservations. Stella missed all of that too. But when her father had dried his eyes, he'd kissed her hand and thanked her for being there. As she'd finally seen the corners of his mouth lift, she'd been glad she was there.

She was grateful that she could talk to Michael—she couldn't confide these feelings to anyone else—but she missed seeing the signs of understanding on his face as they sat together on his sofa, and having him put his arm around her. He often said that he missed her when they spoke on the telephone, but did he miss her in quite the same way that she missed him? His life was so busy, so full, so high-speed, and then there was Lucien. Stella had begun to suspect that there might be some variance in their interpretation of the words "I miss you."

Chapter Two

When Stella had told Michael and Lucien that she'd moved into a property called Celandine Cottage, they had laughed at how twee it sounded and a particularly hideous garden gnome had arrived in the post the following week. Stella supposed they imagined inglenooks and mullioned windows, crooked quaintness and hollyhocks, but Bethesda Row was a terrace of old weavers' cottages, with smoke-blackened stonework and cellars that regularly flooded. What a fright they'd have if they saw her cracked kitchen sink, the rotting window frames and the bloom of mold on the pantry walls. When Stella thought of the bright, modern flat that she'd left behind in Pimlico—everything so comfortable and efficient—the contrast couldn't be greater. She wished that Michael could find the time to come up for a visit, but she imagined herself feeling some embarrassment as his eyes took in the corners where the drawing pins were holding up the wallpaper.

She leaned against the range and warmed her hands now. She'd been writing about modern gas ovens this week, with thermostatic controls and easy-to-clean enamel surfaces, but meanwhile she was cooking on a museum piece. If she had a reliable oven, she'd make *génoise* sponges and soufflés, Stella told herself, splendid things *en croute* and *en papillote*, raised pies and marvelous puddings. If her oven behaved itself, if everything didn't emerge from it covered in black smuts, she'd actually test the recipes she wrote. She pictured a sun-lit tabletop jostling with this impressive fare; instead, her kitchen table was presently the home of her typewriter. There were little balls of dust shifting underneath the keys, she'd noticed yesterday, and she couldn't remember when she'd last rolled pastry there. It wasn't good to be a cookery writer who didn't cook, Stella realized. She was well aware of that. Come to think of it, she hadn't done too much writing recently either. It was just so difficult to find the motivation at the moment.

Stella filled the teapot and stood with her hands around it. Celandine Cottage was altogether a mean little house, she considered, definitely not worth two pounds a week, and very possibly haunted. Mr. Outhwaite, her landlord, had openly told her that his father had passed away here and the property was still furnished with the old man's rugs and armchairs, all suspiciously stained and dinted and marked with tobacco burns. When Stella sat down, she settled into old Mr. Outhwaite's hollows, she ate off his plates, saw her reflection in his mirrors, and her clothes emerged from his drawers with a faintly sour smell. She was fortunate to have a bathroom—several of her neighbors still had outside privies—but there were handles on the walls and, for all of her efforts with white vinegar, she couldn't get rid of the gray limescale ring in the bathtub. She'd once woken in the night and thought that she'd seen old Mr. O standing at the end of her bed, a wheezing shape in a rumpled nightshirt. In the morning she'd told herself that it had been just a dream, merely her overactive imagination, but had it been? Did old Mr. Outhwaite resent her being here? Stella did want to believe in an afterlife—she clung to the idea of being able to see her mother's face again—but Outhwaite Senior wouldn't have been her first choice of ambassador from the other side.

She could smell old Mr. O as she stepped into the front room now, a faint but distinct whiff of pipe tobacco, wintergreen and long-unlaundered underclothes. Stella had taken to exorcizing him with lavender pomanders, pots of hyacinths, sprays of Mitsouko and gardenia-scented candles. She lit one now and a cigarette for good measure. Didn't they puff smoke at bees to keep them in abeyance? Might it work on the ghosts of unwashed old men too?

It was perishingly cold in here. She tried to stir the fire back into life with the poker, but smoke billowed into the room and she had to open a window. Stella hugged her hot-water bottle on her knee and cradled her teacup in her hands. What would people think of her, sitting here huddled in one of her mother's old jumpers? In London, Stella had been known for her bold prints, her daring taste in hats and her *joie de vivre*, friends told her that, but had she even remembered to put lipstick on this morning?

If this property was her own, she'd throw out all the

shabby, sticky furniture she contemplated now. It would give her pleasure to make a bonfire of it in the garden, to pull up the carpets, whitewash the walls and scrub the floorboards. She often liked to think what she might do to the cottage if it were actually hers and she had the money to remodel it. She spent evenings hanging hypothetical curtains, choosing paint colors and Hepplewhite chairs. It was pleasurable to ponder how one might spend imaginary money. But if she had the option, would she really stay here? Wouldn't she go back to London?

Calderdale was the wet watercolors of her girlhood, all ink and earth colors. This village was old stones stained green, crow caw and lapwing cry, the smell of coal fires and leaf mold, sodden moors on the skyline, and factory chimneys in the valley below. It was a place where the past always seemed to be looming darkly over the present, a landscape of ghost stories and standing stones, massive with forgotten meaning, a difficult silence hanging around the cenotaph, and the Roman roads over the moors shining like lead in the rain. It wasn't that Stella disliked Hatherstall—it was a fundamental part of who she was and always would be, she knew that— but she longed for lighter skies, brighter conversations and bed sheets that didn't always feel slightly damp.

She sat up in her chair now and pulled the handbrake on this chain of thought. Such thoughts did no good, she told herself in her most sensible magazine columnist's voice. Instead, she deliberately refocused her attention on the patterns of the Chinese shawls that she'd picked up in an antiques shop yesterday, their peonies, pagodas and birds with fantastical tail feathers. (The blue-green silk was the precise color of Michael's eyes, but she shouldn't linger on that observation.) They were just the thing to hide Mr. Outhwaite's upholstery, bringing a quirky, artistic touch to the room, and hadn't the man in the shop mentioned that he might be able to source some Kashmiri-embroidered cushions too? Stella reminded herself that sometimes in life one just has to throw an interesting textile over inconvenient realities, put on a red lipstick, take a deep breath and look forward.

Chapter Three

Stella looked at the newspaper spread on the table, the pressed-glass sugar bowl, the sauce bottles and her father's reading glasses, and thought it might make an eloquent little composition in pastel crayons. She remembered how he used to like to set the table for breakfast before he went to bed at night, smoothing a clean tablecloth and putting the cutlery out. It had been a point of pride to him to lay an orderly table for the morning. What would her mother think of him setting his knife and fork out on a sheet of newspaper now? Was the world full of widowed men eating on their own over yesterday's headlines?

"Would you like me to mix up some mustard?" she asked, as she placed the pie down. She'd gone to the trouble of decorating the crust with a glazed pattern of pastry leaves (and pick off the smuts), and there wasn't anything here that might move him to tears, was there? Stella couldn't recall that her mother had been especially noted for her pork pies.

"That was a kind thought. And I promise not to cry over it. I owe you an apology for Saturday."

"Don't be silly." Stella put her arms around him. "Apologizing is the last thing you need to do."

"No, I upset you. What must you have thought of me? I felt ashamed of myself after you'd left."

"You loved Mummy. You miss her. I do too. You shouldn't feel ashamed of that."

"I am a daft old fool."

Stella placed a kiss on his cheek before she sat down. He smelled of shaving soap and peppermints. "You're a lovely old fool, my old fool, and I wouldn't have you any other way."

She nodded her head as her father raised the teapot. The winter sun dappled the leaves of the geraniums on the window ledge behind him and she couldn't help but think of her mother taking cuttings with her mother-of-pearl-handled penknife. This room was all as it had been—the potted ferns and dangling spider plants, the enamel tea caddies and brass toasting forks, and the mantel clock chiming on the quarter hour—only her mother's absence now seemed to shadow everything. If she were here today, she'd be bustling around the table, buttering bread and complaining that her father had been mean with the tea leaves. It was too quiet in here now, too still. The silence seemed to be turned up to full volume and filled with static, like the crackling space between programs on the wireless. Stella found herself waiting for the clock to chime.

"I worry that you're lonely, Daddy." There, she'd said it. "You wouldn't like me to move back in with you, would you?"

"What, and have you under my feet all the time again? How can I be lonely when you're always here cadging a bacon sandwich?"

When he rolled his eyes she could tell that he was in better spirits today. He shook his head and spooned sugar into his tea. It would get easier with time, wouldn't it?

"I spoke to Michael on the telephone at the weekend. He asked to be remembered to you."

"That was kind of him." He passed her the milk jug. "He's a good lad, Michael. You could do far worse for yourself, you know."

"Daddy!" Where had that come from? "He's a friend. Platonic. Like brother and sister," she added for emphasis. "As you well know."

"Aye, your mother was my friend. It's best if you are friends. I don't say it applies in every marriage, but I reckon it helps."

"I don't think of Michael like that." Stella knew, as she said the words, that it wasn't *entirely* true. Occasionally, inadvertently, accidentally, she did succumb to a momentary lapse, but she'd learned to shake herself out of such thoughts. "Besides, he's far too busy to be interested in that sort of thing. He's working all hours at the restaurant." She decided not to attempt to explain the complication of Lucien to her father. She couldn't quite explain that one to herself.

"Are all young people obsessed with working these days? I can't remember that we were like that." He lifted his eyes to the window and looked like he might be searching back through memories. "We used to make the time to go for walks and go to dances. We did courting, went on day trips and had conversations. There should be more to life than work."

"And when did you last take a day away from the farm? You've got no room to lecture anyone on working too hard."

"That's different."

"Is it?"

After the funeral, friends had asked her father if he might consider selling the farm. He'd given these suggestions short shrift, and had been determined not to let things slide, but was his heart still in it? He moved like his back hurt these days, and he'd needed help when it had snowed last month. Stella had driven over, but it had taken them hours to get the sheep in and they'd both been soaked through. There were times when their conversations seemed to be nothing but foot rot, intestinal parasites and declining prices, and she knew that he'd been struggling to balance the books for the past year. Stella remembered newborn lambs placed in front of the fire here, the smell of them, the wobbling bleat of their voices, and her mother smiling as she held a baby's bottle to their eager mouths. Her mother had stayed up all hours when it was lambing time. She'd helped with the shearing, the trips to market, and her parents had shared the day-to-day cycle of feeding, mending fences and worrying over veterinarians' bills. It wasn't just grief that was deepening the lines around her father's eyes, was it? Was he coping? Her conscience told her that she ought to be here helping him. But hadn't her mother always said that she must hold fast to her own ambitions?

"Talking of working too hard, are you still slogging at the coalface of literature?" her father asked.

"Not so much recently."

Stella had launched into her new book with enthusiasm, but had somewhat lost her head of steam. It was difficult to sustain momentum when she had to worry about her father eating his greens and remembering to close the gates, and the sales figures of her last book didn't exactly inspire confidence. Stella hadn't told her father that *The Marvelous Mrs. Raffald* had sold less than five hundred copies.

"Who is this new one about again? I know you've told me more than once, but I keep forgetting the woman's name."

That wasn't the best sign. "It's a biography of Hannah Glasse. She wrote the best-selling cookery book of the eighteenth century."

"Have you ever thought of writing about a person who the general public have actually heard of?"

"They ought to have heard of Hannah Glasse. She's much admired by other cooks. She published the first recipe for Yorkshire pudding, you know, but she ended up in a prison for bankrupts. Her life story is like the plot of a Dickens novel."

"Perhaps it's just me, then? You know your mother would be proud of you, don't you?"

"Do you think so?" It mattered that he said that.

"I do."

Her father had pushed a pound note into her hand as they'd parted on the doorstep. Stella had stocked up on flour and butter at the Co-op, dried fruit, sugar, soap, matches and tea. It was a slight extravagance that she also bought a bottle of gin, and a piece of brisket from the butcher's, she knew that, but it was good to frequent the local tradespeople, to be seen to be passing the time of day in one's Astrakhan coat, and to have a little motivating luxury. The wheels must be greased, after all.

When she got home she decided to bake herself a curd tart. She took pleasure in making an enriched pastry and lining the tart case tidily. She turned on the wireless set while she waited for the pastry case to bake, sipped a gin-and-vermouth and the kitchen smelled of hot baking beans. Hannah Glasse had a recipe for a curd tart, didn't she? Didn't it include crushed macaroons and orange-flower water? And couldn't she write an interesting piece about the evolution of cheesecakes?

Grating lemon peel and nutmeg into the curds, Stella sang along to a ludicrously jolly Noël Coward song that required a lot of farmyard animal noises. But then she saw her mother's face smiling as she held the bottle for the lambs, and a shock of love and loss jolted a sudden pain in Stella's chest. Like a physical blow, it took all the breath out of her lungs, and she had to sit down at the table. Would this get better too? With time, would these rushes of awful realization stop coming? She sat still, concentrating on the rhythm of her breath until the world stilled again, a world without her mother in it, and the audience applauded obliviously on the radiogram.

Chapter Four

There's a particular effusive but slightly bossy voice that one must adopt when writing for a women's magazine. Stella didn't find it especially difficult to switch into the finger-wagging mode, but the breathless fulsomeness was harder to pull off these days. Living in London, where the shops were always full of new and exciting products, one could enthuse over vegetable-processing devices and the latest cheese being imported from Italy. She still had the requisite alliteration and the compound adjectives off pat, but some days, as she listened to the Hatherstall voices around her, Stella felt like an actress prattling out a script, and was no longer certain that she was convincing the audience.

Today she was writing an article about smoking kippers. In last week's piece she'd constructed a smoke box, prepared oak chips and filleted herrings. Her magazine persona was now removing lines of bronzed kippers from the box and making plans to eat them with the wholemeal bread that was presently proving in her kitchen. Stella had consulted books on kipper mechanics, so she knew that her advice was correct, even if she hadn't actually tried it out herself.

Beyond her reviews of labor-saving devices and musings on modern culinary trends, Stella was also required to come up with five new recipes for *Today's Woman Magazine* every week. She was always on the lookout for ideas for fork luncheons and after-the-theater suppers, for sherry-party nibbles and picnic portables. Today, extending from the smoked-fish theme, she typed out recipes for a kipper quiche, a potted sprat, a smoked haddock soufflé omelette, a soused-herring salad and a cleansing lemon mousse. The mere thought of it gave her a hiccup of indigestion. Stella concluded her article with tips for keeping table salt running smoothly, removing stains from sinks, and reviving parsley. She made up the word count with some homemade heartburn remedies, and there, the thing was done.

She sat back and lit a cigarette. Developing the recipes had once been her favorite part of writing the column. She used to go around the London markets and then cook up dishes with Michael. It had been great fun, working recipes out together and trying to give them suitably glamorous-sounding names. (It was a running in-joke that at least one of her weekly recipes had to sound slightly risqué.) But the market up here in Hatherstall was all sprouts, swedes and boiled beetroot in vinegar, and it was very difficult to be glamorous or remotely risqué about that. Hatherstall market had never seen an artichoke or an aubergine. She knew people here who still regarded tomatoes with suspicion.

Stella daydreamed about Continental delicatessen stores and the scent of ripe tomatoes. She and Michael had liked to go to Covent Garden and Billingsgate together, to Fortnum & Mason, and to the little foreign grocers' shops around Golders Green, Soho and Camden Town. She'd loved to see the sacks of pistachio nuts and the jars of crystallized ginger, the bottles of orange-flower water and distillations of rose petals, suggestive of the flavors of dishes from *The Arabian Nights*, the barrels of pickled herrings and the sides of salt beef. Together they enjoyed talking about what they might do with the star anise and the brined green peppercorns, the tarragon vinegar and the bottled bilberries. People had sometimes given Stella questioning looks when she took her sketchpad to the markets, but there was a pleasure in trying to capture the textures of the piled oranges and peaches and the glimmer of mackerel scales. Some of the stallholders told her that she ought to buy the produce if she wanted to draw it, as if her sketching devalued it in some way, as if she had bruised the fruit just by looking, but others would occasionally throw an apple and a smile in her direction. Sometimes, when they did so, she would give them her sketch. That life, those images, those flavors, seemed like a foreign country to her now.

There was a certain glamour in being a food writer in London, she used to like telling people that was her trade, but it had all seemed to become rather mundane over the past year, and Stella couldn't help wishing for something more. Potted sprats and simulated kipper smoking was as stimulating as it got these days. It wasn't that she wanted to be a hair-shirt intellectual, or a writer who doggedly pursued injustice, but was expertise in vol-au-vents as much journalistic acclaim as she would ever attain? Hearing the postman at the door, she was glad to break away from dwindling ambitions and the dubious allure of a kipper quiche.

Looking down at the envelopes on her doormat, Stella instantly recognized Fleet, Everard & Frobisher's embossed Basildon Bond. She had been expecting a royalty check, but just how bad would this one be? Stella had been passionate about her biography of Elizabeth Raffald and, in truth, couldn't understand why the book-buying public weren't similarly enthused. She'd given Mrs. Raffald the spirit of a bold female lead in a picaresque novel, overcoming an unpromising start and the restrictions of her sex and of eighteenth-century society to become a celebrated business woman and cookery writer. There ought to be statues of Elizabeth Raffald, Stella felt, a Hollywood film of her life (could Joan Crawford pull it off in a powdered wig?), and young girls should be taught about this indefatigable woman in schools. But, seemingly, the reading public were underwhelmed by Mrs. Raffald's marvelousness. How could that be?

Stella added a slug of rum to her tea before she opened the envelope. It wasn't yet ten o'clock, but didn't soldiers have a stiffener before they went over the top? More than anything, she didn't want to disappoint her editor, Mr. Williamson. When *Mrs. Raffald* had first been published, he'd said he had confidence in it, and had advised Stella that she must push on with her next project. Did he now feel that his confidence had been misplaced? She supposed that the figure on this check would tell her.

The envelope did indeed contain a check, but the amount was even more embarrassing than she'd feared. As she blinked at the figure, she imagined Mr. Williamson's confidence wilting. This check wouldn't cover a week's rent, but, more than that, she worried about what Mr. Williamson had to say. Stella took a mouthful of her tea. She'd put rather a lot of rum in it. Thus fortified, she unfolded the enclosed letter.

Could we arrange a meeting? Mr. Williamson wrote. *Would you be free to come down to London before Christmas? I think it's perhaps time that we had a little chat.*

Stella couldn't help feeling that the phrase "little chat" was like gift-wrapping a scythe. Would *Mrs. Raffald* be remaindered? Might she be pulped? It seemed like an awful indignity. Stella could sense that Mrs. Raffald was frowning at her, perhaps even shaking her head. She had let this excellent woman down. Stella knew that if she were a character in a modern novel this moment would count as A Crisis. If this was a scene in a radio play the orchestra's string section would now be swelling in a minor key.

But in modern novels, the heroine isn't obliged to have a conversation with her Weekly Help in the middle of her moment of crisis. Stella could hear Mrs. Pendlebury putting the vacuum cleaner away and so tried to look busy with her papers. The narrative arcs of real life are so much bumpier than they are in fiction, she mused.

"All done, Miss Douglas." Mrs. P put her head around the kitchen door. She was a formidable woman of indeterminable age, with steel-gray hair and a fondness for bouclé tweed. Stella had a vague recollection that Mr. Pendlebury (now deceased) had had something to do with cattle feeds.

"Thank you." Stella rose from the table. "I do appreciate it. I've got such an awful lot of work on at the moment and I am glad of your help."

"Not at all. I see the way you hammer out those pages. I said to Mrs. Hughes, the noise of the typewriter never stops! Poor Miss Douglas, she's wearing her fingers out!"

Of course, Mrs. Pendlebury would have discussed Stella's typing with Mrs. Hughes. She'd probably discussed the contents of her kitchen cupboards and her bathroom cabinet too. Stella was well aware that she was being inspected by Mrs. Pendlebury on Friday mornings and that her findings would be broadcast across Hatherstall. But, on occasion, Mrs. P's transmitters could be favorably manipulated.

"Same time next week, then?"

"Actually, I'll probably have to go down to London for a meeting with my publisher next week, so perhaps we might skip until the Friday after? If that's not inconvenient?"

"Of course, dear."

Stella waved Mrs. Pendlebury off at the door. Sometimes she pretended to work while Mrs. P was cleaning. She'd just clatter out shopping lists, letters to Michael, and whatever came into her head. Stella was conscious of wanting Mrs. Pendlebury to see her as diligent. She knew, given her present accommodation, that she couldn't pull off Successful Writer, but at least she might look like she was trying hard.

Moving back up to Hatherstall had made Stella conscious of how impressions mattered. She wouldn't have dreamed of stepping out of her door without lipstick and an appropriate hat. The good folk of Hatherstall might be aware that she was still sitting on old Mrs. Outhwaite's upholstery, but no one must know how she worried about her sales figures and the price of Tio Pepe. Just occasionally, as now, Stella longed to be able to whisper her worries to someone, to let her guard down and to hear words of sympathy and advice. She'd be able to talk to Michael when she went down to London, though, wouldn't she? She must telephone him tonight and ask if she might stay in the flat.

Stella turned and looked at her typewriter. The figure on the check and the summons to London meant that there wouldn't be a second book, didn't it? It was time to put those aspirations aside. She was a woman who wrote a popular magazine column, who was financially independent (just about) and understood the use of the subjunctive, and that was reason enough to hold her chin up, wasn't it? Hannah Glasse wouldn't happen now, Stella realized that, and she must let those ambitions go. She would adjust herself to that, but at this moment it smarted.

Stella composed a melancholy little lunch from a reheated dollop of leftover macaroni cheese and two wizened carrots grated into a vinaigrette. The lettuce was beyond reviving. She made a pot of tea afterward, ate a handful of dried apricots, and reflected that no man would exist like this. Certainly no man who wrote about food would accept it. A man would have to have meat, a sauce, and to conclude with brandy. It's rather depressing how women cheapskate themselves, Stella thought, how we make do with a wizened carrot. She could write an article about that, she contemplated—but maybe this window into her personal life ought to be kept discreetly curtained?

Chapter Five

"Could I borrow a cigarette?" Stella asked on Dilys' doorstep.

Dilys McCready lived five doors down from Stella, and as Dilys had published two books on esoteric matters and wrote articles for a magazine called *The Other Side*, they had come to regard themselves as fellow jobbing penswomen. In some ways, Dilys was a model for the career that Stella didn't want, but there was sufficient overlap in their worlds that she might be able to offer some advice. Besides, Dilys' house was dependably full of alcohol and pleasingly soothing herbal cigarettes.

"You look perturbed," said Dilys. She gave Stella an evaluating look as she beckoned her in. Dilys was wearing a paisley dressing gown, fingerless gloves, a string of Egyptian beads and hiking socks, and Stella would have liked to reply that this ensemble was rather perturbing, but she bit her tongue instead.

"I've been summoned to London."

"Your publisher?"

She followed Dilys through the hallway, picking a passage between piles of newspaper, crates of bottles and the cats that circled around her ankles. "I have a feeling that I'm about to get my cards."

"Do you think? Seriously?"

"I do."

"But would that be the end of the world? It might to do you good to break out of the mold."

Dilys had a complicated relationship with the world of publishing, in the sense that she admired it when it was being earnest, but generally despised it when it was profitable. On occasion, the word prostitution had been voiced when she'd spoken of Stella's magazine work, but for the sake of alcohol and cigarettes, Stella chose to let these comments pass. Dilys' own books were published by an outfit in York, effectively a collective of friends who shared an interest in the folkloric, the supernatural and the vaguely occult. The Pentagon Press sounded a bit like a religious cult, Stella thought, and she sometimes feared that Dilys might be on a mission to recruit her.

"Not the end of the world, perhaps, but if it happens—and I think it will—I'll feel disappointed with myself."

"Disappointed? You must change your mindset, Stella. Think of it as a liberation, not a termination. Plus, I could always put a word in for you with the Pentagon."

And there it was again. Dilys' books never paid for themselves, she freely admitted as much, but she shrugged at this fact as if it wasn't quite the point. *The Ghosts and Folklore of West Riding* had thus far sold thirty-seven copies, Dilys had told Stella recently. That hadn't deterred her from pushing ahead with *More Ghosts and Folklore of West Riding*. Dilys had an educated accent and an oriental silver cigarette case, but never had any money in her purse. Stella hadn't yet fathomed the mystery of Dilys' finances. While she enjoyed holding forth on ley lines, sacred springs and the injustices inflicted on eighteenth-century agricultural laborers, she tended to be more reticent with personal history.

"Come through," Dilys went on ahead. "I've had my head in boggarts all day, a most interesting manifestation, so you mustn't mind the mess."

Stella might worry about the smell of old Mr. Outhwaite, but Dilys' house had a distinct pungent fragrance of incontinent elderly cats and fermenting homemade wines. She could taste it at the back of her throat now. Crowds of demijohns burped gently in the corners of Dilys' kitchen, bunches of herbs hung down from the ceiling and there were various pieces of ancient distilling apparatus that looked like they might once have been employed in the laboratory of an alchemist. Stella kept her eyes on these curiosities and averted her gaze from the unsavory-looking cat beds by the back door.

"You've cut your hair."

"I'll admit that it's shorter than I intended." Dilys tilted her chin from side to side as she examined her reflection in the window. Her long silver earrings glimmered. "Still, it will last."

"That shorter length is very much *à la mode*, I believe." But it wasn't all the same length, was it? Was the asymmetry intentional? It was a good inch longer on one side than the other. Stella dithered as to whether she ought to point this out. Dilys' dark hair fell into a natural shiny wave and it was a shame that she always insisted on cutting it herself with the kitchen scissors.

"A medicinal one?" She raised a glass that didn't appear to be altogether clean.

"Yes, please," said Stella, reminding herself of the antiseptic properties of alcohol. "What's your latest vintage?"

"I'm launching the dandelion, finally. It's been a long fermentation."

"Isn't the French for dandelion *pis-en-lit*? It doesn't, does it?"

"It is very cleansing for the system."

Dilys had made excellent walnut, damson and cowslip wines last year, and they'd got gleefully tipsy on her elder-flower champagne, but her experiments could be hit and miss. When she sold her wines in the weekly market, she decanted them into little bottles and applied inventive labels, promising cures for bronchitis, arthritis, insomnia and dyspepsia. Stella wasn't sure about the dyspepsia, but could see how they might give some relief from pain and sleeplessness. How might she label the dandelion, though? A purgative? A diuretic?

"Your good health," said Dilys, raising her glass.

"And yours."

Dandelion wine was surprisingly delicious, as it turned out. Stella had expected it to be bitter, like dandelion leaves in a salad, but it tasted of orange peel and raisins, a little like mead.

It could be marketed as bottled early-summer sunshine, Stella thought. Perhaps she could make her own homemade wines next year? If she wasn't working on another book, she'd have time to gather dandelions, wouldn't she? But that thought soured the taste of the wine in her mouth.

They took their glasses through to the front room and Dilys shooed cats from the sofa. Stella had tried to furnish her own sitting room to maximize the limited light from the small front windows, but Dilys had painted her walls deep purple and hung emerald-green curtains. The arrangement of brass candlesticks and antlers on the mantelpiece was suggestive of an altar and the numbers of fringed cushions and potted ferns seemed to be multiplying. There was a hint of the oriental opium den about this room, only damper and with more cat hair. Stella knew that Dilys took the cats up to bed with her at night and couldn't help wondering at the state of her sheets.

"I'm giving up on Hannah Glasse," she said. "They won't be interested in taking it and I'm not sure any other publisher would want it either."

Dilys seemed to give this some consideration. Or maybe she was evaluating the flavor of the dandelion wine. "If you're passionate about this project you shouldn't give up on it."

Stella supposed that passion must fuel Dilys' ghosts and folklore, but how did she pay her bills? You couldn't trade passion for water and rates, could you? Or, at least, not in any respectable sense.

"I'm starting to lose the passion for writing," Stella admitted. "I'm realizing that I need to adjust my expectations, to accept that vol-au-vents and fashions in table napkins is as stimulating as my career is going to get."

"Don't say that!"

Dilys took Stella's wrist, cocked her head to one side and appeared to be measuring her pulse. She had terribly dirty fingernails again. Stella always tried not to notice Dilys' hands, particularly when she insisted on gifting her a loaf of her homemade bread. She sometimes talked about how life had become unhealthily sterile these days, and said that it would do people good to see a bit of chicken shit on their eggs, but Stella wasn't entirely certain she agreed. It was curious how Dilys could be resolutely rustic in some areas and particular in others; Stella couldn't recall that she'd ever seen her without her pillar-box red lipstick.

"Is my body as ailing as my career? Should I take to my bed?"

"A purge might do you good. I'll mix a tonic for you."

"If I sprinkle it on my books, will it revive them too?"

Dilys creased her brow, but Stella did sincerely wish that she might revitalize *Mrs. Raffald*. Was there more that she might do to make the book sell? When it had first come out, Stella had put on a couple of dinners in London. She'd invited the old crowd from college and, assisted by Michael and Lucien, had cooked Mrs. Raffald's recipes for transmogrified pigeon and calves' head surprise. With everyone well lubricated with sherry, they'd all agreed that Mrs. Raffald was a hoot, and Stella had easily sold her stack of copies. Stella knew that the book might have done better had she still been living in London. There were journalists and influential hostesses who she could have invited for luncheons, and she might have taken baskets of Mrs. Raffald's fruitcake into bookshops. There was frustratingly little that she could do from up here in Hatherstall, but she had to be here still, didn't she? She needed to make sure that her father was eating three meals a day and that he had seven ironed shirts for the week. That was the reality of it. Anyway, it was probably too late to think about reviving *Mrs. Raffald* now.

"Do you want a Culpeper?" Dilys asked.

"I worried I might have to beg."

Dilys made her own cigarettes from a combination of mysterious greenery which she called Dr. Culpeper's Fancy Mix. She liked to maintain a mystery around her herbal blend, but there was something remarkably soothing about her cigarettes. They made one feel pleasantly woozy, and all worries seemed to waft away with their smoke. Stella thought that Dilys ought to market them, rather than writing books about holy wells, stone circles and ectoplasmic manifestations, but had never liked to say so lest she take offense.

"You're only supposing that you're going to get terminated, though, aren't you?" Dilys passed the cigarette lighter. She pursed her red lips and let out a long ribbon of smoke.

"I can't think why else my editor would want a meeting."

"I feel they might offer you a new contract." Dilys narrowed her eyes. "That's what I sense."

Dilys liked to tell people that she was psychic and was given to such pronouncements. She was also inclined to wear a quantity of amulets about her person, though, and Stella saw a contradiction here. As she watched the cigarette going to Dilys' mouth now, she noted the various crescent moons, scarabs and all-seeing-eyes that hung from chains around her neck. If one is psychic, if one knows what's coming, why the need for luck and protection? And why were people who claimed to be psychic not always betting on horses and selecting the winning tombola ticket?

"You do? Seriously? I can't see it myself."

"Would you be glad if they did?"

"Of course I would!"

"Well, perhaps you can convince them. Play the part. Sell your next book to them. Show them your passion."

Stella breathed in the Culpeper. She pulled the sweet smoke deep into her lungs. Whatever was in them, it was marvelous stuff. They really were better than Gold Flake. She pictured herself being assertive in Mr. Williamson's office. She would talk passionately about Hannah Glasse, about her trifle and piccalilli, her time in debtors' prison and her turn of phrase. Stella saw herself in a Worth plaid skirt-suit and a matching hat, wagging a manicured fingernail. Could she do that? Could she have that confidence? Her younger self could have done it. She must have her hair set this week, and press her best silk crêpe blouse. If she was to make an impassioned case, would Mr. Williamson listen? Could it yet be possible? Would Dilys let her have some Culpepers for the journey?

Chapter Six

Stella was thinking about hats as the train pulled out of Halifax. She'd seen a very nice velour hat trimmed in petersham, with an asymmetric brim, in a color that the shop called Lido Blue. Stella could imagine herself being assertive in Lido Blue, but she'd struggled to justify the expense; her felt cloche with the ostrich feather would have to do. She'd decided to wear her Liberty & Co. coat today, with the chinchilla collar and the fringe trim. It always made her feel rather *rive gauche* and there was something jaunty in the way that the fringed hems swished. Did erudite authors wear velvet lamé, though? Her black woolen overcoat would have suggested more gravitas, wouldn't it? But the train platform slipped away and she would just have to work the bohemian aesthetic.

Goods yards and factories blurred past and clouds reflected in canals. There were allotments, hen runs and corrugated-iron shacks, muddy cart tracks and sodden fields, and rain splattered against the glass. Stella watched the droplets stream and stretch, bending the colors of the clouds. It was a Turner sky, all elemental movement and washed with rain. It made her long for a box of watercolors—and wish that she'd remembered her umbrella.

The train went into a cutting and, refocusing, Stella glimpsed her own reflection in the glass. She saw a well-maintained woman of twenty-eight, with tidily waved light brown hair and carefully applied *maquillage*. She was good with lipstick and rouge, and really quite expert with an eyebrow pencil. She arched a brow experimentally at her own reflection now, but the attitude the look suggested didn't match how she was feeling inside. She had to maintain this mask today, though, must remember to refresh her lipstick and her smile, and not let her self-doubts show.

Stella shut her eyes, listened to the rhythm of the train over the tracks, and remembered the trepidation she'd felt when she'd first set out on this journey a decade ago. Her mother had talked to her about confidence as they'd waited on the platform, had told her that she'd earned her place at art college, and then had given her the fiercest embrace as they'd parted. Was her mother watching over her now, willing her on once again? Was she responsible for the rain clouds parting and the train running on time, and would she be there with Stella in Mr. Williamson's office? Remembering how passionately her mother had believed in her made Stella's eyes prick, but it also strengthened her resolve to be courageous today.

The train was busy this morning and she had found herself sharing a compartment with three commercial travelers in mackintoshes, an apologetic woman with a constantly fidgeting child, and an elderly nun. Stella had smiled as the nun had taken her seat (there is always reassurance in finding oneself sharing a railway carriage with a nun), but it was regrettable that the man who had then sat down opposite had decided to be chatty. Stella suspected that her fellow passengers would gladly have occupied themselves behind their newspapers, periodicals and books of prayer for the duration of the journey, but the man in herringbone tweed and brown shoes was determinedly and unrelentingly chatty. Stella hid behind her papers as the plays of George Bernard Shaw, various methods to alleviate symptoms of the common cold, and the extra-marital dealings of David Lloyd George were debated around her. But it was difficult to concentrate on Hannah Glasse when there must be talk of Sybil Thorndike, nasal douches, and improperness with a private secretary. (Surely not an appropriate topic for the ears of an elderly nun?)

"And you, shy young lady? Are you going down to town for a nice day around the shops?" Stella lowered her book and saw that Mr. Herringbone Tweed was addressing the question to her. The eyes of her fellow passengers now triangulated upon her too.

She hesitated. "No, I have a meeting with my publisher."

"You write? Oh, how delightful! Stories for ladies? Charming happily-ever-afters? Let me see—yes, I imagine you might write about beauties in crinolines and dashing but dastardly cavalry officers. I'm right, aren't I?"

He smiled at her as he said it. His eyes glittered with

enthusiasm for this version of Stella. He clearly didn't mean it as an insult, but . . .

"No, you've got it quite wrong. I write novels set in Russian prisons," she lied. "Lots of Bolshevism, syphilis and rats. I'd give you the titles, but they're really not everyone's cup of tea."

It briefly silenced Mr. Herringbone Tweed and for a moment the carriage seemed to be full of blinking eyes. Had she gone too far? (Should she have said syphilis in front of a nun?) It was her nerves that had made her say that, wasn't it? But she couldn't begin to explain that to a train compartment full of strangers. Stella buried her head in Hannah Glasse and felt her cheeks burning. Struggling to recover her focus, she seemed to spend much of the next hour repeatedly reading the same paragraph on syllabubs.

As the train approached London, Stella looked out at suburban gasworks, chimneypots and grimed attic windows, at limp lines of washing across cindered yards—slowing now—and slogans about soapflakes, Horlicks and Guinness on billboards. Opaline with white mist and yellow fog, London was an enchanted city, a place of infinite possibilities, endless rooflines and the gravestones of poets. The city ahead of her was a quicksilver curve of river, bristling with barges, and a ceaseless tide of passing faces—faces straight out of Hogarth engravings and Cecil Beaton's studio—each of them with their own secret stories. London was thousands of stories told in thousands of accents; it was the smell of slow-moving water, fried-fish shops and cosmetics counters;

it was the crescents of dirt under fingernails, neon lights and ancient darkness, fear and hope, and a future that she'd once hungered for. Stella saw domes and cranes on the skyline now; there were warehouses and tenements, signal gantries and church spires, so many criss-crossing railway tracks, and then it was all lost in steam.

For eight years London had been her home—her shared student bedsit, the boarding house in Bloomsbury and then her flat in Pimlico. There had been pennies in the gas meter, milk bottles on window ledges and stockings dripping over sinks; it wasn't all gallery openings and canapés, but there had always been new conversations and invitation cards on the mantelpiece. Looking back at that made the past eighteen months in Hatherstall seem very quiet, narrow and rather colorless. But stepping down from the train onto the platform, Stella was jostled by the push and shove, the speed and the noise of London, and suddenly felt that she was far from home.

She sat on the top deck of the omnibus and smoked a cigarette to calm her nerves. There'd been much talk of "belt tightening' on the wireless recently, about the looming shadow of income tax payments, and the need for prudence this Christmas, but none of that seemed to be going on in London. Stella looked down at the wet, shining streets and watched people hurrying with parcels and pausing to frown at lists. There were displays of hampers, tea caddies and fancy tins of biscuits in the windows of a department store, and everything was decked out with colored paper and baubles. Stella decided that London at Christmas was like a woman in a Norman Hartnell party dress; as some women become more intensely and confidently themselves in strong colors and prints, so London suits Christmas. The only odd note was the "Buy British" banner in every shop window. Walking from the omnibus stop, Stella passed a butcher's where little Union Jacks on cocktail sticks had been pushed into the balls of lard, and the mutton chops looked curiously demure tied with red, white and blue bows.

As Stella rounded the corner, the shiny brass doorplate of her publisher flashed like a warning light. She vaguely wished that she had a hipflask in her pocket, but she pulled up her chinchilla collar and took a deep breath instead. The frontage of the building was darkly Gothic with lots of lacy tracery and sooted trefoils. Grotesque gargoyles glowered down at Stella as she approached the door, and she wondered how many other slightly unsuccessful authors had looked up in trepidation. It was the architecture of a publisher which ought to publish Edgar Alan Poe or Sheridan le Fanu. Was this where Stella Douglas, famed for her vol-au-vents, belonged? Did she imagine the gargoyles shaking their heads?

"Good afternoon," she tried to sound more confident than she felt as she approached the girl on the reception desk. "I've got an appointment with Mr. Williamson."

The girl nodded at her name in the diary and asked her to take a seat. "Miss Salter will be here to meet you in just a minute."

The offices of Fleet, Everard & Frobisher smelled of leather and wax polish. The company seemed to be staffed by tremendously elderly men looking sleepy in wood-paneled offices, and by extremely young women very busy at typewriters, Stella observed, as she followed Miss Salter's well-tailored shoulders along a corridor. A tea trolley was going around and the young women were all talkative and bright. They looked impressively happy in their work, and Stella rather envied them for that. It would have been nice to linger and talk with the bright young women, but she was being led into the region of the mahogany-paneled men.

"How busy you all look to be."

"Oh, horrifically! It's bedlam in Biographies at the moment. I don't know how we're ever going to finish for Christmas."

Fleet, Everard & Frobisher published fiction of a self-consciously modern variety, poems written by librarians, illustrated books about moths and orchids, and the memoirs of recently retired generals. Mr. Williamson looked after the biographers and historians, and was disquietingly knowledgeable about all centuries and all regions. Stella's biography of Mrs. Raffald had been a bit of a departure for F, E & F; the only women who'd previously been deemed worthy of their own volume were Eleanor of Aquitaine, Queen Elizabeth and Catherine the Great, but this seemed to place Mrs. R in staunch and glittering company. When Stella had first met Mr. Williamson, he'd asked intelligent questions and had seemed passionate about her project. He'd been pleased with her proofs too. The edits had been minor and fairly painless, and he'd complimented Stella on the thoroughness of her research. He'd told her that he expected the book to do well and had been delighted by the reviews. Did he now feel disappointed too?

Miss Salter knocked on the door of the office and Stella saw Mr. Williamson looking up from the papers on his desk. She made an effort to put on her best smile, but felt it to be faltering at the corners.

"Would you bring us some tea, Miss Salter?" he asked. "And perhaps you might purloin some of those special ginger biscuits too?"

Heck, Stella thought, his expression was inscrutable. And why was she being given special ginger biscuits? Was this compensation for the difficult news that she was about to receive? A sweetening of the bitter pill? She breathed deeply and pushed her fingernails into her palms. She could do this, Stella told herself.

"Mr. Williamson," she said, and stretched out her hand. "How delightful to see you again."

He stood and smiled. "Miss Douglas. Always a pleasure."

As he took her hat and coat, Stella noticed that he had a copy of *Mrs. Raffald* on his desk, the pages multiply book-marked. What did that mean? Had she made mistakes? Were there things that he must now query? She hadn't expected that. Hell, should she have done homework for this meeting? She was relieved when he put the book aside now and said, "Quite charming."

"Oh, thank you." Stella took a seat, as instructed. Her emotions were up and down like a rollercoaster.

She saw that the sheet of paper on top of his pile was headed with her name. There were bullet points below, many of them terminating with a question mark, but his handwriting required studied decryption at the best of times and was entirely unintelligible upside down. Evidently, she was to be interrogated, though. Stella sat up in her seat, pulled her skirt down, and tried to look professional.

"I hope your journey wasn't too arduous?" He offered her a cigarette from the case on his desk and leaned toward her with the lighter. He lingered slightly longer than was necessary and she thought how his teeth were the color of old ivory piano keys. She'd forgotten that he always smelled faintly of mothballs.

"Pleasantly uneventful. I'm always glad to have an excuse to come down to London. It's a treat to see the shops before Christmas."

"I'm glad we haven't dragged you down against your will, only I thought it might be a good time to have a discussion about your next project."

Her next project? Did that mean there was to be one? She'd heard that right, hadn't she? "Excellent. Yes. I'd be most happy to discuss it."

Miss Salter knocked and came in with the tea tray. She took an awfully long time to pour the tea, lifting the spout of the teapot high and then lowering it, as if she was keen to demonstrate her waitressing proficiency. This was clearly a skill she had practiced, and her expression suggested she was confident it would impress, but couldn't she hurry up about it? Stella suddenly found herself keen to push on with the proposed discussion. Instead, they made small talk until the tea-pouring ceremony was concluded, and Stella noticed how Miss Salter smiled at Mr. Williamson. There was something most unexpected in that smile and it struck Stella. She had to look away for a moment. He was surely old enough to be her grandfather, but if Stella had been writing a romance she'd have made notes on the blush on Miss Salter's cheeks and the angle of her eyelashes.

"You must try these biscuits, Miss Douglas. Miss Salter gets them for me from a baker's in Golders Green. You see, I'm rather spoiled." Miss Salter was reversing out of the door with the tea tray, but not before they'd exchanged another of those looks. "They're the closest thing to Grasmere gingerbread that I've had in years. Are you familiar with it? Tasting these made me think of you and your projects."

He had used the plural, hadn't he? Stella smiled too now. This was safer territory. "I know it well. We used to have family trips to the Lakes when I was a child and my mother and I spent much time trying to analyze the particular flavor and texture of Grasmere gingerbread. It's frustratingly enigmatic, isn't it?"

"Another spice in there other than ginger, don't you think?"

Did he want her to write a book about gingerbread next? That might be jolly. "There's definitely crystallized ginger in there, and perhaps some candied peel?" Stella hadn't imagined that they might be debating the ingredients of gingerbread today. She might not have dreaded this meeting quite as much had she known this was the agenda. "I've read that powdered liquorice used to be added to gingerbread in the Middle Ages, but the conundrum is in the warmth of Grasmere gingerbread, isn't it? Ginger was used in potions to ward off the plague, you know, and the Romans believed it had aphrodisiac properties," she went on—but perhaps she shouldn't go on too far in this direction?

"Excellent," said Mr. Williamson. "That's just the ticket."

Was it? Stella had been fully prepared for him to tell her that this meeting would be the end of their relationship, but she sat a little taller in her seat now. Did Mr. Williamson still see potential in her? Had she misinterpreted the purpose of this meeting? Could Dilys really be psychic after all?

"Have you given much thought to what you want to write next?" He snapped a biscuit in two and nibbled pensively as he regarded her. She noticed him glancing at her legs, but in the circumstances, she could forgive him.

"I have," she replied, now feeling much more positive about her folder full of notes on Hannah Glasse's girlhood. "I've begun work on another biography. Hannah Glasse is better known than Mrs. Raffald. *The Art of Cookery* is still in print and the public might find her more accessible."

Mr. Williamson nodded, but his mouth seemed to be communicating something other than affirmation. What did that mean?

"I have been thinking that we ought to launch you on a more ambitious project."

"More ambitious?"

"Something broader, all-encompassing." He made a fulsome gesture with his hands.

"Mrs. Beeton?" she offered.

"I was thinking more of the whole shebang."

Whatever did he mean by that? Stella wasn't sure that Misses Raffald, Glasse and Beeton would have liked being grouped as a shebang. Was that an appropriate collective noun for cookery writers? "A history of eighteenth-century female cooks?"

"More like *all* history." He said it almost casually. "A history of English food—of what is particular and peculiar to our nation." He took a sip of his tea before he pressed on. "Why we've come to eat what we do and what it says about us. An examination of our favorite dishes and an explanation of where they've come from. That sort of thing, do you see?"

Making a brief mental list, Stella thought that many of the most popular dishes came from abroad, but perhaps this wasn't the time and place to share that observation. "Of all history?" she repeated. "The *whole* thing?"

"It is ambitious, yes, I appreciate that. But you're more than up to it." He gave her a look that demanded a nod in response. "I'm not talking about a PhD thesis; don't run it to three volumes and footnote every last line. Keep it light and panoramic, a sweep through our whys and wherefores.

I thought *How the English Eat* might be a pithy title. What do you think?"

Did he realize that in order to be light and sweeping one had to first probe all the detailed whys and wherefores? "I'm sure it could be done, that it could make an excellent book, but it would be a lot of work, a lot of research and travel," she said, thinking of the twenty-pound advance she'd been given for *Mrs. Raffald*. Twenty pounds wouldn't allow her to do much sweeping, would it? Still, Mr. Williamson was giving her another chance and, at this moment, she could rush around the desk and kiss him for that.

"It could do very well," he mused, stroking his side-whiskers, "if you keep it accessible and positive, and aim for a broad appeal. Think of the average woman in the street and what she might be keen to read."

"I understand." That woman would probably prefer a new Hercule Poirot, or another chunk of *The Forsyte Saga*, Stella thought, but didn't say it.

"With the right tone, it might hit a nerve. Zeitgeist, do you see? I think the market is ready for a book like this."

There seemed to be an emphasis on tone. She couldn't help feeling there might be a critique of *Mrs. Raffald* in these words. Was that why there seemed to be so many bookmarks in Mr. Williamson's copy? Were those the places where she'd got the tone wrong?

"Accessible and positive," she repeated.

"Quite. What we need is something uplifting. Think about what Cecil Sharp has done for folk song and what

Lady Gomme is doing for folk games. People are interested in the countryside and tradition just now, our old customs and ceremonies, and there's a chance for you to tap into that. Nostalgia is potent stuff and it's fashionable at the moment. See if you can't find some stories that remind us of ourselves at our best, that boost national pride. I know we're not presently regarded as one of the world's great cuisines, but why not? I know you can deliver that."

Stella nodded, but this task seemed to be getting larger by the moment. She stubbed her cigarette out in the ashtray and contemplated the corners of the ceiling. Was she meant to single-handedly restore national pride and the reputation of English cuisine now? Put alongside the folk songs and the folk games, it all sounded rather Merrie England, she thought. Ruddy-cheeked children in smocks skipped around maypoles in her mind (all of them fed on wholesome, home-grown food, of course) and mugs of cider were raised. Well, if that's what he wanted, that was what she'd give him.

"Celebratory, yes. Folk tradition. I do follow."

"I suspect you might have been disappointed with *Mrs. Raffald*'s sales, but a broader project will give her a push."

Oh dear. Must they talk about *Mrs. Raffald*'s sales figures? It had all been going so well. The accordion hit an off-note and the merrie dancers suddenly slumped around the maypole. "But I was delighted by the reviews," Stella urged.

"And I'm sure that the reviews of your next book will be even better. However, perhaps we can learn a little from *Mrs. Raffald*? I'd advise against footnotes with this one. I know you're a stickler for your sources, but I'd suggest that you should paint with a broader brush this time. Think about charming your reader. Bring in quaint anecdotes from farmhouse kitchens, picturesque characters, and lots of local color—you know the sort of thing. We'd be willing to offer you an advance of forty pounds for this one, on the under-standing that you'd be able to have a draft completed within twelve months."

Forty pounds? That was five months' rent, Stella quickly calculated, and twelve months in which she could call herself an author, focusing on a serious, scholarly project (even if it must have cheering and maypoles). "I'd be happy to accept those terms." She didn't dare haggle for more. She was aston-ished enough to be getting another project, never mind one with a forty-pound advance.

"Capital!"

Stella took another ginger biscuit with Mr. Williamson's encouragement. Possibilities seemed to be shifting around her and suddenly there was an adventure in prospect. She saw herself motoring around the country, visiting museums, archives and flour mills, rooting out stories about eels and stargazy pie. She pictured herself at the kitchen tables of ancient farmers' wives, listening to tales about feast days of yore, and being handed their grandmothers' handwritten recipe books. What fun it might be. But this would be an erudite book too, wouldn't it? A book with some intellectual heft? She could find serious things to say about Englishness, soups and sauces, and hold her chin up as she told people about her research. She imagined sober, learned faces nodding at her as she spoke of vellum manuscripts, lampreys and marchpanes. Would it be extravagant to buy a new hat?

Church bells seemed to be tolling all across London as Stella stepped back out onto the pavement: a Salvation Army band was playing in the street; there was a smell of chestnuts roasting and the twinkling lights were coming on in the shops. In a novel, gentle snowflakes would probably start to flicker down at this moment, but at least it had stopped raining. Stella looked up at the glowering gargoyles and grinned.

Chapter Seven

Stella treated herself to toasted teacakes in a Lyons' Corner House, bought a box of Turkish Delight for her father, and a bottle of gin on the way to Michael's flat.

"But I thought we were meant to be commiserating?" said Michael in the doorway. "We were all ready to do tea and sympathy. We were going to build up your reserves with a hearty stew and then comfort you with syllabub."

"I hope it's Mrs. Raffald's recipe?"

"Dare we attempt anything else?"

He smiled as he pulled her into a hug. His Fair Isle sweater smelled vaguely of fried onions and he'd sprouted a new moustache which tickled her cheek. She stepped back and looked at him.

"How heavenly it is to see you! But what's going on with the soup strainer? Are you trying for a Ronald Colman look?"

He rubbed at his top lip, giving Stella the impression that he perhaps hadn't yet fully committed to it. "Don't you like it?"

"I'm deliberating." She'd read that moustaches of the "Hollywood" variety, imparting a dashing or Spanish aspect, were being cultivated on the upper lips of Mayfair's gilded youths, but Stella always suspected facial hair might be a little unhygienic. "Actually, perhaps it's more Douglas Fairbanks than Ronald Colman. It would look better with thigh-high boots and the cavalier hat. Do you get to do much swash-buckling around Covent Garden?"

"Only on Friday nights. Come on up. Lucien's in the kitchen."

Michael's flat was on a slightly seedy street off Covent Garden and the entrance was up a linoleum-covered stair-case with scratches up the walls. He might have been able to afford somewhere nicer now, but it was convenient for the restaurant, he said. The sitting room was rather disorderly: the sofas were long overdue re-covering, the ashtrays needed emptying and there were discarded books and magazines scattered about everywhere. It was cozy with the electric fire on, though, and there was a comfort in seeing Michael's old paintings on the walls and all the familiar ornaments that had migrated from one property to another over the decade they'd been friends.

"It smells of Gauloises in here. Wherever do you find them in London?"

"Lucien has his uses." He winked as he took Stella's coat.

She and Michael had first been drawn together in a room where nothing had felt familiar. A grammar-school boy from Bradford, he'd been at the Slade on a scholarship, and their similar backgrounds had made them instant allies. He'd admitted to her in confidence that he'd grown up in an end-terrace house with worker bees in the stained glass of the fanlight and that his father managed a shoe shop in Bingley. There had been a joy in discovering the things they had in common, where their lives overlapped, and in those first few months of their friendship they'd often talked until the dawn light was creeping over the rooftops. He would jokingly curse her then as he rushed off to early shifts on markets and in hotel kitchens. Michael always had jobs on the side, and as she'd watched him sprint between them, Stella had thought about those stained-glass bees.

The pair of them had taken pleasure in discovering the London markets together, stretching their fingers out to touch the pineapples and pomegranates, sketching the stalls piled high with herrings and cockleshells, and holding clementines to their noses at Christmas, each fruit crackling in its wrapping of foreign lettering. But Michael had transitioned from sketching compositions of artichokes to having a job in a kitchen off Covent Garden. As well as composing still lives of vegetables, he had an aptitude for cooking them, as it turned out, and so he'd quickly been promoted from *plongeur* to *commis* to *entremétier*. He'd done longer and longer hours at The Oubliette, until he'd ended up dropping out of college altogether and working in the restaurant full-time.

Stella had envied him when he'd been offered the opportunity to work in France for a year. She'd traveled out and stayed with him for three months through the summer of 1925 and Paris had dazzled her. There was an exhilarating otherness to it all; the colors seemed brighter, the scents different, the voices louder, and the food all so unexpected. She and Michael had walked arm-in-arm through the Paris markets then, pointing at the piles of apricots and melons and the pink-tinted heads of new garlic, the bunches of mint, tarragon and basil, every shade of green in the palette, and the morning bells had clanged out from the churches all around.

It was three years now since Michael had moved back to London to take up the head chef's job at The Oubliette. Stella had been delighted for him when he'd written with this news; however, she'd been slightly surprised to read that Lucien, his flatmate, was moving to London with him. She'd asked herself—had she perhaps misunderstood the parameters of their friendship? When she'd lived with them she'd noticed how Lucien looked at Michael (how could she fail to notice?), but did it work both ways? Stella hadn't quite figured this out.

"*Ma poule!*" said Lucien, turning from the stove now. He planted *bises* on her cheeks and stood with his hands on her shoulders. "How delectable you look." Lucien's mother had been from Brighton, so he spoke perfect English, but he could occasionally be rather Gallic. Stella understood that flirtation was part of *politesse* in France, and didn't take it too seriously, especially since Lucien was inclined to address similar comments to Michael.

"You look rather sweaty, my sweet, but in extremely good health. How are you enjoying Le Chabròl? Michael told me you'd got the head chef's job. Are the pair of you fearfully competitive now?"

The lines of Lucien's face were more defined than they had been last time Stella had seen him, but his dark eyes sparkled with merriment, and he smelled most deliciously of beef daube.

"Absolutely. We're beastly to each other and never miss an opportunity for sabotage or slander."

"Do you spit in each other's soup?"

"Whenever we get the chance." There was a hint of mischief in Lucien's grin and Stella wasn't entirely convinced that he was joking. "Anyway, never mind about my news—has Michael told you his yet? The scoundrel has acquired a *woman*!"

"But . . ." Stella hesitated. What was this? She must tread carefully here, mustn't she? "A woman?" She turned and looked at Michael, who was leaning in the kitchen doorway. "In what capacity?"

"The conventional capacity." He smiled rather shyly.

"You should see the woman, though," Lucien went on. "Beyond her womanliness, there's nothing remotely conventional about her."

"How you gossip!" Michael protested.

"Stella loves it," Lucien said. "Look at her face. You can, at the very least, let us have some amusement at your expense."

"You'll have to tell me all the details now," said Stella. Had Lucien's flirtations been a red herring, then? Were they not reciprocated? She suddenly felt a little foolish. "Do we get to know the lucky lady's name?"

"Cynthia Palmer!" said Lucien and widened his eyes.

"You've heard of her, of course? You'll have seen her photograph in the picture papers."

"What, *the* Cynthia Palmer?" She looked at Michael. "CP from the Slade?"

"The very same," he said.

Cynthia had been a life model when Stella and Michael were at college. She'd been walking out with Harry Owen back then, Stella remembered, though her eyes always seemed to be touring the room for a better offer. Stella recalled being struck by Cynthia's voice the first time they'd spoken. While most of the models were London girls, Cynthia's accent was moneyed Home Counties. Rumor had it that she'd been estranged from her family since she'd run away with a circus strong man at seventeen. Cynthia fancied herself as an artist too, and although her Hercules had long since been traded in, she painted images of luridly lit circus tents, acrobats in implausible contortion, miserable-looking tigers and the crumbling face paint of clowns. In more recent years, Cynthia had made a name for herself as a celebrity beauty and the hostess of bohemian parties. She'd modeled for Lanvin and Patou, and was regularly photographed on the society pages in evening gowns, sables and sequinned headdresses. What did that flamboyant woman see in quiet, modest, earnest Michael? But then, perhaps it was simply the case that she'd noticed his sweet, shy smile and the excellence of his gratins too?

"But you *can't* go out with CP!" Stella remonstrated, half amused and half horrified. "You're from Yorkshire and have made a reputation for your vegetable dishes."

"And?" Michael crossed his arms over his chest. "Cynthia says I'm authentic. She says that so many of the people she meets these days are terribly bogus."

"Oh, Michael! Does she make you flatten your vowels and pretend you've worked a day down a coal mine?"

Lucien spluttered into a wineglass.

"Don't be nasty!"

Was she? Stella didn't want to be nasty to darling Michael. She was concerned for him. That was all. "Good Lord!" she said. "I'm seeing you in a whole new light. Is she nice to you?"

"Do you think I'd choose to spend time with her if she wasn't? Of course she's nice to me."

"I'm surprised she's your type." Somehow the idea of Michael coupled up with Cynthia Palmer was more shocking than the notion of him responding to that coquettish thing that Lucien did with his eyelashes. And Cynthia was such an obviously, emphatically *womanly* woman.

"It surprised me too," said Lucien. Stella couldn't help noticing that he momentarily looked a little downcast. "But they're in amour." He stretched the word out, pronouncing it with sufficient feeling and phlegm that it seemed rather lewd.

Michael smiled and shook his head. "Do you see what I have to put up with? I've had no end of ribbing since I told him. Stella, I'm so glad you're here. Please, can't we gang up against him?"

Lucien turned back to his stove. "Go and tell Stella all about it. I'll interrogate her for the most salacious details later."

*

They settled on the sofa together with glasses of vermouth. Stella tucked her feet up and looked at Michael. "Cynthia Palmer! I will admit that you've stunned me." She gave him a prod with her foot. It had surprised her, and was that a stab of jealousy that she felt too? She had, more or less, settled her mind to the idea that Michael didn't do relationships with women, that all of that was off-limits, but something seemed to shift as she imagined him with Cynthia.

"She's not always like she is in the magazines," he said. "That's Cynth's public persona. It's what people expect of her. Behind closed doors, she's sensitive and thoughtful. She likes poetry, simple Italian food and Spanish guitar music." He smiled into his glass.

Cynth, indeed! "You have got it bad. But if you're happy, I'm glad for you, darling." Stella reached for his hand. She told herself that she could make herself be glad for him; she must try to be, even if it was disquieting to imagine him lifting forkfuls of spaghetti to Cynthia's lipsticked mouth.

When Stella looked at Michael, she could still see him at eighteen, his hair shiny as liquorice and his eyes bright and hungry for life. She remembered when he'd first spoken to her, how she'd thought his profile was like Michelangelo's Adam in the Sistine Chapel and she'd wanted to mix a paint color to match his eyes. She'd hitherto assumed that gentian-blue eyes only existed in the pages of a certain type of novel. With his height, his broad shoulders and his handsome-as-a-fresco face, Michael ought to have looked out at the world with confidence, but there was an occasional shyness in his smile, and the way that he let his fringe fall in front of his remarkable eyes made Stella want to hold a mirror up so that he might see his own worth. She still felt like that about him—but she really wasn't sure about the moustache. Was that Cynthia's influence? It was annoying how it kept drawing her eyes to his mouth.

"I can't recall when I last saw you with a woman on your arm," she said, cautiously. She could say that, couldn't she? For a decade they'd been allies, confidantes, trusted and trusting, but they'd never had this conversation. "Is it that you've always been too busy with the restaurant?"

"I've not exactly been falling over offers—possibly because I've spent most of the past ten years with *you* on my arm!" He laughed, but then some thought seemed to crease his brow and he looked away.

"Don't imagine you'll shake me off easily!" Had she embarrassed him? Had she held him back? This felt rather awkward. "Well, you've bagged yourself a famous beauty now. Didn't *Vogue* dress her up in white feathers last summer and use lots of similes about swans?" And didn't they say that a swan's wing could break a man's arm? Stella blinked away an image of a sharp beak hissing. "You've certainly set your sights high."

"There's more to her than looks."

Was there? "Yes, of course."

"Enough about me, anyway," he said. It almost sounded like a plea. "What did your editor say? What happened? I'm assuming it all went rather better than anticipated?"

"Gingerbread and good fortune happened. Mr. Williamson

seems to believe in me, which is frankly astonishing. I'm not at all convinced that I believe in myself. Apparently, he thinks I've got a best-selling book hiding somewhere inside me. I think it might be buried quite far inside, but he's giving me an advance to coax it out."

"But that's brilliant news!" He clinked his glass against hers, leaned over and kissed her on the cheek. "I'm so proud of you. Is it another biography?"

"No, you'll laugh—it's a history of English food."

"All of it?"

"Well, quite!" Had she just said "Yes' to an enormous undertaking? "It has to be a nice book with broad appeal," she went on, quoting Mr. Williamson. "It will be a comforting book that will make people feel sentimental for their grandmother's cooking, all Bath buns and Bakewell pudding, that sort of stuff, and lots of flag-waving."

"English food?" said Lucien from the kitchen doorway. "Did I hear that right? Is it a comedy? A mystery? Or perhaps it's a tragedy?"

"It's going to be called *How the English Eat*," said Stella, making inverted commas with her fingers, and nearly spilling her vermouth in the process.

"I can summarize that in one word: badly. Can you stretch that out to fill a whole book? Or will it just be a pamphlet?"

"It won't be a pamphlet; it will be a success. And don't be so bloody rude. I'm well aware that our reputation isn't up to much, but I'm going to restore that. This book will make people feel proud of their national cuisine."

"So it's a work of fiction, then?"

"Michael, will you tell him—"

"Proud of your overcooked cabbage?" Lucien sat down on the arm of the chair, still laughing. "Proud of your milk puddings? Your suet dumplings? Your lamb and mint sauce? Have you ever read your beloved Mrs. Beeton? She recommends boiling carrots for an hour and a half. Woe betide an undercooked vegetable enters an Englishman's stomach. You know, I saw a lunchtime menu the other day that sought to lure me in with 'surprise rissoles' followed by 'prune whip.' What sort of a country entices with prune whip? As a race you may be known for your table manners but, I'm sorry, you are not known for your food."

"You may have to push a large boulder up a steep hill," Michael agreed. "I'm not sure that *restoring* our reputation is quite the right word."

"And thank you for your support, dear friends! I'm not beyond a journalistic challenge and I mean to make this one work, even if it does require me to defy gravity a little. Anyway, people love their mint sauce and suet puddings, and you two are just food snobs."

"*Moi*? Snob?" Lucien raised his hands and his eyebrows. "Have I been complimented or slandered?"

"It will be a likable book, a popular book," Stella went on, "and I mean to make my publisher pleased with me."

"Popular, unlike poor old Madame Sabayon?"

Lucien insisted on calling Mrs. Raffald Madame Sabayon. He also took pleasure in turning through the pages of *The*

Experienced English Housekeeper and pointing out that many of Mrs. Raffald's recipes were French. Did he do this just to provoke her, or did he genuinely believe that? The thought disturbed Stella slightly. Hannah Glasse could be distinctly rude about the French (what was it she called French chefs? Overpaid boobies?), but her book was full of daubes, *ragoûts* and *fricassées* too. Stella had already begun to worry about how she might deal with the French—but, all in good time.

"It will be a thoroughly nice, thoroughly English book," she said, "with some serious observations to earn me some credibility and sufficient sales to allow me to stop worrying about paying my rent. I'm damn well determined to deliver that."

Michael put his arm around her. "And you will. It will be a brilliant book. I have absolute faith in you." He gave her his most darling smile.

Bloody Cynthia Palmer, Stella thought.

Stella stretched out on the sofa after dinner and listened to them talking. She'd always enjoyed doing this. If she closed her eyes, it was like listening to a play on the wireless, and she deliberated which actors might best be cast as them. She made Lucien Maurice Chevalier tonight and Michael a subtly Yorkshire Cary Grant. The one disturbing theme in this evening's play was the recurrence of Cynthia's name (Stella cast her as a particularly vampish Theda Bara). She asked herself why this rankled.

She had a vague memory of sketching Cynthia wearing

a snake bangle around the top of her arm. It had nasty red glass eyes and a little flicking tongue, Stella recalled, and Cynthia had extended a kohl line out from the corners of her eyelashes, evidently wanting to give a flavor of Cleopatra. They'd all sniggered about that in the coffee room afterward, but Cynthia had been deadly serious. Cynthia was always serious. Stella wondered if she had a sense of humor. She might be famously beautiful, but surely she wasn't much of a giggle?

She listened to Michael talking and the sound of his voice was home, safety, trust and her best memories. His laughter took her back to nights when they'd tried out new dance steps in Montmartre jazz clubs, to meandering, inebriated moonlit walks around London, and to all those times when idiotic jokes had tipped them over into hysterical tears. His voice had been there when she'd needed comfort and support too. She'd telephoned and told him when her mother had gone back into hospital for the last time and he'd driven all the way up to Hatherstall that same night. He'd held her hand through the funeral service and stayed on for a fortnight, administering sweet tea, whiskey and hugs at appropriate intervals. Michael was her truest and most trusted friend, but the fact that he kept saying Cynthia's name made Stella feel oddly irritable tonight. Must she acknowledge that this feeling was envy?

Chapter Eight

"And how was Michael?" her father asked, as he crouched to put another log on the fire. He tapped his pipe out on the grate.

"In love, it seems." Was he really? The words felt awkward in Stella's mouth, both too sugary and sharp, like the jagged edge of a boiled sweet under her tongue. She watched the lengthening flames flickering. The wood was damp and it hissed as it caught. "He's walking out with a woman who used to be one of the life models."

"A stunner, eh? I suppose he is a good-looking lad." Her father sat back down and dusted flakes of ash from his trousers. "It's a pity you were slow off the mark there."

"Daddy!" Stella heard an outraged note in her own voice. "Michael's my oldest friend and I'm very pleased for him."

"A friend who makes you blush and who you telephone every other day?"

"We're good friends."

"So you're always telling me. He won't be spending hours on the telephone to you now that he's got a stunner in his life."

Stella supposed her father was right. "And I have a book to write. I won't have the time to spend hours on the telephone either."

He leaned back in his chair and gave her a look that was a shade too astute. "I found some of your mother's books the other day. Have I told you this already?"

"Her books? No, you haven't said. Go on." She would be glad to change the direction of this conversation.

"Cookery books, I mean—the notebooks that she used to keep, where she'd write out her recipes." He reached his tobacco pouch from his pocket and began to fill his pipe, frowning slightly with concentration. "I've left them in your room. I thought of them when you were telling me about your new project. You might find something useful in there."

Stella's school books were still on the shelves in her bedroom at the farm, the Japanese woodblock prints were still pinned on the walls and the doll that said "Mama" when you tipped it was where she'd left it on the rocking chair. Sparrows fluttered in the gutters, the wind was whistling under the roof tiles and she could feel the cold breath of it around the window frames. She looked out at the pewter-colored fields and at the treeline smudged with rain, and remembered lying in this bed, dreaming of a world where the pages of books didn't always warp with the damp, a place that existed in bright oil-paint pigments. Her mother had encouraged her to reach for that, and she'd known that place for a while, but then her mother's cancer had pulled her back into this room and all the colors had darkened.

There had been a year of frightening conversations with doctors then, explanations of medical words that seemed to make the floor give way, days that felt like months sitting in hospital waiting rooms, and morphine tablets were always spilling out of her mother's pockets when she reached for a handkerchief. All those hundreds of pills she'd swallowed didn't soften the signs of pain on her face, though. They didn't even touch the edges of it, she said, and Stella had felt that in the grip of her hand. That had been the worst part, seeing her mother's pain, and being powerless to ease it. If she concentrated on the patterns of the curtains and the wallpaper now, might she rewind time and think herself back to before all of that began? To when life was uncomplicated, when her mother was downstairs in the kitchen, and the beat of music from the gramophone was coming up from the floor below? In the photograph on the nightstand her parents were young and laughing, bright-eyed and wind-blown on a beach. That was how Stella wanted to remember her mother, as a young woman in a gingham dress, seashells in her lap, and her hand on her father's shoulder. She tried to blank out all the parts where there were nurses and dressings and falls; she tried to keep those scenes at bay, but they flashed back unbidden and she couldn't now be here without recalling the sound of her mother crying in the next room.

Her father had left the notebooks on the bed. As soon as Stella saw them, she remembered their marbled-paper covers. She could picture them open on the kitchen table as she stirred bowls of cake mixture for her mother. There were five of them, notebooks ruled with blue lines and crammed with her mother's handwriting. She'd written her name inside each book, *Elizabeth Douglas*, in a neat, deliberate hand. Stella could see her biting her bottom lip as she concentrated on her letters. How strange it was to look at her writing again now. The sight of that familiar script made tears instantly flood Stella's eyes, but as the shapes of the words formed into a sentence said in her mother's voice, she found herself smiling.

Stella turned through the pages and saw the pikelets, pea-and-ham soup and the boiled mutton and capers of her childhood. Here was her mother's wimberry pie, her damson jam and her gooseberry fool. Where recipes came from relatives and friends, her mother's handwriting noted the case: the method for hot-water pastry had been handed down from her grandmother; the parsley in her suet dumplings came from her cousin; the parkin was her great-aunt's recipe. Stella remembered how she and her mother would always share the first slice of roast lamb at the stove and the secret glass of sherry they'd drink as they made a trifle. Those moments of everyday togetherness were now precious memories and they were preserved in the pages of these books. As Stella read, the shadows in the room lightened, the gramophone played again distantly and order seemed to return to the world.

She also saw sketches as she leafed through: a study of honeysuckle flowers here, an arrangement of wooden spoons there, and now details of her own infant face. Stella couldn't remember that she'd seen these before. She'd never been aware that her mother drew, but she had a confident line and captured a good likeness. Had she once had ambitions that she'd wished to pursue? Is that why she'd encouraged Stella? Had she been disappointed that she'd let those dreams go, then? When Stella had come home and told her parents that she'd taken a job with a magazine, emphasizing the routine and the regular pay day, had her mother felt as regretful as she, in truth, did? Her mother's personality was captured in these notebooks, all the love and hope that she'd invested in Stella. At this moment, loss felt like a hard, clenched knot of muscle, or a stone, in her chest.

In Stella's memories of childhood mealtimes, they all sat at the big old mahogany table in the kitchen, extended out to its maximum length back then, and always with neighbors and relatives there too. After her mother had gone, her father had taken the leaves of the table away, one by one. Had he looked inside these books? How had that made him feel? Stella remembered how her mother would ruffle her father's hair, raise her eyebrows at his jokes, and kiss the top of his head as she passed his chair. She recalled the way that her mother looked at her father, that particular smile that she only gave to him. She also remembered how her father had cried after her mother had gone, those great racking sobs. "What am I meant to do now?" he had asked Stella, and she didn't have the first clue how to reply. In the weeks afterward, Stella had lain awake in this room listening to him crying in the night, and hadn't known whether she ought to go to him. Should she have comforted him, or did he need to let it out? She hoped her mother had known how well she was loved.

For the past year, Stella had kept herself busy. She'd not allowed herself to have idle, reflective, self-pitying moments. She'd focused on making sure that her father was eating and shaving, and not letting things slip on the farm. She'd made sure to deliver her magazine articles on time, tried to maintain a bright tone, and had been careful not to let her grammar slide. Stella hadn't let herself sit and think about missing her mother, but hearing her voice on paper hit her now. The thought of the table leaves gathering cobwebs in the barn suddenly had a bleak finality. For five minutes she might let go, mightn't she? Stella turned the key in the door, crawled under the blankets of her childhood bed and, for the first time in months, allowed herself to cry.

"I MISS"

[From the notebook of Elizabeth Douglas, 1923]

I miss my mother's pastry.

I miss Aunt Lucy's boiled beef and dumplings.

I miss watching my grandfather eating pickled walnuts.

I miss Annie's sticky ginger cake.

I miss my grandmother's potato scones.

I miss my grandfather making rum punch at Christmas.

I miss helping my mother to make a trifle and both running our
   fingers around the mixing bowls.
I miss my father being finicky and noticing my mother
   rolling her eyes.
I miss looking up and seeing my parents' faces at the table.
I miss having my daughter at home.

Chapter Nine

Resolved that she must now devote undivided attention to her new project, Stella made an initial list of the dishes that she meant to investigate. Sitting at the kitchen table, she flicked through Mrs. Raffald, Eliza Acton and Hannah Glasse and it was already turning into rather a long list. A more affluent version of herself with no deadline could have a thoroughly enjoyable time researching this book, she considered. She saw herself peering into bread ovens, beside a cider press, and poking into lobster pots, talking with gamekeepers, market gardeners and pork butchers. She closed her eyes and pictured herself zigzagging across the country in her motor, staying in half-timbered inns and farms that offered bed-and-breakfast accommodation. In the less brightly tinted real world, she would have to manage the budget for this project carefully. She opened her eyes and poured another cup of tea. Forty pounds had initially seemed like a generous sum, but this project might potentially require a lot of traveling and that wouldn't be cheap. Still, there were excellent resources in the British Museum, and she could stay with Michael while she worked in London. (With her thoughts *fully* focused on her book, she wouldn't let herself be disturbed by his romantic entanglements. Stella had taken to telling herself this every time her thoughts strayed.)

She didn't just want to reproduce material that was already in print. As Mr. Williamson had suggested, she'd like to weave in the voices of home cooks and quaint, colorful anecdotes. She'd decided to reach out by placing notices in regional newspapers requesting recipe suggestions. This would cost her a little money, but might allow her to cut back on travel expenses. In deciding which newspapers to approach, she'd observed that it was the peripheral regions that seemed to have the most distinct culinary cultures—the far north, remote south and the eastern and western edges. Was that something to do with population mobility? Or was it linked to imports and external influences? There were regional accents to food, it was already apparent to her, but Stella couldn't help noticing some foreign lilt in those voices too. The jars of spices in her kitchen suddenly seemed challenging and every time she looked at a potato now, it provoked difficult questions. At what point did a foreign flavor become native? Where should that line be drawn? As Stella considered ingredients, there seemed to be a returning Crusader, a Dutch horticulturist or a Tudor privateer at the starting point of every story.

We are a mongrel nation, Stella thought, as she made lists of recipes and ideas, a jumble of imports and influences. She sat back and chewed the end of her pencil. She rather liked that idea, as it conjured an image of a colorfully dressed crowd, all chattering away in different languages—but was that what Mr. Williamson had wanted? Was he hoping for something more suggestive of the village green and the church spire? Wasn't that religion once an import from the Middle East too, though? The longer Stella pondered these matters, the more slippery they seemed to become. Writing the biography of an eighteenth-century cook was an altogether more straightforward business, she realized now. She hadn't anticipated wrestling with semantics, botany and several millennia of population movements.

Stella had long since discovered that writing about food gives one a raging appetite. She'd brought a piece of Roquefort cheese back from London and her thoughts turned to it as she put down her pencil. It had made her best velvet beaded handbag smell like a midden, but she couldn't buy these things in Hatherstall, and it was perfectly ready to eat now. Looking at the clock, she could still sprint to the baker's for a loaf before it closed, and then she'd take the time to dress a green salad properly. For the past few days she'd been eating over her papers, casting toast crumbs between her typewriter keys, but there was a blue sky today, so she'd put on a warm jumper and take her lunch at the garden bench, she decided. (Yes, Mrs. Booth would think her peculiar if she looked out of her kitchen window and spied her eating in the garden in January, but then Stella's eccentricity was already well established among her neighbors.) She would eat slowly and thoughtfully today, she planned, and there would be pleasure in that. Should she be savoring an Aveyronnais sheep cheese, though? Was this a disloyal choice of lunch? In the interests of focus and professionalism, Stella resolved that she would write an admiring paragraph about Wensleydale cheese this afternoon—and perhaps not mention it first having been made by Cistercian monks from Roquefort.

Chapter Ten

What exactly were pinto beans? Stella thought that she probably ought to know, though she was pretty sure she'd never eaten them. They certainly weren't something used in English cookery, were they? Dilys had given her the details of a health-food shop off Regent Street and a list of mysterious pulses and grains. Stella had found it interesting to wander among the shelves of bran and buckwheat, the millet and the spelt and the yeast extract, but how unrelentingly brown healthful living seemed to be.

"They look like something from *Jack and the Beanstalk*," Stella said, as she passed the paper bag over on Dilys' doorstep now. "What precisely do you do with them?"

"You soak them, boil them, pulp them, and then you can eat them as a paste on toast," said Dilys. "They contain all essential nutrients and are high in dietary fiber."

"How marvelous." Stella thought that sounded like an awful lot of work to top a slice of toast, and hoped that she wasn't going to get another of Dilys' speeches about the importance of roughage. The last one had been excruciatingly graphic.

"I intend to plant some of them and see if I can get them going in the greenhouse. If they're a success, I might sell them on my stall. Of course, I'll have to write a little pamphlet to tell people how to use them."

"That might be wise."

Stella wondered: was Hatherstall ready for pinto beans? The Co-op always had a sack of split peas, but butterbeans were considered to be a bit fancy and you had to go to Huddersfield for anything as outlandish as lentils. Dilys' pamphlet would need to make some impressive claims. Stella followed her through to the kitchen.

"Anyway, how did the meeting with your editor go?"

"Considerably better than anticipated—in fact, astonishingly better. I have to say that you were right: he gave me a new commission. I'm writing a cookery book—or, rather, it's a history of English food."

"You see, I sensed that." There was momentarily something sphinx-like in Dilys' smile. "I've got an excellent recipe for pottage and a stew of turnip tops. That's extremely ancient. I'll write them out for you."

"Thank you," said Stella uncertainly.

Dilys had great confidence in herself as a cook and, at the slightest opportunity, she would tell people about the wholesomeness of her food. She made a great fuss over this, as if she felt superior about it, and loved to talk about how she was nearly self-sufficient (with a caveat for Huddersfield's lentils). But everything that Dilys cooked was the color of sackcloth and it all tasted more or less the same. Perhaps that was the flavor of virtue? Stella idly wondered if Dilys ever secretly craved a shop-bought sausage roll.

"It's a big subject the history of English food," Dilys said, but then frowned and looked like she was reevaluating her words. "Or perhaps it isn't—most things are imported, aren't they? If you wind it all back, I guess there's not much that truly is native. I suppose, when it comes down to it, our only indigenous foods are fungi, worts and seaweeds. I've given you my recipe for nettle dumplings, haven't I?"

"You have. Thank you."

If she took it back that far, this really would be Dilys' sort of book. Stella had spent much of the past week pondering where to draw the line. She'd realized that if she was over-vigilant with her definition of Englishness, she would end up with nothing but a pamphlet.

"Do sit down. I'll make some coffee."

The range was burning brightly in the kitchen and there was a bitter smell of wood smoke. It made Stella's eyes smart for a moment. Dilys was in the habit of gathering fallen branches on her walks and liked to talk about this right being enshrined in the Magna Carta. Stella often saw her coming back up the lane laden down with boughs and looking like some sort of half-tree, half-human figure from a Norse woodcut. An enamel dish on the hearth tiles appeared to contain a variety of nut roast. One of the cats sniffed at it, blinked slowly, and turned away with an expression that could only be described as disdainful.

"My chickens are off laying at the moment," Dilys said,

as she filled the kettle, "so I had to buy eggs from the grocer's this week. Do you know, he's selling Australian eggs? Eggs from the other side of the world! Are all of England's chickens on strike? They can't be fresh, can they?" Her long earrings swung with feeling. A cigarette was unraveling into shreds at the corner of her mouth, as was perennially the case, and she didn't seem to notice as ash fell onto her bosom. "His Cheddar is from Canada—he seemed to be rather proud of that—and he offered me what he called Empire Lard. I remarked on how international his shelves seemed to be and he told me that the butcher's Yorkshire beef comes from Argentina in a deep freeze. Judging by the shop counters of Hatherstall, English food seems to be going the way of the dinosaurs. Are you allowed to say that in your book?"

"My editor likes the idea of it being a rallying cry. That's how he wants me to position it."

"A rallying cry? Good luck with that! I fear the horse may have already bolted."

Stella dusted Dilys' breakfast crumbs from the oilcloth and thought about dinosaurs and bolting horses. Dilys wasn't wrong, of course, but that was why Mr. Williamson believed this book would be timely, wasn't it? Perhaps she might inject some urgency and imperative into her text; she could beat a drum for English eggs and Yorkshire topside—though, it mustn't sound *too* strident, must it? Mr. Williamson had also talked about it being an enjoyable read for the average woman in the street, and she wouldn't have much patience for a lot of finger-wagging, would she? Stella was beginning to feel like this book had a lot of boxes to tick.

"It will be a matter of getting the angle and balance right," she said, as much to herself as to Dilys.

"And how are you at gymnastics? Did I ever tell you that I once interviewed a circus contortionist?"

With Dilys' back turned, Stella quickly checked her cup just to make sure there were no mouse droppings in the bottom. She'd made that error once and wouldn't repeat it. She could still picture the thing's slow circumnavigation on the surface of her tea and Dilys' voice telling her not to let it go cold. Dilys said that her cats were great mousers, but evidence seemed to suggest otherwise. Stella pondered: were mouse droppings acceptable in a vegetarian diet?

"It really is quite a tricky commission when you start to think about it, isn't it?" Dilys sat down with the coffeepot. She pushed her spectacles up her nose. "I mean, who even are the English? The descendants of the Germanic tribes? We're a great hotchpotch really, aren't we? A mishmash of Celts, Anglo-Saxons, Danes, Normans, et cetera, et cetera, so a complicatedly hybrid ancestry, barely united for centuries, and our borders always shifting. We're not a pure, homogeneous race sprung from English soil, are we? When people talk about Englishness, I often get a whiff of frowsty Victorian velvet," she mused, articulating more expansively with her hands as she warmed to her theme. "It makes me think of paintings of King Alfred, *Ivanhoe* and Tennyson, people putting on dressing-up clothes to do archery, and

William Morris tapestries. Perhaps Englishness is less about geography and historical dates and more about symbols and emotions? There are lots of tripwires and misty hollows between the lions and unicorns, aren't there? When you begin to think about what Englishness means—and, by extension, English food—it all starts to become rather precarious and complicated, doesn't it?"

"It does," Stella agreed. It seemed to be getting more complicated by the second.

Chapter Eleven

Stella pushed a drawing pin into Clitheroe. She'd pasted a map on the kitchen wall and now felt a little like a general embarking on a military campaign. She had targeted Yorkshire, Lancashire, Northumbria and Cumbria, for a start, placing advertisements in the newspapers with the largest circulation. There was something comforting about the practicality of the map and the drawing pins. Dilys had made her head spin with all her whirling conjectures and questions about Englishness (Stella had an unsettling suspicion that Dilys might be more equipped to write this book than she was), but posting letters off to local newspapers had seemed to bring her feet back down to the ground.

Thus far—and it was still only a month into her campaign—she'd received two recipes for oatcakes from the West Riding, three variations on the theme of parkin from Preston and a rather ordinary meat-and-potato pie from Blackburn. Rochdale had yielded a thrifty rissole, Ambleside had offered a currant pie, and in this morning's post she'd had a surprisingly sentimental letter about bone soup from Clitheroe. There were no tripwires here, Stella was glad to sense, but opening these envelopes also didn't set off fireworks of excitement. There was some potential in the Yule cake recipe she'd received from Ripon, ditto the frumenty from Kirkbymoorside, and she'd look more closely at the letters from Morecambe, both of which were meditations on potting shrimps. Three correspondents from Northumbria all provided slightly varying origin stories for pan haggerty, and an elderly gentleman from Bolton had written a poem about boiled sheep's trotters. There were no huge surprises, and no recipes that Stella found herself longing to cook, but it began to piece together a history and a character for the different counties. Most of the letters she'd received suggested a hard history of eking out and scraping by. The food of the north was thrifty, for the most part, she was concluding. It was every-bit-of-the-beast food. She would find few enriching egg yolks and marzipan layers here. It would be curious to see how it shifted as she moved south.

Stella poured herself another cup of tea and contemplated oatcakes as she put her drawing pins away. Her imagination arranged the oatcakes, rissoles and dumplings into a still life, and even with complimentary lighting, it was a rather cheerless composition. She found herself wanting to add a single satsuma to the canvas to give it a splash of color and a contrast of texture, a pomegranate, an aubergine, or even a humble tomato. But that wasn't English cooking, was it? She looked at the pile of letters. "We are not a country that cooks in primary colors," she said aloud, experimentally, testing the words as her mouth formed them. How pleasurable it would be to write about a ratatouille made from sweet end-of-summer tomatoes, apricot-colored chanterelles fried in butter with flecks of bright green parsley, or red mullet grilled over vine prunings and served with spoonfuls of golden aioli—but Stella shook herself out of her reverie. She must put such things out of her mind. This was just the beginning, she reminded herself, and waterfalls of envelopes would cascade through her letterbox yet. They would contain all manner of curiosities, she reassured herself, revelations about suet pastry, dozens of ways to feed a large rural family with a rabbit, and surprising inventiveness with sprats. Still, it was annoying how Dilys' and Lucien's voices were now alternately chorusing "frowsty velvet" and "prune whip" in her head.

Stella had been reflecting on Mr. Williamson's fondness for gingerbread and considering whether she might be able to justify an investigative tour of Westmorland. She foresaw stories of sailing ships unloading cargoes of nutmegs and cinnamon sticks, anecdotes about Wordsworth and Coleridge, and a pursuit of potted char. If she could uncover the recipe for Grasmere gingerbread, that would be a coup, wouldn't it? She pictured herself returning triumphantly to the offices of Fleet, Everard & Frobisher with a box of gingerbread and her typescript in hand. Mr. Williamson would be impressed by that, wouldn't he? Yes, Westmorland seemed like the place to start. (She would worry about where the ginger and nutmegs had sailed from later.)

Dear Miss Douglas,

As part of your history of British food I am sure you will be giving consideration to the variation in—and chronology of—regional choices of bread grains. This is a fascinating study, and much overlooked, don't you agree? I would be glad to send you a copy of my doctoral thesis on the cultivation of barley in later-medieval Cumberland.

DR. WILFRED MYERS, Lancaster

Madam,

Having seen that you are writing a book about English food, I am certain you will want to cover the demise of our national loaf. Over the past two centuries our bread has been degraded and adulterated, stripped of its natural vitamins, iron and mineral salts, a process which has arguably done more damage to us as a race than the invention of the machine-gun. I enclose my pamphlet on the pernicious and urgent dangers of the toxic white loaf. Remember, wholegrain for health—the future depends upon it!

MR. H. V. ATHERTON, Harrogate

Dear Miss Douglas,

In response to your notice in the Hull Daily Mail, *I enclose my grandmother's recipe for a Yorkshire breakfast loaf. Is anything nicer than a fresh white loaf? You may be too young to remember the filthy brown stuff that they made us eat during the war. It played havoc with my digestion!*

ENID PRICE (Mrs.), Cottingham

Good Taste

Muffins, teacakes, tea rolls, morning rolls, batch rolls, stottie cakes, barm cakes, wigs, bridies, huffkins, oven-bottom muffins, baps and cobs ... It says something about us as a race, doesn't it? (But, frankly, I'm not sure what.)

HORACE DAVIDSON, Ripon

Chapter Twelve

The hills loomed high over the slate rooftops of Grasmere, silhouettes in gray chalk against the white sky. The church spire had a stalwart look about it, Stella considered, but it was diminished by the backdrop of the fells. How was an architect meant to compete with that? She passed under the ivy-grown lych-gate and walked between the yew trees. The graves were clustered together in groups, as if they had secrets to share and were turning over-the-shoulder eyes on incomers. The newly mown grass was cadmium green oil paint squeezed straight from the tube.

Stella leaned on the railings as she read the inscriptions on William and Dorothy's graves. The light made the lettering crisp and brought out the purples and golds of the lichens. Shadows bowed the head of the lamb on Dora Quillinan's gravestone; the trees beyond were full of the trilling of blackbirds, and lines of Wordsworth's "Lucy" poem came into Stella's mind.

"No motion has she now, no force, she neither hears nor sees," she whispered. *"Rolled round in earth's diurnal course, with rocks, and stones, and trees."*

There was a timeless quality to the landscape around her, to the lines of the fells, the shapes of the yews, and the lichened stones, as if clocks might not tick down the minutes in the conventional way here, but Stella's memory took her back to specific times when she'd been here before, and to her mother's presence—and now absence—at her side.

She stepped into the church, and sight and memory aligned. There was something prosaically agricultural about the black crossbeams of the roof space; it might be some great medieval barn. The crisscross shadows cast against the brightness of the whitewash made Stella's palm itch for a stick of charcoal. She toured the walls, conscious of the sound of her own footsteps, reading the stone tablets, and recalling her mother's voice talking about rush-bearing rituals and ginger-bread. She could hear her words and inflections so distinctly that she might be a ghost whispering into her ear. In turn, Stella told her mother that she wanted her to be here with her now, that she needed her here, that she wasn't going to manage well without her. Could she hear? Churches listened, didn't they? After all, what were all those beseeching carved words and prayer benches for? Stella lit a candle and stood with her arms folded across her chest as she watched the light quivering against the walls. She found herself holding her breath, waiting and searching for a sign. But then her mother's recalled voice was telling her to be sensible, that she must pull herself together, and Stella knew that she had to push on with the task in hand.

She remembered much furrowing of brows over the

secrecy of the recipe for Grasmere gingerbread (she imagined a butter-stained paper padlocked in a casket), and the smell of this place was a memory too. How evocative that was now as she approached the door of the bakery. Could she work the recipe out? Or was there a way of loosening those padlocks?

Stella checked her lipstick in the mirror of her compact before she pushed the door. She'd taken care over her hair and makeup this morning because—well, one never knows. She remembered that the counter of the gingerbread shop had been staffed by indomitable women back in the day, but one can always hope for a corruptible youth. She breathed in the smell as she pushed the door. It was so particular and so teasing.

The woman behind the counter smiled as the shop bell rang, but it was a brief, professional smile. She was a redoubtable-looking woman, stout with a scrubbed complexion. She looked resolutely incorruptible. Still, Stella turned up the dial and assumed her most charming manner.

"Isn't this the most delightful shop? I remember coming here as a child and it hasn't changed a bit."

"Thank you," the woman nodded. "We do like to keep up the old standards."

"As I can see—and rightly so. Please forgive me for asking, but I can smell something other than ginger, can't I?" she chanced. "Oh, how tantalizing it is! There's another spice, isn't there? A pinch of allspice? Maybe nutmeg? No, it's spikier, isn't it?" She was aware that she was now sniffing the air like a hunting dog. "A touch of pepper perhaps?" Was that possible? It was used in early gingerbread recipes, and wasn't there a Westmorland pepper cake?

The woman's smile straightened. "I couldn't say, dear. How many packets?"

"It isn't only powdered ginger, is it? There's definitely crystallized ginger in there. And a bit of candied peel too? You don't have to say," Stella cajoled. "You could just give me a nod."

The woman neither smiled nor nodded. There was no response at all. She stared blank-faced at Stella. She didn't even blink. Damn it, she was a sphinx.

"It's a mix of oatmeal and wheat flour, isn't it? I'm not wrong about that, am I?" She looked at the woman's eyes hoping for a flicker. The eyes narrowed. Something in the line of her square jaw reminded Stella of a mantrap.

"That'll be thruppence," she said.

Dash it, she'd got nothing here. She was in and out of the shop within seconds. Stella stood on the pavement feeling like she'd been spat out. She so wanted to be able to produce this recipe for Mr. Williamson. She pictured herself in his office and his face lifting from her typescript, his features up-lit and enraptured, like those of a man experiencing the revelation of a miracle in a Renaissance painting. Having come this far, Stella didn't mean to go home empty-handed. She wanted to deliver the miracle of the gingerbread.

She sat on a bench and listened to the blackbirds as she nibbled appraisingly. She'd forgotten quite how assertive the ginger was. It wasn't a child's ginger biscuit, no mild-mannered gingerbread man; it was decidedly grown up. It tasted like a biscuit made by a woman with a mantrap face. Doggedness and astringency were certainly among its ingredients. She nodded at her calculation of oats and golden syrup, and she'd been right about the candied peel, hadn't she? The smell of ginger mingled with that of damp privet. Ivy scrambled over slate walls, brackens made prehistoric shapes and the branches of the yew trees dripped into indigo shadows. Between the black needles the sky was streaked with wind and incoming rain. She wondered if the bake house had a window.

Stella clambered through a hawthorn hedge. This wasn't her finest hour, she considered, as she straightened her hair and dusted a cobweb from her chest, but she did feel thrillingly like a proper journalist pursuing a lead. As she was rounding the corner of the building, she heard the creak of a door opening. She crouched behind a privet as she watched a youth stepping out. He untied an apron from around his waist before he shut the door behind him, pulled on a cap and reached a packet of Woodbines from his pocket. He was only about seventeen, skinny and with a rather doughy-looking complexion. Bingo, Stella thought.

She watched the youth head down the path and close the gate, and she followed in cautious pursuit. Bicycles swerved away, ringing their bells, as she shadowed him across the street, and she narrowly avoided being tangled in a dog lead, but she wasn't going to let her quarry get away. He walked down the road and headed into a public house. Excellent. Alcohol was always a useful lubricant.

It was dark inside the pub. It took her a moment to blink the room into focus, but there he was—the youth was leaning on the bar. At the tables there were hikers in boots and a selection of variously whiskered elderly men sat on horsehair benches. Several eyes were appraisingly cast in her direction and lingered there unabashed. Stella had thought to dress appropriately and elegantly this morning, in slacks, a fitted tweed waistcoat and her knitted beret, but she suddenly felt conspicuously like a *Tatler* version of the modern country miss.

"Good day." She stood elbow-to-elbow with the youth at the bar. He glanced at her as she ordered a whiskey and soda and she gave him an unobtrusive smile. "The clouds aren't lifting today, are they? Do you suppose we'll have rain this afternoon?" She reversed back into her girlhood northern vowels.

"Aye," said the youth into his tankard. With the look of alarm on his face, she might well have asked his opinion on advanced calculus or the philosophies of Confucius. God, this could be easier.

"The whole village smells of gingerbread, doesn't it? I'd forgotten that. I have to say, it's the most delicious gingerbread I've ever tasted. Don't you think?"

"Aye." He sipped quickly and nervously at his drink. His shifting lowered eyes reminded her of a cornered dog. Were the bakery staff threatened with thumbscrews if they spilled the secrets?

"I'd love to be able to make it at home, only I can't quite

figure the recipe out. Is there some candied citrus peel in there, would you say? Or perhaps a little lemon zest?"

"I couldn't say." His expression suggested she'd asked him some embarrassing intimacy. Good Lord, this was worse than the time when she'd tried to wrestle the Fat Rascal recipe from a waitress in Harrogate. Was it all going to be this difficult?

"Perhaps another spice. Cloves? Nutmeg?"

The youth gave a conspicuous sigh and leaned away from her.

"And golden syrup? That has to be there for the texture, doesn't it? Perhaps not treacle, though. What do you think?"

The barman came back to the beer pump and laughed. "Nice try! I admire your persistence, but you won't get it out of him. Do you know how often they get asked? They're under strictest instructions. If he blabbed it to you, he'd be out of his job by midafternoon. Wouldn't you, Alf? And possibly subjected to some minor forms of torture. You wouldn't want the poor lad to go through that, would you, miss?"

"Aye," said Alf again. This seemed to be the extent of his repertoire. He took his chance to bolt now, and shouldered his way onto the benches of agricultural types. Stella saw the whites of his eyes as he glanced back toward her.

"I'm not sure if that was a thrill for him or whether you've genuinely terrified the kid." The barman grinned as he leaned on the pump.

Stella sighed. It was no good. She'd get nothing here. She'd just have to take the packet of gingerbread home and experiment until she could reproduce it.

"Do you know of anywhere where I can get potted char? Are there places that still do it?"

"You want to head over to Windermere for that. Try the Royal Hotel. Do you mean to strong-arm a recipe out of them too?"

"I just like cooking," she said and shrugged. Men liked that, didn't they? Wasn't that a womanly virtue?

He gave her a knowing smile as he turned away. "Are you staying in the village?" he asked over his shoulder. He appeared to be writing something down on a piece of paper.

"Yes, I'm at the Red Lion tonight."

"Excellent," he said.

He pushed the paper toward her before he moved down the bar to serve another customer.

Flour, oats, butter, dark sugar, golden syrup and ginger, he'd written. *And now you owe me a kiss.*

Oh, hell's teeth! When she looked toward him, he actually winked. She supposed he was quite handsome, but in a rustic and overconfident sort of a way. Why had she told him where she was staying? Was he going to make a nuisance of himself? Did Mr. Williamson have any notion of how secretive, complex and potentially perilous English food could be?

Chapter Thirteen

Stella had been able to write a nice piece about gingerbread and how the evolution of its recipe reflected the history of the British Empire. Reading her pages through for a second time, she'd deleted the references to the gingerbreads of ancient Rome and the traditions in Germany and Holland, but she had to acknowledge that the key ingredients were imported, didn't she? Deletion and conscious omission was starting to make her feel *slightly* uncomfortable. This was the mandate that Mr. Williamson had given her, though, and she must deliver Englishness.

It was most dissatisfying not to be able to reproduce the Grasmere gingerbread shop's recipe. The barman had turned up at her hotel that evening and she'd had a job shaking him off. If he'd had something more specific to offer, she might not have minded so much, but she wasn't going to give him anything in exchange for a vague list of ingredients. There was no trade to be done there. Through experimentation, she'd worked out an approximation of the recipe, but she would have liked to be able to cite something authentic. It was a pity that neither Mrs. Raffald nor Hannah Glasse had holidayed in the Lakes.

Stella looked up as she heard the post landing on her door-mat. Her notices in newspapers were proving fruitful; she was receiving lots of letters, but they weren't exactly yielding the colorful and varied accounts that she'd hoped for.

In response to her advertisement in the *Yorkshire Post*, a Mr. Lumbut of Skipton had penned a letter to the editor reminiscing about his grandmother's oatcakes. He wrote evocatively of the warming bakestone, the bubbling batter, the flipping, the stacking and the smell of toasted oatmeal. That was pleasingly picturesque, Stella could use some of that, but then a Mrs. Wright from Pickering had replied saying that Mr. Lumbut's grandmother was committing a gross blunder in flipping her oatcakes. Furthermore, a Mrs. Hemshore had then responded, saying that both Mr. Lumbut's and Mrs. Wright's ancestors were in error and that yeast should never—"under no circumstances"—be added to the batter. The tone of the last letter was rather tetchy. People seemed to be getting somewhat overheated about oatcakes.

Oatcakes might not be exhilarating, but at least this text was wholesome. That was more than could be said for Stella's breakfast. She'd cut the green bloom off the crust of the loaf, but this piece of toast still tasted musty. She'd been so occupied in editing her chapter on the history of breadmaking this morning that she'd forgotten to go to the baker's. She idly conjured up an image of a fresh baguette, the crisp of the crust and butter yielding on the still-warm crumb inside. Just occasionally, in cheering for the superiority of English food,

Stella felt like she was pushing against the evidence of her senses. However, she must banish baguettes from her mind. This would never do.

She opened this morning's post and read a letter from a Mrs. Haddon from Salford, saying that it was immoral to be writing a cookery book when nearly three million people were unemployed in this country and suffering hunger and hardship. She suggested that if Stella was determined to pursue this course, it ought to be a book of thrifty recipes for those living on the "dole' and any profit ought to be going to charity. The letter pricked Stella's conscience. Was Mrs. Haddon right? Was Tudor gilded gingerbread obscene? She needed the means to pay her rent too, though, didn't she? She wanted to reply to Mrs. Haddon and tell her that she was eating moldy toast this morning.

And she wasn't unaware of what was going on. Joan Blake, her editor at *Today's Woman,* had telephoned yesterday and told her about a meeting they'd had in the office. A decision had been made that the magazine must do something to reflect the present economic climate. With the newspapers full of headlines about collapsing exports and closing shipyards, it didn't seem quite nice to be carrying pieces about Continental holidays and the latest fashions in furs. The magazine had to be careful in its tone now, Joan had said. Accordingly, Agnes was being dispatched to the northeast to write an article about welfare work, Juliette would be publishing a piece on how to pep up last year's fashions, and it had been suggested that Stella should give some advice for the financially challenged kitchen. She'd dug out a selection of soups, and thrifty ways with potatoes and dried peas, and was quite happy to heed Joan's guidance, but it struck her how everyone seemed to be talking about tone at the moment. The word resounded in Stella's head like a solemn bell.

She'd be on soup too for the next week. She'd written down all the costs for her Cumbrian trip and, even though she'd been mindful of her budget, the bottom-line figure still made her wince. She was planning to go down to the British Museum next week and she'd have to be careful about her spending in London. Michael had said she could stay in the flat, but still there'd be the train fare, omnibus fares and the cost of eating out. (Did D. H. Lawrence worry about train tickets and the price of cheese and pickles?) She looked forward to talking about Grasmere gingerbread with Michael, about parkin, soul cakes and Bonfire Night—there were childhood memories here that they shared—but would he be going on about Cynthia again? Stella knew that she really ought to make an effort to like Cynthia, but the thought of Michael rattling on about her poems and her sensitivities was presently as unpalatable as her green toast.

Dear Miss Douglas,
   In response to your letter published in the Sheffield Daily Telegraph, *I thought you might be interested in my late mother's recipe for oatcakes . . .*

                              BERYL WHITWORTH, Tideswell

Miss Douglas,

As I understand you are compiling a collection of traditional English recipes (I saw your notice in the Shipley Times*), I am sending you my recipe for proper West Riding oatcakes . . .*

EDWIN DENTON, Shipley

Madam,

I was interested to see your advertisement in the Leeds Mercury *and would be glad to share our family recipe for Yorkshire oatcakes with you . . .*

FLORENCE HEYSHAW, Otley

Dear Miss Douglas,

Having seen your letter in the Yorkshire Post*, I have pleasure in enclosing my grandmother's recipe for a Skipton oatcake . . .*

R. S. BURTON (Mrs.), Skipton

Dear Stella,

How lovely that you're writing a book about traditional English foods. Would you like to include my recipe for oatcakes? I would be glad to share it with you and your readers . . .

MILDRED BRIERFIELD, Silsden

Chapter Fourteen

Stella had spoken with Michael on the telephone only three days earlier, so it had shocked her when Winifred Palgrave mentioned his engagement to Cynthia in a letter dated that same day. (Indeed, the fact that Winifred had terminated this sentence with five exclamation marks didn't seem remotely excessive.) The letter related that Michael had gone down on one knee at Rupert Snelgrave's sherry party. It had silenced the room, Winifred said, and Stella wasn't surprised. She'd had to pull out a chair and read Winifred's letter through again.

Stella had spoken to Michael on the telephone several times since her last trip to London. He had talked about Cynthia, she'd been well aware of that, but she hadn't picked up that things were advancing quite so speedily. She certainly hadn't foreseen an engagement. Having read Winifred's letter for a third time, Stella poured herself an emergency measure of brandy.

The invitation to the engagement party had arrived the next day, confirming that Winifred's information was correct. Of course, Stella would go to the party, but it smarted that Michael hadn't told her on the telephone. Why hadn't he said anything? And how could he have advanced from initial experiments in coupledom to marriage so swiftly? Shouldn't someone tap him on the shoulder—promptly—and tell him that it wasn't necessary to go so fast?

Stella had made a list of the materials that she wanted to consult in the British Museum Reading Room and it was exciting to have a scholarly plan for the week. She felt privileged to be permitted to sit under that mighty dome, with the names of the great men of English literature picked out in gold letters above. (It was a pity they'd forgotten the women, but still . . .) There was something temple-like in the atmosphere of this room with its rings of lights and the reverentially lowered eyes, and the whisper of pencils on paper was its murmur of prayer. As she turned through pages penned by seventeenth-century traders and eighteenth-century agricultural pioneers, Stella had a curious sense of being both very distant from the lives of these writers and within touching distance. She felt great reverence as she unpicked the tangles of a handwriting describing food served to Queen Elizabeth and Sir Walter Raleigh's guidance on how to preserve beef at sea. When no one was looking, she had bent over the desk and sniffed the vellum of *The Forme of Cury*. Was that the smell of a fourteenth-century kitchen? Her eyes had widened as she'd unrolled the manuscript and deciphered recipes for whale, porpoise and peacock—but it was rather annoying how peacock tails took her back to a memory of Cynthia Palmer posing in a feathered headdress. It didn't seem quite appropriate to be thinking of Cynthia in a bejeweled *brassière* in the British Museum.

She was grateful that Michael had offered her his room for the week, but it was peculiar to turn the key in the door now and to step into the empty apartment. She heard her own footsteps on the linoleum, and the hallway was all still air and shadows. Stella had never known these rooms silent before; they'd always been full of laughter and chatter and music. Had this stage of Michael's life already finished, then? Would there be no more nights of experimenting with cocktail recipes, winding the gramophone and tipsy dancing? That thought left Stella feeling thoroughly glum.

She'd slept in this room many times before. It was quite normal for Michael to take to the sofa when she came down to London and let her have his bed, but it was unsettling to look around now and to think that Cynthia might have been here too. There was a tartan blanket over the bed, and a poetry anthology topped the stack of books on his nightstand. Had he carried out a seduction on the tartan blanket and whispered rhyming couplets into Cynthia's ears? Or perhaps she had seduced him in her peacock feathers? Why would Cynthia want a man like Michael, though? He made an impressively reliable soufflé, and his Béarnaise sauce never split, but Stella could hardly imagine that these were virtues Cynthia might value. There was the matter of his smile and his long eyelashes too, though, wasn't there? Then there were his broad shoulders, his warm, calm voice and his clever hands. The restaurant was successful—he'd achieved some reputation—and, yes, his fringe was like a glossy blackbird's wing. Upon deliberation, Stella had to concede that there were several reasons why Cynthia might have decided to acquire Michael. She found herself examining the cigarette ends in his ashtray, scrutinizing for lipstick prints, but then she caught her own reflection in the mirror and saw how pitiful this looked. What was she thinking?

Sun slanted through the window and the iron bed frame cast bars of shadow across the floorboards. There were framed photographs of Michael's parents on the nightstand, smiling faces in Sunday clothes and eyes squinting into holiday sunshine. Stella crouched at she looked at the stack of books. He'd been reading *Mrs Dalloway*, Aldous Huxley and Evelyn Waugh, and there was a bookmark in a volume of T. S. Eliot's poems. She and Michael had the same taste in novels and had always loved discussing and exchanging books. Did he have those conversations with Cynthia now? Did she get to see how enthusiasm would widen his eyes and how a comic story could make him laugh? As Stella put her suitcase down on the bed, she noticed that his alarm clock had stopped at a minute to midnight. Dilys would read meaning into this, wouldn't she? But what was Stella meant to do with that?

She looked down at the rag rug in the sitting room and pictured their younger selves cross-legged there. With its cobalt-blue walls and leather sofas, this was a masculine room, but the piles of film magazines and candles in bottles made it homely. The way the old sofas sagged always prompted Stella to think of elderly men letting out a breath as they loosened their belts after dinner. Her finger trailed along the lines of gramophone records and she remembered how Michael had laughingly crooned into her ear as they'd danced to "It Had to Be You." The tune played again faintly in her head, but it was scratchy and wobbled and she couldn't hold onto it. There was a fine layer of dust on the cover of the gramophone player now. Stella formed her initials in it and wondered how long it might be until Michael noticed. The etchings of the Gare St-Lazare and the aquatint of the Luxembourg Gardens had been on the walls of his room in Paris, and Michael's sketch of her was still hung by the light switch. Stella recalled the day he'd drawn it, as they sat outside the café on the Rue Mouffetard, and how she'd suddenly felt shy as his evaluating eyes lingered on her features. It was an overly complimentary portrait, she thought, as she regarded it again, and how young and naïve that ponytailed girl looked to be. Might things be different now if she'd had more courage?

Stella opened kitchen cupboards and felt conscious of Michael's absence. There was a pan of Lucien's vichyssoise soup in the larder, but she saw few signs of Michael having been here recently. How long was it since he'd cooked in this kitchen and slept in his own bed? Stella lifted the sash of the kitchen window, leaned out and lit a cigarette. The window looked onto a yard full of dustbins, crates and rags. Smoke was drifting down from the chimneypots opposite, a flight of starlings rushed across, and a pigeon was pecking at something unpleasant. She heard the distant rumble of an Underground train and the voices of a man and woman arguing. Heavens, this wouldn't do for Cynthia, would it? The party invitation gave a smart Chelsea address and Stella supposed that must be where Cynthia lived now. Was Michael already playing host at her bohemian parties? Would he give up his job at the restaurant next and take to touring with Cynthia in her gypsy caravan? Would she dress him up in a stove-pipe hat and embroidered waistcoats, as she had done with Niall Kavanagh, her ex-husband? As Stella pictured Michael in that ensemble, his eyes shifted to a more intense blue and his smile seemed to gain in comeliness. She wasn't absolutely sure what caused this optical illusion, but it was really rather annoying. She stubbed her cigarette out and heard herself sigh.

Stella stood in front of Michael's mirror in her aquamarine crêpe de chine. She'd admired a black chiffon dress in the window of Selfridge's that morning. It was beautifully cut in the new silhouette, but she couldn't justify spending the money and mustn't look funereal. She took time painting her nails the same coral pink as her lipstick, and fixed her hair up into a chignon. Her bohemian beaded jewelry seemed appropriate for this evening and she gave herself a generous confidence-boosting spritz of Mitsouko. Fastening her high-heeled sandals, Stella told herself that she mustn't have too much to drink and fall over. She must also remember to smile at Cynthia.

Lucien had come straight from the restaurant and was waiting downstairs in a taxicab. "You look extremely elegant," he said, as he held the door for Stella. "*Très belle soignée.*"

"Not too much?"

"I'm from Paris, do remember. There is no such thing as too much."

He kissed her cheek and squeezed her hand. He'd changed into a rather loud checked suit, and a brown fedora with a scarlet silk ribbon, and smelled of a woody eau-de-cologne. He hadn't bought those red patent brogues in London, had he?

"So you'll get your first sighting of Michael with La Belle Cynthia tonight," he went on, as they settled side by side in the taxi together. "You'll find it fascinating. It's better than the cinema or a trip to the zoo."

Stella was reassured to sense that she'd be in the company of an ally this evening. "I have to admit that I'm still recovering from the shock. I can hardly believe that we're on our way to Michael's engagement party. Did you see it coming?"

"I had to have a cognac when he told me. I asked him if he'd been hit over the head and we had a row. We didn't speak for several hours, and then I felt I ought to apologize, but I really didn't want to. He told me that she sang some sort of Portuguese lament for him on the day that he proposed, then she took him back to her apartment and laid lumps of rock on his chest." Lucien shook his head. "*Pauvre idiot!*"

Stella leaned her head back and saw the sun flashing between rooftops, pale pearly clouds and then the corner of Peter Jones', the windows full of hats and dresses in the new spring colors, all geranium reds, hyacinth blues and Parma violets. Watching the military capes, tennis frocks and boleros blur past made her feel slightly like Alice tumbling down the rabbit hole. "Rocks?"

"Well, geological specimens, you know."

Stella wasn't sure that she did. "She put geological specimens on his chest? Whatever was that about? Was she trying to crush him? Did she take his shirt off?"

Stella imagined Cynthia's fingers unbuttoning Michael's shirt. She'd never actually seen him without his vest, but she gave him the physique of Michelangelo's Adam for the purposes of this visualization, and pictured Cynthia placing chunks of turquoise and malachite on his smooth fresco breast, her eyelashes trembling as she muttered some hocus-pocus above. Had it been like that? It was a disconcerting image.

"It was something about focusing the energies of the earth," Lucien said. "That's not Michael. I do wonder if she might have hypnotized him."

Could that be true? Cynthia might have picked up some old magic from the gypsies or the circus folk. Stella wouldn't rule it out. "But *marriage*! What was he thinking? It's such a rush. It's so extreme."

"I suppose people do it every day."

"And they get divorced every day. Cynthia has done it

twice already. Can it be an addiction? Does she need to put on a wedding dress once per year? Or perhaps it's good for business?"

"I can't say I'm impressed either, but you do sound rather cynical, you know. Weren't you writing romantic stories for magazines at one time?"

"I've also written articles about polygamy and goat breeding," Stella replied. "Writing about a subject doesn't mean that you believe in it."

"I'd suggest that we ought to make a plan to rescue him; I have considered it, only I'm not sure he wants to be rescued," Lucien said, rather solemnly. "I suppose he's a grown-up and we have to let him make his own mistakes, test his wings, all those clichés."

"Do we? But I don't want to watch him making mistakes, and frankly I'm not sure that marrying Cynthia Palmer is a grown-up choice."

"I believe that some of her parties are very grown up."

"Quite! Can you imagine Michael at one of those?"

The taxicab swung around a corner and paused at a crossing for a gaggle of nannies pushing perambulators. Would that come next? Would Michael be rocking a cradle by next Christmas? Forsythia and cherry blossom were out in a garden, flickering in the light, and there were pots of golden crocuses by doorsteps. Stella saw sticky-looking buds on a horse chestnut and climbing roses were sending out fresh pink shoots. Everything seemed to be resurgent. Burgeoning. Fecund. Had sap risen in Michael too? Is that what it was? Had some primitive, undeniable man urge surged in his loins? Stella found her imagery heading in a *Lady Chatterley* direction, so she tried to think about the spring fashions instead.

"I can appreciate how Cynthia might value Michael's looks, but surely he's a little modest and quiet for her taste? Doesn't she normally go in for fractious poets and petulant sculptors? Types who have tantrums, who like to throw crockery and stand in corners glowering?"

"His niceness is probably a novelty to her," Lucien replied. "Though I do wonder how long that novelty might last. Perhaps she regards him as exotically northern and daringly lower class? The English do normally like to mate within their own class, don't they? Were you in love with him too?"

"I'm sorry?" Stella swiveled her head so fast that her earrings swung against her cheeks. For a second, she questioned whether she might have misheard him. Had he really just said that? But the look on Lucien's face told her that she hadn't misheard.

"*Tiens,* I shouldn't have asked you that. I apologize. You don't have to tell me. But I felt it within five minutes of first meeting him." Lucien's dark eyes met hers and he smiled rather sadly. "I have no idea whether he knows—though, frankly, if he hasn't noticed, he must be blind and deaf. For goodness' sake, I followed the man to London! Did he really imagine I was that keen on smog, flat beer and boiled cabbage? I'm obviously not his type, I realized that long ago, but *cette femme!* Wait until you see her. I know she's a famous beauty, and everyone talks about how fabulously she wears her clothes, but I'm not certain she isn't a witch. Seriously, could she have put a spell on him?"

They pulled up in front of a white stuccoed row. It was a smart address, in a square overlooking a railed garden with tall plane trees, and was a striking contrast to Michael and Lucien's flat over a pie-and-mash shop. Cynthia had clearly done extremely well for herself. This wasn't earned on a life model's wages, was it? Perhaps this was the rumored family money? Or maybe this was what two divorces did for a girl? Stella briefly wondered if she'd been foolish in her abstemiousness. As far as she was aware, Cynthia didn't really *do* anything for a living apart from being photographed and talking about herself to magazines.

They stepped out of the taxi and exchanged meaningful looks. From the pavement Stella could hear a good deal of noise coming from a first-floor window, loud voices, eruptions of laughter and the beat of music.

"Have you been here before?" she asked as they ascended in the lift.

"No! I've never been deemed worthy of an invitation. Is it just me, or do you feel like we're entering the spider's lair?"

The floor space of Michael's flat would easily have fitted inside the entrance hall. The ceilings were high and Stella looked up at fine plasterwork moldings. The highly polished wooden floors were covered with antique Afghan rugs.

Lucien whistled. "*Putain!* Has she earned this by taking her clothes off? I wish I'd tried it myself now."

Stella linked Lucien's arm. "I seem to remember that when you're inebriated you're very keen on taking your clothes off. I have an unfortunately vivid memory of you sprinting a circuit of the Place Monge wearing nothing but a pair of espadrilles and a spotted bowtie."

"And yet no one has ever offered to pay me for it." He shook his head and smiled. "*Incroyable, n'est-ce pas?*"

They followed the sounds of revelry into a room which was decorated with dark, brass-studded furniture, emerald-green silk sofas and ostentatiously large vases of freckled orange lilies. It smelled of patchouli and pollen and Stella stifled a sneeze. Potted palms occupied the corners of the room, incense burners trailed smoke, and a line of bronze deities squatted on the mantelpiece. A man in a purple satin suit was playing a white piano, his facial expressions suggesting that he was putting much feeling into the piece, but its notes were barely audible above the *fortissimo* voices.

"Doesn't it remind you of that Indian restaurant on Regent Street?" Lucien whispered into Stella's ear. "Do you think we could order a lamb Madras?"

He'd brilliantined his chestnut-brown hair smooth, but curls were already starting to spring out. Stella fought an urge to smooth them down. "I know what you mean. I also feel like I've blundered onto the stage in the middle of a Noël Coward play."

Stella was relieved to see Michael heading toward them through the vociferous crowd, but slightly alarmed to spot

Cynthia on his arm. Michael hugged her and gave Lucien's hand a hearty shake. Cynthia planted dry, cool kisses that smelled faintly like Dilys' herbal cigarettes.

"You remember Stella, don't you?" Michael asked, turning to Cynthia.

"I think so." She sounded hesitant. "Michael talks about you a lot and he was most insistent that I ought to remember you, but I couldn't place your face."

It was strange to have Cynthia's eyes trained upon her. There was something penetrating but also inscrutable in that gaze. Stella remembered being stared at by an owl in a bird sanctuary once. She felt similarly studied now and couldn't read the emotion behind the eyes.

"Congratulations!" She made an effort to put on a friendly smile and stretched out and squeezed both their arms. "I hope you'll be blissfully happy together." She did sincerely want Michael to be happy, but might he really achieve that with this intense, owl-eyed woman?

"Oh, we shall. Don't you worry," Cynthia said.

She certainly was dazzling, Stella had to concede that. She was wearing black silk georgette threaded all over with gold bugle beads (was it Schiaparelli?), and a whole workshop full of jewelry. The bangles extended a good six inches up each arm and her fingers were clustered with emeralds. Cynthia looked expensive, sleek and like she might have taken hours to get dressed. Her *maquillage* was flawless, and she had film-star cheekbones, but whatever did she and Michael talk about?

"Stella is living back up in Yorkshire again now," he ploughed on.

"Of course, you two had that Yorkshire thing going on, didn't you? I do recall that now. Darling, do you remember your vowels?" She turned to Michael and laughed. "But surely Yorkshire is somewhere that people leave? I know that one goes there to shoot pheasants in October, but no one actually chooses to live there, do they? Can one live there?"

"I had family reasons to go back," Stella said.

"How tiresome for you." Cynthia's green eyes were ringed with kohl and she widened them theatrically as she spoke. There was something altogether theatrical about her. Her gestures all seemed to be self-conscious, she might have spent time fine-tuning her poise in front of a mirror, and she spoke as if she was pronouncing lines from a play. Was she in character tonight, or was she always like this? Surely she didn't use that voice behind closed doors?

"Stella's working on a new book," Michael went on. She could hear him making an effort. "She's staying in our flat this week while she's working in the British Museum."

"Isn't their flat perfectly horrid? I think it's so funny that they live over a shop that sells meat pies! Could you invent anything more ghastly? People don't believe me when I tell them that the bedclothes smelled of gravy. Too, too vile!"

"They're actually rather good pies," Michael said.

"Darling, you are hilarious."

Stella noticed Cynthia's fingernails as she lifted her glass. They were conspicuously long, painted dark red and had been filed into points. There was something unsavory about these nails, Stella thought. How could one do the washing-up or make pastry with talons like that? But then she supposed that Cynthia didn't go in for much of that sort of thing. Did she take staff with her when she set off in her gypsy caravan? Stella had seen artistically grainy photographs of Cynthia poking a stick at a camp fire. She couldn't have done any camp-fire cooking with those nails, though, could she? For all the talk of the romance of *la vie gitane*, there'd be a maid out of camera shot with a wicker luncheon-basket, cans of hot water and a pile of nice clean towels, wouldn't there?

"Anyway, we must circulate, but do help yourselves to drinks."

"There, you've been Cynthia-ed," said Lucien, as they walked away. "You seem to have come through it relatively unbruised."

"She's . . . extraordinary," said Stella. Further polite words presently evaded her. "How on earth are she and Michael a couple?"

"*Ex-ac-te-ment!* I'm so glad you see that too. Has he told you that he's painted her portrait?"

"Michael has? But he hasn't painted for years, not since he left college, and he's rarely voluntarily done portraits." Michael's subject was the glinting scales of mackerels and the shapes of pomegranates. Portraits weren't really his thing. Stella remembered how his cheeks had blushed in life-drawing classes. Had Cynthia emboldened him then? "Have you seen it?"

"Apparently, she's not wearing much clothing. I'm not sure I want to see it."

"No," Stella agreed.

She felt a little better when Lucien had placed a glass of gin-and-bitters in her hand and put an arm around her shoulders. But she noticed that her glass trembled slightly when she lifted it to her lips and she asked herself why that was. Had Cynthia really rattled her that much? Stella gulped at her drink, willing it to kick in and steady her nerves.

"Is there going to be food, or was that it?" Lucien asked. "She doesn't really look like she eats, does she?"

"I imagine she has supplies of frightfully expensive vitamin pills and swallows them down with the driest martinis."

"Perhaps the odd stuffed olive?" Stella suggested. "I'm trying to picture her eating a meat pie, or a Scotch egg. I'd pay a guinea to see that, but I just can't visualize it."

Stella had written many articles about cocktail-party canapés—it was one of her specialisms—and so she now wondered if that made her difficult to please. But it wasn't that, was it? Beautiful young men in Pierrot costumes had circulated with trays of blinis, all prettily polka-dotted with various kinds of fish eggs, but they tasted of disappointingly little and no further food was forthcoming. Stella got the impression that more care had been invested in the costumes than the canapés, and Michael clearly hadn't arranged the catering. She scanned the room for him, expecting to see embarrassment on his face, but he was standing on his own, looking out of a window, and she couldn't read his expression. Did he look happy? Like a man at his engagement party should? She wasn't absolutely sure.

Stella left Lucien talking about new restaurant openings with Claude Comyns, and toured the walls as she sipped at her gin. There were large abstract canvasses, slightly alarming erotic prints (Stella squinted and stepped closer, but then wished she hadn't. Cynthia hadn't contorted Michael into that position, had she?) and photographs of Cynthia herself. She was looking intense on the steps of her gypsy caravan, being *bohème* in turbans, smocking and a swan-feather headdress, and waving her arms at moody skies. Wasn't it a bit peculiar to decorate your walls with your own image? The thought of her own face on the walls of Celandine Cottage made Stella wince.

She eavesdropped on conversations as she examined the artwork, and watched the room in the reflections of the glass. People were talking about exhibitions, commissions, catalogs and art dealers. It was awhile since Stella had heard that vocabulary and she remembered how she'd once hungered for it too. Where would she be now if she'd stuck with it? At eighteen, arriving in London for the first time, she'd imagined a future in which she'd have a studio of her own and paint canvasses of big seas, wide skies, and foreign cities where the twilights were scented with spices. But by the age of twenty-one, Stella had known that she didn't have the talent—or, more importantly, the confidence—to pull it off. Michael had told her that she ought to believe in herself more, and Jack Graves had observed that it was very middle class of her to worry about money, but the job with the magazine offered a regular wage, and she'd felt that she would have been reckless to refuse that.

"Of course, he's gone abstract," a voice was saying, "frightfully intellectual, really pushing the boundaries. He's renounced the third dimension entirely. So stimulating. So now."

It was all about confidence, wasn't it? So much of it was illusion fueled by faultless self-belief. As she looked around the room, Stella concluded that success seemed to have a lot to do with how a person held their shoulders, how adept they were at wielding the fashionable lexicon and carrying off bias-cut silk georgette.

Much of the old crowd from college were here. Stella hadn't seen some of them for a decade and it was curious to observe the signs of time upon once-familiar faces, how lines and shadows subtly alter. Her former classmates looked like they'd been doing a lot of living, and to hear them speak, they were all busy being marvelous and modern, having bright, full, amusing lives and violent passions. And what was she doing? Still fretting over her father and writing articles about new ways to fold table napkins? For a moment, Stella had a sensation of standing still while the room rushed around her.

Aside from the college crowd, there were a number of Cynthia's people here. There was a tendency for crushed velvet and silk cravats in this brigade, and several of the men were wearing makeup, Stella suspected. They all had the look of actors who had just come off stage after a long performance. In Yorkshire, Stella was sometimes conscious of being conspicuously patterned and colorful, but in this company she felt insipid. She'd forgotten quite how competitive the dressing was in London. And queen of it all was Cynthia. She was smiling as she put her fingers through Michael's hair now. This was a trifle too intimate to watch and Stella found that she had to look away.

"What are you working on now, Stell?"

She turned to see Rupert Snelgrave regarding her over the rim of a cocktail glass. It had always annoyed her how he must abbreviate her name. How taxing were two syllables? She'd also heard that Rupert had made a face at *Mrs. Raffald*, calling it a fuddy-duddy baking book. But then Rupert was painting pastel-colored semi-abstract landscapes in which the clouds all looked like blobs of mashed potato. She'd gone to see his last exhibition with Michael and they had joked that this must be Rupert's *pomme purée* period. Stella felt a little sad as she remembered how they'd linked arms and grinned their way around the gallery.

"I've been commissioned to write a history of English food," she said. "It's a heck of a lot of history to cover, but it's an exciting project." She felt an urge to fling her arms wide to demonstrate a great expanse of centuries, a broad swathe of research and scholarliness. "The history of food is the history of civilization," she added, just to make sure that Rupert had grasped the scholarliness.

"So are cookery books your thing now? Jeremy Pemberton

told me you'd gone all domestic. 'She's written a book about some woman who makes custard!' he said." Rupert snorted at this. "A Mrs. Ruffles, wasn't it?"

"Elizabeth Raffald."

"Have to say, I hadn't heard of the old dear."

It wasn't the first time Stella had been told this. It was annoying how regularly people reacted to the title of her book with a baffled "Who?", but Stella wasn't sure that she could be bothered escorting Rupert through Mrs. Raffald's marvelousness. She suspected he wouldn't be capable of appreciating it.

"I must admit, it did surprise me to hear that," Rupert went on. "I mean, it's not the sort of work that one would have expected of you back in the day. Weren't you given to making statements about feminine self-assertion? Storming barricades of masculine entitlement? But now you've gone all baked goods and periwigs?" He smiled tightly. "All crinolines and homeliness? Still, I suppose that asserting one's femininity must be tiring."

"Homeliness? As a father of three, I'm surprised how pejorative you make that word sound, Rupert. You must like Julia being homely?" Rupert and Julia lived in a basement flat with three children under five, Michael had told her.

"Julia adores homemaking, but then she's never pretended to be anything else."

"Does she?" Julia was presently flopped on a sofa with drooping eyelids and rusk stains on her blouse.

"But I mean, it seems an unambitious sort of book, not

very modern, rather safe, and perhaps a little dusty and twee, dare I say?"

Stella tried not to splutter her drink. "Not very modern? But open any newspaper at the moment and you'll read politicians talking about food. I think you'll find that it's a very current issue—and it's fascinatingly revealing too. What we eat says everything about us. It gives us away—just look at Cynthia's canapés," she added, and then worried whether she perhaps ought to have kept that thought to herself.

Rupert's mouth did a *moue*. "It's nice that you're passionate about your puddings."

Damn him. She had an urge to hiss *pomme purée* in his face. There was something thoroughly patronizing about the way he pronounced the word nice.

"It must be nice for Julia to have a night off," she replied. "The poor girl appears to be having a nap. She does look terribly exhausted. Don't you think you ought to go and rescue her glass, Rupert?"

Stella finished her drink, the words "dusty" and "twee" still buzzing around her like troublesome wasps. She felt affronted on behalf of Mrs. Raffald and really rather riled. If she could write a successful book, a book that sold well, would people treat her differently? Would they take her seriously then? Friends from college had published volumes of poetry and criticism that had been taken seriously, and even Effie Petherbridge, who seemed not to have a thought in her head, had written a novel that reviewers called "insightful." But then this crowd all had connections, contacts in the right places, and could afford to lock themselves away for a year and focus uninterrupted energies on analysing Gerard Manley Hopkins' sprung rhythms. Perhaps she'd been foolish not to exploit the connections that she had here, not to shake hands a little more warmly, and grasp the courage to ask favors. Did they all think that she wrote twee books, though?

"Stella Douglas! Good Lord, you're more like a Rubens Venus than ever these days. You ought to have a flight of cherubs around you and be dressed in something altogether more diaphanous." Jack Graves chewed on the end of his pipe as he gave her an appraising look. "Brava!" he said.

Stella hesitated as to the appropriate reply. She wasn't certain that she wanted to be a Rubens Venus and neither was she keen on how Jack had decided to converse with her chest. A lot of young men seemed to suffer from insufficient neck musculature these days. It was unfortunate how it prevented them from conducting a conversation with a woman's face. "How are you, Jack?"

He looked sleek as a plump herring in his pin-striped suit and had arrived with a new wife on his arm. Lucien had whispered that the wife was an American, obscenely wealthy, and reputed to have an issue with white rum. Stella had read an article about Jack's stringed geometrical forms being exhibited in Venice to some acclaim, but if she hadn't known better she might have guessed him an insurance salesman in his slightly shiny serge suiting.

"Still no wedding ring, I see," he went on. "What's wrong with the manhood in Yorkshire? Are they all blind, or is it that they're damn fools?" He gave her an unabashed up-and-down look. She might be a heifer coming into the ring at Malton Cattle Market and she almost expected him to give her flanks an appraising slap. "I say, didn't you and Michael have a 'thing' back in the day?" Jack made quotation marks with his fingers and looked amused. "I suppose this must be a bit awkward, what?"

"Not at all!" Where had that come from? Other people didn't think that too, did they? "I'm afraid you've got that quite wrong."

"Of course, you wouldn't want to admit it here, would you? Say no more!"

Stella wanted to say more, considerably more, but feared arousing suspicion with excessive protestations. She wished that Jack would stop smirking at her like that. She felt horribly seen. "Will you excuse me, Jack? Lucien is waving a drink at me. I must unburden him."

"Certainly. But don't have too many drinks, eh? We don't want tears later. It can be awfully embarrassing if the ex starts unburdening! By the way, you blush awfully prettily, you know."

Stella stepped into the hallway, glad to break away from the chatter and appraising eyes, and refreshed her lipstick in a rather covetable Venetian mirror. As she did so, she spied Michael watching her. She lifted a hand to his reflection and saw him smile as he began to walk toward her. She wasn't blushing, was she?

"Are you unscathed?" he asked. "I saw Jack giving you

the once-over. It was embarrassing to watch. I dithered over whether you needed rescuing."

"I wish you had. His poor wife! Do you think he's driven her to drink?"

She turned toward Michael. Cynthia's fingers had styled his hair into a center parting. He looked handsome tonight in an ink-blue silk suit, but Stella didn't like the idea of Cynthia stealthily remodeling him. He didn't need that, did he?

"I wouldn't pity her too much. She's in a huddle with Cynthia and they're critiquing everyone's clothing. They seem to be enjoying themselves."

"You know, I'd forgotten what the old college crowd are like. It's so fiercely competitive, isn't it? They're all watching each other out of the corners of their eyes and measuring themselves up. It makes me want to run away and hide under a rock."

He laughed. "It is a bit like that, but you should have no fear of not measuring up. You're still the golden girl. You always were. Every man in our year had an infatuation with you at some stage—and some of the women too, I'd hazard. We all set our caps at you, but you were far too busy being studious and infuriatingly talented. I bet you never even noticed, did you?"

It was sweet of him to want to boost her confidence, but *he'd* never set his cap at her, had he? "You are a darling, and wonderfully loyal, but I don't believe you for a second. Anyway, are you having fun? You and Cynthia make a glamorous couple."

"You do like her, don't you? I want you to be friends."

Stella tried to picture herself coming over for dinner, making amicable chitchat over a casserole, perhaps organizing a shopping trip together, or meeting Cynthia for tea in Lyons. It didn't seem plausible. "I am a little intimidated by her, if I'm honest, but if she makes you happy, I will learn to love her." Could she? This presently felt like quite a stretch.

"You mustn't be intimidated by her. You need to get to know her. Yes, she puts on a bit of a front—there's a persona that she maintains in public—but she's an interesting and creative person, passionate and intelligent."

Interesting? The choice of word struck Stella. Men in the first throes of love didn't describe the objects of their desire as interesting, did they? But if he'd asked Cynthia to marry him, he must be in love with her. "You are going to carry on working, aren't you? You're not going to throw it all in?"

"You're giving me a look!" He smiled at her over his glass. "You don't have to worry about me, you know. I'm getting married, not having a mental breakdown. Cynthia doesn't mind that I'm at the restaurant in the evenings. She understands, and accepts, that that's what my life is like. She goes out with her friends at night. It actually works out rather well."

It sounded like it was going to work out tremendously well for Cynthia. "I do worry about you. I can't help it. All of this is happening so fast. I'd hate to see you hurt."

"And who is going to hurt me? Cynthia?" He looked

slightly rattled suddenly. "Hell's bells, Stella, I am nearly thirty, you know. I've had all this from Lucien. We're not going to fall out, are we?"

"No, of course not. I'm sorry. Let's be friends and go and find another drink. I'm going to need to get quite blotto if I have to undergo another interrogation as to why I'm not tidily coupled up."

"But I thought that question was an easy one for you? How did you describe marriage? An 'outmoded institution'?" He held his arm out for her to link. "I can't presently bring to mind all of your argument, I'm afraid, but I do recall that it involved subjugation and brood mares. Actually, that reminds me, I haven't told Cynth about the subjugation bit yet. I'd better warn her, I suppose. I wonder how that will work out?"

"I said that?" Stella turned to him. She couldn't recall it.

"Don't you remember? It was when you came down in the autumn, that day when we'd been drinking daiquiris in the Savoy. You were a bit tipsy at the time, but you wagged your finger at me and were impressively fervent."

Had she been too fervent? What precisely had she said? "Golly. I recall having an almighty headache the next day, but I can't remember speechifying at you. Did I bang on? I am sorry."

"No need to apologize. It was most enlightening. *In vino veritas* and all that, eh?"

"How embarrassing. I think I've gone off daiquiris."

*

Stella found Lucien by the potted palms and they passed a whispered commentary together as they watched the room.

"They all had different partners last time I saw them," she said. "Some of them appear to have done direct swaps. Doesn't that strike you as incestuous? I could do with a schematic so that I don't put my foot in it."

Lucien laughed. "Is Cynthia about to dance a flamenco?"

"I'm not sure. She looks like she's revving up for something, doesn't she?"

Cynthia seemed to enjoy the jangling as she moved her arms in dancer's arabesques. Her hands made elegant shapes in the air, which she appeared to regard with self-admiration. The coterie of obedient men around her watched too, and there was Michael in the middle of it all.

"Why do you suppose he proposed?" Stella asked.

"She's one of those women who marries, isn't she? A serial marrier. She probably dropped heavy hints, beckoned and then barred certain gates, et cetera. You know how they do it."

"I'm not sure I do. Does he love her, do you think?"

"I suspect he's trying hard to convince himself that he does."

"But why? How utterly depressing!"

"It's what people do, isn't it?" Lucien shrugged.

"Is it? You know, I was contemplating renouncing alcohol a few minutes ago, but I'm now thinking that I might take it up full-time."

"What?" Lucien looked at her. "Renunciation is the last thing we ought to be contemplating. Only strong liquor will get us through this." He put his hands to her shoulders. "I'd happily renounce this crowd, though, and I can only take so much of watching her twiddling his dials. What say we dig an escape tunnel and find a nice, ordinary public house, filled with unthreatening, ordinary people?"

"That's the most attractive offer that anyone has made me in a long time."

They walked arm in arm and ate salty fried potatoes out of newspaper. It was pleasant to stroll through the dark streets of London like that, watching the glitter of the lights in the puddles, pointing at Parmesan cheeses in the window of an Italian grocer's shop, and laughing as they tried to visualize Cynthia eating a Scotch egg.

"You will keep an eye on him, won't you?" Stella asked.

"Don't worry. I plan to keep a particularly sharp eye on him. I will survey his movements and transmit relevant bulletins to you at regular intervals. I live in hope that Cynthia's spell might wear off in time."

"But if they're already married before it wears off!"

"*Eh bien*, she rarely stays married for long, does she? I think Niall was the record at two years. Give it a few months, and Michael will have served his purpose for her and she'll hand him back. He'll be vulnerable then and he will need us. *J'ai tout réfléchi.*"

"Haven't you?" Stella glanced at Lucien. He appeared to be quite sincere. "But poor Michael!"

"Like a tenderized escalope," Lucien added and shrugged.

"But I don't want him to be a tenderized escalope!"

Lucien stopped, turned and looked at her. He examined her face a little too closely and lengthily, and then gently put his hand to her cheek. "*Ma pauvre chérie,* I do believe that you're suffering from it even worse than me."

Stella wasn't entirely sorry to be leaving London behind. She'd thoroughly enjoyed working in the British Museum, and had gleaned excellent information on Jacobean pastry, the evolution of the plough and the history of herring fishing, but at times it had been hard to concentrate. She'd had a useful morning studying turnip cultivation; however, in an indulgent moment she'd drifted into a daydream in which she was motoring around the Mediterranean with Michael, writing about salty hams and sweet Charentais melons, slicing into glistening apricot tarts, and cracking crab claws by glittering harbors. When Stella had resurfaced, she'd made herself sit up and copy out a whole page of turnip statistics. Though she was grateful to have the use of the flat, she was having troubled, sleepless nights in Michael's bed. Lucien spent the evenings being far too candid and giving her penetrating looks, and she must drag her thoughts away from recalling Cynthia talking about Michael's sheets. This simply wouldn't do, Stella told herself. All in all, it would be good to get back home, she decided, and to completely immerse herself in contemplating the evolution of pottage ingredients and regional variations in ham curing. She closed her suitcase, gave herself an admonishing frown in Michael's bedroom mirror, and pressed her fingers against her eyes.

Caroline Scott

"SIMNEL CAKE"
[From the notebook of Elizabeth Douglas, 1922]

Stella came home for the Easter weekend and brought her friend Michael with her. I was a little nervous to cook for him, as Stella had told me that he has a job in a restaurant kitchen, but he had lovely manners, was very appreciative and even volunteered to do the washing up. (I made sure that Charlie heard him say that.)

I roasted a leg of lamb and baked my Simnel cake, a good rich fruit cake, with a layer of almond paste, topped with eleven marzipan balls to represent the loyal disciples. I remember making it with Stella when she was a child and her fingers getting all glued up with marzipan. I told Michael that story and he asked me if I'd mind writing my fruit cake recipe out for him. I think there's much to be said for a young man who takes an interest in cake and who smiles so fondly at my daughter.

Charlie and I agreed that Stella seems to be a bit sweet on Michael. She didn't say anything, but it amused me to watch how she looked at him, and to notice how he returned those glances. He's a fine-looking young man, evidently a hard worker and from a respectable family. Stella might be keen on him, but she has no talent whatsoever for courting. As I listened to her holding forth on the rights of women workers and the shackles of conventional aspirations, I felt a little sorry for the lad. I might have to elbow my daughter.

It surprised Stella to see those words in her mother's handwriting. She remembered her father raising an eyebrow when

Michael had helped her mother with the washing up, but Michael hadn't been giving her special smiles that day, had he? It hadn't been like that, had it? Stella felt her mother's elbow connecting with her ribs as she read the last paragraph. But it was ten years too late, wasn't it?

Chapter Fifteen

Stella had been making notes on the Roman occupation of Britain and compiling a list of the foodstuffs they'd imported, the oil and wine and spices, all the plant varieties and the livestock. It had turned into a long list. She'd then read about the Saxon ways with bacon, the Viking methods of preserving fish, and the Arabic influence in the food of the Normans. There seemed to be an awful lot of importing and intermingling going on through these centuries, and it was difficult to draw a tidy border around what Englishness meant—but, for the moment, she'd turned the page on these niggling ambiguities. This week, she would write about Banbury cakes and Bath buns. That surely was uncontroversial and entirely English (whatever that was)—wasn't it?

Stella looked out at the passing countryside now. It was like England as it is depicted on exported biscuit tins, a country of little valleys and beech copses, of gilded fields and mellow, misted hollows. Green hills rolled evenly, as if they'd been landscaped by Capability Brown, and oak-framed vistas presented themselves for her approval. Even the sheep here appeared to have been shampooed and set. Stella thought that if she'd grown up in Gloucestershire, she might be painting watercolor landscapes and infinitely contemplating variations of green. But then, looking at the honey-colored houses on the hilltops, she supposed that one had to be rather wealthy to live here. She was still recovering from the shock of having paid 2*s*.1*d*. for a pot of tea in Banbury.

It had been a successful morning, all in all; she'd had a fruitful tête-à-tête with a baker, a tip-off about where to find an authentic Sally Lunn in Bath, and then a pleasant hour lingering in a teashop while she wrote up her notes on currant cakes (having paid that price for a pot of tea, she was damn well going to eke it out). She would have put it down as an altogether satisfying day, had the engine of her motor car not started making an alarming whirring sound just as Banbury disappeared from the rearview mirror.

Stella was finding it difficult to get into gear now and the car seemed to be losing power on hills. And there were such a lot of hills here. What they lacked in height, they made up for in profusion. A horse and cart had overtaken her moments ago as she slowly chugged to an ascent. Whatever was wrong with the engine? She'd put petrol in, hadn't she? Was there a problem with the petrol? Oh damnation, Stella thought—this was the last thing she needed.

The whirring was becoming more insistent and, though she put her foot to the floor, all the power seemed to have gone from the engine. She managed to pull onto the verge just as the motor ceased altogether and shuddered to a halt. Stella stamped her foot on the accelerator, but it whined a brief complaint and then gave up. She beat her fists on the steering wheel and released a rather Anglo-Saxon selection of vocabulary. Why couldn't this have happened while she was driving through a village? How long was it since she'd passed somewhere that looked inhabited? All she could see was billowing green hedges and fields of barley.

Stella lifted the bonnet and stared at the engine. It gave her no answers. She could change a tire quite proficiently and top up the oil, but she had no idea what to do about a spluttering engine. She tapped a piece of metal experimentally with her knuckle. It was hot. Should she hit it with a spanner or something? She walked around the vehicle and kicked the tires, but beyond relieving some exasperation, this did no good.

Her resources were deserting her now. Damn and blast it; her father would know what to do. Perhaps she might telephone him? But how far away was the nearest call box? She really ought to have done a motor car maintenance course at some time. She should be capable of such things. She shouldn't need help. But, drat it, she did. She could hear the cooling engine ticking faintly, and then nothing. Silence. Branches shifted, birds arced above and Stella was alone on a country road. She kicked the tires again.

There was no point walking back in the direction she'd come, as she hadn't passed a house for miles, but perhaps she might find a farm further along the road? Stella took her overnight bag, shut the car door and set off. Finches flashed in the tops of ancient elm trees and rooks lifted on gleaming wings, while the verdant landscape rippled sweetly all around her.

Sheep bleated peacefully, cow parsley billowed at the roadside and celandines shone poetically. A cuckoo called and an answer echoed back. She really ought to be drinking it in; it was like benign nature was spreading its arms for her, but Stella was in a foul mood now. There were still no houses in sight. Damn the countryside, she thought. Damn the blithe, smug, under-populated wilderness of it all. As she let rip with her damning, her ankle twisted over. Why had she worn heels today? Damn agriculture, damn rustication, damn Banbury cakes and damn Cynthia Palmer! She could cry tears of frustration.

Stella stopped and made herself take a deep breath. She closed her eyes and paused for a moment, breathing in the scent of new-ploughed earth and hawthorn blossom, hearing the swishing of branches above and the cooing of wood pigeons. She could hear her own pulse banging too, and then . . . was that the sound of an engine? She turned to see a vehicle, a good distance down the road, but unmistakably heading toward her. As it got closer, she saw that it was a van with a load on the back. Please let it be a friendly driver with a spare seat, she prayed. Please let him stop and not be a murderer or a pervert. (Though, right at this moment, she'd take her chances with a pervert.) She tried to adopt a striking attitude, something both imperative and appealing—but how to convey that with arms and legs? In the end, she waved her hands. Would the van stop? She waved her hands more frantically, faintly aware that she probably looked ridiculous. Dear God, please let it stop.

As the vehicle slowed and pulled over, Stella felt that she

could hug the driver. That impulse intensified as he cut off the engine and stepped down. She noted height, broad shoulders and a face straight out of a *Vanity Fair* photo spread. She blinked her eyes, but, no, she hadn't dreamed him up. How deliciously fickle fate can be, Stella thought.

"Interesting makeup," the improbably handsome stranger said as he walked toward her. He took his hat off and smiled. He was dark, with angular features, had expensive-looking teeth, exemplary eyebrows, and his brilliantined hair was like patent black leather.

"I'm sorry?" she said.

"Your face. You look like a glamorous advertisement for engine oil."

"Oh, hell." She took out her compact. She'd evidently put her hands to her face after she'd been poking inexpertly under the car bonnet. What a sight she was.

"Here," he said, and passed her a clean white handkerchief. "Whatever have you been doing?"

"My motor has broken down. It lost all power and hiccupped to a halt. I don't suppose you could give me a lift to a garage, or a telephone, could you?" His handkerchief smelled of lavender. Perhaps he had a pretty little wife who layered his laundry with lavender bags? But he wasn't wearing a wedding ring, was he?

"Ah, it was you. I did see a poor Baby Austin looking dejected on the verge. Do you want me to go and have a look at it? Come on. Hop in. I'll take you back and we'll see if we can get you moving."

"Do you have the time? That's awfully kind."

"Freddie Langham," he said, and offered her his hand
to shake.

Stella looked at her own oil-smeared hand and his black-
ened handkerchief. She could hardly give it back like that.
She wiggled her grimed fingers at him. "You don't really
want to shake my hand, do you?" But then his fingers were
around hers. It was a firm handshake. No wet fish here. He
was clocking up points by the second. "Stella Douglas,"
she said, "and thank you. I try not to play damsel in distress, not a part that I enjoy, but I'm extremely grateful that
you stopped."

"What sort of a no-good reprobate would I be if I drove
past a damsel in distress?"

He grinned at her again. His smile was like the beam of
a lighthouse (how did he do that? What toothpaste did he
use?) and his dark eyes sparkled. Mind you, even if he'd had
a face like a gargoyle and been dressed like a rat-catcher, she
could have kissed him at this moment. He gave her a hand
up into the van and nodded his head in a most chivalrous
way. What delightful manners he had. Stella decided that the
day was brightening.

"I'm so sorry," she said, as he climbed up beside her. "I
hope you weren't pressed for time? I'm not delaying you
getting to lunch, am I?"

"Nothing that can't wait."

"I've never sat in a van before. It's quite jolly, isn't it?
Are you moving house?" She glanced back and saw a lot of

Victorian mahogany furniture. Perhaps he lived in one of those hilltop houses? He had the right accent for it.

"I'm on my way back from an auction." He did a three-point turn in the lane. "It's stock for my shop."

"You sell furniture?"

"Antiques and collectibles. I specialize in furniture, treen, kitchenware, studio pottery and the odd stuffed parrot. I sold one of those last week..." He paused and seemed to consider. "Only, he might have been a cockatoo. Are they the same thing? I'll admit that my parrot expertise is a bit limited. Apparently, he belonged to an English professor in perkier times and had quite an extensive vocabulary of Middle English."

"How astonishing."

"Isn't it?" He turned to her, his eyes lingering on her face for a moment as he smiled.

They pulled up by her car. He lifted the bonnet and she heard him sigh deeply. He took off his hat, rubbed his forehead and bit his lip as he contemplated. Stella hovered at his elbow, glancing between his remarkably attractive profile and the mysterious mechanical parts. He prodded and knocked at various pieces of metal and looked thoughtful.

"Is it something serious, do you think?" she eventually had to ask.

"I ought to be able to deduce that by sheer power of masculinity, shouldn't I? I'm well aware that, as a male of the species, I'm expected to attack this with know-how and gusto, and to have you back on the road again within five minutes, but I'm afraid that my masculinity is failing me at this moment. Can you tell that I'm floundering? Ask me to glue a broken vase together or re-upholster a chair, and I'm your chap. I regret to say that motor car engines are mysterious to me, though. How terribly embarrassing." He put a hand through his hair and gritted his teeth as he turned to her. "I'll admit, I feel rather unmanned."

"Don't worry, I wouldn't know where to start. I'm sorry, have you got a cigarette?"

"How about I take you to a garage? There's a trustworthy fellow in town. He can come out with a tow rope and we could have a bite to eat while you wait." He leaned in with the lighter. "Here. Let me. With those oily hands you might combust. I assume you haven't had lunch yet? The King's Arms does a decent pie and pickles. Can I tempt you?"

She watched him raise half-closed eyelids to the sun, the cigarette smoke curling from his lips, and thought that he could definitely tempt her. All too much.

"That sounds like a plan." The idea of having lunch with this man was appealing—Stella couldn't deny that—but, hell, how much was a mechanic's bill going to cost?

"Splendid. It seems to be turning into my lucky day."

Freddie pulled up in front of a shop and invited her to come in and wash her hands. She looked out and saw his name painted in black Gothic lettering. There was a display of brass kitchen scales in the bow-fronted window, copper jelly molds and hinged tins for making raised pies. They were the sort of items with which Stella might furnish her ideal kitchen, decorative but also giving the right impression. She liked people to think of her as a woman who might arrive at a party with a spectacular game pie.

"I've just picked up some scrumptious hand-carved butter stamps," Freddie said. "Darling things. They make me long to buy a dairy cow and a milk churn and to revert to a simpler life. Would you like to see?"

There was momentarily a glint of something wolfish in his grin—just briefly—and Stella was reminded of mischief-makers in fairy stories who lured innocent children with gingerbread. He had a deep voice with an edge of amusement to it, and there was a velvety and alluring quality to its tone. But a temptation of butter stamps—how heinous could that be?

"I do have a weakness for kitchenware," she admitted.

"Excellent," he said.

It was a very nice antiques shop. Though it was crammed with stock, everything was polished and well dusted. It gleamed with pewter and brass and quality cut glass, and she could smell beeswax polish and Brasso. There was a lot of dark oak and elm furniture, slipware pottery and rustic domestic items that looked as if they had been salvaged from farmhouse kitchens. Might he have salvaged any recipe books too? There was nothing overly ornate here, nothing frilled, or fringed, or transfer printed. His stock gave an impression of integrity, of quality and care. Stella pondered, perhaps as one may judge a person by their bookshelves, so too might one evaluate an antiques dealer by his stock?

"If I was furnishing a fantasy house, I might go for Jacobean oak," she considered. "It's sturdy and honest, isn't it? I can't help wondering what domestic scenes it's witnessed."

"It's not always honest. There's a lot of Victorian fakery around, all treacled up to look older than it is. It's wily stuff. You've got to know what you're looking for."

Stella had never imagined that a chest of drawers might be wily before. Freddie spoke about the fakery as if he disapproved of it, his brow briefly creased, but did she detect a twinkle in his eye? Had he ever fraudulently "treacled up' a dresser, as he put it?

"I'm renting a furnished cottage at the moment and it's full of reproduction Gothic. Everything has twiddles and fretwork and bulbous legs, and it's all an unpleasant golden-syrup color. It makes me think about actors hamming it up in heavy stage makeup."

"How utterly ghastly. If you want to shift anything on, I might be able to help."

"As I say, I'm renting, so I'm stuck with it. Besides, I'm up in Yorkshire. Rather off your circuit, I expect."

"That is a pity," he said. "But I'm always keen to see a new part of the world. Come through to the back." He parted a beaded curtain. "I'm sorry. I'm afraid it's a bit of a mess out here. This is my Aladdin's cave."

The back room was full of stock and shelves lined with tins of waxes and stains. A sideboard stood on a paint-splattered sheet. He looked like he might be midway through giving it the treacling treatment.

"It's the door on the right. There's soap in there, but shout if you need anything more industrial."

He showed her through to a little WC and Stella was impressed that he had a spotless towel and a new bar of scented soap. Having washed the grease from her hands, she tidied her hair in the mirror and wiped a streak of engine oil from her cheek. She could hear Freddie humming as she refreshed her lipstick. She hadn't given him the best first impression, had she? But then why should she want to be making an impression on this man? Shouldn't she be focusing on finding a garage or a telephone instead? "What am I doing?" Stella mouthed to herself.

"All sorted?" he asked, as she stepped out.

"Yes. Thank you."

"These are the butter stamps I mentioned. Don't you think they're sweet? I picked them up in a house sale last week." He reached for a newspaper-wrapped package and produced blocks of wood from it, variously carved with corn sheaves, hearts and thistles.

"I see what you mean about wanting to buy a cow and spending your days playing at printing butter pats." Stella ran her fingers over the textures. They were the sort of thing that she'd love to collect.

"If you'd care to skip off into an alternative life with me, I'd buy you a lovely milkmaid's outfit."

"That's an offer I don't get every day."

"Really?" A smile twitched his mouth. "You surprise me."

"How much are they?" She felt she ought to steer him away from playing at milkmaids.

"As you've been kind enough to agree to have lunch with me, consider them a gift. I know a bunch of roses is more conventional, but heck, we have to work with what we've got."

It was a public house with low beams, brass-topped tables and stuffed pikes in glass cases. There were china barrels behind the bar, murky photographs of shepherds in smocks and faded prints of hunting scenes. Women looked up from writing postcards and men lifted their eyebrows as they took a table.

"I have a secret liking for taxidermy," Stella admitted, as she eyed the pikes. "I'd quite enjoy the company of a long-since-expired pheasant or a sparkly-eyed fox, but there's something nasty about stuffed fish, don't you think? They always look like they might be on the verge of putrefaction."

"I've got a stuffed fox up in the flat. I've had him for years. He wears a fez and he's called Crispin. I must introduce you."

"Somehow that doesn't surprise me."

Freddie left her with a drink and went over to the garage. He seemed to have arranged everything before Stella could evaluate the merits of the situation. He said he knew the mechanic, and would have a man-to-man talk with him, but should she not be the one dealing with the garage? How much might all of this cost?

She listened into other people's conversations while she

sipped at her ginger beer. A couple who had just finished eating were discussing a child who had hives, and a party of elderly men were having involved debates about swine fever, Ramsey McDonald, and whether it was appropriate for a curate to take a widow to see a Clark Gable film. Stella couldn't help making a note of the occasional phrase. People suppose that writing is a noble and romantic profession, but they really have no idea how parasitic it is.

"All sorted," Freddie said, as he returned to the table. "Watkins will go out with his tow rope now. He'll assess the damage and said he should have a verdict for you if you call in after lunch."

"Thanks most awfully. I am grateful."

"Not at all. Fret not. Everything is in hand."

He took off his hat, smoothed his shiny hair, and did that grin again before he turned to the bar. How simply resolved he made it all sound. There was a glossiness and ease about him that suggested most things in his life might be simply resolved. He exuded a sense of faultless confidence and seemed to be thoroughly enjoying demonstrating his efficiency.

"So Yorkshire, eh? You're a long way from home," he said, as he settled back at the table with a tankard. Stella had decided to have a fortifying measure of whiskey with her ginger beer this time. "What brings you to Gloucestershire?"

"I was halfway between Banbury cakes and Bath buns," she said.

He raised an eyebrow in response, which made her feel

like she'd let a double entendre slip out. "I say! You're going to have to elucidate." He settled his chin on his hands as he regarded her and looked rather amused. His habitual expression seemed to be one of expectant amusement.

"I'm a writer," she said. She could say that now, couldn't she? "I'm working on a history of English food and, well, I'm meant to be here on a research trip."

"And there's me banging on about pie and pickles! How pedestrian you must have thought me." He hesitated. "But then I'm not sure that Geoffrey can summon up marchpane, comfits and a surfeit of lampreys."

Freddie turned in his seat and looked to the man behind the bar, but he seemingly wasn't listening to their conversation, or if he was, he didn't intend to get involved in lampreys. He carried on polishing glasses.

"Well, yes, it's that sort of stuff. I was intending to head down to Bath next to scrutinze the difference between a Bath bun and a Sally Lunn."

"That sounds like tremendous fun," he said, and seemed to mean it. "What a delightful thing to do for a living. You know, I've seen the graves of William Shakespeare and William Blake, but I've never met a living writer before. Or one who isn't called William. I feel in awe of you now."

"Heavens, don't! I write for a women's magazine mostly," she admitted. "A good part of my working life is inventiveness with vol-au-vents, the wonders of the pressure-cooker and ways to stretch out the Sunday sirloin. I do have ambitions for this book, though. I want it to be engaging and colorful, but it's all slightly beige at present. I seem to be spending a lot of time writing about oatcakes and gravy."

"But doesn't gravy run in our veins? Isn't that the elixir of Englishness?" He clinked his glass against hers. "I'm sure that in your hands the oatcakes will sparkle. You know, I had a potted-char dish pass through the shop a few months ago. One so rarely sees them these days. And I had some cracking gingerbread molds last year. I can't resist bidding on that sort of thing. I do hope you'll tell me more about your book."

There was something both eager and earnest in his expression then. He really did have heavenly eyes.

"It would be my pleasure," Stella said.

The mechanic sucked on his teeth and gave her a top-to-tail look. Stella could almost feel his eyes scraping over her and this didn't seem to bode well. Her Austin was now sitting over a pit, and an oily youth was being noisy with a spanner beneath it. Poor car, Stella thought. She felt that she was rather at the mercy of these men, the evaluation of their eyes and their casually flourished spanners.

"Have you been able to diagnose the problem?" she asked, hoping against hope that it might be something cheap and easily remedied.

"Clutch gone," he said, pronouncing the word in a way that made it sound vaguely lewd.

"The clutch?"

Stella knew that a clutch was something to do with a gearbox, but wasn't precisely sure what. The way that the man now frowned his brow made it seem that this might be something crucial and expensive.

"You drive with your foot on the pedal too much. Women do that."

Did they? Was there an implied insult to womankind here? Stella wasn't entirely certain, so she resisted the urge to retort. Hadn't Freddie said this man was honest, that he was a decent chap? "And you'll be able to fix that?"

The man stared at her. Must he do that? It was a blunt stare, like a cow's. "Aye," he said eventually. "Won't be cheap, though."

"Can we quantify 'not cheap'?"

Stella tried her best smile, but it made no disernible impact on his expression. She had no idea what a clutch ought to cost. Was it just a little piece of metal, or was it one of those complicated parts that was all winding tubes and pistons? She wished that her father was here by her side. He would know all about clutches and the going rate for replacing one. He might even be able to do it himself—but how to get the car back home? She could hardly ask him to come down on the tractor and drag her two hundred miles north.

"I'll have to take the back axle off; the clutch plate will have to be relined, and it'll need decarbonizing too. With parts and labor it should come out around seven pounds. That's the normal rate, you'll find. I'll have to order parts in, so it will take the best part of a week."

"*A week!*" She wasn't sure which to be more horrified by,

the seven pounds or the week of being stuck in a distant southern county.

"Course, you could always take it elsewhere," the man said, knowing that she damn well couldn't.

She called her father from the telephone box.

"Daddy, what should a clutch cost?"

"What sort of clutch?" He was shouting. Stella could hear the cricket on the wireless in the background. Did he have to have it on quite so loud? She wondered if he was perhaps going a little deaf.

"For my Austin. I'm stuck. I've broken down."

She listened to the rumble of the Bradford crowd and the noise of Frank Sibbles taking a run up. "That's a six!" her father said.

"I'm sorry? Six pounds?"

There was an unfortunate whiff of gentlemen's lavatories about this telephone box and she didn't want to touch her face with the receiver. She was surprised that men who lived in picture-postcard Gloucestershire villages didn't have more decorum and bladder control.

"Six runs. Sorry about that. No, to reline a clutch on an Austin should cost about three pounds." He seemed to recall himself to the conversation. "That's up here, mind. How far south are you? Have you been keeping it serviced?"

"Not really." They always found something vital but expensive to repair when she had the motor serviced. She'd been keeping her fingers crossed instead.

"That's bad luck," he said.

She wasn't sure if he was talking about the cricket or the motor. It might have been both. Heck, this was going to make an almighty dint in her advance. Figures wheeled around in Stella's head like the spinning reels of a slot machine. Bloody Bath buns, she thought.

She found Freddie unpacking the furniture from the back of his van. "My clutch is caput," she said.

He whistled through his teeth. "Hell, that sounds painful."

"It is painful, to the tune of seven pounds, and it's going to take a week to fix. Are you sure your Mr. Watkins is honest? It does seem rather expensive."

"He is a bit oily, isn't he? He's a good sort, though, and is thorough. I am sorry to hear it's a big job—but silver linings, eh?" he straightened and smiled down at her. "Well, for some of us, at least. I'd gladly offer you my spare room, but wouldn't want to sound presumptuous. If you're amenable to a bit of tapestry and taxidermy, the rooms are comfortable at the Crown."

She nodded. Tapestry and taxidermy it would have to be.

Her room had flock wallpaper and a slightly depressed-looking stuffed owl in a glass case. Stella knew how it felt. At least there was a dressing table that might serve as a desk, she supposed, and she'd brought a new notebook with her, so she could use this time to write.

She leaned on the windowsill and lit a cigarette. There was a view of mixed borders and apple blossom below, and a savory smell was rising from the kitchen. In other circumstances, it might be pleasant to have a week away in a country hotel, but adding the room rate to the price of the clutch, Stella felt things to be running away from her. Why did her life always have to turn into a drama?

She'd arranged to meet Freddie in the lounge bar at six. She got there early and ordered a double gin. He was easy company, and the distraction was welcome, but she also felt like she needed the anesthetic of alcohol tonight.

"You look delectible, but glum," he said, as she came in. He kissed her on the cheek, which took her by surprise and was perhaps a little forward. This afternoon already seemed like days ago, but she had still only known him for six hours, hadn't she? Was this acceptable etiquette in the Cotswolds?

"Money," she replied. "Isn't it a bore?"

"It is when there's not enough of it." He frowned sympathetically. "We're going to have to do something to put the smile back on your face. It's too nice a mouth to be turned down at the corners."

"Don't have any cut-price clutches squirreled away at the back of your shop, have you? Right now, I'd rather have that than a casket of emeralds."

"Really? How refreshing you are."

She wasn't feeling very refreshing.

"For a start, let me buy you dinner tonight, and then I'll endeavour to keep you entertained for the week. My skill with spanners might be limited, but I'm talented at distraction. Let us make some good out of the bad, eh? What do you say? You know, you might even be thankful for your malfunctioning clutch by the weekend."

She couldn't quite see it, but she smiled at him for the encouragement.

"Come on. I've booked a table for us."

As she followed Freddie through to the dining room, Stella noticed his eau-de-cologne. It was the scent of green cardamom pods, nutmeg, cloves and orange peel. She couldn't recall ever having met a man who smelled so delicious—or so redolent of a fifteenth-century Venetian spice galleon. He pulled out a chair for her and then that lighthouse-beam grin caught her again. It sent her off balance for a moment. It was a damn shame that he wasn't better with spanners, but he certainly had other charms.

Freddie seemed to like talking about food, was knowledgeable and enthusiastic, and made a great show of explaining the menu. It was all bread-sauce-and-gravy fare, but he said it was good honest stuff, and meanwhile he recommended local inns where she might be able to sample potted trout and a rabbit terrine. He was evidently accustomed to impressing women with his culinary *savoir faire*; he went into great detail about braising oxtail, making brawn and told a long story about a ten-bird roast. Stella had noticed that when men talked about their cooking it was always meaty and ostentatious, the kind of dishes that she'd only cook for a crowd. They made complicated curries, hot-water pastry and roasted whole suckling pigs. Men never talked about making the dishes that sustained the world from Monday through Friday, she reflected; they never boasted about making a superlative scrambled egg or a perfect mashed potato, but such things done well kept the world turning.

Still, Freddie was diverting company. It gratified her that he'd taken trouble over ordering the dinner and that he found such obvious pleasure in his food. She couldn't stand to see a man poking about at his plate. His conversation was light and positive; he paid her a lot of compliments, and when he wasn't bragging about his prowess in making brawn, he was charmingly self-deprecating. He was easy to talk to, his enthusiasms animating his face, and he made her feel slightly embarrassed in a way that was peculiarly and piquantly pleasurable. By the end of the bottle of Claret, the steak-and-kidney pudding and the rhubarb fool, she'd almost forgotten about the clutch.

They sat at the bar to drink a brandy. He swirled his glass and smiled into it. "I'm happy to provide wheels for you while you're here. Did you want to go down to Bath?"

"That had been my intention, but I don't want to put you out. You've got a shop to run."

"Exceptional circumstances," he said. "I don't get to rescue a fair damsel every day, and if you're going to disappear back up into the wilds of Yorkshire next week, I mean to make the best of these few days."

Stella thought of the writing that she'd planned to do at the dressing table in her room, but being driven around the countryside by Freddie could count as research, couldn't it?

They'd be talking about food and she'd be keeping a lookout for medieval field systems and manorial bread ovens.

"You'd do that? That's tremendously kind."

"Nonsense. It's self-interest. You're very original, you know. You amuse me and you twinkle like a cut-glass decanter. I could do with catching up in the shop tomorrow, but I'm entirely and devotedly yours from Wednesday. It might be fun to have a day in Bath together. What do you say?"

He put a hand through his hair and Stella recalled Cynthia's fingers in Michael's hair, but she must push such thoughts aside. Might Freddie distract her from that too? She'd never been compared to a decanter before and wasn't averse to the idea of being twinkly. It was certainly an improvement on dusty and twee.

"Thank you. I'd enjoy that," she replied.

"Excellent. I am glad we have an interest in common," he said, and smiled as if it satisfied him. It pleased Stella too, even if she wasn't absolutely sure why. Could a mutual interest in butter stamps be a basis for something more? Was it time to close certain doors and explore others?

Stella said goodnight to him at the bottom of the stairs. He bowed gallantly and swooped down to kiss her hand. With a brandy, a double gin and a half a bottle of wine inside her, Stella thought this delightfully old-fashioned behavior and he looked a little like Rudolph Valentino in the candlelight. Perhaps Freddie Langham might be just what she needed right now? Could the fickleness of fate contrive mechanical malfunctions?

*

Stella opened her eyes as the light was creeping around the curtain edges. She ought to have had a sleepless night, worrying about the cost of repairing the car, but she'd slept like a hibernating dormouse, and supposed that was down to alcohol and nervous exhaustion. The big old bed was rather lumpy (she decided not to turn back the sheets and examine the mattress), but it was also beautifully soft. It had been like sleeping on a bed of mashed potato and she'd dreamed about Rupert Snelgrave's paintings.

Stella always woke up ravenous after she'd overindulged in the fermented grape, and her thoughts turned to the flaky layers of croissants now, the smell of brioche freshly out of the oven, and thick real coffee—but this would be a bacon-and-sausage sort of a hotel, wouldn't it? Still, that was an indulgence that she rarely enjoyed. And isn't hotel toast somehow always nicer than at home?

She opened the window and breathed in the morning air. It had rained a little overnight and everything had been washed clean. Ivy leaves looked lacquered, bee wings hummed in hawthorn blossom, strings of birdsong seemed to garland the garden, and all was sweet, fresh and bright. Stella could smell newly mown grass, honeysuckle, breaking buds of lilac—and, yes, frying bacon. As she turned, she caught the eye of the saturnine owl.

"What? Well, I've got to make the best of it, haven't I? Wouldn't you?"

Chapter Sixteen

Stella pushed her plate away. She was glowing slightly and, good Lord, she did feel full. At her dressing table, before coming down, she'd written some notes on the history of breakfasting, about Good Queen Bess eating a pottage made with mutton bones and Samuel Pepys' oysters and ale, and was glad that she'd done this before she'd eaten such an enormous breakfast. The thought of Victorian sideboards laden with deviled kidneys and veal galantines made her feel rather green around the gills now. She would work in her room today, write up the Banbury cakes and musings on currants, but decided to take a stroll around the square first. She needed to do something to jiggle down the sausages, bacon, black pudding and the contents of two toast racks.

Stepping out of the door of the inn, Stella thought that this might be an England manufactured expressly for the camera lenses of American tourists. It had that sort of higgledy-piggledy eighteenth-century architecture that looks charming in its exuberant inconsistency of roofline and gable. The houses were constructed of a honey-hued limestone, and the finely dressed lintels and pilasters spoke of old affluence. Slate roofs glinted in the sun and the lines of shiny motor cars indicated that fortunes hadn't dipped here. Roses draped themselves around doors and blue lobelia frothed from hanging baskets, while all of the shops were prinked to look like images on toffee tins. There were three antique shops in the square, other than Freddie's (how many majolica plant stands did one village need?), a baker's with a window full of iced buns, a surprisingly chi-chi dress shop and the cleanest butcher's shop she'd ever seen. A sign for "Ye Olde Tea Shoppe' seemed to sum the place up rather neatly.

The architecture suggested that this village must have prospered from the wool trade two centuries ago, but who lived behind its well-polished door brasses now? Stella pictured sitting rooms with William Morris wallpaper, prints of Admiral Nelson with an empty sleeve, Lord Kitchener on horseback entering Khartoum, and Mafeking being relieved. She peopled these spaced with purple-cheeked retired colonels who studied the racing papers and women who sipped from Crown Derby and wore their mothers' pearls midweek. What recipes might they submit if she were to send an appeal to their local newspaper? Stella supposed there would be many preparations for partridge and venison, and superior trifles decorated with pansies and nasturtium petals. They certainly wouldn't want their neighbors to hear them being sentimental about oatcakes, would they? The church bells pealed up and down the scale, wood pigeons fluttering and settling, and Stella wondered at how one's own country can occasionally feel like a well-mannered play on the wireless.

Freddie was leaning in the doorway of his shop as she approached, talking to a woman in riding tweeds and a felt beret. Stella heard the woman's throaty laughter before she saw her and her voice calling him "adorable, absurd Freddie. Too, too naughty!" Stella smiled as she listened. Good heavens, he did flirt! It was quite outrageous. Was he like that with everyone? It would have made Lucien blush. Stella saw that look that her mother sometimes gave her over the top of her reading glasses and the phrase "frightful bounder" came into her mind unwilled. But she had no intention of getting tangled up with Freddie, did she? It wasn't like that. He was just helping her and being friendly. That was all, wasn't it? The woman kissed him on the cheek before she departed.

"Keeping your customers sweet?"

"Sophie is a darling. She collects Coalport and silver sugar tongues. I do like to get something in for her."

"I'll bet you do." Sugar tongues, indeed! Stella imagined that Freddie might have a whole seraglio of Sophies who he serviced with silver novelties, lacquered curios and delightful little *objets d'art*.

"Do you want a cup of tea? I was just about to put the gas ring on?"

"Is this how you ensnare your Sophies?"

He raised an eyebrow at her before he turned.

Stella followed Freddie through to the back of the shop and sat in a rush-backed rocking chair while he set a kettle on the ring and dabbled with tea leaves. He had a silver tea caddy and a fine willow-pattern teapot, but as he lifted the lid she could see that it was all brown and crusty inside.

"You need to bleach your teapot," she couldn't help saying. "It looks most unsavory."

"Bleach it? Sacrilege, woman! Is that what you tell people in your magazine column? How perfectly horrid. The accumulation of tannins improves the flavor of the brew, much like whiskey maturing in an old sherry cask."

Stella wrinkled her nose. Was this his sales patter? She wouldn't be surprised if he tried to charge his Sophies extra for a stain at the bottom of a cup. He'd make up some elaborate story, Stella imagined—how Edward VII was the last person to drink out of the cup, or how Turner had used it to clean his brushes.

"If you can put up with my dubious standards of hygiene, perhaps you'd let me make dinner for you tonight? I've been hanging a hare and have a most interesting eighteenth-century recipe."

Stella pressed her lips together and suppressed the urge to laugh at this enticement. She'd never been lured with an eighteenth-century hare before. "How intriguing that sounds."

"I'm only an amateur in the kitchen, of course, but I'd like to think that I do have a reputation as an epicure in my circle."

Stella thought him faintly ridiculous, but she couldn't tell how much of it was self-mocking. Was she meant to laugh in these places? Or was he being entirely serious? Still, he made good strong tea and looked quite outrageously handsome this morning. He was wearing a sky-blue shirt and she'd detected the scent of lavender pomade as he'd leaned toward her with the teapot. (Isn't there a line in Shakespeare about lavender's aphrodisiac qualities?) As Stella tried to resist the urge to reach out and touch Freddie's shiny, scented hair, she realized that she hadn't thought about Cynthia Palmer for over twelve hours.

I'm sure you are aware of the history of the Crusaders bringing spices and dried fruits back to England. While these would have been luxuries at first, with the establishment of regular trade routes, spiced cakes would eventually become affordable treats for the common people, and were often associated with the festivals of the religious calendar. Spiced buns, marked with a cross, were being eaten on Good Friday in the fourteenth century, the origin of our Hot Cross Buns, and there are also many local peculiarities linking spices, currants and the church. Banbury cakes, baked for the town's St. Luke's Day fair, are made in an oval shape to signify the cradle of the baby Jesus . . .

REV. SAMUEL WAVERLEY, Banbury

Eccles cakes were originally made for the town's Wakes Fair. This festival commemorated the foundation of the local church, but over time it became a notoriously rowdy affair. It's sometimes said that Oliver Cromwell tried to ban Eccles cakes. It's true that Puritan reformers did crack down on

*boisterous feast days, and frowned on lavish use of spices, but
the cakes continued to be baked. The Wakes Fair was still
known for its unruliness in the nineteenth century, its bull-
baiting, cock-fighting and general licentiousness, and it was
only finally banned in 1877. Memories of it have faded now,
but the irrepressible Eccles cake still thrives here. Incidentally,
I understand that the three slashes traditionally made on top
of the cakes refer to the Holy Trinity—a curious story of the
sacred and profane, eh?*

THOMAS EDGERTON (schoolmaster), Eccles

*Please note—a Chorley cake is not a squashed Eccles
cake! The two are quite distinct. My family have been
baking them for three generations, so I can speak with
some authority on this matter. Chorley cakes are less sweet
than Eccles cakes, our spicing is slightly different (those
details I can't divulge), and, fundamentally, they are made
with shortcrust instead of flaky pastry. They are normally
eaten either buttered or with a slice of Lancashire cheese.
The difference is more than twenty miles of geography.
Do you see?*

LILLIAN SYKES (Mrs.), Chorley

*In Coventry we make currant pasties called Godcakes. Both
their triangular form and the three cuts on the top nod to the
Holy Trinity. They are unique to Coventry, I believe . . .*

CONSTANCE HARPER, Coventry

God's Kitchels are a traditional currant pastry baked in Suffolk. They are made for New Year, and are given by godparents to their godchildren. Here in Aldeburgh, bad luck is foretold for anyone who doesn't eat a Kitchel on New Year's Eve, but they must be consumed before midnight. To eat even a crumb afterward could put a curse on the new year . . .

MRS. IRENE BAXTER, Aldeburgh

A Godcake, a triangular currant pastry, is unique to the East Riding of Yorkshire. As my parents and grandparents did before, we eat them on New Year's Day with a glass of rhubarb wine. It is considered bad luck to pick rhubarb and drink the wine made from it within the same calendar year, so the timing is important. Only a reckless soul would attempt this on New Year's Eve!

GLADYS DAVIES, Pocklington

Chapter Seventeen

It håd been a satisfyingly productive day. Stella had consolidated her notes on currant cakes, made a plan for the week, and had spent a profitable couple of hours with Eliza Acton. She'd washed her stockings in the bathroom sink, had procured an electric iron to press her blouse, and had finally sat in the bath for an hour enjoying a particularly gossipy parish magazine. For some of that time she'd also managed to forget about the clutch.

When she'd paid for the repairs and her hotel bill for the week, there would only be twenty-six pounds of her advance remaining. Stella dreaded what might go wrong with the car next. If she needed to make any further research trips, perhaps she might go by train? But that was so limiting. She would have to rely more on second-hand sources, she'd decided, and whatever she might glean from her advertisements in newspapers. If only there weren't so many inconsistencies and contradictions in the responses she was receiving. As she'd reviewed the letters on currant cakes, she'd again felt like she was required to referee competing legends. There did seem to be rather a lot of that in English food.

Stella took her time getting dressed for dinner and amused herself by imagining the sight of Freddie in an apron and oven gloves. She was ready to be distracted from thoughts about clutches and budgets, and the etiquette of eating Godcakes, and looked forward to an evening of antique talk and harmless flirtation.

"Come in. Come up to the flat." Freddie flashed his brilliant smile, smoothed his hair back and beckoned her in.

They passed through the shop and to a door at the back which opened on to a staircase. There were watercolors of Victorian nudes on the walls of the stairwell, déshabillé women looking listless around fountains and ponds, and Stella could smell the gaminess of the hare. As she followed Freddie up, noting his well-polished brogues, his tidy trouser hems and how fetchingly his braces showcased his *derrière*, she thought of stories of innocent maidens being lured into a philanderer's lair. Was the Victorian nudity a danger sign? But that was silly, Stella told herself. She was hardly an innocent, or a maiden, and what dangers could there be from a man who was passionate about earthenware and treen?

The style of Freddie's living accommodation wasn't a significant transition from the shop. His sitting room was full of dark, shiny furniture, wingback chairs and potted palms. He had a good selection of slipware pottery and a cabinet of curiosities and the teal-green walls set off the gilt-framed paintings. He seemed to collect seventeenth-century portraits and Stella couldn't help but step toward them. They were mostly women with spaniel-like hair arrangements and rakish-looking men in large lace collars.

"Now all my foibles are exposed," Freddie's voice said behind her.

"Aren't they, indeed? Are these your illustrious ancestors?" Stella glanced at him over her shoulder. Was there a resemblance between him and the raffish men? Could she see him with an earring and a velvet jerkin?

"God, no!" he laughed. "My grandfather was a pig farmer. We're nothing so grand. They're just pieces I've picked up at auction, simply faces that I found interesting."

"Really?" Stella turned to him and smiled. It's curious how one can suddenly feel more comfortable with a person knowing that their grandfather was a pig farmer. "You surprise me. I'd imagined there must be a family pile somewhere. I pictured a drawing room with paintings of your mother in her debutante season and your father posing with dead pheasants."

"In fairness, I will concede that there is a painting of my father with a wild boar, but you might be disappointed by the modesty of the familial seat."

He poured her a glass of sherry and she toured the walls, musing as to why these particular faces might have appealed to Freddie. Were the spaniel women his sort of thing? She refocused on her own reflection and found herself mercifully lacking in bulging eyes and curly ears. All the men looked like they might have their hands on their hips just out of shot. There was perhaps something of Freddie in that. Still, his accommodation was impressively polished and he evidently had a way with houseplants.

Stella took the opportunity to be shamelessly nosy while he went in and out of the kitchen. She peered into his curiosity cabinet. It contained flint arrowheads and ammonites, standard schoolboy stuff, but also a shark's jawbone and a seahorse with a ribbon around its neck. There was a slightly mangy-looking stuffed magpie, a fly whip and what a label declared to be a finger bone of Saint Barbara, nestling in a cigar box.

"Make yourself comfortable," said Freddie's voice from the kitchen. "And help yourself to another sherry. I won't be long."

"I'm having an enjoyable snoop."

There were framed images of women on the mantelpiece, all tightly corseted and somewhat stern in daguerreotypes and silhouettes. Were these his female relatives?

"My mother," he said, coming back into the room. He picked up a pale photograph in which a slim young woman was smiling wanly. Stella supposed that she ought to say something nice, something complimentary, but the photograph reminded her of skimmed milk. It was like one of Dilys' spirit photographs where everything was hazy with ectoplasm.

"She looks delicate." Stella finally decided that adjective might do. "Rather gauzy. She could be a fairy." Yes, that was better.

"She was bodily delicate, always succumbing to one malady or another, but she was terrifically strong mentally. My father didn't stand a chance."

Stella could imagine that: the delicate Mama lying languid

on a chaise longue, but with the sharp eye of a lizard and the steely will of a general. Stella pictured a slim white arm lifting, waving frailly, and a household jumping to attention. She thought of her own mother and her poor thin white hands at the end, hands that had been so capable, but which had lost all of their strength, and then finally had slipped from her own.

"You lost her?"

"When I was twelve. My father passed away too last year. It's strange to think of oneself as an orphan."

"You poor boy. I am sorry."

"I'll permit you to comfort me with soothing words and caresses later."

She'd genuinely pitied him until he winked. She'd had a sense of fellow feeling, and had wanted to put a consoling hand to his chest, but—had he deliberately set that one up? Amontillado seemed to stimulate this part of his personality and he twinkled at her now. It struck her that he had that air of perfect self-assurance and subtle degeneracy which certain leading men wield so effectively on the cinema screen. It was fascinating to observe up close. One rarely encountered it in West Yorkshire.

"Am I permitted to see the chef at his work?"

He'd been making a good deal of noise in the kitchen, banging doors and clattering pans, but, even so, Stella was a little taken aback by the chaos that greeted her eyes. For a man who had such an elegant sitting room, he was surprisingly messy in the kitchen. The doors of a dresser were hanging open, every surface seemed to be covered with used pans, and a great pile of washing-up was stacked by the sink. She could hear her mother tutting. Freddie was studiously stirring a bubbling brown sauce and a pudding basin full of blood waited at his elbow. Stella found herself mentally roughing-out a portrait of him in this attitude. There was something slightly macabre, but also intensely *him* in this composition, and it amused her to imagine putting its lines down on canvas. "The Epicure," she'd call it.

"Can I wash up for you?"

"Do you mean to imply that I'm slovenly?"

"Not at all." She hesitated. "Well, maybe a bit?"

"In that case, you certainly may not. Go and arrange yourself in a decorative position at the dining table. I'll be ready to serve in just a minute."

His dining table was in a corner of the sitting room, but he'd set it nicely with a heavy damask cloth, silver cutlery and Georgian wineglasses. Stella liked that he knew how to do things properly. Freddie was never going to be a man who had crusty-topped sauce bottles on his table, or who ate off yesterday's newspaper, but she was impressed by the cleanliness of his cruet and his floral centerpiece. That was what one called an epergne, wasn't it? How many bachelors possessed one of those these days?

"It has amused me to cook you something quintessentially English," he said, placing a plate in front of Stella. He'd made a ham-hock terrine set in a bright green parsley jelly. She bit her lip not to observe that it was *jambon persillé*, but he'd clearly gone to a great deal of effort, and she was grateful and complimented by that. He sat down opposite, filled the wineglasses, and nodded before he set about his own plate. It was agreeable to observe a man who ate with gusto, Stella thought. Freddie didn't hide the fact that he relished his food, even if he'd cooked the dish himself, and he wiped bread around his plate to scoop up every last morsel. Watching him eat, Stella couldn't help but smile; it made her want to cook for him, to place food in front of him that would please him. She'd cooked for some terribly disappointing men in her time. There is nothing worse than going to lengthy efforts only to have a person poke at their plate. Englishmen can be terribly finicky sometimes.

"Where did you get the recipe from?" she asked. She resisted suggesting Burgundy.

"I had it in a restaurant in Bournemouth."

"Well, one can't get more English than that."

"It's marvelous what you're doing," he said, pushing his emptied plate away, and sitting back with his wineglass in his hand. "I truly believe that. I think the history of food is quite as important as the order of Henrys and Edward and the dates of battles. It defines who we are and we ought to preserve and celebrate that."

Stella judged this a fine statement and rather wished that she'd had Freddie on her arm as she'd faced Rupert Snelgrave last month. She might have felt braver facing Cynthia too. But what would Michael have thought if she'd arrived with a man on her arm? (It was his engagement party, though, wasn't it?)

"It's a history that seems to be shifting rather fast at the moment," she replied. "I arrive in places just as the last bakers' and butchers' shops have closed, and there are so many traditions and flavors that are already only vague memories. I can buy butter from Poland and Estonia in my corner grocer's now, and three different brands of tinned pineapple, but can I find a recipe for Collop Cake? That does make it feel like a worthwhile project."

"Hurrah for your arrival, then. Miss Douglas, savior of the Collop Cake! Whatever that may be." He touched his glass against hers. "And if I'm able to assist you in your research, I will do so with the greatest of pleasure. I want to be helpful to you."

Freddie had cooked the hare very well, with cloves, juniper and red wine. It was succulent, rich and complex, but it was slightly marred by the detail with which he talked through the shooting, hanging and butchering of the beast. He spent some time listing all the varieties of creatures he'd shot for the pot, and went to great pains to describe how a hare must be hung by its hind legs with a basin placed below it to catch the blood that drips from its mouth. Stella wasn't squeamish, but she had to suppress an image of red teeth and circling bluebottles.

"The key thing is to save as much blood as possible. That's what makes it sumptuous. I pounded the liver to a paste and pushed it through a sieve."

Wasn't that a *civet de lièvre*? Might he be offended if she were to suggest that? "Hannah Glasse would be proud of you." It seemed a safer observation.

Freddie went on to describe the hanging and aging of various game birds, reminisced about making his own pig's head brawn, and went into raptures about a stew of lambs' tails. When the conversation moved on to casseroled hearts, Stella began to wonder if she was perhaps undergoing some sort of offal-tolerance evaluation. He also mentioned the various women he'd cooked these dishes for. Clearly, there had been a lengthy back catalog of Sophies. Was he testing her by talking about them too?

"Hare is an aphrodisiac, you know," he said. "It keeps you at your peak for nine days after consuming its flesh."

"Nine days? Goodness." Where on earth was she meant to go with that? Did he expect her to ask for a demonstration?

"Our food is the most honest and wholesome in the world. Don't you agree?"

"In the world? Do you think?" What would Lucien say to that?

"I sincerely believe that." Freddie waved his fork as he spoke. He clearly meant to make a point. "It's hearty, nose-to-tail cooking—only it's all going wrong because everyone is lazy and squeamish now. They won't attempt to make a dish that takes some time to prepare, or that might require them to look an animal in the eye. It will all be forgotten, just because people have become such ninnies and it's easier to open a tin. England's exceptional cuisine will all be lost. It will be shipwrecked on a doom bar of canned spaghetti, Danish bacon, pineapple chunks and squeamishness."

"Shipwrecked?" He looked entirely serious, but a laugh

escaped from Stella's mouth. He did have a way with metaphors.

"I'm not wrong, though, am I? Part of the problem is that young women aren't taught to cook now. It used to be an essential preparation for marriage, but women suppose they needn't bother these days. If they can open a can, they're happy. A can opener seems to be the essential item in the dowry now, but I refuse to have one in my house—and any girl who means to brandish one at me."

Stella suspected that any Sophie eyeing Freddie as a marriageable prospect would need to be highly qualified. And rather patient. As she listened to him making speeches, she noticed that there was something occasionally pedantic about his voice. He took care over certain words and was strikingly free with his opinions. At points, Stella found him sounding slightly boorish, but he had gone to a great effort for her and the wine had given him such pretty ruby-red lips.

"I've liked cooking for you," he said. "It's been a great pleasure. So many women think that they can impress a chap with silly sensitivities, as if that's a desirable feminine quality. Cecily was a nightmare. Do you know, she once burst into tears over a lamb chop."

Stella could well imagine the scene and how Freddie might have scoffed in response. Poor Cecily, whoever she was. "Cecily?"

"She's gone back to Cambridge now. She didn't last. We were never going to. I mean—a lamb chop!"

"But what is dessert?" Stella asked. It didn't seem polite to linger on Cecily's sensibilities. "Have you made some elaborate construction from sugar paste? A model of Hampton Court Palace in blancmange? RMS *Queen Mary* made in marzipan? I shall be disappointed if it doesn't involve at least ten challenging culinary processes and gold leaf."

"Dessert? How deliciously northern of you! I suppose you have dinner at midday too, don't you? And tea at six o'clock?" He looked amused by this thought. "For *pudding* it's treacle tart and custard. I do hope that's complicated enough?"

It said something about the English class system, and the strength of regional identity, that they couldn't even agree on the names of meals, didn't it? Stella made a mental note that she must look into this further, but she didn't feel like manning a barricade just at this present moment. "If *dessert* is good enough for forty million Frenchmen and half of my own countrymen, it's good enough for me. And treacle tart sounds agreeable too."

His pastry was excellent, she couldn't fault it, but the filling of the tart was tooth-achingly sweet. "Was it a favorite school pudding?" she asked.

"How did you guess?" He smiled rather boyishly then. "Every Thursday lunchtime, regular as clockwork."

"I can picture long tables full of little Freddies all licking their plates."

"You bet!"

"You don't cook like this all the time, do you?"

"Of course! One should never skimp. I have friends who eat off trays, sitting on sofas, but I think that's the beginning of the end, don't you? Would we ever have had an empire if we were the sort of people who sat around nibbling Welsh rarebit off our knees? No, I always make myself three courses, and cheese, and sit at the table with a napkin."

"Women don't go to the same effort when they're on their own. I'll often have just a grilled chop and a green salad." Stella decided not to add that she sometimes ate it off a tray.

"But that's tragic!"

Was it? She laughed uncertainly. "There are worse things, aren't there? Surely, tragic is suicide, natural disaster, opera. I'm not sure that a grilled chop really qualifies as tragic."

"I feel I need to rescue you now. I bet you don't open a bottle of wine either, do you?"

"I sometimes have a bottle of beer."

"Oh, stop it, or you'll make me sob!"

He carried dishes into the kitchen and Stella caught her reflection in the mirror over the mantelpiece. I am somewhat intoxicated, she thought, as she looked at her face framed in mahogany. The mascara had smudged slightly under her eyes and her mouth kept breaking out into a slightly silly smile. She tidied a wisp of straying hair away and told herself to be sensible. What would her mother say?

He brought out his cheese after the dessert, and she restrained herself from observing how barbarous this was considered to be in France. He also placed a bowl of grapes on the table and it amused Stella to watch him using grape scissors. How many people still possess grape scissors, never mind use them?

"English cheeses are the finest in the world, don't you think? I don't know why anyone eats foreign cheese. Why on earth would you want a flaccid Camembert when you can have a fine, flinty farmhouse Cheddar? Most foreign cheese isn't fit to bait a mousetrap. Much of it is adulterated, you know."

Stella was partial to a well-aged Camembert, a Comté and a Cantal. The fact that one could buy Continental cheeses had been one of the pleasures of living in London, and while she'd been in Paris she'd practically lived on the stuff. But as Freddie was feeding her, and it was an excellent Cheddar, it would have been churlish to retort.

"This is particularly good. You must tell me where you bought it. I'm assuming that you didn't milk the cow yourself and age it in your pantry?" She could tease him a little, couldn't she?

He was keen to introduce her to local cheesemakers, but she tried to steer him away from the subject as they took to port. She could only politely listen to so much of him being contemptuous about Camembert. Perhaps it was time to divert to safer waters?

"Is the antiques trade in the family?" she asked.

"No, not at all. I opened the shop here three years ago. I was a stockbroker before, but you can do that only for so many years."

It didn't entirely surprise her. She got the impression that money wasn't an object and that he could comfortably fund a life of pursuing his interests. She thought again of the clutch, and of how much more complicated her own project had just become, but she didn't suppose Freddie would understand that.

"I used to walk out with a girl called Olivia in my London days," Freddie said, as he lit a cigarette. He shook the match out and smiled. "She was a dashed good-looker, a real head-turner, but her hands always smelled faintly of garlic and it was too much in the end." He reached across the table and took Stella's hand. He turned it and seemed to examine it. "Her mother was Italian, but all the same."

"Perhaps she suspected you might be a vampire?"

"An Englishwoman's hands should never smell of garlic." He lifted her hand to his face. Stella raised her eyebrows to him as he sniffed her palm and was even more surprised as he then kissed it rather tenderly.

"No offending indication of alliums?"

"I've never kissed a writer's hand before. Mind you, keen as I am on Ernest Hemingway, I feel no urge to fondle his fin. I dread to think what they smell of—manly sweat, fish and rum, possibly?"

He tried to press her to brandy, but Stella knew that if she had more to drink she'd find herself succumbing to his flirtations. Although she felt she understood Freddie pretty well by the end of this evening, she reminded herself that she'd only actually known him for two days, and would probably never see him again after this week. After all, he had a circuit of Sophies to service, and some of his opinions might become grating, but as he held her coat for her she couldn't help noticing his fine eyes and the scent of his eau-de-cologne.

He insisted on walking her back across the square, warning of marauding hoodlums and ruffians. Stella couldn't imagine that much marauding had gone on here in recent centuries, but if he wanted to be chivalrous—and he clearly did—she didn't object to that. They took a route around the edge of the square, the night air being deliciously cool and fresh, and it was amusing to peer into the houses. Lamps had been lit, but not all curtains were drawn yet, and Stella enjoyed looking in at the interior decorations, noticing the patterns of the wallpaper, the framed landscapes and the candlesticks, the coronation jugs and the shrouded birdcages. It was like peeping into so many dolls' houses and she speculated as to the family groupings and the conversations within these interiors, the passions and the secrets that hid behind the framed samplers and the seashell collections. And what had they eaten for their dinners? Was it really all pheasants and public-school puddings here? White moths flickered against windowpanes, and she saw herself reflected in the pool of light from a streetlamp—him and her—and his arm sliding around her shoulders now.

Freddie moved to kiss her as they got to the door of the inn. Stella had suspected that he might, as they had seemed to be heading in that direction, and she wasn't entirely averse to the experiment. As it turned out, he was a remarkably good kisser, really first rate, but then she supposed that he'd probably had rather a lot of practice. She hoped that her mother wasn't looking.

Chapter Eighteen

Freddie was wearing a long, herringbone-tweed coat and it swished as he walked. It was an elegant coat, but Stella couldn't help thinking that it gave him a rakish air. Had he deliberately decided to dress as a dandy for this trip? Did he see himself as a bit of a Beau Nash? There had been some innuendo around being in Bath together on the drive down, which may have enhanced this impression. Still, it had amused Stella to mimic the name of the town in his accent, drawing the vowel out to inordinate lengths.

Bath delivered all the Georgian elegance that she'd hoped for. It was a town of Palladian terraces, pillared porticoes and polite teashops. It was full of satisfying symmetries and the colors of old gold, and was no doubt inhabited by people with ostentatiously long vowels. Stella thought of Jane Austen and rambunctious young Georgians hoofing and gossiping their way around Assembly Room socials, but it all seemed very well-behaved this morning, rather gracious and emphatically respectable. While there were crowds in the streets, American accents and camera flashes, Bath rose above it like a dignified dowager duchess who had seen it all before. The populace of this town might well live on sugared buns, but they would eat them with excellent table manners, Stella was sure.

"Have you ever had a Sally Lunn?" Freddie asked. "I'm well familiar with a Bath bun, but I'm not sure I'd recognize a Sally Lunn if someone aimed one at my head."

It didn't take them too long to find a baker's shop with pastries in the window and a sign promising authentic Bath buns and Sally Lunns. They ordered a plate of buns of both pedigrees and took a table in the attached tearoom. Every surface was covered with a chintz print, or a crochet cloth, and china figurines clustered between the aspidistras. The tables were principally occupied by elderly ladies (similarly upholstered in chintz) and there was a tinkling chatter of well-mannered conversation. Stella had to tell Freddie off for lifting one of the figurines and examining its underside. In this company that seemed like a most improper gesture.

"So Sally is a plump but plain version of the conventional Bath bun?" he proposed, spreading butter on a toasted bun now. "Like a stout and slightly dowdy elder sister?"

Stella was pleased to see that he wasn't parsimonious with butter. She'd come to the conclusion that a Sally Lunn was an impoverished brioche and so it probably was best spread with butter. "Curious that sugary buns became a fashion in a resort where people came to take the health-giving water, isn't it?"

"Virtue and vice are never far apart." Freddie licked butter from his fingers and gave her one of his looks. It was slightly alarming to be in receipt of such a look in a respectable tea-room. "Who was Sally Lunn, then?"

"There are several different origin stories. Some people say she was a Huguenot. I keep encountering this," Stella mused. "As I pursue the origin of what I assume to be quintessentially English foodstuffs, the trail often leads back to a Huguenot refugee, a Venetian galleon or a knight returning from the Crusades."

"I say, if it tastes good and people believe it's English, don't dispossess them of that belief. Surely there can't be anything more English than a fruit bun? That's the gist of what you're meant to be delivering, isn't it? English fruit buns rule the waves, et cetera?"

"Well, to a degree. But . . ."

Could she really just leave out facts that didn't fit the brief? Personally, she found it fascinating that English kitchens had always been full of foreign influences, and how much more dull it would be without the nutmegs, the currants and the barrels of sack. But would it be better to play down the foreign names and the trade routes? Ought she to be waving the Union Jack a little more vigorously? Was she overthinking it?

"Anyway, on with the origin story." Freddie wafted his hand, indicating that she must push on. "Give me the Huguenot bit, and we'll decide what you ought to do with it."

"So, yes, some people say she was a Huguenot refugee, actually called Solange Luyon. She introduced the baker who she worked for to French enriched dough. With time, her name was corrupted to Sally Lunn."

"God bless dear Sally," said Freddie, and dunked his bun in his tea. Was that allowed? Was that acceptable etiquette? Stella looked around the room to see if anyone had noticed. "To me she sounds like a fine, buxom, rosy-cheeked English girl," he went on. "I see her in a mob cap, with a basket over her arm, and a comely Somerset brogue. Loose the refugee bit. You don't want her being French. Perhaps you could make up a story in which she has a passionate but ill-fated dalliance with Beau Nash? Are we around the same era? That would be fun, wouldn't it?"

How fast and loose he would have her play with history! Stella thought of all the stabilizing footnotes in *Mrs. Raffald* and felt slightly dizzied by Freddie's casual approach to historical authenticity. "There's no paperwork to document that she ever existed; no real evidence that a woman with that name was ever working in Bath. Moreover, neither Solange nor Luyon are Huguenot names, so it might all have been a tall story to glamorize a humble local bun."

"Well, there you are, you see. Now you've done yourself a favor. No need to bring the dubious Frenchness into it at all. French patisserie is all far too sickly, anyway. English baked goods are far more subtle and satisfying."

"The alternative theory is that the name Sally Lunn derives from the word *solilem*, which is a type of sweetened bread from Alsace." Stella took a sip of tea. "That's what Carême believed."

"Are the French determined to dispossess us of our bun? I tell you, never take the word of a Frenchman on trust. Is there not a nice, patriotic, indisputably English origin story?"

Stella considered protesting that she'd known a good many thoroughly decent and trustworthy Frenchmen, but decided to take this as a jest on Freddie's part. "And that's narrative number three: another story says that they were invented by the physician William Oliver—he of the Bath Oliver—and that he used to give them to patients taking the cure in the Roman baths."

"Dunk 'em in the eggy water and then feed 'em the eggy bread? I like Mr. Oliver. He sounds like a reliable sort and he does make excellent crackers. I reckon you should go with Mr. Oliver. Forget the French girl and Monsieur Carême's Alsatian."

"But I'm not sure that one is at all plausible. Is a man who invented a plain biscuit also going to recommend a buttery bun? It doesn't seem likely, does it? All three versions of the story are flimsy, really," she said. "None of them can be pinned down with facts. The truth probably lies somewhere in between them."

"A right old bun fight, you might say?"

"Quite," Stella agreed. She stirred the teapot and refreshed their cups. Freddie lifted the milk jug to the light and squinted at its hallmark. "Anyway, by the later eighteenth century, they were being sold on the streets of Bath. Poets wrote about the women with their bun baskets and composers set their cries to music."

"Like so many sticky-bunned Nell Gwyns? Most picturesque."

"There's a Gilbert and Sullivan song about them. 'The

rollicking bun and the gay Sally Lunn! The rollicking, rollicking bun!'" Stella resisted the urge to actually sing, though Freddie's company inclined her to flights of silliness.

He grinned. "I'm partial to any bun that rollicks."

"In the eighteenth century Bath buns were flavored with rose water, orange water and caraway and were sprinkled with comfits." Stella tried to sound scholarly again. The rollicking bun had prompted looks from the women on the next table. "It's the Victorians who replace the caraway with currants. I'm not sure that was progress."

"But what can you expect of people whose loins were stirred by the sight of table legs?" Freddie lifted the tablecloth and peered beneath. He winked when he sat up again. "Second-rate chaps, the Victorians, I've always thought. You know, that's the thing that I enjoy about you, Miss Douglas. It's like conversing with a particularly decorative encyclopedia. How the devil do you know all of this stuff?"

"Books?" She shrugged. She supposed it was a compliment, of sorts.

"I have to say, it's all sounding thoroughly English to me. You should keep the perfidious French well out of it."

"You are rather rude about the French." She had to say it. "Some of my best friends are French."

"My condolences to you." He sat back in his seat. "No, I don't mean to be rude. It's just the assumption that everything French is superior that rankles. In so many restaurants one needs a French degree to decipher the menu these days, and it's all self-congratulatory nods and winks with the waiter.

It's the most ludicrous snobbery! Half of the restaurants in London seem to be called Chez Someone-or-other now, and, of course, they're all staffed by foreigners. I'll warrant that there are some London kitchens where you won't find a single English accent. I don't blame them, but—"

"Oh, I'm sure they'd be most relieved!" She couldn't help but retort.

"Don't misunderstand me—French food is fine in France. The French have determinedly preserved the individuality of their cuisine, and good luck to 'em; we could learn something from that. But an Englishman should eat a broth, not a *consommé*, a stew, not a *ragoût*, and I certainly don't want a sauce with peeled grapes in it. You can't honestly say that isn't nonsense!"

Stella looked at Freddie. She wondered whether to tell him that her best friend was head chef in a French restaurant and known for his *consommés* and *veloutés*. If she were obliged to attend Cynthia's parties in the future, she wouldn't mind having Freddie at her side; he'd be able to handle that crowd and would boost her value in other people's eyes—but would he be beastly to Lucien? And what would Michael think of him? She couldn't really see the two of them getting along—they had such different values and manners—but then, Stella told herself it was perhaps time to stop worrying about pleasing Michael.

"Apparently, Jane Austen 'disordered' her stomach with Bath buns," she said. It might be best to deviate away from the French.

"What's the story?" Freddie asked. "You can't leave it at that. I'm concerned for poor Jane's constitution."

"It's just a sentence in one of her letters. There's no further detail. But I'd love to know more, wouldn't you?"

Freddie steepled his hands and looked thoughtful for a moment. "You ought to make something of it. People love that sort of thing."

"Make something of it?"

"You know, pad it out a little." He licked a finger and picked up the last few sugar crystals from his plate. "Embellish it. Have dear old Jane enjoying a jolly escapade in a teashop, a bit of a flirtation perhaps, a mischievous to-and-fro of wordplay, and then needing to take to a chaise longue. You could make a nicely piquant episode of it, don't you think?"

"Piquant?"

"Stimulating to the taste buds and the imagination."

He clearly had quite an imagination. "You're saying make something up? Lie, you mean?"

"Lie is such an ugly word, an unfinessed sledgehammer of a word. It's heavy with disapproval. I mean be creative, apply some charm. People love a celebrity and a story, don't they? That's the sort of stuff that sells books. And who would know that it wasn't true? A handful of academics? If you fib a little, insert some anecdote that nobody can easily dispute, what's the harm? No one will get hurt and you'll give the reader a more diverting experience. Isn't that to everyone's benefit?"

What a light and flimsy word *fib* was. It was a childish word. It suggested a young girl's rosy-cheeked pertness. Did fibbing come easily to Freddie? Stella couldn't entirely disagree with what he'd said, though—adding a charming anecdote here and there could lift the whole text. It would be like adding a spoonful of baking powder. If her sources were obscure enough, veiled in sufficient antiquity and non-specificity, would anyone know? But it went against Stella's ethics. She was a footnotes-and-bibliography sort of a writer. Wasn't she? In *Mrs. Raffald* she'd anchored her text with footnotes; those pointers to authenticity and scrupulousness had given her confidence, they'd been like guy ropes—however, Mr. Williamson had said this shouldn't be the sort of book that needed notes. He'd been clear about that, hadn't he? So could she get away with a bit of elaboration? The thought of it made Stella feel somewhat untethered, slightly light-headed, like she was floating in a hot-air balloon some height above verified reality. Mischievous little zephyrs seemed to be buffeting her one way and another, but could she learn to enjoy this freedom?

"I'm not sure it's ethical."

"You'd hardly be defaming Jane, would you? It's an innocent little story, merely a bit of fun."

Was he right? Could she do that? Stella had been reading Dorothy Wordsworth's journal while she was up in Westmorland and had greatly enjoyed the bread-baking, the rum-bottling and the gathering of wild strawberries. It was just annoying that Dorothy didn't go into more detail. Stella would have loved to have a great Lakeland poet kneading barley bread in her text, but the information was teasingly scant. Could she get away with flouring William Wordsworth's hands? Could she extend his participation in the rum-bottling? As Freddie said, it would hardly be defamatory, would it?

"How conveniently flexible your morals are."

"What?" he laughed. "It's the way of the world! And you are under pressure to make this book salable, aren't you?"

"I am," she replied. Mr. Williamson had been clear about that too, hadn't he? And with the bill for the clutch looking likely to eat up a sizable chunk of her advance, it was going to be all the more difficult to rigorously research the remainder of the book. Perhaps a little flexibility wasn't out of order?

It was agreeable to walk through genteel Bath on Freddie's arm and develop the Jane Austen story together. Freddie suggested that Stella ought to work in a handsome curate, a playful badinage, hilarity and then blushing cheeks. They laughed as they invented the narrative together, and it became all the more outrageous with the retelling. Stella was impressed with his facility for fiction. What stories he must spin around his gateleg tables! But could she really get away with it? Could Jane Austen forgive her?

Hot toast, buttered scones, slices of plum cake and a fire crackling in the hearth—is there anything nicer than a country tea? What a pity it would be if we lost these habits! I hope your book will be a success, Miss Douglas, and that the old ways might be preserved. I'd be glad to contribute my great-grandmother's recipe for a reliable pound cake . . .

MR. V. M. HALL, Burford

Good Taste

The English have more recipes for cake than any other country. (I can't verify that, but I'm certain it's true. Don't you agree?) I have copied out my grandmother's recipe for a good plain seed cake below ...

IVY AMBROSE, Frome

I am sending you my mother's recipe for a Dorset apple cake. My mother never wrote the quantities down, she wasn't good with her letters, and it was just a cake that she was in the habit of making. I hadn't written it down myself until today, but it gave me pleasure to make it again and to remember the smell of my mother's kitchen ...

GRACE SPEEDWELL, Bridport

As a society we could have managed quite well without the invention of the cake fork, but isn't it fun, just occasionally, to use one? I am pleased to enclose my mother's recipe for Maids-of-Honor. She made beautiful pastry, such a light touch, and this was a great treat in my childhood. She liked to tell us that this cake dates back to Henry VIII's time (he was fond of his maids, wasn't he?) and that the original recipe is padlocked inside an iron box in Richmond Palace. Could that be true?

CHARLES WEST, Surrey

Your letter to the Evening Chronicle *made me think of all the hours we spent in tearooms in the years before the war—all our fervent hopes and speeches, the gallons*

*of tea and the endless plates of buttered toast! I was a
member of the Women's Social and Political Union and
teashops were sympathetic spaces where we could congregate
and freely debate. Will historians one day write theses
on the importance of teashops in the history of female
enfranchisement—or will all of that be forgotten? (I hand
this on to you!) I assume you are aware of* The Women's
Suffrage Cookery Book, *compiled by Mrs. Aubrey
Dowson, in 1912? I was proud to have my own recipe
for wholemeal scones published there and I've copied it out
below . . .*

ELSPETH BRIANT, Newcastle

Chapter Nineteen

Freddie was lolling on the sofa with an auctioneer's catalog. He always seemed to have one of these somewhere about his person. Stella looked over his shoulder and saw that he was marking up lots with a pen, circling the numbers of items, and writing down figures in the margins. It was all done in tidy, deliberate handwriting.

"Sheraton satinwood Pembroke table, crossbanding and boxwood ..." he muttered to himself. His brow was furrowed, but the way that he said the words made it sound as if they were delicious to him, like honeyed words served on a golden spoon. "A George III satinwood serpentine commode," he went on, speaking softly, "inset with mahogany flame veneers."

Stella wasn't precisely sure what these words meant, but they sounded lovely, all silky smooth and glossed to a toffee shine. She wondered: what did it say about a man, that he was so moved by fruitwood veneers?

"What are you chanting? Does a George III commode appear in a puff of smoke if you incant it thirteen times?"

"There's a sale at Harrup Hall next week. Actually, you

ought to come with me." He put the catalog down and looked up at her. "We could make a day of it and have a luncheon somewhere. You'd enjoy it."

"Tempting though it sounds, I am hoping not to be here next week. Not that I dislike listening to you murmuring about tulipwood crossbanding, but I need to get home and back to work."

"Pity," he said, and looked like he meant it. He reached out and took her hand. "Do you really have to go? You know, there's an eighteenth-century recipe called 'Love in Disguise.' If you stay, I could be persuaded to make it for you."

"I've read that recipe. It's made from a calf's heart, isn't it? Is that a romantic gesture?"

"The heart is stuffed with breadcrumbs, lemon zest and herbs. It's roasted and then rolled in crushed vermicelli, so that it looks all prickly. Doesn't that sound like fun? Aren't you intrigued?"

"Not as much as you evidently are!"

Within five days, they'd become comfortable in one another's company. Freddie was easy to be with, made her laugh and it really was very pleasant to sit on his sofa eating buttered crumpets. He was attentive, positive and didn't seem to take anything terribly seriously, which, Stella supposed, was what she needed as she worried about the looming cost of the clutch.

She'd watched him in the public bar last night and observed how he was supremely charming to women and chummy with men. There was much back-patting and arms around shoulders. Perhaps there was something tribal here, some display of virility or clan-bonding (perhaps she'd read too many books about anthropology?), but it was impossible not to notice how people liked Freddie. That had to mean that he was a decent sort, didn't it? That he was respected and dependable? Stella had found herself smiling as she'd watched him from across the room. However, they'd taken a moonlit stroll through the churchyard after they'd left the pub, and he'd reminisced about a girl called Arabella, who liked to read the inscriptions on the gravestones and listen to the owls. Where was she now? And quite how many other women had he walked through that graveyard? Stella imagined a long line of them picking through the shadows behind her. She kept hearing the word "lothario' said in her mother's tones, but it was just that the upper classes were more light-hearted about these things, wasn't it? They took life casually and weren't shackled by the conventions of respectability. (Her mother's voice observed that *they* could afford to be casual.)

Freddie stood up as the telephone rang and Stella listened to him speaking in the hallway. Questions about costs and readiness suggested that this might be something to do with her motor.

"Is it fixed?" she asked, as he returned to the room.

"It will be ready on Friday. Does that mean you'll leave on Friday?" He put his hands on her shoulders.

"I can't keep accumulating hotel bills."

"Damn it. To hell with propriety!" He curled a strand of

her hair around a finger. "You ought to have stayed in my spare room. Why don't you move over here? There's a lock on the door and I wouldn't try anything improper. I promise. Not unless you want me to be improper?"

The fact that he raised an eyebrow at that fixed her resolve. She definitely heard her mother's intake of breath then. Did he have no regard for the decencies? "And don't your neighbors talk? Or perhaps they expect to see random women appearing out of your shop door in the mornings? Thank you for the kind offer, but I ought to get home."

"You should never listen to idle gossip. Most of it stems from bitter jealousy."

"Really?"

"It has been fun, though, hasn't it?" He rolled a sweet on his tongue and his words smelled of peppermint. "At least say we'll do this again? Don't force me to have to sabotage your tires. I'll employ foul means if I have to, but I'd rather we were straightforward."

"It has been fun," Stella said, and smiled as she looked up into his excellent eyes. She could almost taste the peppermint on his breath. Just occasionally, it was a pity that she felt her mother watching.

"MINT PASTY"
[From the notebook of Elizabeth Douglas, 1924]

Charlie's mother used to make what she called a mint pasty. She told me this was an old Yorkshire recipe and it isn't something that I've ever seen sold in a baker's shop. She once showed me how she made it, lining a shallow pie dish with pastry and then filling it with currants and a big handful of fresh mint chopped up with a little brown sugar. She grated nutmeg over it, dotted it with butter, then it was topped with another layer of pastry and baked. Charlie's family were very fond of this and washed it down with endless cups of fiercely strong tea.

My mother used to put a leaf of mint in a jug of milk to keep it fresh in warm weather and a bunch of mint in a kitchen was meant to keep flies away. She was a great believer in a drop of peppermint oil in a glass of hot water to relieve stomachaches. I was given that often as a child, and do still associate the taste of mint with bellyaches.

My grandmother used to say that mint could heat up a man's blood. She told me that it was used in love potions in the olden times and soldiers weren't allowed to eat it lest they run amuck with lust. I remember her expounding on this subject over the Sunday roast and the cautionary look that she gave my grandfather as he reached for another spoonful of mint sauce.

Chapter Twenty

Freddie was moving an awl over a chest of drawers and repeatedly striking it with a hammer. It was a serviceable old piece of furniture and he seemed to be committing a deliberate act of vandalism upon it.

"Whatever are you doing?" Stella asked, as she pulled the beaded curtain aside.

"Being a woodworm."

"I thought you were meant to treat woodworm, that you were meant to patiently fill in the holes, not make them?"

"Not necessarily," he seemed to ponder this. "Sometimes it can give a piece more story." He smoothed his hand over the wood and blew dust away.

"Story? Make it look older than it is, you mean?"

"Put bluntly, yes." He looked up and shrugged.

"Isn't that cheating?" she asked.

"Ouch! Don't use such filthy language, Miss Douglas! If we must give it a word, let's call it 'antiquing.' Everyone does it."

"Everyone?" Was that true?

"Yes," he laughed. "Don't give me that disapproving look!"

Stella liked the smell of Freddie's workshop, its scents of

sanded wood, of paraffin and beeswax. There were jars of shellac, linseed oil, gold size and rabbit-skin glue on the shelves. Where did one buy such things? Did he cook them up himself in some cauldron? Many of the jars contained his own proprietary concoctions, colors of wax he'd blended himself, stains, putties and solvents. He'd painted names on some of the jars, but these words only served to make their contents more mysterious. "Dragon's blood," Stella read (surely not?), "Garnet." "Pumice," "Van Dyke" and "History." Whatever was "History"? Stella lifted the jar up to the light and turned it between her hands. It contained a dark, viscous liquid that was slightly grainy in the bottom. It might have been a gravy that had caught badly on the hob, something drained off an engine or dredged from a primeval swamp. Was this what he used to "antique" pieces of furniture? Was this the patina of ages that he painted on after he'd finished the job of the woodworm?

"It's not illegal to make a piece of furniture look older than it is, is it?" she asked, turning toward him again. "You can't get into trouble for fraudulently aging furniture?"

"Fraudulent! Wash your mouth out with soap and water, miss! It's not like I'm faking a Rembrandt. It's just a piece of brown furniture. *Caveat emptor,* and all that. The buyer has ample opportunity to examine the piece and we negotiate a price. If he likes it, if he can picture his children eating their dinner around it, we shake hands. I don't apply thumbscrews or give them a load of spiel."

Was that true? Stella had heard Freddie in action. He

spoke fluent spiel. "But you're presenting it as something it's not. Fundamentally, you're pretending it's something more valuable."

"It's only furniture, though. If they like it, they live with it. It's not like some Cinderella trick; they don't turn back into Victorian pine at midnight."

"Your conscience doesn't prick at all?"

"Not remotely. If anything, it's fun." He grinned. "If they're snob enough to want something special, something they can brag about, well, they ought to have done their homework more thoroughly. Everybody's at it, you know. Show me a dealer who doesn't do a bit of tinkering."

"Tinkering?"

"Call it what you will, it's just presentation. Don't bakers glaze the tops of inferior pies? Don't chefs call poached eggs *oeufs pochés,* strew on a pinch of parsley, and double the price?"

She wanted to tell him that he was mistaken, that he'd got it wrong, but she couldn't. "So what's in 'History,' then?"

"Well-stewed tea, household dust and sump oil."

"Sump oil!" she laughed. "Listen, fascinating though this is, and much as I'm enjoying watching you being a wood-worm, I'd better make a move." She'd already settled her hotel bill and taken her bag out to the car. She wanted to be on the road and get home before it was dark.

"Do you really have to?" He made a pleading face that very nearly steamrollered her resolve. "Can I do nothing to persuade you to stay?"

"Like cook a cow's heart?" she smiled. "Alluring as that

sounds and as fascinating as your repertoire of facial expressions is, I've got to get going."

"Will you call me when you get there? Will you let me
know that you're home safely?"

He kissed her in the doorway of the shop, rather tenderly,
and then with sufficient enthusiasm that her hat fell off. Stella
was certain that she wasn't the first woman to have been
kissed in the doorway of Langham Antiques—he ought to
install a revolving door—but it was still quite an effort to
walk away.

The bill for the repair work had come to £7 10s. The
mechanic might have had oil-engrained fingers, but he'd had
it typed up into a spotless invoice. Stella had felt obliged to
pay it—after all, she'd agreed to the work—but she couldn't
help asking herself if she'd been swindled. The motor was
nearly ten years old and decidedly rusty in some regions. It
had been her parents' car originally, and in the latter years
her father had taken to pushing hay bales and occasionally
a sheep or two in the back. What could it be worth now?
Surely not much more than thirty pounds? And what might
go wrong with it next?

She spent the miles between Stratford and Stoke thinking
about how she might explain it to her father. Would he think
that she'd been naïve? Would he tell her that she'd been
fleeced? But Freddie had said that the garage was honest,
hadn't he?

From Stoke to Buxton she made calculations. In addition

to the seven pounds she'd spent on the car, the hotel bill had come to five pounds. That left her with only twenty-three pounds of her advance remaining. She'd have to manage her budget very carefully now. There was a list of research trips that she'd planned to make, but she'd have to work through that, prioritize and do some crossing off.

From Buxton to Hatherstall she contemplated household economies. Her *Today's Woman* column covered her rent and her normal household spending, but there was never much left over at the end of the month. At least it was warmer now and she wouldn't need to order coal again. And wasn't washing in cold water good for the complexion? As the miles passed, Stella was conscious of the distance between her world and Freddie's. She couldn't imagine that he'd ever had to worry about the price of petrol.

By the time that she turned the key in the door and stepped into the dark and damp-smelling cottage, she missed the upbeat lilt of his voice.

Foreign acquaintances often like to tell me that English food is bland. When they are guests, I sometimes serve them deviled kidneys for breakfast and that soon puts right their misapprehensions. It seems to me that the fundamental difference between ourselves and our nearest Continental neighbors is this: while the French like their meat cut up and presented in a sauce, we prefer to see our meat in a joint and to add our own tracklements at the table. (Does this suggest that we are of a more suspicious nature than the French?)

Good Taste

We also like our sauces to be spicy. As Chaucer said, "Woe to the cook whose sauces had no sting!" Incidentally, I can't help wondering if there is an ancestral link between our Worcestershire Sauce and the garum sauce so beloved of the Roman legionaries. Could this be another legacy of Caesar's invasion?

REVD. WALTER ALFORD, Chester

When the Venerable Bede was on his deathbed in Jarrow, in 735, he distributed his few worldly possessions to his fellow priests and these included a tiny box of peppercorns. Bede called these "little presents as God has given me." I think of that whenever I fill my peppermill and it makes me thankful.

MARY DENMAN, Hexham

I have been a grocer for forty years and was always proud to tell customers about the curious origins of my trade. The Guild of Pepperers—traders in spices—is first mentioned in records not long after the Norman Conquest. Venetian galleons brought figs, oranges and almonds to our shores, and spices sourced from those mysterious lands beyond the Mediterranean. How exotic their perfumes must have seemed. By the fourteenth century the Pepperers had become the Worshipful Company of Grocers—grocer being derived from "grossarii," and meaning one who dealt in quantities. Who says there's no romance in grocery?

MR. ALFRED COLMAN, Birmingham

Spice was the flavor of affluence in medieval England.
Desire for it emboldened navigators to set out on perilous
voyages, lead to wars between nations, generated trade
"booms" and "busts," and motivated the creation of empires.
Even today, any decent grill room must have a goodly
array of spicy relishes, mustards and chutneys. You'll find
family recipes for a satisfyingly fiery catsup, a piccalilli and
a chilli vinegar enclosed. I have copied these from my great-
grandfather's notebook where they are dated 1818.

HORACE SANDERSON, London

Can we count curry as an English food? We've been eating
it keenly since the mid-eighteenth century, so I'd assert it
ought to be the case. I enclose my own recipe for an excellent
mutton curry. It's very invigorating for the blood circulation
and I believe it was a great favorite of Queen Victoria's.
(Could a recipe have a finer English pedigree?)

DR. CHARLES HAMILTON, Bexhill-on-Sea

Chapter Twenty-one

"Did I tell you that I sold another copy of my book? That's forty now." Dilys took off her glasses and smiled. "It feels like a bit of a landmark."

"Well done," Stella said, touching the rim of her coffee cup to Dilys', and sincerely hoping that she didn't sound patronizing. It must be awfully hard word trying to shift books on a market stall and she'd hate to have to do it herself. She'd witnessed Dilys' sales patter and it was far removed from Freddie's.

"I've decided that I'm going to treat myself. There's a jumble sale at St. Aiden's on Saturday and it's always a good one. I might have a little something."

Dilys was a great one for jumble sales and seemed to derive considerable satisfaction from telling Stella how cheaply she'd acquired a new skirt or a coat. As some of the coats were full of moth holes, and the skirts quite Victorian, she occasionally struggled to summon the positive words that were required of her.

"Why not? We all need to reward ourselves sometimes."

Dilys didn't reward herself very often, but then—could she

afford to? Stella looked around Dilys' sitting room, noticing the places where cat claws had plucked at the upholstery and where the paint was blistering on the walls. She'd pushed rags into the gaps around the windows to keep the drafts out and there was a smell of damp plaster behind the peppery insistence of the incense sticks. How did she get by? Stella knew that she made a little regular income from her magazine articles, but she'd confided that with circulation figures for *The Other Side* declining, she'd had to accept a pay cut this spring. Dilys' living seemed terribly precarious. But then her own career wasn't exactly ironclad, was it?

"I picked up a pair of boots there last winter," Dilys went on. "They'd hardly been worn. They're a couple of sizes too big, but I've filled the toes with newspaper, and so long as I don't have to walk far, they're quite comfortable."

"How practical you are."

The words "jumble sale' conjured a particular smell in Stella's nose, of crusted soup dribbles on a stranger's cardigan, an old mourning blouse gone mildewed in a suitcase and the curling linings of ancient plimsolls. At that moment, she felt a rush of resolve. No, she wouldn't settle for that life. Being a magazine writer who just about broke even every month wasn't enough. And this book could save her from that, couldn't it? Hadn't Mr. Williamson said that this one could be salable? That it could be a success? Even if it meant wholesale fabrication, she would damn well make it salable, Stella decided now. It would be a book that people talked about, smiled at and, most importantly, bought. Newspapers would deem it perceptive, and magazines would call it a charming book. She could hold her chin up and Mr. Williamson would bestow his most beneficent smile. She would bloody well make it a bestseller and ensure that Cynthia Palmer never got to see her wearing a second-hand cardigan. Stella determined that whenever doubt assailed her, she would think of the expression on Dilys' face when she got word of a jumble sale. And she would buy her a new pair of boots.

"Do you ever find a hint of a good story, something that you'd love to share, only to discover that the evidence to fill it out just isn't there?" Stella asked, as Dilys refilled her coffee cup. She supposed that when one was writing of spectral matters, there must be a lot of tenuous evidence. (She was also aware that she'd weighted her question in order to provoke the response that she wanted to hear.)

"Sometimes one has to make informed assumptions." Dilys wafted her hand in a vague way. "Yes, we must try to verify and be complete; however, there are always gaps, and that's where instinct comes in. We all have to bridge the gaps from time to time, but if one does it with understanding, I think that's acceptable practice. History is full of holes."

Yes, that's all it would be: a well-informed bridging of gaps. Stella could glean the facts and figures from books, but she would put flesh on these bones using her empathy and a little imagination. She knew the way that people felt about their inherited recipes and she could conjure up appropriate words. She could so easily imagine those voices in her head. They were there now, making impassioned statements about oven-bottom muffins and bloater paste. It wouldn't be entirely fictionalizing because it would be broadly evidence-based and plausible. It wasn't that risky, was it?

"I received a charming letter from a Colonel Jenkins," Stella wrote, when she got home, *"who has a family link to William Wordsworth and the illusive recipe for Grasmere gingerbread. Much as I have searched, pestered and experimented, I've struggled to find a recipe that delivers the particular fieriness and sandy texture of Sarah Nelson's celebrated gingerbread. I was delighted, then, to receive Col. Jenkins' letter and, upon following the recipe he enclosed, I have been able to produce a convincing approximation of the veritable and estimable Grasmere gingerbread. (Some Hosannas may have issued from my kitchen.) The recipe is detailed below, but I must also share with you a delightful anecdote that this gentleman included with his letter.*

Col. Jenkins' great-grandfather was one of the pupils at the school in Grasmere where the famous Lakeland poet sometimes taught. The two were well acquainted, and young Mr. Jenkins was a regular caller at Dove Cottage. Dropping by this address, one winter's day, Jenkins found William and his great friend Samuel Taylor Coleridge in a state of some merriment on the hearthrug. While Dorothy was away, they had raided the larder and had seemingly spent a very diverting afternoon eating toasted fruit teacakes liberally endowed with rum butter. This is a particularly Cumbrian combination of butter, brown sugar, rum, nutmeg and cinnamon. It's traditionally prepared in a house when a woman enters confinement, and a piece is usually placed in a new baby's mouth as its first taste of earthly food, but it's also generally eaten on bread, oatcakes and biscuits. On this occasion, Dorothy's rum butter was clearly particularly fine (and potent) and the good gentlemen had got through a whole bowl of it. Indeed, such was the indulgence, and the ensuing hilarity of the two illustrious poets, that young Jenkins recalled them in the midst of composing an ode to rum butter. Alas, no manuscript survives, but Jenkins recalled much amusement around certain indelicate rhymes and the sight of the two great men of letters weeping tears of mirth on the Turkey carpet.

Yes, that was the stuff, Stella thought. Of course, Colonel Jenkins didn't exist, but it was plausible enough, wasn't it? It was the sort of thing that Mr. Williamson wanted, she considered—warm, colorful and giving humor and humanity to the text. And, who was to say, maybe Wordsworth and Coleridge had once overindulged? Her only evidence was a few references to rum in Dorothy's diary—but, equally, who might disprove it?

Pleased with her experiment in the realm of hypothetical history, Stella decided that she might do more of this. Why not put in the Jane Austen story? And couldn't she work up something involving Charlotte Brontë and a seed cake? Charles Dickens and a whitebait supper? Robert Walpole and a lamprey pie? She wouldn't need to motor out to the far reaches of Norfolk and Cornwall when she could imagine herself there, and surely it wouldn't be that hard to do? She might invent knowledgeable cheesemongers, erudite eel-catchers and quaint in-service cooks, take fictional tours of dairies, bakeries and kitchen gardens. She'd have to be careful about using famous names, Stella knew that, but with a little artfulness it ought to be achievable. Yes, thinking it through, the possibilities seemed exciting and endless.

She telephoned Freddie and told him the story of Charlotte and Emily walking up to Top Withens and unwrapping slices of seed cake as they debated Heathcliff's table manners.

"This is just the sort of thing! How utterly delightful. Where did you find it? Was it in their diaries?"

"I made it up."

"Ha! Seriously?"

"Is it unwise, do you think? I mean, it *could* have happened. There's a seed-cake scene in *Jane Eyre*."

"I don't suppose anyone could disprove it. You'll just have to be careful how you write it. How likely is it that every line will get picked over?"

"My editor is astute, but I don't suppose he'll take a magnifying glass to every fact."

"Then go for it, I say!"

Stella continued to deliberate after she put the telephone down. If she framed these things very carefully, very cautiously, she could make them convincing. She thought about Freddie's jar marked "History." If he could make a career of getting away with it, couldn't she?

Chapter Twenty-two

Stella stood in the queue outside the butcher's shop and tried to pin a name to all the shades of red. Carmine, cadmium, Venetian red, she thought, vermillion, rose madder, magenta. It gave her a vague longing to be stirring a brush in bright pigments. Mr. Gomersall had a cleaver in his hand, she could see through the window, and a neat streak of fresh blood up the center of his white apron. He might be a butcher in a play, and Stella idly wondered if he deliberately put the scarlet splatter on his apron. She pictured him doing so, as purposeful as Turner placing a red dot on a canvas. It might be one of the stages in his morning routine, like hanging up the strings of sausages and turning the "Open" sign on the door.

A memory of sketching in Smithfield Market came back to her as she contemplated the window, an early-morning trip when she and Michael were both still new and keen students. She remembered the swinging carcasses and the bustle of the porters with their trolleys, a smell of blood, sawdust and disinfectant, and feeling like they were in the way. She could picture Michael's nineteen-year-old face so clearly still, his eyelashes cast down in concentration, but then turning and smiling at her. The memory of that expression brought a smile to her own face now, and then a bittersweet sensation. It was three weeks since she and Michael had last spoken. She'd counted that up last night. She couldn't recall that they'd ever gone so long between telephone calls, but, as her father had predicted, his focus was elsewhere now, wasn't it? Still, Stella couldn't help hoping to hear his voice every time she lifted the telephone receiver, and she wished she could discuss her book with him and ask his advice. But he'd caution her, wouldn't he? If she admitted that she was leaning on the evidence, he'd tell her that it was unwise. She didn't really need to hear that, did she? And, besides, the last time they'd spoken, he'd talked about preparing *saumon en croûte* for Cynthia, and Stella had felt envious of his attention and his puff pastry. Could this long silence between them be for the best after all?

"I read your article about dinners for slimmers," said Mrs. Schofield, over her shoulder.

"Did you?" The voice brought Stella out of her reverie and back into the queue. She'd written the magazine article with London acquaintances in mind, not Edith Schofield who worked in the confectioner's and who was known for a certain overkeenness in taking the "stales" home.

"My Harold's not opposed to pickled cabbage, but I've no chance of making him eat a chopped salad. He doesn't trust tomatoes."

"No?"

"No. His mother had a nasty incident with one before the war."

"Oh dear. I'm sorry to hear that."

Stella turned back to the window. It was full of slabs of beef, trays of rolled roasts, and the row of plastic sheep with soapflake-white fleeces and upturned smiling faces. Glassy-eyed rabbits dangled by their feet, while chops were stringed into rounds and trotters were arranged into tidy lines (what was Mrs. Raffald's delightful word for them—pigs' petti-toes?). Stella watched the lazy, impudent bluebottles crawling on the sawdust floor.

"It was right what you said about linoleum, though," Mrs. Schofield added, turning back again. "And I swear by carbolic."

"Good. I'm glad we agree."

Stella meant to make a chitterling turnover tonight (she'd received the recipe from a Suffolk vicar) and wanted suet to make a Westmorland herb dumpling. It was a good job that so many English recipes required cheap cuts. Stella felt that she might be eating a lot of offal over the next few months. She made herself look at the hairs in the pigs' ears, and how the bluebottles rubbed their legs together, and told herself that she wasn't really craving a bacon sandwich.

"My feet are killing me," complained Mrs. Midgley behind. "How long has Elsie Holmbridge been at the counter? Is she going to buy the whole shop? I only came out for a bit of kidney."

Mrs. Thorncliff made sympathetic noises. "I just want some honeycomb for Edgar's tea. It slips down nicely, doesn't it?"

Mr. Gomersall sold a lot of tripe, which the older people

liked, all curled and folded like slightly soiled-looking blankets. Stella had been force-fed various textures of tripe as a child. Her father extolled its health-giving properties, and liked to eat it generously doused with white pepper and malt vinegar. Stella thought that any food that must be drowned in vinegar to disguise a whiff of urinals wasn't really something that she should voluntarily put in her mouth. But for the sake of the book and her budget, should she make a renewed effort with tripe? Could she get beyond the slither and the quivering, the squeak against the teeth and the cartilaginous lumps?

"How's your sister getting on, Beryl?" Stella heard Mrs. Thorncliff's voice again.

"Oh, she's not so bad, but it's hard times up there at the moment. The shipyard where her Alfred works let four hundred men go last month. It doesn't bear thinking about, does it?"

Stella had read Agnes Blenkinsop's *Today's Woman* article about silent shipyards and rusting cranes last night, and it had left her reflecting on how many people were presently much worse off than she was. Her column ought to reflect these realities, she'd thought. She'd accordingly compiled a selection of recipes that stretched out a bit of suet or a few rashers of bacon, nutritious, wholesome and inexpensive dishes, but as Stella had typed them out she'd recalled the butcher's shop in the square where Freddie lived. How odd it was that in one part of the country, people were queuing for soup kitchens, while in another they ate beef tenderloins and shopped for antique sugar tongues.

Stella stepped up to the counter and asked for her chitterlings. As she looked down at the crown roasts and the lamb chops, she couldn't summon much passion for chitterlings. A need for financial prudence can so quickly take the pleasure out of food, she reflected. She remembered how Freddie had called eating a pork chop tragic. She might be able to talk to him about historical offal recipes, but she couldn't confide in him about her finances. He simply wouldn't understand. She wondered what menu he might be preparing tonight. A slow-braised oxtail? A roast chicken with bread sauce? A rabbit with a good brown gravy? It would be pleasant to have an evening in his company, she considered, a light-hearted conversation over a partridge or a pheasant. But, if she was honest, she'd still rather be having *saumon en croûte*.

On seeing your notice in the Western Morning News, *I was reminded of a debate that took place across the correspondence pages of* The Times *some five years ago. A passionate discussion ensued around the definition of pie, in particular whether a pie requires pastry beneath its filling, above or both. I recall that the manager of Simpson's in the Strand was eventually summoned to make a ruling (a pie must have an upper pastry crust, it was decreed), but the strength of feeling this argument provoked suggests that the demise of English food may be overstated . . .*

SIMEON FORSTER, Falmouth

Your appeal in the evening paper reminded me of the four-and-twenty blackbird pie of the nursery rhyme and I believe this was a dish served at the Tudor court. I have been unable to find an English recipe in my library, but would refer you to "Epulario" (1598), "To make Pies that the Birds may be alive in them, and flie out when it is cut up." Of course, it was an entertainment, a novelty, not something that was actually eaten. We're not as barbaric as the French!

EDMUND DELAFIELD, Cirencester

Please find my father's recipe for a blackbird pie enclosed. I have never made it myself, but he told me that he used to trap blackbirds, sparrows and lapwings as a boy. They were a family of ten children and I suppose you had to be glad of what you got in those days. Poor folks couldn't afford tender feelings back then, could they?

MRS. MARGARET ELLERTON, Gloucester

In response to your advertisement, I am sending you a recipe for rook pie. I seldom hear of it now, but there was a time when it was a popular Whitsuntide dish here in Lincolnshire. Rook takes some preparing, there's not much meat on them, but cooked with care, it's as tasty as pigeon, and they are a farm pest . . .

HAROLD DALBY, Grantham

I am sending you my mother's recipe for a starling pie. Starling can be bitter to the unaccustomed palate, but the Wessex housewife knew how to prepare it and it was a regular feature of the rural diet when I was a boy . . .

ALFRED WHITE, Dorchester

Chapter Twenty-three

The honk of a motor car horn broke into Stella's pie contemplations. Looking down from the window, she saw a van pulling up by the gate, piled with an assortment of furniture. Her first thought was that it must be Freddie's van. She hadn't given him her address, though, had she? And why might he come here laden with mahogany table legs?

But then she had the most peculiar sensation. As Stella looked out, she recognized those particular table legs from her parents' sitting room. That chest of drawers looked awfully like one that used to be in their bedroom, and surely that Turkey rug was normally in the kitchen at the farm? Then a man who looked very like her father stepped down from the van. As he opened the gate and came down the path, it obviously was her father, but why had he brought all of his furniture with him? What had happened? Had the house burned down? Had some awful tragedy occurred? Stella ran to the door.

"Daddy, what has happened? Why is your hearthrug on top of that van?"

"I couldn't leave it behind. I know it's full of burn marks, but it was one of the first things your mother and I bought when we set up home together." He wiped his feet on the mat and smiled. He was looking rather pleased with himself.

"Whatever is going on?"

"In here, Ted!" her father called over his shoulder to the man who was now untangling ropes from the rear of the van. "Stella will help you. My daughter isn't short of a bit of muscle. Weren't you school arm-wrestling champion?"

Stella raised her hands. "Daddy, please stop. Please tell me what's going on."

"I'm moving in, aren't I?"

"What?"

"The farm was getting too much for me. I told you. I'm not a young man any longer, I struggled last winter, and every time I go to market, prices are down. I've never known them as low as they are now. So when Bill Baxendale made me an offer, I reckoned I'd be daft to refuse it. I know you have to be careful about money. You never say too much—you're proud, like your mother—but I can see the signs." He put his arm around her shoulders. "So this solves a problem for both of us. Instead of inheriting the farm in another ten years or so, you can have the money in the bank now. You'll be financially comfortable and we'll be snug as two bugs in a rug here. You are pleased, aren't you? Only, looking at your face, I can't tell."

It was too much information. Stella felt herself reeling slightly. "You've sold the farm?"

"That's what I just said, wasn't it?"

"And you didn't think to discuss that with me?"

"Bill made me an offer. It came out of the blue. Some folks reckon the market has hit the bottom now, that it could start to pick up, but I'm fed up of running at a loss. It's been getting me down. I have been thinking about putting it up for sale for a while and I was intending to discuss it with you, but it all happened rather fast. Bill offered me a decent price. I was quite surprised by just how decent it was. Well, you didn't propose to take the farm on, did you? You've never shown any interest in doing that."

It was true, but ... "And so you've decided to move in with me?"

"I thought it would be nice for us both to have some company. You're always asking me if I'm lonely and I began to suspect that you might be yourself. I'll admit, I wasn't expecting you to look so shocked."

Lonely? Had she given him that impression? The man called Ted was now standing behind her father with two suitcases in his hands.

"Top of the stairs, door on the left," her father said.

"Beg pardon." The man nodded an acknowledgment, but then jostled past Stella. She couldn't quite comprehend that a stranger was jogging up her staircase into the room that she called her "study," and that this great stockade of furniture was now going to be following him into that room too.

"You cleared the house without telling me?"

"I did telephone you last week, but you weren't here, and then I didn't want to worry you while you were having problems with your motor. It sounded like you'd got enough on your plate. Bill and Mary bought some of the furniture, the big old wardrobes, the dressers and the dining table, but you wouldn't have had space for those, would you?"

Stella began mentally inventorying her parents' home. She thought about her mother's wardrobe and all her clothes hanging in there. What had happened to them? He hadn't passed her mother's winter coats on to Mary Baxendale too, had he? Surely he hadn't done that?

"You didn't think that I'd like to go through it all with you and decide what we should keep?"

"I've brought most of it." He was starting to look slightly crestfallen. "I thought you'd be glad. This place always looks a little bare. It will be cozy now."

Cozy was one word for it. The contents of a four-bedroom farmhouse were on top of the van, she saw, and rather a lot of her father's collection of scrap metal from the barn. Was he planning to squeeze that into her study too?

"Where's it all going to go?"

"Oh, we'll jiggle down. And I do mean to see you right. We'll make an appointment at the bank. Think of it as getting your inheritance early in return for giving your old father a bit of help. That's not a bad deal, is it?"

"'Scuse me, love." Ted shouldered his way past her and Stella felt like she could cry. It was true that she could use the money, and that was no small thing, but how on earth would she work? And where was all this furniture going to go? "I wouldn't mind a cup of tea," Ted suggested. "Then perhaps she could give me a hand?"

"Aye, our Stella will have it sorted in no time. She's a marvel, she is."

It took Stella by surprise as the man called Ted reached out and squeezed her bicep. "You've bred her well, Charlie. A fine strapping lass. You're a lucky fellow."

"I know I am. You're going to take care of your decrepit old father in his twilight years, aren't you, love? Your mother would have been so pleased. I know this is what she would have wanted."

Was it? Hadn't her mother always encouraged her to be independent? Hadn't she argued for Stella's right to go to London? She tried to conjure up her mother's face and it wasn't looking pleased. Her expression was rather stern. But what could Stella say in reply to him now? She felt like she'd been ambushed. She could hardly turn him away, could she?

Three hours later, her house was full of chests of crockery, blanket boxes and travel trunks. It was most peculiar to see all the furnishings of her childhood home now crammed into the cottage, and her father installed in his armchair by her fireside. It seemed to confuse and challenge Stella's memories. Her father was talking about getting the chimney swept now, and fixing the slipped tiles on the roof. He was saying that he'd have a talk with Mr. Outhwaite, would ask him if he could take away old Mr. O's furniture, and perhaps he might do some decorating. Stella had to admit that would be welcome, but could the two of them really live here together?

Stella had sometimes daydreamed about restyling the cottage with pieces of rustic eighteenth-century furniture. She'd paint the ceilings and the beams white, and would try to maximize the light from the small windows; however, her front room was now crammed full of dark Victorian veneer. It looked like a mahogany assault course. All the light seemed to have left the room, and the subtle but unmistakable smell of sheep and generations of collies had entered.

"I noticed that the window frame in that bedroom is rotten. I'll scrape the worst of it out and fill it with putty. It'll look better once it's painted."

"Thank you," said Stella vaguely. She felt like she was spinning in a vortex of table legs and best intentions.

She was struck with a twin contrary shock at being over-crowded with her parents' possessions and a slow realization that so many familiar items were missing. He'd left her mother's dressing table, garden bench and kitchen scales back at the farm. Didn't it occur to him that these were important things, that so many memories were attached to them? Why had he let these go, but opted to bring his corroded coal scuttle, a bail of barbed wire and several sets of moth-ravaged curtains? How could he have chosen cobwebbed oil lamps and saws with rusted teeth over her mother's washstand? Why had he not thought to discuss this with her? Stella stepped over a pile of fire irons, the wind-up gramophone, and the barometer that always forecast rain, and settled herself into the chair that now faced her father's. He'd put an antimacassar on the back of it. In fact, as she looked around, she saw that antimacassars had appeared on all the chairs now, like hand-embroidered territorial flags. She hugged her glass to her chest.

"Is that a gin-and-bitters? It's not four o'clock yet."

"It's only tonic water," she lied.

"I didn't know you used that room as a study. I thought it was just a spare bedroom and couldn't recall that you'd ever had anyone staying in there. I do realize that I ought to have asked you first," he conceded. He was fiddling with his pipe and strands of tobacco fell onto the rug. "I'm sorry. But I thought it would be a nice surprise for you to have the money. I wanted to please you with that. I was excited about telling you."

She could hear it in his voice, and also a note of disappointment. "I've not said thank you, have I? No, I'm the one who ought to apologize, Daddy. I am grateful, the money will make a big difference to me, but I wish we could have talked about it first. Of course, I would have been glad to have you here—I always would have said 'yes'—but you might have given me the chance to get ready and let me help you sort through the house."

When she'd first viewed the cottage, Stella had imagined that the spare bedroom might become her study. She'd pictured herself writing her Hannah Glasse biography there. As it turned out, it was warmer to work at the kitchen table—but still, that room was the place where she laid out her papers and lined up her library books. It was now full of suitcases, two slightly balding armchairs and her father's collection of tankards. She would excavate her books and papers, but where could she put them? Where would she have the space and time to work now?

Her father seemed to have assumed that in return for "getting her inheritance early," as he put it, she would spend her days looking after him. He evidently regarded this arrangement as a form of paid employment for Stella. But at what point had she applied for this job? Stella knew that it was probably selfish of her to even have this thought—after all, this was what unmarried daughters were expected to do—but she presently felt like she could sob. Could anyone blame her for needing a midafternoon gin?

Chapter Twenty-four

"And you hadn't had a conversation about it?" Michael asked.

"We hadn't so much as exchanged a word on the subject." Stella had needed to talk to him—her first instinct had been to telephone him—but was that Cynthia's voice in the background? She now found herself distracted by trying to pick out the backdrop sounds. "Apparently, Bill wrote a figure on the back of an envelope; he mulled it over for twenty-four hours, and then accepted it. Just like that. I was away; my motor had broken down, and I was stuck in Gloucestershire for a week. He said he didn't know how to get in touch with me. I wish I'd been here."

"You suspected he was lonely, didn't you? Maybe it was about more than his cash flow and sciatica?"

"I think you're right. He needed someone to talk to in the evenings. The funny thing was, he told me that he was worried *I* was lonely, like that was one of his motivations. When am I meant to have time to be lonely?"

"But, darling, aren't you? I've worried that too. You do seem to be isolated up there. You so rarely talk about friends and I miss hearing the laughter in your voice. I always used to be able to hear that, that little ripple of amusement, but it's not been there recently. Your voice sounds flat. Should I be worried about you?"

Stella heard concern in his voice and found herself holding the receiver closer to her cheek. "I'm just a little tired and busy, that's all. I've got too much work on to sit around feeling sorry for myself, or to be having a hectic social life. With juggling the column and this book, I'm working full time at the moment."

"But are you happy?"

The question took her by surprise. Was she? She hesitated. "Can anyone say that?" She knew it wasn't a proper answer.

"It's not that complicated a question. Listen, you would tell me if you were feeling blue, wouldn't you? I do get concerned for you. You haven't called me for three weeks."

Stella bit back the urge to remind him that, equally, he hadn't called her. "I know you're up to your ears in work and wedding plans."

"I'm never too busy that I wouldn't be glad to hear from you. You're always on my mind. You know that, don't you?"

Stella wasn't sure what to reply for a moment, but then Cynthia's voice (yes, it was her voice) was there in the background again and it disordered her thoughts. "Well, I'm certainly going to be fully occupied now. He's set up side-by-side armchairs for us in front of the fire. We're going to spend our evenings playing cribbage and listening to the wireless together."

"Oh God, I can just picture it! I want to rescue you! What can I do?"

"Recommend a wholesaler who delivers gin by the crate?"

"Seriously, I am worried about you. How are you going to manage?"

"Oh, we'll sort ourselves out. I'm just in shock at the moment. And you should see the state of the house! It looks like a bric-à-brac shop."

It had been instinctive to dial Michael's number. She hadn't for a second thought of calling Freddie, she realized now. There was a significance in that, wasn't there?

"I wish I could do something," Michael said. "I feel so far away. You'll call me if you're feeling down, or want to let off steam, won't you? Please promise that you'll telephone. You can call me any time, day or night. Don't leave it three weeks again."

Stella was glad he said that, but she could also hear him sounding distracted.

"I will—but I must let you go now. Are you on your way out to the restaurant?"

"I had better ring off. I've actually taken the night off for once. We've got tickets for a play, something Russian and bleakly intellectual, but Cynthia is keen to see it. Let's speak again at the weekend, eh? Cynth says to tell you that she sends her love."

That wasn't true, was it? Stella could hear Cynthia in the background, making sounds like she wanted Michael to wind the call up, but she wouldn't be directing love toward the telephone receiver, would she?

"I hope the play isn't too grim. Enjoy your evening."

"I'm glad to have heard your voice. I've missed it. Say hello to your father for me—and you will look after yourself, won't you?"

"I will, I promise. Goodnight."

The line crackled and he was gone. Stella stood with the receiver to her chest. She'd wanted to speak to him, his was the one voice that she needed to hear tonight, but when he was concerned and sweet to her it just smarted all the more. Perhaps it was for the best that they spoke infrequently now?

Chapter Twenty-five

A week on, some progress had been made with the furniture rationalization. Her father had proved to be rather efficient at negotiating with Mr. Outhwaite, and Stella hadn't been sorry to see old Mr. O's stained armchairs and sticky rugs exiting the property. A lengthy bargaining process had resulted in Stella and her father agreeing that they must sell certain items of furniture, and Mr. Harris had already taken away a van full of chairs.

The front room still looked crowded, though, and it was very strange to suddenly find herself living in a reshuffled version of her parents' home. Every chest of drawers and box of crockery was full of memories. Half-forgotten conversations and the sound of her mother's voice fell out of crates of linen and rolls of rugs. Mostly her mother's recalled voice seemed to be saying that she must be brave and pursue her dreams. What would she think of this arrangement? Stella put the question to her in her head and her mother's voice had a few choice words for her father.

But there were parts of this new existence that weren't disagreeable. The two bedding chests had proved to be full of her mother's clothes and, as her father had arranged his room, they had reminisced together. On occasions, they had cried together as they shared memories. It was pleasant to have someone to talk to in the evenings, and Stella had moved her typewriter and scrubbed the kitchen table so that they might eat there together. Her father was appreciative, and she found herself making more effort in the kitchen, but, as well as space, all of this took up so much time and emotion. Stella realized that she hadn't added a single word to her book since her father had arrived. Was this how it must be now? Should she telephone Mr. Williamson and tell him that her circumstances had changed?

She'd brought the typewriter up to her dressing table. Looking up from the keys, she would face her own reflection in the mirror. It was sometimes useful to look herself directly in the eye; but at other times it definitely wasn't. In the end, she'd draped a pillowcase over the mirror. Stella reminded herself that the Brontës had jostled elbows as they worked around the parlor table, and hadn't many writers produced masterpieces from chilly garrets? Still, it wouldn't be terrifically inspiring to be typing in between her tins of cold cream and face powder. There was a page still in her typewriter, half finished. She'd looked at it earlier in the day and seen the words, "*I was recently in Bath . . .*" It seemed a world away.

The sound of the wireless wasn't especially conducive to working either. Over the past year her father had become accustomed to the company of the BBC. He had the radio on all day, be it for the cricket, an afternoon concert or an evening play. Stella was convinced that he wasn't always listening (was he really interested in discussions about Bauhaus architecture and Norwegian theater?) and it often seemed to send him to sleep. She hadn't objected to the swing jazz concert in the background as they'd unpacked suitcases and found places for her mother's soup tureens—it had been quite jolly at times—but how was she meant to work with the voices constantly competing for her attention? Hoots of audience laughter billowed out from behind her father's door, cheery strains of signature tunes and interminable academic debates about the Gold Standard.

There was also the noise of her father and Mrs. Pendlebury chattering. Mrs. P had looked aghast when she'd walked in last Friday and found the house jammed full of furniture. She'd said that she didn't know where to begin with the dusting, and how was she meant to hoover? In the end, Stella had apologized, paid her and sent her home. But Mrs. Pendlebury and her father seemed to be getting on rather well this morning. Stella had never heard Mrs. Pendlebury laughing before. It was an unexpected sound. She also heard her father speaking in a voice that she didn't recognize, as if he wanted to make Mrs. P laugh. The expression on his face was new too. This left Stella feeling slightly confused. Was she mistaken in detecting flirtation there? An unexpected territorial sensation asserted itself, and she found herself hoping that her mother wasn't watching.

She walked into the front room now to find her father

observing as Mrs. Pendlebury sprinkled a white powder all over the rugs. He looked up at Stella and smiled.

"It's a magical product that Mrs. Pendlebury has mixed up herself. It draws out all the dirt and smells. I've told her she ought to market it."

"The rugs smell of the farm. I don't mind that."

"Give it ten minutes and then I hoover." Mrs. Pendlebury stood with a hand on her hip. "I've added some eucalyptus oil, so it will all be nice and fresh."

Stella wasn't sure that she wanted her house to smell of eucalyptus. Her father's rugs smelled of Border Collies, wood smoke and muddy boots. She remembered a whole dynasty of dogs lying there, their legs gamboling as they chased rabbits through their dreams, and her mother looking on with an indulgent smile. When the rugs were first unrolled Stella had been aware of that smell; however, after a couple of days, she'd begun to find it oddly comforting. It was a memory of younger, healthier, noisier times—but now the room was beginning to fill with the scent of bronchial chest rubs and Stella stifled a sneeze.

"Would you like a cup of tea, Mrs. Pendlebury?"

"Very kind of you, dear."

Her father followed her into the kitchen. "She's a grand woman, isn't she?"

In her father's parlance, this was high praise. Earlier that morning Mrs. Pendlebury had observed that her father was a smashing chap, and didn't he have a cheeky sense of humor? The question had briefly derailed Stella.

"Mrs. Pendlebury? Yes, she's a demon with that hoover. You must be careful of your feet. You don't want to get in her way."

"She was being dynamic with a feather duster earlier. I'm not sure I've ever witnessed such vigorousness. Did I tell you that Mary was hanging new curtains?"

"You did."

He'd driven over to the farm the previous day to see how Bill and Mary were settling in. He'd invited Stella to go with him, but she'd found an excuse not to. She didn't want to see it. Not yet. When she contemplated the word "home', the rooms of that house were what came to mind. It was most peculiar to imagine relative strangers living in the farm now, sitting around their dining table, and doing Lord knows what in her childhood bedroom. Unfamiliar faces would be looking out of the windows and a woman other than her mother would be standing at the stove. Stella wasn't ready to see that. And if the farm wasn't "home' now, where was?

"Didn't it feel odd to you to go back in there?" she asked. Her father had settled down with his crossword at the kitchen table.

"A bit, but I have to say that I don't miss my alarm clock going off at six every morning."

"You could have sold the land to Bill, but kept the house. Did you not think of that?"

"An old chap on his own doesn't need a four-bedroom house. It's a house for a family. Besides, Bill wouldn't have been interested in the land without the house. It was worth more as a working farm."

"It's sad," she admitted.

"You never expressed any interest in taking the farm on, though. Not once. If you had done, of course, I would have discussed it with you."

"I might have felt like it one day."

"Don't talk daft, Stella."

She pictured herself pulling on wellingtons and a cardigan as the six o'clock alarm went off. No, she'd never seriously considered that life, but perhaps she ought to have looked out for a handsome young farmer. It was a pity that they all had ruddy faces and were so keen on talking about silage.

"Won't you miss your garden?"

"I can get the garden here into shape, can't I? I thought I might put in some borders and those vegetable beds are just going to waste. The rhubarb is taking over. It's crowding everything else out."

It wasn't the only thing, Stella thought.

"RHUBARB FOOL"
[From the notebook of Elizabeth Douglas, 1908]

We have a glut of rhubarb at the moment. I made a rhubarb fool last night, stirring the cooked fruit through whipped cream, and we ate it with ginger biscuits. The first of the rhubarb is a great treat, but I've been chopping, cooking and bottling it all morning, at the same time as doing the laundry, and am beginning to feel like a slave to rhubarb. I was finally folding the sheets and putting the jars away in the pantry, when Charlie came in and said that the sheep had got out again and the mare was going to foal.

I shouldn't complain, I don't complain, but I do occasionally long to sit quietly with a book, or to go for a walk simply for the pleasure of it. We don't do that any longer, and I'm usually so tired at the end of the day that I never seem to be able to concentrate on a book. Charlie was brought up knowing that the farm would be his and I don't think he's ever thought about an alternative life. When I married him, my mother warned me that I'd find myself tied to the farm. I've never regretted coming here to share this life with him, this place is so much a part of who he is, but it does occasionally strike me that all our conversations these days are about the price of feed and veterinary bills.

Stella follows her father around, he lets her carry a bucket sometimes, and it amuses me to hear her chattering away at him. If she decides that she wants this life when she's older, I'd be happy for her, but I don't want her to feel trapped by a sense of obligation. I'd like her to see other places, to visit foreign countries and big cities, and if after that she chooses to come back here, all well and good. But I do want her to feel that she has choices.

Chapter Twenty-six

For the first couple of weeks it had been a pleasing novelty to have someone to cook for. Her father ate heartily, made appreciative noises, and it had been comforting to smell a chicken in the oven and to take the time to make bread sauce. Stella realized that she'd largely been subsisting on cheese and crackers for months, on tinned pilchards and something quick that might be rustled up with a couple of eggs. She now found herself reproducing the dishes that her mother used to cook, her pea-and-ham soup, her jam roly-poly and her rhubarb fool, and it was reassuring to pour gravy into a sauceboat and to have a cake ready to cut in the tin.

But her back ached from leaning over the sink this morning. As Stella looked at her hands in the greasy washing-up water, she felt slightly overwhelmed at the thought of another twenty years of frying black pudding at first light. Her father had told her over breakfast that he'd be happy to have shepherd's pie again for lunch, but hadn't they only finished the last one three days ago? There was something slightly depressing and institutional about shepherd's pie, particularly if one was obliged to eat it every week. She'd told him how

Victorian workhouses bought mincing machines so that they might feed all the nasty bits to toothless paupers. Surely he ought to be encouraged to masticate and eat a more varied menu? That was what her mother would say, wasn't it? In the end, she'd put lamb shanks in for lunchtime, she would cook them long and slow, and the meat would be as tender as butter—but did she need to be spending quite so much time in the kitchen?

There was a talk about an Everest expedition on the wireless now and he was sleeping soundly in front of it. She could sneak out and have a cigarette with Dilys, couldn't she?

"The fig wine is ready. Shall we try it?" Dilys asked.

Stella nodded. Right now she would be glad of an anaesthetic—and possibly some medication that might induce memory loss. She'd witnessed the sight of her father leaving the bathroom in nothing but his combinations that morning. When she'd advised him that he ought to wear his dressing gown, he'd told her not to be prudish. The time would come when she'd need to bathe him, he had said, so she ought to start casting aside any silly sensitivities. Was he teasing, or would it really come to that? Stella gulped at the glass of wine.

"It's got an interesting flavor, but it is one to imbibe in moderation," Dilys cautioned.

"Is it terrifically alcoholic?"

"No, but it goes straight through you. Not something to drink if you're planning a long journey."

Stella tried to imagine what sort of day might begin with the quaffing of fig wine and then proceed with a long journey. Perhaps a day that started with bathing her father? They pulled out chairs and sat down at the kitchen table. There was a smell of yeast and overripe fruit and the demijohns gurgled softly all around them.

"I saw that Mr. Harris took some furniture away," Dilys said. She tapped her cigarette on the table and passed Stella the lighter. "You must still be packed to the rafters in there, though."

"We have to climb over things. It's probably highly unsafe. Father is talking about building a shed to accommodate the overflow, but we're going to have to let some more of it go."

"It is a permanent arrangement, then?" A black cat clambered onto Dilys' lap and draped itself around her throat like a fur tippet. She barely seemed to notice it.

"I couldn't ask him to leave now. He thinks he's done me a great favor and, in many respects, he has. It would break his heart to think I didn't want him." Stella pictured the look on her father's face if she were to query the desirability of their current arrangement. She couldn't do that. It wasn't a choice.

"So that's it? That's how you live now? I have to say, it does seem a little Edwardian, father moving in with the spinster daughter. I always thought you were rather more modern than that. You don't mind me saying that, do you? Is it the end of your writing career too?"

Was it? Stella had been asking herself the same question. Earlier that morning, she'd inadvertently found herself typing the word "*HELP!*," but that was the only word she had typed for days. Last week's *Today's Woman* article had been an embarrassingly slapdash effort and her book had stalled entirely. Would she be able to restart it? She'd had ambitions for it, she realized now, and she hated the thought of letting Mr. Williamson down. She pictured herself at a party in London being asked how her book was progressing. "It's not," she heard herself say. "I don't do that any longer. I look after my father now." But then, she wouldn't be going to parties in London, would she?

"I've written more than half of it. I would like to finish it, even if it's the last thing I write."

"The last thing you write? Dear me. That's sad," said Dilys, and refilled Stella's glass.

"It is rather," she agreed.

"Miss Douglas," said Freddie's voice. "How brisk you sound on the telephone. I'm not dragging you away from rhyming couplets or watching a rising soufflé, am I?"

"No." She'd been darning the heels of her father's socks, but she wasn't going to let Freddie imagine her in such an unflattering light. How bright his voice sounded. She pictured him in his flat, perhaps in the middle of larding a pheasant, or making a layered terrine, a glass of something civilized at his side and possibly with plans for entertaining a Sophie. "I was just preparing a leg of lamb for the oven," she lied, "but you're not disturbing me. It's nice to hear your voice."

"I was thinking, I'm free this weekend, and you'd talked

about making a trip over to East Anglia in pursuit of an eel pie. That sounded like fun. You might already have plans, perhaps you have some lucky young beaux lined up, but if you're not busy, I could drive us over there. It might be a giggle? What do you think?"

Her father was snoring in the next room while the wireless debated tea farming in Ceylon, recruitment to the navy, and foot-and-mouth disease. At this moment, eel pie had never sounded more attractive. Could she ask Mrs. Pendlebury if she might keep an eye on him for a couple of days? That wasn't an appalling dereliction of daughterly duty, was it?

"I might be able to reshuffle my plans."

How agreeable it would be to have some easygoing company and the open road stretching ahead. She might even do some writing.

"Do the necessary, shuffle the beaux, and give me a call back, eh? I've read about an inn in Worcester where they still do potted lamprey."

Stella resolved that she must make potted lamprey happen.

Chapter Twenty-seven

"So your old man moved in with you, just like that?" Freddie asked. He glanced toward her again. Stella wished he'd keep his eyes on the road.

"It all seemed to happen rather fast. One minute I heard a car horn and the next minute he was installed in my spare bedroom, had adopted a seat by the fire, and his toothbrush was there in the glass next to mine."

Freddie whistled. "Hell's bells!"

Stella put a hand on her hat again and debated whether she might say something about his driving. It was rather fast too. As she'd stepped out of the railway station, she'd looked for Freddie's furniture van, but he'd pulled up in a shiny Bentley. It had royal-blue paintwork and was shaped like a bar of soap—a bar of soap which occasionally slithered on the bends. Freddie laughed when he skidded and when the brakes squealed, and he seemed to have a very casual attitude to keeping both hands on the wheel. Could she say something, or might that just encourage him?

"And the old rascal didn't even mention it first?"

"He thought it would be a nice surprise for me. He was

excited about it. Bless him, when he saw my face it popped his balloon." Stella wished that she could rewind and reorganize her features into a less obviously shocked response.

"I can picture it! Why the sudden decision, though?"

"He got an offer for the farm and decided to take it. It was all getting too much for him, I realize now, and it didn't make financial sense for him to carry on."

"The government needs to bring in quotas on meat imports. I'm not surprised that your old man has waved the white flag. No wonder the country's on its back. But do you not have some sympathetic aunts that you might move him onto? Isn't he driving you dotty?"

"Oh, only mildly dotty." She'd admit that much, but she wasn't sure that she liked the idea of off-loading her father onto relatives. It made him sound a little too much like a surplus sideboard or a badly trained dog.

"It must put the kibosh on the young, free and single life, though, doesn't it?" Freddie looked toward her. "I mean, it must be awkward to ask chaps back to your house now if the old man is installed as a permanent fixture?"

What sort of a life did Freddie imagine that she led? Did he suppose that she had a revolving door of amiable young chaps? It seemed to reveal a lot about his relationships with women. "You make me sound like some gadabout girl around town."

"Aren't you?" Freddie angled one of his excellent eyebrows at her. "God, you look like an irresistibly sassy matelot in that outfit. Do you know how confusing that is for a man?"

Stella had dressed in a striped Breton jersey and wide-legged navy slacks today, a broad-brimmed straw hat and red sandals. The fashion pages said that a maritime motif was *de rigueur* for an away day anywhere watery, but she was rather regretting her sartorial choices now.

"I haven't been a gadabout girl around town for decades."

"Shame," he said. "We must do something to put that right. You know, there's a tantalizing hint of pantomime-boy about that outfit. I am struggling to concentrate on the road."

Stella wished he'd try harder to concentrate. She'd be enjoying the scenery much more if Freddie would keep his eyes on the tarmacadam and not on her nautical stripes. He also couldn't help talking with his hands, and for much of the time his right elbow perched casually on the edge of the window. Stella's father had taught her to drive with her hands at ten-to-two, and she'd never lost the habit. She supposed that Freddie's casualness and brake squeals were meant to impress her, that this was deliberately done to demonstrate bravado, but she thought of peacocks spreading their tails and bellowing stags, and wondered if perhaps it was time that the female of the species had a quiet little word with the male.

"Anyway, assuming it approximately eel-central, I've booked us into a nice old inn in Ely. I'm at your disposal as chauffeur, lackey and dining companion, but I leave the agenda up to you. Just tell me what direction you want me to point the motor in, and I'll do it. The only itinerary item I'd add is that there's a house sale north of Cambridge on Monday. I thought we might call in on the way back. You wouldn't mind, would you? There are some interesting kitchen lots in the catalog. You might enjoy it."

"That sounds like fun." While Stella felt guilty that she wasn't getting on with writing, it was agreeable to have five pounds in her pocket and not to be worrying about balancing out her income and expenditure. She might even treat herself to some kitchenware. Yes, she would go with the flow, keep off the subject of French food, and trust that they wouldn't end up in too many scrapes.

"Eel fun in East Anglia, eh? Hell, you do know how to entice a man."

Freddie gave her a sparkling, slightly wicked look. If he was in possession of a waxed moustache, he might have curled it. Must he make things sound slightly unsavory? Was there an off-switch for his innuendos?

"If I can gather a little history, an anecdote or two, and soak up some local color, I'll be pleased."

"So how's the tome coming along?"

"It's not," she admitted. "I'm afraid it's stalled. I don't seem to have had any time recently and I've lost my writing space. It wasn't ideal, but I was settled at the kitchen table. Only, I'm now required to cook and eat there. Imagine, having to *cook* at a kitchen table! It's a bit of a shock to the system."

"You mustn't let it stall altogether. You must make a priority of finding the time and the space." Freddie's voice sounded serious suddenly and she had to look across at him to make sure that he really was in earnest. "You must be determined, Stella. It's an important book that you're writing.

I keep telling people about it and everyone is terrifically interested. A few people have even given me recipes and insist that I must pass them on to you. Don't let me forget to give them to you."

Was he telling his Sophies about it? Stella imagined them flocking into the shop wanting to impress Freddie with their handwritten, handed-down recipes for venison pasties.

"None of them are recipes for oatcakes, are they?" she asked.

"I think one of them might be a Staffordshire oatcake."

"They get everywhere!" Did Freddie genuinely believe that it was an important book? He'd looked entirely serious as he said it. Stella sat a little taller in her seat and couldn't help a silly little smile stretching the corners of her mouth. "Thank you," she said. "You're good for my sense of resolution."

"No woman has ever said that to me before." He glanced toward her and grinned. "I'm not really sure if that's a compliment."

The landscape had now become strikingly flat. Only the odd copse of trees rose above the horizon. They passed between fields of wheat and sugar beet, and roadside signs pointed to farms offering new potatoes, peas and gooseberries. They drove over ditches, dikes and canals. The road ahead was perfectly straight, and the mackerel sky seemed high and clean and sublime. It was like driving through a seventeenth-century Dutch landscape painting, Stella thought, and she found her eyes scanning for windmills. She imagined the red farmsteads inhabited by stout families with Bruegel faces.

"And are you managing to keep the foreigners out?" Freddie asked.

"I'm sorry?" She turned back to him.

"Those beastly Huguenot refugees and interfering French chefs who want to pass their opinions all over the place?"

"I am going all out to emphasize Englishness." The way that Freddie put it made Stella question whether she'd been doing too much emphasizing. His words left her with a slightly uncomfortable sensation.

"Good. You must. That's the right message to be getting across."

The right message? Stella did mean to fulfill the brief; however, she wasn't sure that she wanted to be conveying a message. That sounded a bit too like deliberate manipulation of the facts to hammer home an agenda—but then she couldn't deny that she'd edited out a Portuguese trader and a Dutch plough last month. Should she have done that? This landscape reminded her of all those Flemish Protestant refugees who'd come over with their experience of irrigation and crop rotations and market gardens. They'd made permanent marks on the English landscape and diet, hadn't they? Wasn't that too significant to be written out?

"Is that the cathedral?" She saw the shape of it rising on the skyline. It was like a beacon in the flat land and Stella grasped the chance to change the direction of the conversation. "Isn't it impressive? It makes me think of Excalibur rising up from the waters and I can almost hear the orchestra crescendo. I might blink and have imagined it. It looks like some sort of fairy-tale kingdom."

"Doesn't it?" Freddie's mouth curled into a smile. "They call it the ship of the Fens. It was an island before the land was drained, only accessible by boat. King Canute used to have his knights row him nearby because he liked to hear the monks singing. Rather an enchanting image, isn't it?"

"It is. Have you been here before?"

"A couple of times. I do a lot of mileage," he said. "I like to go to house sales in different parts of the country. One sees different things that way. I find it a great pleasure to travel. Don't you?"

"I do," she said. She looked across at him. It might be a pleasant life traveling around England and accompanying Freddie as he examined brown furniture in country salerooms. She couldn't imagine that she'd be doing much traveling for the next few months, though, so she must make the most of this weekend.

Freddie locked the motor and Stella looked around at the square. It was surrounded by buildings that might house monks or scholars, and there was an atmosphere of hushed antique learnedness. She imagined men bent over illuminated manuscripts behind those windows that now blinked back the setting sun.

"I want to look through the windows," she admitted. "Don't you?"

He laughed. "You always want to peer in through people's

windows. Tell me, is that journalistic curiosity or are you just nosy?"

Freddie carried their luggage over to a hotel, a pleasingly symmetrical Georgian building, which did indeed look very nice. Stella felt a momentary alarm as they approached the door, though, and then his voice was affirming her apprehensions.

"You are happy to be Mrs. Smith in the hotel register, aren't you? Damn it, I should have brought a ring. Why didn't I think of that? Best put your hand in your pocket, eh?"

"What? You haven't, have you?"

"Oh, Stella, your face!" He grinned. "That's ripping! I'm teasing, of course. I wouldn't do that to you. You know that, don't you?"

Did she? It was with some relief that she found herself looking out at the cathedral tower from the window of her own room. What would she have done if he'd expected her to be Mrs. Smith for the weekend? She wasn't sure. Freddie was charming, and she felt a frisson in his company, but he also left her with a sense that she was driving with her wheels close to the edge.

Stella changed into her aquamarine crêpe de chine and remembered wearing it to Michael and Cynthia's engagement party. She'd felt insipid and rather a failure that evening, lacking in courage and color, but Freddie had been so effusive with his compliments today, and she felt taller and bolder tonight. It was a fortnight since she'd last spoken to Michael, and she was missing the sound of his voice, but despite promises, he hadn't called her, and when she'd tried to telephone him the line had just rung out. Stella told herself that she really did need to let it go now. Remembering his arm around Cynthia strengthened her resolve to be more assertive—and why the hell would it have mattered if Freddie had required her to play Mrs. Smith? Nobody knew them here, and if Freddie wanted to put his arm around her later, she might let him. Stella looked at herself in the mirror, put on extra lipstick and her diamanté dress clips. She was possibly a little overdressed for a country inn, but what the heck. She blinked hard to erase the image of her mother's raised eyebrow from her mind.

"You're incapacitatingly lovely in that color," Freddie said, as they met on the turn of the stairs. "If I had an ounce of artistic talent, I'd beg to paint your portrait, but I'm afraid that I'll just have to stammer and stare a little instead."

"What a ridiculous man you are!" she laughed. But how charmingly he groaned and rolled his eyes.

They walked through to the dining room and Freddie insisted on pulling a chair out for her. She was rather enjoying this show of chivalry and attentiveness, and he did look terrifically handsome in a dinner jacket.

"I took the liberty of telephoning the proprietor in advance to order the smoked eel. I wasn't certain they'd have it on the menu, and I did want you to be able to have it tonight. I hope I did the right thing? It would have been a shame to come all this way only to have your eel curiosity frustrated, I thought."

"That was most considerate of you." She was touched by the effort he'd evidently gone to—even if expressing thoughtfulness through eels was a little unconventional.

"I am, you know. People don't always appreciate it, but I am tremendously considerate." He winked at her over the menu. It was a pity that he did always have to go a little too far.

Freddie made a fuss over ordering the dinner, asking the waiter detailed questions about where the lamb had been farmed, how it would be cooked, and wanting a guarantee that the peas wouldn't be out of a can. Stella felt sorry for the young man as he stammered uncertain responses. Was Freddie always so pernickety with waiters, she wondered, or was this a performance for her benefit?

"What would you order for your last supper?" she asked him, as the waiter headed for the kitchen, no doubt relieved to be released. She often asked people this. It tended to be revealing.

"I can't decide whether to go for something beautifully simple or fiendishly elaborate." Freddie's expression suggested that he was enjoying contemplating the question. He bit his bottom lip in thought. "Do I have the perfectly executed steak, or the ten-bird roast? You know, I'll just have the steak, medium rare, with chipped potatoes, an assertive English mustard and perhaps a little wilted spinach on the side. It's good for the blood, I believe. Though, as this is my last supper, why am I worrying about that? What hideous crime am I being put to death for, anyway?"

"Oh, probably some form of fraud."

"Slander!"

His glower reminded her of Mr. Rochester looking down on Jane Eyre from his rearing stallion, and Stella didn't entirely dislike it. "You're fond of meat, aren't you? Perhaps if you ate less of it, you might not need the spinach." She imagined that Freddie's blood might run very richly. Hadn't he talked about gravy running in an Englishman's veins?

"Are you concerned for my health? How endearing. That bodes well. But a man should eat meat. It keeps a chap virile, you know."

That again. "Does it?" How he liked talking about virility. "Do you want to stand up and put your hands on your hips as you repeat that line?"

"I believe you're laughing at me, Miss Douglas."

"Just a bit."

The smoked eel came with a green salad and malty brown bread. When ordering in a restaurant Stella was always inclined to choose an obscure or a time-consuming dish, something that another person had to marinade for twenty-four hours, which involved lots of stages and fiddly processes. She never understood why people went to restaurants and ordered chops. She would have liked to have eaten the eel slowly and analytically, but Freddie ate fast and must always be talking. It was astounding how he could talk so much and clear his plate in minutes.

"It's gone out of fashion, hasn't it?" she mused. "I believe some smart London restaurants are now selling jellied eels as a novelty, but I can't remember the last time I ate it."

"I suspect that most people don't know how to prepare them these days. They are awfully slippery buggers and it's damned easy to cut yourself as you wrestle with them. A feller I know is rather an eel aficionado. He showed me how you should nail them to a door, and then with a quick slip of a knife the skin slips off, easy as anything, just like peeling down a lady's stocking."

A waitress was leaning against a wall, picking varnish from her fingernails. Stella noticed Freddie giving the girl a quick look. She wondered how many stockings he might have peeled down. Quite a few, she suspected. "I have to admit that I've never cooked them myself."

"There's a widespread misconception that eels must be skinned alive, and I guess that's too horrifying for people. Plus they can't cope with bones. The pyrotechnics I've known some women create over a fishbone!"

Not for the first time, Stella found herself feeling a little sorry for Freddie's female friends. She could imagine some poor young woman choking and Freddie shaking his head as he looked on.

"The appeal of jellied eels is rather lost on me, I have to say. I can't recall that I've ever craved chilled eel-bone jelly."

"I must concede that, likewise, I'm not the greatest devotee. Is it unmanly to admit that?"

"Do you worry very much about your manliness?"

"Only when I'm in the presence of a disturbingly lovely woman. Are you at all aware of just how lovely you are?"

She smiled and shook her head.

"I almost forgot. I brought you a present," he said.

"You did?"

He produced a small wrapped parcel from his inside pocket and passed it across the table. Stella could tell that it was a book. But what book? One can discern a lot about a man by the books he gifts. She half expected it to be a volume on wood finishes, or recipes for offal, so was slightly taken aback to unwrap a book of poems.

"John Donne's love poems?" She looked up at him. "I will admit that I'm surprised. I didn't have you down as a man of poetic sensibility."

"Don't underestimate me, Miss Douglas! I've got quite a repertoire of slightly uncouth limericks, I'll have you know. Didn't you tell me that you wrote for a poetry magazine when you were a student? I thought you might like that sort of thing. It's a collectible edition, I believe."

"What a treasure." Stella turned the book in her hands, wondering what to make of this gift. "We studied him at school and I think every girl in the class was a little bit in love with him. All those hemispheres and compasses and interlocking eyeballs! He's catnip to adolescent girls."

"Well, well," Freddie said, managing to imbue the word with great meaning. "I am making notes of all the above."

Stella flicked through the pages—but then stopped as she saw the inscription on the flyleaf. TO DARLING FREDDIE, FROM PHYLLIS, WITH MUCH LOVE, it read. Oh dear. Who was Phyllis? Aunts and godmothers didn't gift John Donne, did they? Had Phyllis looked into Freddie's eyes and felt the spheres shift? Where was she now? If Phyllis was a former love, it didn't seem nice that Freddie was now passing on her tenderly inscribed John Donne. That seemed like rather bad taste. He might as well have gifted Stella some intimate item of Phyllis's clothing.

"Phyllis?" she asked. "Did you break her heart?"

"What? No!" He lifted his eyebrows. "Nothing of the sort. Oh, you don't mind that, do you? I'd entirely forgotten it was there. She was just a friend from university. It doesn't make you feel uncomfortable, does it?"

"I'm more amused than shocked." Stella smiled, but what a peculiar gift it was. If he'd forgotten the inscription was there, had he forgotten the existence of poor Phyllis too? A warning sign blinked faintly for Stella; however, she was having a jolly evening, was thinking about her book again, and she'd rather be here than cooking shepherd's pie and darning socks.

"I like being around women," Freddie mused, as he swirled the wine in his glass. "I always have—women's conversations, women's opinions, women's humor. That doesn't bother you, does it? You don't strike me as a jealous type. Jealousy is a horrible emotion, don't you think? It spoils people."

Was she a jealous type? She wouldn't have said so before this year, but . . . "No, of course, that doesn't bother me. If you respect and admire women, I'm glad," she said. Was that quite right, though? Was that really Freddie's attitude?

"It's refreshing that you don't take yourself too seriously. Much as I do admire the female of the species, I find that many young women suffer from earnestness these days."

Stella put the book aside and swallowed a mouthful of wine. "You sound like you've suffered from womanly earnestness."

"I have. Young women can be so severe now. They must constantly be evaluating how they're perceived and looking for ways to take offense. I think it's a modern affliction."

"You do?"

"Of course, it's more of a town thing," he said, looking thoughtful. "They are less prickly out in the countryside; however, there one does find oneself having to have a lot of conversations about ponies. I mean that's pleasant enough for a while—those girls are all tremendously sweet—but I crave the company of women who have interesting opinions, women with whom one can have a stimulating discussion and not be afraid that she's going to be affronted by every other word."

Did he think that *she* was interesting, then? She hadn't been feeling especially interesting recently. It pleased Stella if Freddie saw her that way, but she felt a little sorry for the sweet girls who wanted to tell him about their ponies. She imagined them having stilted conversations with Freddie while their mothers looked on. The countryside can be very cruel.

"You should join some social groups," Stella said, in her women's magazine voice. "A choir, a local history group, or a book club maybe. You'd meet women with opinions there."

"But I don't want to meet other women. I want to be here with *you*!"

They laughed a lot over the course of the evening. Freddie didn't take anything seriously, least of all himself. The names of female friends appeared regularly in his stories, but he was a good raconteur and knew how to deliver a punch line. Stella was happy not to think about obligations, impediments and her father's breakfast for a while.

After dry martinis over the menu, they'd drunk a bottle of white Burgundy, then claret with the lamb, and had finally ended up in the residents' lounge with brandies. (Freddie's scorn for the French seemingly didn't extend to the cellar.) He put his arm around her as they sat together on a sofa, and insisted on reading selections from John Donne aloud to test their aphrodisiac effect, as he put it. When he moved in to kiss her, she wasn't surprised or resistant.

Chapter Twenty-eight

Stella's head felt like it might be made of eggshell. If she moved too fast, it could crack. A bluebottle banged against a window and its drone was like a zeppelin. Sometimes the zeppelin seemed to be inside her head too. Cautiously opening her eyes, she squinted up at an unfamiliar ceiling and remembered that she was in a hotel room in Ely. Yes, this was the room where she'd unpacked her suitcase yesterday, with her aquamarine dress draped over the back of a chair (golly, that color was bright), but what was Freddie Langham's head doing on the pillow next to hers? It rolled toward her and grinned now. Stella suddenly felt very wide awake and the cracks in her skull were fracturing. Ye gods and little fishes! What had she done?

"And now good-morrow to our waking souls," he said.

"Did we . . . ?" she began, though the answer was all too obvious.

"Don't tell me that you can't remember! I'm most affronted," he glowered exaggeratedly and then laughed. "You were entirely engaged in the matter last night. My face in thine eye, and all that?"

But, yes, she did remember. "Bloody John Donne," she said.

Stella closed the bathroom door. She was tempted to bang her head against it. Why had she had so much to drink? Why had she let him recite love poems and talk her into bed? Had he planned that all along?

She sat down on the edge of the bath. He was a very handsome man, she considered, educated, well tailored, with beautifully polished shoes and always smelling pleasantly of eau-de-cologne and shaving soap. He was possibly the most agreeably aromatic man she'd ever met, and, as it turned out, he was extremely proficient in the bedroom department too. Quite remarkably proficient. But then, Stella supposed, he'd had plenty of practice. She thought of all the women whose names had cropped up in the conversation last night. Beyond Phyllis with her loving inscription, there'd been a Cristobel with whom he'd gone boating, a Lavinia who had choked on a prawn, a Dinah who had hiked around the Highlands, and an Iris with whom he'd had an indiscretion in the royal bed chamber of a stately home. Stella imagined herself standing in a long line, so many women behind her and possibly a great number ahead. Was Freddie a philanderer? Was he a frightful bounder? Enjoying women's conversation was one thing, but just how many of them had he bedded?

Stella asked herself if she could trust Freddie. Could she confide in him? Would he confide in her? No, she reflected, this wasn't that sort of relationship—if it could be called a relationship at all. She knew that he would always be charming and flirtatious with other women and spend many nights in various hotel rooms. This was a casual arrangement, merely social, recreational, and she must never think of lines of John Donne when she looked into Freddie's eyes. He hadn't meant it like that, and she mustn't take it that way.

"What are you doing in there?" His voice came from the bedroom.

"Pondering."

"I say, don't do that for too long, it's really not healthy. It ruins a woman's complexion."

She put her head around the door. "I'm going to have a bath."

"Is there room for two?"

"No, but you could have a look at my Bath bun chapter, if you like. It's in my bag there. Tell me what you think."

"Damn it, woman. How you tease!"

Stella let the taps run and poured in lots of bath salts. Her head was now pounding, like the zeppelin was ricocheting off the sides of her skull. She ducked under the water and counted the seconds until she had to surface. When she did, she could hear Freddie talking to himself in the next room. When he'd suggested this trip, she'd never imagined that they might end up in the same bed on the first night. He was a flirt, and, yes, she'd flirted back, but she wasn't in the habit of inviting men into her bed. She prided herself on exercising discernment in these matters. Was it because she'd been thinking about Michael and Cynthia as she went down to dinner? About missed opportunities and not having been assertive enough? Or was it all John Donne's fault? No, there is only so much blame that one may heap upon metaphysical poets. Oh God, what would her mother think?

When she stepped out of the bathroom Freddie was still in bed. He'd propped himself up on all the pillows and seemed to be studiously absorbed as he worked his way through her papers with a pen.

"I was starting to worry that you might have drowned in there." He flashed her a smile as he looked up. "I was about to ask if you needed me to come in and rescue you. I've got my life-saving certificate, you know, so I am fully qualified. I can do the kiss of life and everything."

"I'm sure you can."

Stella sat down on the bed and pulled her papers toward her. She'd thought that reading them might keep him occupied. She hadn't expected him to set about editing them.

"You don't mind, do you?" he said. "I've scribbled down a few thoughts."

"So I see."

In truth, Stella wasn't sure how she felt—perhaps surprised, more than anything, at this moment. He clearly had a lot of thoughts and they swarmed all around her typed text. Mr. Williamson didn't edit that intensively.

"You didn't take the Huguenot out," he said. "You ought to. As you say, there's no evidence that this woman ever really existed, so why credit her? Just blur her out and keep it a marvelous English bun. That's what people want. Your average person wants to read a book that makes them feel good about themselves, and all of these murky foreigners are diluting that."

Should she delete Solange? He'd drawn a line through the quotes from Carême too, Stella's ponderings on brioche and her suggestions about Alsatian sweetbreads. He'd then moved on to her chapter about the complexity of "Englishness' and he'd deleted most of that.

As Stella looked at Freddie's bold round letters, his question marks and cuttings, she felt a perplexing mix of feelings—somewhat outraged, slightly embarrassed and distinctly unsettled. Yes, Mr. Williamson wanted the band to be playing "Rule, Britannia', but was Freddie suggesting that she edit out something intrinsic? Stella asked herself, not for the first time, whether she ought to be listening to Freddie. Was he a healthy influence? Shouldn't he be told to write his own book rather than scribbling all over hers? But, damn it, he could sell spectacles to a blind man, couldn't he?

Freddie talked about eels as they dressed and went down to breakfast. There was rather a lot of double entendre tangled up with the eels, and Stella wasn't sure how she'd ever dissociate that now.

He ate a hearty breakfast, lifting an eyebrow as he turned to her and musing as to how he might have worked up such an appetite. He lamented that he couldn't call upon the landlord to serve him chops and ale, a virile manly breakfast, as he put it. Stella wasn't certain that his virility required further fueling. He watched Stella eat too and wasn't satisfied until she'd cleared the last forkful from her plate. Women ought to have curves, he said, and she'd need energy for later. Stella wasn't sure how she felt about that.

"You should write a chapter about the history of the English breakfast. It's quite unique."

"I already have." Would he want to edit that too?

"Excellent. You must let me see it. Englishmen shouldn't be eating croissants for their breakfast. And as for puffed wheat and Grape-Nuts! What sort of a day does that start? An Englishman ought to begin his day with sausages and bacon, kidneys and cutlets. That's the stuff that gets the blood up. That's the breakfast of empire builders. It's bad enough that everyone is buying horrid Danish bacon these days. You must celebrate the English pork butcher," he insisted. "Your book ought to be a rallying cry for our cured meats."

Stella pictured a flag-draped Britannia on her book cover, her trident aloft and the bellow of a battle cry almost audible on her lips. Lions roared around her, and the swelling crowd at her feet held flitches of bacon and hamhocks in their outstretched arms. A rallying cry for cured meats? Really? She might draw it and gift it to Freddie. Or, perhaps, he shouldn't be encouraged?

"I'm complimented by the fact that you're so interested."

"Your book is very timely. Your publisher chap was right about that. We've been complacent, but we need to wake up to that now. Do you know that the Germans set up a program of importing elvers from the Severn in the years before the war? They imported millions of the little wrigglers and restocked all of Germany's waterways with them. They were perfectly of a size to eat by the time that war was declared. Underhanded Hunnish behavior, yes, but you do have to admire them sometimes."

"That wasn't planned, though, was it?" Stella took a sip of tea. The cracks in her skull finally seemed to be fusing back together again. "The outbreak of war wasn't down to the eels of Westphalia attaining requisite inches?"

"Perhaps the two aren't linked precisely, but it makes us look rather naïve, doesn't it?" He buttered another slice of toast and waved his knife in emphasis. "We were on powdered egg and rissoles and they were having smoked eel."

"From what I remember reading, they were mostly living on turnips, weren't they? I don't think eel fattening had a significant impact on military strategy."

He shrugged. "But, you see, they keep an eye on that sort of thing, and that's where we've gone wrong. Listen to what Adolf Hitler is saying about self-sufficiency now. Old man Mussolini knows what he's doing. We ought to be observing and learning. It's time to reeducate people here. The average English working man needs to be taught how to eat patriotically. That's why your book is important."

Stella had read about Mussolini's efforts to wean the Italians off pasta. She'd also read about the mayor of Naples holding aghast hands in the air and protesting that the angels ate vermicelli in heaven. A little of what Freddie said was true, she supposed, but didn't the freeborn Englishman have a right to macaroni cheese if he fancied it? And surely Hitler was a beastly, shouty little man?

The height of the cathedral made the old houses below it seem to huddle. There were a lot of bric-à-brac shops, and black-beamed teashops, and businesses which seemed to be a fusion of the two. The sunlight highlighted the architecture at unexpected angles, cast sharp, slanting shadows, and so many of the faces that she passed might have stepped out of early Flemish portraits. Stella wished she could linger with a sketchpad.

"The cathedral doesn't look English, does it? It reminds me of a tiered wedding cake, doesn't it you?"

"Women always say that about cathedrals."

Did they? Was that true? They stepped through the doors of the building and it was full of a pale gold radiance. The lines of the nave were mathematical and musical; there was a smell of candlewax and incense, and a sense of ancient peace. They walked on and the sunlight through the stained-glass windows projected patterns of ruby, emerald and sapphire onto the flagstones at their feet.

"The tower is a replacement," Freddie said. "The original Norman tower collapsed. This new one was built from eight almighty oak trees."

Stella could have replied that men always liked to have facts about cathedrals, but she looked up at the lantern windows instead. "What an alarming thought."

"I say, you don't have tendencies, do you?"

She glanced at Freddie. His eyes were raised to the stained glass too. "*Tendencies?*"

"Religion, I mean. I have a great-aunt who became a nun. She was mad for it, absolutely potty for all that wimple and incense stuff. It's always been regarded as rather a tragedy in the family."

Stella smiled. "No, I just like old buildings."

"Good. Me too. It's useful that we like the same things."

"Useful?" What did he mean by that?

"We speak the same language, don't we?" he went on, reaching out and curling a strand of her hair between his fingers. "We have the same sensibilities. I think we understand each other pretty well and have similar tastes and values. Don't you think so?"

His arm slid around her shoulders as they walked on. Did they have the same values? It was strange to look at Freddie and to consider that he thought her a like mind. Stella didn't see herself reflected there. The cathedral bells struck the quarter hour, and as their arm-in-arm shadow lengthened ahead Stella tried to work out why his words unsettled her.

They drove out to the Fens in the afternoon. The flat, wet land stretched for miles and there was something somber and primeval-looking about this country. Freddie stopped the motor, and as the engine silenced, Stella heard oozing and gurgling, sounds of lapwings and shrills of plovers. It seemed a mysterious, somehow secretive place, rather melancholy, and neither land nor sea, perhaps only borrowed temporarily from the waves. There might be Vikings hiding out there, or the ghosts of Anglo-Saxon armies. Stella would have liked just to stand here for a while, taking in the atmosphere, the sounds, the scent and the strange light, but then Freddie was talking again. He did so rarely stop talking.

"Savage-looking country, isn't it? I can imagine how it might have been a refuge for brigands and insurrectionaries."

"Yes," she said. It was warm this afternoon and she felt her headache coming back. She fanned her face with her hat. As Freddie put his arms around her waist, she could smell his skin, hot from the sun. It was a little too humid to be entangling limbs.

"I believe there's an inn in Littleport where the landlord will rustle up a roasted eel, if you ask nicely." He kissed her neck. "I'm sure you're more than capable of asking nicely."

"I might have reached my surfeit of lampreys."

"Now, they're a different zoological species, you know."

"I know." Stella rolled a stone under her shoe. She enjoyed Freddie's fondness for facts, but he was inclined to do a little too much explaining and correcting. After a while, it became slightly wearisome. He'd launched into a lecture about elvers now, and she found herself listening to the lapwings instead.

"Back to the Sargasso to spawn . . ." he went on.

Stella's thoughts turned to Michael and how she missed his voice. It was always so pleasant to have a conversation with him, always an equally balanced dialogue, a duet of voices. He was a good listener—she could tell him anything (almost), and when there was a silence it was never awkward. Freddie must always fill the silences. Always there must be the sound of his voice. She vaguely wondered if he might perhaps have some sort of nervous problem.

"I suppose you know the story about King Henry?" he asked.

"I do."

It used to be the case that Stella could spend days in the cottage without speaking to another soul, but now there constantly seemed to be instructing and requesting voices around her. How she would like the space and the quiet to think. That was what Virginia Woolf had said, wasn't it? That a woman needs a room of her own if she's going to write? Stella would be glad of just one room to herself and a few hours of peace.

She put on her apple-green dress and her orange glass beads for the evening. As soon as she stepped into the dining room, Freddie observed that she made him long to sink his teeth into a juicy Granny Smith. It set the tone for the evening. He was outrageously flirtatious over his plate of oysters, openly debating their efficacy, and Stella realized that he expected this evening to conclude as the previous one had.

"You are amused when we're together, aren't you?" he asked, as they took their whiskies through to the lounge. "I know you are," he prompted. "I see it on your face. I think you're a ripping girl and we do have fun, don't we?"

"We do," she said.

He frowned as he plaited a strand of her hair. His hands had been in her hair all evening. "Can I cut a little piece off and keep it?"

"Like a character in a Jane Austen novel?" Stella looked at him. Did he collect locks of hair from all his women and keep them in some sort of trophy cabinet? Was it a very large cabinet? "How bizarre you are."

"Don't you find it romantic?" He blew smoke at the ceiling and then seemed to be contemplating. He took his cigarette from his mouth and looked at it. "I'd quite like a strand of it set into a ring. Like those pieces of Georgian mourning jewelry, you know?"

"Are you planning my death? Should I be concerned?"

He laughed. "But wouldn't it be a delicious idea? Don't you think your Mr. Donne would approve?" he whispered in her ear.

Hell, not ruddy John Donne again. "I think it sounds rather morbid."

"You can have some of mine in return," he offered.

"And have it set into a ring? It wouldn't be especially hygienic if I was making pastry."

"How damned practical you are! What does it take to make you swoon?"

Freshly boiled langoustines and mayonnaise, Stella thought—or perhaps a perfectly set *omelette aux cèpes*? A long lunch on a shady terrace, the scent of thyme, a violet sky and the sound of cicadas? She could do a bit of swooning for that. Or one more day around the markets in Paris with Michael? One more evening in his calm, easy company? But she mustn't have thoughts like that. Freddie's arm was around her shoulders now and his hand was making exploratory forays south. Was he not aware that people were watching them? Or did he simply not care?

"Would you mind awfully if I turned in?" she asked,

trying to disentangle herself from his arms. "I am sorry, but I'm tired tonight. I'd just like to get an early night."

"What a marvelous idea. Yes, let's go up."

"I want to *sleep*," she said, looking at him directly. He did hear the emphasis, didn't he? Must she explicitly say that she wanted to sleep on her own?

"Oh. I see. I get the message."

He pulled his arms away and looked put out. Yes, he'd paid for the dinner, but he didn't think he'd paid for the right to spend the night with her too, did he?

Freddie put on a jokingly dejected face at breakfast, made doe eyes at her, and talked about how cold the sheets had been as he'd climbed into bed.

"You ought to have sent down to reception for a hot-water bottle."

"But I didn't want a hot-water bottle!"

Stella glanced around the breakfast room and felt embarrassed. Could he not be more discreet? She couldn't blame him for what had happened on Saturday night—she had been a willing participant—but it did now feel like an error of judgment.

"So have you garnered sufficient eel material?" he asked.

"I think I could write a book on eels now, never mind a page."

"And so where are you off to next?"

"I really need to crack on and do some writing," Stella

said. Saying it aloud made it seem more firmly a commit-ment. "But I'm contemplating heading down to Cornwall next month."

"I know a nice old inn with rooms in Mousehole. It's years since I've been down there. Have you ever had stargazy pie?"

Would he want to set the agenda there too? She shouldn't complain about Freddie's interest, but she was starting to feel a little territorial. "I've arranged to meet my friend Lucien in London. We're going to take the train from Paddington together."

"Oh," said Freddie. "Lucien, eh?" He narrowed his eyes. Stella couldn't tell if he was making this face for comic effect. "I didn't know there was a Lucien in the frame. I ought to have guessed, I suppose."

Of course, she'd made no such plans. Freddie also didn't need to know that Lucien kept a framed photograph of Ivor Novello on his nightstand. Stella pictured herself sitting alone at a table by a harbor, no noise except the sound of waves, the cries of gulls and a jangle of rigging, no voices apart from her own thoughts. What an enticing image it was. But then she glanced across the table and saw Freddie looking crestfallen. Had she been beastly to him? "He's only a friend. Don't look so downcast!"

"He might tell you that he's only a friend, but he's a Frenchman, isn't he? You do know they're not to be trusted?"

"While Englishmen are all entirely honorable?"

Oh dear, this was getting rather awkward.

Chapter Twenty-nine

The hallway was full of crates of books, hockey sticks, croquet mallets and watering cans, every item with a label attached. They walked into a dining room where tables were covered with canteens of cutlery, marquetry boxes, bronze nymphs and framed family photographs.

"Doesn't it strike you as terribly sad?" Stella asked, as she opened the cover of a photograph album. "They're selling off their own history. Has there been some tragedy in the family?"

"Rumor has it that the old man has got himself chin-deep in debt. If he can sell off enough of the contents, he'll manage to keep the house."

"But these objects seem so personal."

She looked more closely at a photograph of small boys in sailor collars by a boating lake. Removed from this place, these faces would lose the chance of ever being connected with a name and the structure of a family again. There were homemade birthday cards pasted into the album and pressed flowers that must once have had significance. It didn't seem right to be selling these memories off to the highest bidder.

"You are a sentimental old thing, aren't you?" Freddie put an arm around her. "The good news is that everyone knows he's desperate to raise money. It'll keep the prices down."

"Good for you, you mean?"

He shrugged and picked up a chamber pot painted with blousy pansies. He turned it over and peered at the potter's mark.

"Why ever would you want that?" she asked.

"People like them. They plants hyacinths in them these days."

"Do they really?"

Stella watched Freddie making notes in his catalog as they toured the room. He paused in front of ink stands, japanned trays, carved seashells and paintings of dead stags. It was curious to see what attracted his attention. He made annotations next to some rather ordinary pine commodes now.

"They're nothing special, are they?"

"Precisely. And I'll pick them up for nothing." He lowered his voice. "But with a bit of work, I can add a century and a nought or two to the price." He winked, and Stella thought about his jar marked "History." "I'll tell you the truth: this game isn't about making great discoveries; it's about keeping the stock moving. And there's fun in getting away with it."

Getting away with it? Stella was struck by how casually Freddie did these things. Did his conscience never smart? But then, she thought of the pages she'd been working on that morning, the story about the old eel fisherman who had shown them his traps and invited them onto his houseboat.

She had laughed with Freddie as they'd invented the interior of the boat together, the nicotine-brown ceiling, the bottle of homebrew, the old man's story about an encounter with a giant pike, and his talk of the eels running with the moon. Of course, this man didn't exist. He was a fictional character that they'd cooked up together, but which she would now pass off as a truth. Stella asked herself: were she and Freddie as bad as one another? Was it true that they were of like minds?

Stella knew that when these stories were published she would feel a certain nervousness, that she would be conscious of just how much was invention. But, as Freddie said, it didn't hurt anyone, did it? It was merely "coloring-in," as he put it, and these characters were based on some facts and research. She just happened to be animating the facts and making them more engaging for her readers. It wasn't an outright lie, was it?

"These old jam pans might make nice garden planters," she said.

"There, see. You're getting an eye."

Stella's fingers trailed over wooden sewing boxes, chintz armchairs, needlework-covered stools and the room was full of the unsynchronized ticking of clocks. Everyone around her was lifting the lids of boxes, and looking at the underside of vases, appraising and evaluating. Her fingertips traced the facets of a cut-glass ink bottle. It was part of a Victorian desk-set, such a pretty thing with its gilding and hand-painted forget-me-nots, and she considered treating herself. But then, she didn't actually possess a desk to place a desk-set upon, did she? Might she, though, one day? At some point in the future, could she have a room of her own that she might call a study and a book worthy of desk accoutrements? She pictured herself sitting in that place, orderly piles of papers in front of her, and a perfect silence all around. She still wanted that, Stella realized now—a book that she could feel proud of and a room of her own where she might write more. She had to keep on coloring-in.

"Could you age that one?" She watched Freddie examining a carved linen chest. "Is it a likely candidate?"

He put a finger to his lips as he shushed her. "Hell's bells, keep it down!" She could hear an exclamation mark and admonition in his voice. "It's not a matter for open debate."

Stella noticed that Freddie would sometimes pick up an object and examine it thoroughly, but on other occasions he would become furtive. She guessed that he was furtive when he was genuinely interested in an item and believed that he might make a decent profit on it. He wasn't at all furtive in his relationship with her. What did that mean? But, then, this wasn't exactly a relationship, was it? She realized, as she watched him, that it would hardly break her heart if she were to see him in the street with one of his Sophies. It wouldn't be like watching Michael with Cynthia. Why had she let him talk her into bed, then? But Cynthia was part of that equation too, wasn't she? If Stella hadn't been thinking about Michael's arm around her waist, she wouldn't have let Freddie keep on refilling her glass. If she hadn't been recalling Cynthia's fingers in Michael's hair, she might not have been so amenable to Freddie's maneuvers. Stella knew this was true, but didn't enjoy admitting it to herself.

They walked through to the kitchen and Freddie pointed at good pieces of slipware, creamware, Dresden and Belleek. The table was stacked with decanters, tarnished cruets and toast racks. He picked up willow-pattern serving platters, soup tureens and sauce boats. She looked through boxes of ice-cream molds, pastry jiggers and carved breadboards, and unfolded bales of embroidered table linen.

"One for you, Miss Douglas." Freddie handed her a book.

Opening the cover, Stella found it was a handwritten recipe book. She turned the yellowed pages and saw recipes for plum cakes, ices and possets, and the name ABIGAIL FOTHERGILL, COOK inscribed on the flyleaf. "I don't think it contains many revelations, but it's lovely to imagine her cooking in this kitchen, isn't it? Do you suppose that she did?"

"Only you know there's nothing revelatory in there."

"What do you mean?" She looked at Freddie.

"Well, you could cite it, and edit it as you do so, couldn't you? 'I found this recipe in a handwritten book that I picked up at a country sale, et cetera, et cetera.'" He made inverted commas with his fingers. "Who would ever know that it wasn't the truth?"

She *could* do that, Stella thought, but would Abigail Fothergill mind?

"I've made a note of the number," Freddie said.

They walked into the drawing room as the auction was beginning. It amused Stella to see how Freddie communicated with the auctioneer using only the slightest nod or movement of his catalog. Other bidders did the same, she noticed, and it was like a competition to see who might indicate an interest with the smallest gesture. Freddie did a lot of bidding, and seemed pleased with himself. But, then, he generally seemed pleased with himself.

"Don't let me forget, there's a basket of gooseberries for you in the boot of the motor," he said, as they stepped out of the house. "It's been a good year for them. I've had far more than I can use, but I was sure you'd be able to give them a good home."

"Do you have a garden behind the shop?"

"No, this is from my house. There's the most delightful walled garden. I was down there pottering on Thursday. You must come over and see it."

"I didn't know you had another house."

"There's a lot that you don't know about me yet." He raised an eyebrow at her and his mouth curled up at one side. His facial gymnastics were occasionally rather impressive. "You've barely seen the top of the iceberg yet. You'll find I'm complex and profound. Like a fine claret," he added.

"Really?" she laughed. "You're in danger of getting your metaphors in a tangle."

"Oh, Miss Douglas, you've had my metaphors in a tangle since the moment we first met."

As they drove away, Stella asked herself: why was it that she liked him more for the gooseberries? It was nothing to do

with the other house, but the idea of him pottering in a vegetable garden was curiously alluring. It was slightly unexpected
too. Maybe he was more complex than she'd given him credit
for? She also contemplated what it said about her own personality that the gift of a basket of gooseberries was seductive. She
pictured Freddie in corduroy trousers, picking runner beans,
and it was a peculiarly pleasing image. She gave him a trug, a
slightly soiled neckerchief, and a leather waistcoat—but then
it was all becoming far too D. H. Lawrence and she had to tell
herself off. Perhaps it was time to stop comparing him with
Michael? Should she not simply enjoy the company of a man
who wanted to be with her at this moment?

*As you may be aware, eels were a staple of the medieval diet.
They were particularly abundant in the marshy areas of the
Fens and the Somerset Levels, and in both of these regions
they provided sustenance for religious orders. Land rents
were also often settled in eels in these areas; 60,000 eels
were paid annually to the monastery at Peterborough, and
Ely received about 93,000 eels per year from local fisheries.
They were exchanged as a currency too. Ely Cathedral is
built from stone quarried at Barnack in Northamptonshire.
This land was owned by Peterborough Abbey and Ely
delivered 8,000 eels a year to pay for the stone. I recently
presented a paper on the importance of eels in the finances of
medieval monasteries to our local antiquarian society and I
would be glad to send you a copy . . .*

REVD. LEONARD BURNHAM, Somerset

Your notice reminded me of the London pie-and-eel shops of my youth. I understand that the first of these establishments, Henry Blanchard's Eel Pie House, opened in Southwark in 1844. The shops sold hot stewed eels in winter and chilled jellied eels in summer. For one halfpenny a working man could fill his stomach with six or seven long pieces of eel and wash them down with the flavorsome liquid in which they'd been stewed. My children make horrified faces when I tell them this. How times do change!

ALBERT MORTON, Deal

When I was a child we would sometimes take the steamer to Eel Pie Island, in the Thames, near Richmond. The hotel there was famed for its food and, of course, its eel pie. I recall that it contained hard boiled eggs, along with the eel, all in a parsley sauce and under a puff pastry crust. It was a great treat and I can still picture my father licking his whiskers . . .

MRS. ELSIE BOOTH, Bermondsey

I worked for the Ministry of Food during the war and remember being involved in cookery demonstrations with which we were trying to convince people to eat eels. They are quite as nourishing as a loin of beef, and there was a strong case to be made for them, but beyond London we found people reluctant to try them and aversion intensifies as you travel north. The association with serpents, and a conviction that eels must come from muddy, unwholesome places, ultimately proved more powerful than the grumbles of hungry stomachs . . .

VERA HEMSWORTH (Miss), Bristol

Madam, You may already know of our association, Ye Ancient Order Eel-Gobblers? We have been gathering since 1921 (not so ancient, really) and our aim is to promote the interests of eels and those who admire them. We hold a monthly "eel-gobble" in Battersea, often attended by more than one hundred gourmets, in which we enjoy an array of eel dishes; our bill of fare generally includes eel soup, eel pie, stewed eels and boiled eels, but jellied eels is always our principal dish. We often get through 100 lbs of eels in a sitting. Our numbers include members of parliament, trade union leaders, magistrates, surgeons, authors and senior men of business, and our slogan is "good spirits, good fellowship, and good fish." On behalf of the Gobblers, I would be delighted to invite you to one of our banquets . . .

HARRY FANTHORPE, London

Chapter Thirty

As she'd had her head buried in eels and dumplings for the past month, Michael and Lucien had volunteered to cook Stella a thoroughly French menu. They started with Michael's sorrel *velouté*, Lucien had made his grandmother's *fricassée de poulet*, and they ended with Grand Marnier soufflés. It was a warm evening and they sat in the flat with all the windows open, the curtains billowing on the breeze, the sky like pale blue porcelain, and voices coming up from the street. Stella could hear people laughing, the occasional phrase of a piano playing in a neighboring flat, and now and then there was the smell of the pie shop below. But that brought Cynthia's voice into her mind—her voice making comments about Michael's bed sheets—and Stella didn't want to think about that tonight.

"We ought to have made you tapioca pudding for dessert, really, shouldn't we?" Lucien suggested. "Or do you perhaps prefer sago? I could have done it with a nice skin on top, and as you've been such a good girl, I might have let you stir in a spoonful of strawberry jam. Just like nanny made, eh? Wouldn't that have been a treat? That's how children get rewarded in England, isn't it?" He grinned. "No wonder you're all so emotionally constipated."

"Steady on," Stella said. "Do remember you're outnumbered here."

She could picture Freddie eating sago pudding with a spoonful of jam. That had probably been on the school menu too, hadn't it? But she didn't particularly want to think about Freddie this evening either.

"I actually love the skin on a rice pudding," Michael whispered. "If there's lots of nutmeg, that's the best bit."

"Quite! I couldn't agree more." Stella touched her glass to his and they laughed together at Lucien's look of horror.

One of Michael's old paintings was hung on the wall facing her seat, a watercolor sketch of St. Anne's, Limehouse, uncannily white as the dusk closed in. She remembered that she'd stood at his side in the churchyard, drawing the same view, and then they'd sat in a café, wrapping their cold fingers around mugs of cocoa. It was pleasant to recall that, how they'd talked about Hawksmoor and Wren on the omnibus, and made plans to meet up in York Minster at Christmas.

"Have you found anything that is through-and-through English, though?" Michael asked now, breaking into her memories. "Any one dish that you can say contains absolutely no foreign ingredients or influence?"

She blinked at him and smiled. "There are lots of things . . . and I'm learning to be flexible with my definitions." Should she tell them quite how flexible she was being? "Equally, I return the question to you: is there any dish that is purely and unadulteratedly French?"

"Snails?" Lucien suggested. "Cooked with garlic butter? That's the cliché, isn't it? That's what you English think we eat all the time? What could be more French?"

"A-ha! But the cultivation of both snails and garlic were introduced by the Romans," she said, finding herself sounding a little like Freddie. "Most of what we think of as classical French cookery came from Italy with Catherine de' Medici— and, in turn, much of Italy's food tradition originates from the Near East. To be honest, the more I look into it, the more I feel that we've always been influencing each other. Chefs invariably want to tell each other what they're doing, don't they?"

"But that's not what you're meant to be saying in this book, is it?" Michael asked. "I thought it was meant to be a rallying cry for Englishness?"

"And it will be. I'm being judiciously selective. I might be reaching some alternative conclusions in my head, but I'm determined to deliver the brief."

She'd had a busy day in the British Museum, reading about owl pies and lark pies, and recipes for pottages made with porpoises and seals, but had stepped out and bought a sandwich in a café for her lunch. The bread was like damp wadding and the cheese had tasted of nothing much. Stella had poked it with her finger. It was an alarmingly orange color and seemed to be perspiring. It was quite the most unappetizing sandwich she'd ever encountered. Was this really the best cuisine in the world? She'd imagined the crust of a *pain de campagne* then, and remembered how Michael had once trickled honey over toasted goats' cheese. She'd dreamed about his duck pâté with green peppercorns, and of putting a spoon into a perfectly yielding *oeuf en cocotte*. But then she'd pulled the handbrake on these thoughts. Stella had told herself that these were illicit thoughts, disloyal thoughts, distracting thoughts. She must keep them to herself—at least until she'd delivered her manuscript in November—and carry on banging the drum for dumplings.

Lucien was on good teasing form tonight and had talked a great deal as they ate. Michael had been a little quiet, though, and Stella thought he looked tired. There were dark shadows around his eyes and he seemed to be refilling his wineglass more regularly than he was accustomed. When Lucien went back into the kitchen to make coffee, she couldn't help asking if something was wrong.

"Have you been burning the midnight oil?"

"We're short-handed at work and we've all been sprinting this week. I've had a few late nights too, if I'm honest." He reached for another cigarette and passed Stella the packet. "I'm happy for Cynthia to be out with her friends, but I do feel that I ought to show my face. I was out four nights last week after I'd finished at the restaurant. If I stop moving, I'll fall asleep and might not wake up for a fortnight." When he exhaled smoke it sounded like a sigh, but he looked at her and smiled.

"Michael, you can't carry on like that. You're going to keel over. Is Cynthia not concerned?"

"She's like a trained athlete when it comes to socializing. I'm not sure how she manages it. Lots of practice, possibly?"

Stella thought of replying that Cynthia was probably sleeping soundly all day while Michael was sprinting through the luncheon and dinner service, but decided that perhaps he didn't need her to point this out. "Do you have to do the service every night? Could you not deputize occasionally?"

"There's no chance at the moment." His fingers twisted the silver paper of the cigarette packet. "The restaurant is doing well, though. We've had some good reviews recently. Some of that is down to Cynthia pulling strings. We're fully booked for the next week."

"Then perhaps leave Cynthia to the company of her friends? She'd understand, wouldn't she?"

He refilled both their glasses and sat back in his seat. "I left them to it in the Café Royal the other night. I waved the white flag at midnight, I'd been on my feet all day and I wanted my bed, but Cynthia told me that I lacked stamina, and then all her friends had great fun describing scenes of our married life in which she'd be tending to my pipe and slippers."

"Stamina? She does know how hard you work, doesn't she?" Stella could hear Cynthia's voice repeating those words and the mocking calls of her hangers-on. How could she say that to Michael? "Don't drive yourself into the ground trying to keep up with her partying as well." She could go further, she wanted to say more, but she told herself to stop.

"Don't pity him!" said Lucien, returning with coffee cups. "He's just spending too many energetic nights with Cynthia. Look at the dark circles around his eyes! I'm not certain that she isn't trying to kill him. Is it the praying mantis that bites the head off her mate once he's done the business?"

Michael threw a piece of bread at Lucien.

"Anyway," Lucien went on, "you've been boringly discreet about your rescuer with the furniture van. We do require all the details, you know, and assurances that he's being suitably gallant. Didn't you say that you've been away with him?"

Stella wasn't entirely sure why she didn't want to talk about Freddie with Michael and Lucien. She'd always shared her embarrassing stories with them, let them laugh and then listened to their advice. But, for some reason, she didn't want to tell them about Freddie. She didn't want to share too much about his personality or the way that she was with him. Stella asked herself why that was.

"Don't wiggle your eyebrows at me. It's nothing serious. It's only a bit of fun. He has strong opinions about walnut veneers and game birds."

"You being a game bird?"

"But do you like him?" Michael asked. "Is he good to you? Do you want it to be more serious?"

"Has he got you plucking pheasants and wearing his mother's pearls?" Lucien put on a Noël Coward accent.

"Is he all tweedy, and lisping, and given to Latin mottoes?" Michael winked at her as he joined in.

"He's very handsome, actually, and he enjoys plucking his own pheasants."

"Does he, indeed!"

Ye gods, that was enough! Stella didn't want to be having

to defend Freddie. She wasn't sure that she could do that for too long.

"He's encouraging, interested in what I'm doing, and occasionally it's good to get away from my father's needs for a few days." That was pretty much it, wasn't it?

"And how is your dear father?" Michael asked. "Poor old Charlie, is he still feeling down?"

Stella smiled at Michael. She was grateful for the change of topic. "He's better—much better, actually. He's working on the garden and I heard him whistling last week. I haven't heard that for a long time. We're crammed in together, very short of space, but it makes me happy to put a biscuit in his saucer, and a roast dinner in front of him on a Sunday, and to see pleasure on his face."

"But would you rather be slipping biscuits onto your antiques dealer's saucer?" Lucien gave her a quizzical look. "Can you see a future version of yourself roasting his pheasants?"

Stella pictured herself carving bloody joints of meat and presenting a dish of brawn to Freddie. She wasn't sure that her digestion could take it. But then, would Freddie actually let her cook? Perhaps he might permit her to arrange salad leaves or serve a pudding?

"No," she admitted. "It's not like that. He's amusing company, but the needs of an aging father can sometimes be a convenient excuse for a woman."

They talked more about her book over coffee and cognacs. She considered confiding that she had some concerns, that her research and approach perhaps weren't everything that they ought to be, but found herself reluctant to say this out loud. What would Michael and Lucien think of her if she confessed that she'd been leaning on facts to make them fit? Stella decided not to say it, but did admit that she felt under pressure.

"I didn't think they'd give me another chance, if I'm honest. I know they've been disappointed by *Mrs. Raffald*'s sales figures, so I feel I have something to prove with this book. I need it to pick up favorable reviews, and for those reviews to make cash tills ring. I need this one to sell. I need people to like it."

"And they will." Michael put his hand to her shoulder. "You sound like you're putting a lot of yourself into it. You're clearly going all-out to make it charming. People will respond to that."

But was she going too far with the charm? She'd dropped a sample chapter off at the offices of Fleet, Everard & Frobisher that morning, and had arranged to have lunch with Mr. Williamson at the end of the week. Stella had felt rather nervous handing her envelope of papers over, but did she need to be? Following on from their discussion about gingerbread, she'd judged that her chapter on the culinary peculiarities of Cumbria might appeal to Mr. Williamson. She'd worked hard to get the recipe for Grasmere gingerbread right (her father had obligingly critiqued his way through seven batches), and had attributed it to her fictional corre-spondent, Colonel Jenkins. She'd put a recipe for potted char in too and had credited that to Mrs. Fothergill. Of course, it wasn't really hers, but Stella had been able to embroider a nice story about finding this volume of handwritten recipes at a house sale, and Mr. Williamson need never know that Mrs. Fothergill's book contained mostly chutneys, invalid foods and paragraphs copied verbatim from Mrs. Beeton. Stella had also worked up the anecdote about Wordsworth and the rum butter. She was well aware that there were risks here; however, she'd been cautious about her wording, and it was just the sort of thing that Mr. Williamson liked. It wouldn't be problematic, would it?

My grandfather liked to call himself a gentleman farmer. He was a great one for experimenting with feeds, and entering agricultural competitions, and I've inherited several portraits of marvelously corpulent cows. There was a great pride in English beef in that era. All the visiting foreigners remarked upon it and how even the lowliest English working man could sit down to a joint of meat. The French started calling us Les Rosbifs at that time, I'm told, which stemmed from envy, I'm sure. I assume you are familiar with Mr. Fielding's verse "The Roast Beef of Old England"? It might make a nice frontispiece for your book, don't you think?

CAPTAIN FREDERICK HOWARTH, Cheltenham

Madam, I trust you will be mentioning The Sublime Society of Beefsteaks in your volume on English food? I am proud to count an ancestor as a founder member of this noble institution (est. 1736). There was a great fashion for ragoûts and fricassées at that time, extravagant, effete stuff, all messed up with sauces, and rather suspect—you know? However, the Beefsteaks celebrated honest English beef at their dinners, the food that fueled the bellies of our heroic ancestors at Crécy and Agincourt. It was a fine patriotic association and not frightened of plain speaking (particularly about the Frenchies!). If only we had more like them now, eh?

REGINALD BATHURST, London

My mother was employed as a good plain cook, as they used to be called. She had no time for fancy foreign cooking and no regard for gentlemen who employed French chefs. She cooked simple, honest fare, economical and wholesome. That's as English cooking should be, isn't it? I don't hold with these restaurants that must have French words all over their menus now. It's not right in England, is it? I wish you good luck with your book. It's about time that someone set these matters straight.

ROWENA ROBERTS, Somerset

People like to talk about the roast beef of olde England, but do you know that fifty per cent of the beef that we consume in this country today has been imported from Argentina? I ask you: what's to be done about that?

WILFRED EWART, farmer, Hereford

Chapter Thirty-one

Lucien pushed his plate away. Gravy and grease were already congealing. Stella's whitebait had been excellent. For a chef, Lucien was very bad at ordering from a menu, but then, perhaps he wanted to be disappointed? He had certainly seemed to enjoy denigrating the plate that now lay between them. It had been like watching an autopsy.

"Whitebait used to be sold by the pint pot," Stella said. "People would eat hot fried whitebait and drink cold punch on the riverfront at Greenwich. Cabinet ministers came down from Westminster on special barges."

Lucien nodded. "I'm not saying that sprats aren't fascinating, but when you talk about food, you're sometimes diverting. Do you know that you do that?"

"Do I?" Was that true? "But don't you think *sprats* is a delightful word? It has a fishy flick, a no-nonsense bluntness, and—"

"You're worrying about him, aren't you?"

"Well, aren't you?" Stella couldn't deny it. Michael had met Cynthia in Quaglino's after he'd finished work on Friday night, had stayed out until dawn, and had burned his hand badly during the lunchtime service the next day. It was a deep enough burn that he'd had to go to a doctor and have it dressed. "I'm not wrong to, am I?"

"But what can we do?" Lucien sat back. "If I say anything, he growls at me—and I suppose he has every right to do that. We're in real danger of falling out over her."

Stella nodded. She hated seeing the dark circles around Michael's eyes, the smell of last night's whiskey on his breath, and he couldn't go on like this, could he? She wanted it to stop, for him to snap out of it, but what could she do? What could she say? She really didn't want to fall out with him. Her finger made circles in the spilled beer on the tabletop. "I keep remembering what you said about a praying mantis. I made the mistake of looking that up in a book, you know, and I can't get the image out of my head now. There were diagrams and everything: she *nourishes* herself on his nutrients!"

Stella and Lucien had agreed to meet up with Michael and Cynthia's group in a nightclub off Wardour Street at ten. It had seemed like a sensible idea to imbibe some Dutch courage in advance, but it hadn't kicked in yet. The public house in which they were now sitting was all dark wood paneling, etched glass and button-backed banquettes. There was much sticky red velveteen and a noisy, arty crowd. Considering the prevalence of hand-crafted sandals, beards and enunciation, Stella supposed that many of the clientele might be actors. They could all be part of Cynthia's crowd, and as Stella listened to the voices around her, the self-conscious diction and the laughter that was a little too loud, she continued to puzzle as to how Michael fitted in with this tribe. Were these his people now? Could he genuinely enjoy the company of Cynthia's set?

"How can darling Michael want to be with a woman like that?" Lucien asked, echoing her own thoughts. Stella heard both incredulity and sadness in his tone. "Do you know, when we first moved to London he paid my rent for two months until I got a regular job. I bet he's never told you that, has he? But that's what he's like. He's the kindest, loveliest man I know, and she's not worthy of him. Yes, all her dresses have exclusive labels and she drinks with influential people, but those aren't things that Michael values. Can he not see how shallow she is? Is he blinkering that out somehow? I do start to wonder if he's having some sort of *crise psychiatrique*."

"Are you being serious?" Was that just envy talking, or had Lucien really seen signs that Michael might be unwell? "Do you think we ought to be concerned about that?"

"Of course, it's probably all about sex, isn't it? It's a very physical relationship, I suspect, and she seems to know how to push his buttons. I can imagine she might be rather commanding in the bedroom, can't you?"

Stella blinked at Lucien. She didn't know what to imagine. Even less what to say to this. Was it permissible to voice such thoughts aloud? But then her ears zoned into the surrounding conversations and everyone seemed to be talking about infidelities, urges and libidos. Soho could be rather *trop*.

"I think he might be a little bamboozled by her."

"Hmm, you know all of this rather makes me regret that he didn't just couple up with you."

"With *me*? That was never on the cards. Michael has never thought of me in that way."

Lucien's laugh was slightly mirthless. "*Tu plaisantes?* Are you truly unaware of the way Michael looks at you? Do you know how much I used to envy you? I used to dream that he'd focus his big blue eyes on me like that. I would gladly have given a month's salary for five minutes of those looks!" He drained his glass. "I should have banged your heads together years ago; I thought that when we were having dinner the other night. The pair of you were both doing the corner-of-the-eye thing."

"What corner-of-the-eye thing? I don't know what you mean. Michael doesn't look at me any differently than he looks at anyone else." That was true, wasn't it? But then she recalled her mother's handwriting observing smiles and glances, and her elbow seemed to make contact with Stella's ribs again.

Lucien shook his head. "*Mon Dieu*, this country! What's wrong with you all? Being good-mannered is all very nice, but you people take the reserve to perverse lengths. It would be funny if it wasn't so tragic. Is England full of lonely hearts who missed colliding because it didn't seem sufficiently polite at the time? Is it full of melancholy souls who were just a little too embarrassed to speak up? For the love of God, just say what you feel, people!" He lifted his hands and leaned back in his chair. "Still, it's too late now, isn't it? The mantis has sunk her barbed teeth deep into his flesh and I dare say you've missed your chance."

Stella was glad to be linking Lucien's arm as they approached the club. The man on the door looked down his nose and demanded to know whether they were members, but at the mention of Cynthia's name they were waved in.

"Does her name open doors all over London?" Stella asked.

"Just so long as it opens bottles too . . ."

They descended down a long flight of stairs, past walls that appeared to be perspiring. The club had been set up in a network of old cellars. While overhead there were ancient vaulted arches, below all was glittering, hectic and throbbing with the beat of the music. A bar occupied one side of the room, an American jazz band was playing on a stage, and limbs gyrated on a crowded dance floor. All the dancers were extremely young, furiously energetic, and looked as if they might be auditioning for parts in some cabaret. The chairs were painted gold and the tables were covered with dark-red cloths, while the air was faintly blue with cigarette smoke. There was a smell of Shalimar de Guerlain, spilled champagne and sweat, and an atmosphere of luxurious seediness.

"*Le bordel!*" exclaimed Lucien.

It was noisy in the club, but a particularly high-volume hilarity was coming from Cynthia's table. As Stella and Lucien approached, she couldn't help wondering if some of that laughter was at their expense.

"Sweet of you to have invited the catering staff," said Reggie Houghton.

"Don't be horrid!" There was a note of admonishment in Cynthia's voice, but a smile on her lips. She was wearing a good deal of black tulle tonight, a necklace that looked like it had been made out of Liquorice Allsorts and was wafting an ostentatiously long ivory cigarette-holder. She was a sketch out of *Vogue* brought to life. "It's nice for Michael to have his fan club here."

Stella was of a mind to retort that at least they cared about him, that they didn't keep him out all night and let him have accidents with cooking fat, but then Michael was picking his way across the room toward them. He embraced them both and went to take the chair that had appeared at Cynthia's side. She kissed him rather demonstratively on the mouth, a kiss that was a fraction too ardent for a public place, and Stella had to look away. When she glanced back, he was smiling benignly at the room and Cynthia was making a face at his clothes. He was wearing his old corduroy jacket, the one he'd bought in Paris, worn shiny on the elbows now, and he looked like an out-of-place tradesman next to Cynthia and all her tulle. Her mouth turned down at the corners as she put an appraising hand to his collar. Her blood-red lipstick gave her a rather vampiric look, Stella thought, and she had to blink away an image of Cynthia sinking her teeth into Michael's neck.

Rupert Snelgrave was there, Reggie Houghton and Marcus Ellercot, and three acolytes of Cynthia who the conversation revealed to be a sculptor, a poet and a theater critic. A thick pall of smoke hung over the table and a crowd of empty glasses awaited collection. It was apparent that the group had been occupying this table for several hours and they were already somewhat sauced.

Rupert stood to pour champagne for them all, swaying unsteadily in time to the music, and Stella looked around. Everyone was dressed in a conspicuously fashionable style, lots of ivory satin, black velvet and swansdown trim. She recognized the faces of young aristocrats from the society weeklies, moneyed adventuresses, debutants, notorious *roués* and *demi-mondaines*. Stella imagined that a *Bystander* review might call the place "exclusive but cosmopolitan." It seemed like the sort of joint where any sin might be sampled for the right price.

Stella found herself sitting between Lucien and the theater critic, who, as it turned out, also did book reviews for a London periodical. He was obviously slightly squiffy, but Stella put on her best smile and tried to blinker out Cynthia and shift into professional mode. The critic gave her a penetrating look as she introduced herself, raising her voice above a rather raucous Dixieland number. She felt herself being assessed, or perhaps he was merely long-sighted and had misplaced his spectacles. With his pink-rimmed eyes and protruding front teeth, he reminded her vaguely of a white rabbit that she'd owned as a child.

"Cynthia tells me you write cookery books," the white rabbit said, when his eyes had completed a circuit of her face.

290

"Not exactly. I'm writing a history of English food at the moment." She looked at the pink eyes for a reaction. "It's turning out to be as much a work of anthropology as of cookery. It's very revealing, what we choose to eat, don't you think?" Stella heard herself sounding slightly pompous.

"How interesting," said the rabbit. "I'm a vegetarian myself. It's an ethical decision. I won't bore you, but it does make one eat with consideration."

Stella already felt slightly judged by his considerate eating. She was sympathetic to vegetarians, but hoped he wasn't going to make a speech about the tender emotions of lambs. Could she talk to him about Viscount Townshend's turnips? Might he be interested in Flemish crop rotations? But whatever would he think of all the rabbit pies, jugged hares and porpoise pottages in her book? Perhaps it might be safer if she were to discourage him from reading it? She tried to suppress a picture of him nibbling pensively at salad leaves.

"It does all sound rather cozy," Cynthia said, leaning forward and flicking cigarette ash. She pronounced the word as if it tasted unpleasant in her mouth. "Do people read books about cake these days? I don't think I've eaten cake for decades!" She looked around the group with an expression of amused incredulity. "Still, I suppose there's all those Women's Institute types. All those sensible skirts and spinsters who do handicrafts. They might invite you along to make a speech about the anthropology of the Victoria sponge." The poet laughed at that, but then he laughed obediently at everything Cynthia said.

"It is more than a book about cake." As the eyes of Cynthia's coterie swiveled toward her, resentment swelled in Stella's chest. Why should she have to sit here and be judged and mocked by these people? Why must she justify herself? For a moment, she felt an urge to reach across and pull Cynthia's hair, but then she looked at Michael and saw that he was frowning. Cynthia had gone too far, hadn't she? "My publisher is confident that it will do well," she went on, not feeling overly confident. "It's a zeitgeist thing, you know?"

"Really? Does he think so?" Cynthia didn't look at all convinced by the zeitgeist.

"It's a tremendously ambitious book, actually," Michael spoke up then. His eyes met Stella's and he gave her a smile that was like the sun breaking through clouds. "Very much more than cake. Stella has been telling us about her research. I think your publisher is right. I'm certain it will do well. I'm looking forward to spotting people reading it and feeling proud of you."

Stella wanted to walk around the table and hug him for that, but Cynthia turned to him with a look on her face that was like a warning. Stella knew, at that moment, that they weren't on the same side. That look told her what Cynthia thought of her and why Michael's telephone calls had become so far apart. The sculptor lifted his eyebrows, the critic peered at Stella through a pair of pince-nez, and an awkward silence stretched.

"Anyway, how are the wedding plans going?" Lucien eventually asked.

They all listened while Cynthia talked about the dress she was having made for the wedding. The designer had sourced some rarefied fabric from a remote region of India and a suite of jewelry was being created by a goldsmith friend. She'd sent invitations to several photographers from fashion magazines and had already worked out the choreography of the poses. She spoke lengthily of how her hair was to be styled, her shoes, her flowers, her guest list and of the gypsy caravan from which waiting staff would serve drinks. It struck Stella that Michael seemed to be rather peripheral to all of these plans. Was that really how it was, or was that her selective judgment? But then Lucien said: "And Michael? Is he invited?"

Cynthia narrowed her eyes at Lucien. "What a thing to say!" She put the back of her hand to her forehead, like a stricken woman in a play, but then she laughed and the coterie laughed with her, uncertainly then heartily. She turned the full focused force of her femininity onto Michael now, giving him the sort of look that the film magazines called "smoldering." He was still frowning, and for a moment it seemed that he might resist, but Cynthia's womanly powers had such wattage and insistence.

"Just checking," Lucien said.

Stella turned her chair and watched the dancers. She didn't mean to be ill-mannered, but she could only stomach so much of Cynthia. Various complicated twistings and intersections of limbs were being executed on the dance floor.

"What dance is that?" she asked Lucien.

"Some sort of tango?"

A woman in a fringed shawl was sitting on top of the piano now and singing in a husky voice. Hostesses in sequined dresses circulated between the tables, moving their hips in an exaggerated way and arching painted eyebrows. As Stella looked around the tables, she vaguely recognized actors, playwrights, poets, picture dealers, models and artists. Everyone was either whispering or shouting over the music. There was much posturing and positioning, a lot of social politics in play, and there was something contrived about it all. The whole place seemed slightly unhealthy. If she had to spend many evenings in joints like this, Stella felt that she might have a *crise psychiatrique*. The ever-quickening beat of the music was starting to make her head spin.

She pulled her chair closer to Lucien's and they talked about the trip that she was planning to Cornwall, about saffron, clotted cream and spider crabs. This conversation pushed back the perspiring walls and the painted faces, and brought a stir of fresh, salty air into the overheated club. Lucien's enthusiasm made her look forward to the trip, and as she talked, she became more determined that she would make a success of her book. Of course, it was more than just a cozy little book about cake. She would finish it and feel proud of it. She glanced toward Michael, wanting to tell him that she'd reserved a table in the restaurant he'd recommended, but he was kissing Cynthia again, a lingering, passionate kiss that ought to have a curtain drawn around it. Stella's eyes met Lucien's and they exchanged a grimace.

"Nourishing on his nutrients," he whispered.

Good Taste

"JUST CAKE"
[From the notebook of Elizabeth Douglas, 1920]

"It's not just cake," Charlie said to me, as I cut him a slice this afternoon. "It's <u>the</u> cake. You haven't forgotten, have you, Lizzie?"

But, of course, I hadn't forgotten.

It's my mother's recipe for apple cake, with cinnamon and rum, best butter and brown sugar. I'd made it for Charlie the second time that we met and he asked me to marry him there and then. Or, if I wasn't partial, and she was available, he'd asked if he might marry my mother.

We'd met for the first time at a dance, the previous weekend. It was a potato-pie supper at the Mechanics' Institute, with red cabbage and a dance band from Bradford. My friend Annie had mithered me into going with her, but she'd paired up with Jack Warner as soon as we were through the door and I hadn't seen her for an hour. I wasn't keen on dancing back then. I was too self-conscious, I didn't know how to speak to young men, and I preferred to sit and watch. But then Charlie Douglas stood in front of me, all smartness and civility in his shirt collar and polished shoes, and said that life was too short to sit and watch.

He proved to be a good dancer. He was very considerate and had gentlemanly manners. I laughed when he told me he'd been to dancing classes. I asked why a farmer's son needed to know how to dance. But he'd shrugged and said, "Why not? Why shouldn't a farmer dance? And, besides, how else might I find an excuse to stand this close to a beautiful woman?" He'd given me such a look then and I could feel myself blushing. My mother always said he could charm the birds out of the trees.

The second time we met we walked up the Roman road and onto the tops. We sat on the boulders and ate slices of apple cake and drank tea from a Thermos flask. It was a windy day, I remember, the shadows of clouds scudding fast over the moors, and the silky heads of the cotton grass rippling. We'd danced again up there, our feet treading the heather and him singing into my ear because the wind took his voice away. He told me to close my eyes, just to listen to the rhythm of the music, and to trust him. We danced like that for a long time, with the sigh of the wind and the scent of the heather, and when I opened my eyes again I realized that I did trust him and that I wouldn't ever want to dance with anyone else.

Charlie still says that asking me to dance, that first time, was the bravest and best thing he's ever done. When I look back over the years since, there are chances that I regret not taking and some choices that I'd change, but finding the courage to say "Yes" to Charlie that night still feels like the best decision I've ever made. My second-best decision was baking the apple cake that put thoughts of marriage in his mind. I reckon there's no such thing as "just cake." Cake can have consequences.

Chapter Thirty-two

Mrs. Parr had responded to Stella's appeal for recipes published in *The Cornishman*. In her letter, she'd explained that she was now in her eighties (the ponderously looping handwriting seemed to authenticate this), but had spent most of her life in service in various houses around West Penwith. Since her retirement, she'd been offering farmhouse teas from her cottage, she explained, and she'd be happy to talk with Stella about her experiences. She had dropped the names of various artists and writers who she'd cooked for into her letter, and Stella had thought that Mrs. Parr's effusive indiscretion sounded very promising.

Sitting in Mrs. Parr's kitchen now, with its whitewashed walls and black-leaded range, Stella felt that she might, at last, have struck a seam of gold. An old pine table occupied the center of the room, scrubbed white as a sea-scoured bone, the light from the window casting bright squares between the lines of cake stands and teapots. Scones were cooling on a rack and fruit pies waited under wire cloches. The room smelled of vanilla and strawberry jam, and a pleasant hubbub of conversation came in with each swing of the door. Stella decided that heaven might be much like Dorothy Parr's kitchen.

She'd approached the cottage through a garden planted with catmint and candytuft, forget-me-nots and night-scented stocks. The dappled bells of foxgloves hummed with the sound of bees and columbines were opening purple velvet bonnets. Mrs. Parr had insisted on walking her around to the back of the cottage and showing her the vegetable garden. Stella had watched the hens pecking between the bean rows as Mrs. Parr had talked about early potatoes, peas and salad greens, and how she grew strawberries, raspberries and currants for jam. Stella had felt an urge to send a telegram to Mr. Williamson informing him that she'd found the perfect scene and character for her book. She wanted to telephone Michael and share every detail with him. Here, at last, was that treasure she'd been seeking: the seemingly dwindling farmhouse cookery tradition. Was this how an anthropologist felt upon encountering a supposedly lost tribe? Unicorns whinnied and gamboled in Stella's mind.

"Are you sure I can't help?" she asked now. "I'm feeling guilty sitting here watching you working."

"No, you stay where you are. I know you mean well, my love, but I'm in my rhythm. I'll just take these teas through and then I'll sit down with you."

The crochet fringes on the lampshade shifted as Mrs. Parr went out of the door and Stella couldn't help sketching a quick cartoon. Dorothy Parr had white hair scraped back into a bun, a stooped back and a deeply lined face. In her high-necked blouse and long black skirt, she might well have stepped out of a Mary Webb novel. Occasionally, as she bent, Stella caught a glimpse of worsted stockings, but it wasn't that difficult to imagine how Dorothy might once have been a bare-legged girl nimbly picking between rock pools. For all that she looked like a portrait of ancient, modest widowhood, she had the energy and tumbling word flow of an adolescent, and Stella's note-taking hand had barely been able to keep up. She'd already given Stella her recipes for seed cake, saffron cake and Cornish splits, and had promised a lesson in scalded cream and junket.

Stella followed Mrs. Parr into the larder now. There were great pats of golden butter on the marble slabs, wheels of cheese, sides of bacon and bowls of cream. The walls were lined with bottled gooseberries, chutneys, pickled walnuts and cucumbers, and she'd never seen so many jars of jam. Stella wished she had a camera. Would Mrs. Parr mind if she were to sketch it? Wouldn't it make a perfect cover? (Perhaps in ink and crayon? Or a juicy gouache?)

"I flavor it with brandy and lemon peel," Mrs. Parr said, turning with a bowl of junket in her hands, and ushering Stella out of the pantry, "because that's the way my mother did it, and my grandmother too, I suppose. Of course, in Devon they don't put in more than a scrape of nutmeg. When I worked for Mr. Trevellion he liked his flavored with rum. Made it less like nursery food, he used to tell me. Saying that, he liked a slug of rum in his tea too. Some folks put cinnamon in, others wine. It's whatever you like, really. But you should always eat it with cream on top."

Stella nodded, noted, and followed Mrs. Parr back to the kitchen table. An incident with a young man called Hubert had left her with a horror of set-milk desserts (would she ever delete the memory of those quivering pink shapes set in the form of various body parts?), but Mrs. Parr's junket had a soothing cleanness and a good hit of brandy.

"When my mother made it, she'd put a piece of calf's stomach in the milk to curdle it, but it's marvelous what you can buy in a bottle these days, isn't it?"

"It is," Stella agreed. It was a pity that the calf's stomach had become *passé*, it might have been a picturesquely rustic image, but then again she was quite happy to be eating milk that had been set with clean bottled rennet. Maybe, for the sake of scenic text, she could pretend that Mrs. Parr had demonstrated the older method?

"We do get people from the north coming down here now," Mrs. Parr said, looking at Stella thoughtfully. "It's still mostly the crowds coming in on the train from London, mind, and folks on motor tours. Some people ask me if I object to all the holidaymakers being here, but why should I? I do a nice little trade with the teas and I like to chat to them. My neighbor, Matthew, says I enjoy telling them the tale, but I'm only being friendly, and that's what folk want on their holidays, isn't it?"

As they'd talked, Mrs. Parr had gone in and out with trays of tea, bread and butter and scones—and, every time she went into the next room, Stella could hear her telling the tale. It was evident that she relished the part. Half a dozen tables were set up in the parlor next door, presently mostly occupied by couples in hiking boots and families with jam-smeared children. Stella had come in that way, past the canary in a cage, the ticking grandfather clock and the Staffordshire figure of John Wesley preaching. It had all gone down in her notebook.

"Do you not find it a lot of work?" Stella asked. The teacups rattled precariously on the trays as Mrs. Parr carried them. Could she not get a girl in to help her? The annotations on the wall calendar suggested a busy month ahead.

"Some weeks in August, I can bake as many as two-hundred scones. The oven is going night and day. I pride myself on everything being homemade: the jam is from the fruit in the garden, and I make my own cream. Well, if you make it yourself, you know it's proper, don't you? I don't think of it as work, though—not this. Now, when I was a girl and a scullery maid, *that* was work. Some of these artist types have the filthiest ways, you know. You wonder how they were brought up. It doesn't bother them to eat off dirty dishes, and the women just step out of their drawers and leave them on the floor. That is, when they bother to wear drawers." Mrs. Parr's eyes sparkled. "Some of them have no shame. I've seen some sights, I could tell you."

"Really?" Stella knew she ought to be keeping Mrs. Parr on the subject of scones, but she was enjoying her enthusiastic indiscretion.

"I used to work for a Mr. Lovett in St. Ives. He was a painter, Royal Academy and all that. Ever so lah-di-dah, he was. He was a nice gentleman to cook for, appreciative and never mean with the money, but his wife was a right one. She'd go out pruning the roses wearing only what the good Lord gave her, and think nothing of chatting with her neighbors over the hedge. She was a titled lady too. And the goings on at their parties—well, when you took breakfast trays up, you never knew who was going to be in which bed. They're like that, though, these bohemian types, aren't they? I'm no prude, not one to judge, but it fair made my eyes water sometimes. I could write a book, I tell you. And then there was Major Hemshore . . ."

Stella took notes as she listened. She knew she couldn't use most of this—some of it was outright libelous—but the more that she showed interest, the more extreme Mrs. Parr's stories became, and it was rather entertaining. (Was it beastly of her to hope that Cynthia's family might have holidayed in St. Ives and that some relationship-souring scandal might transpire?) Mrs. Parr was very rude about D. H. Lawrence, talked lengthily of Katherine Mansfield's cough, and became quite girlish over Alfred Munnings' manners. She spoke of apple pies, picking blackberries from the hedgerows, nutmeg-topped rice puddings, family picnics and church harvest teas.

"Is this useful to you, my love?" she asked, as she refreshed Stella's teacup. "Is this the sort of thing you're interested in?"

"Fascinating. Thank you."

"Will you mention my name in your book?"

"That's the way I'm writing it—when people give me recipes and stories, I'm quoting and acknowledging them. Would you rather I didn't?"

"Oh no, not at all—you *must*, dear. Remember to say Mrs. Parr of Bridge Cottage. Say about the farmhouse teas. Fresh every day, homemade cream and jam, and as much tea as they can drink. You know, some places won't let you have another pot of hot water? And I could name some who serve shop-bought scones."

Of course, she'd want the advertisement, but Stella didn't begrudge her that. They were simply exchanging a favor and Mrs. Parr had been splendidly good value.

Stella sat on a bench outside the inn and light flashed on the water in the harbor. There was something restful about the clink of the riggings and watching the boys dangling their legs over the harbor wall, their attention fixed on bobbing fishing lines. She'd just read through her notes from Mrs. Parr and was considering what an excellently useful day she'd had. She'd booked a room here for two nights, and had a reservation at the restaurant that Michael had recommended for tomorrow evening.

Her thoughts again returned to what Lucien had said about the way Michael looked at her (they had been returning there quite often over the past two days), but he'd got that wrong, hadn't he? And surely her mother had too? It was just friendly concern that showed in Michael's eyes. Stella also recalled the look that Cynthia had given Michael in the club and Lucien's theories about physicality. She couldn't help feeling that Cynthia wasn't good for Michael, all those late nights, those seedy places, and the snide aside words of her crowd, but there had been nothing unambiguous in that kiss, had there? If she and Michael were to remain friends—and Stella did sincerely want that—she must let these feelings go.

She narrowed her eyes to the glitter of the water and breathed in the salty air. There was an unusual quality to the light here, crystalline somehow, and the intensity of the colors brought to mind paintings of the South of France. If her book was successful, and she was now resolved that it must be, perhaps she might suggest to Mr. Williamson that she could write a book about French food ("How the French Eat"?). She pictured herself motoring around the Languedoc, visiting markets and out-of-the-way *auberges*, and it was an agreeable image. Talk of saffron and Phoenician trading routes had left her thinking about bouillabaisse and dipping bread into ochre-colored aioli. She saw herself standing over dishes of pork cooked with prunes, chicken flecked green with tarragon, and jewel-like pears poached in red wine. Stella shut her eyes to the dazzling light and felt the warmth of the evening sun on her lifted face. She was full of resolve tonight. She was a writer, she told herself. She had a career. This book would be a success, then there would be others, and that would be enough. (If she repeated this to herself a sufficient number of times, she would make it so.)

*

"I heard you were over at old mother Parr's today," the barman said, when she went in for another glass of cider.

"That's right." Was there something wry in his smile? How villages could talk! "She was very helpful."

The man laughed as he poured the cider. "I'll bet she was! I dread to think what yarns she spun you."

"Yarns?"

"All the goings on at the Lovetts' parties, yes? Major Hemshore in the hayloft with the girl from the dairy? Mrs. Farrah-Jenkins and the traveling salesman?"

"Something like that."

"I thought as much. Be careful what you believe. Dorothy Parr has a mouth on her. She's known for it, always has been. What she can't find out, she makes up, and doesn't she have an imagination?"

Stella recalled how Mrs. Parr had talked so gleefully. She'd heard all about the indiscretion in the hayloft and the scandal with the traveling brush salesman. Could he be right? "Surely not? She seemed a thoroughly respectable old lady."

"Respectable? Do you think?" His eyebrows lifted. "You won't hear that from the folks whose marriages she's split up. She can be poison, that one. I suppose you had all the homemade jam bit too?"

"Yes, she makes it from the fruit in her garden."

"She saw you coming!" He grinned as he put her change down on the bar. "She buys her jam by the crate from the wholesaler."

*

Stella opened her notebook again. She'd filled twenty pages that afternoon and, while there might be a lot of tittle-tattle here, surely the parts that Stella might use were irrefutable? That genuinely was an inherited recipe for saffron cake, wasn't it? And all that lore about the Phoenicians trading saffron for tin must be true, mustn't it? But then Stella recalled how Mrs. Parr had talked of spending hours hulling strawberries for jam. She tried to rewind her memory back to standing in the larder and bring its shelves back into focus. There were an awful lot of jars of jam in there—and had there been printed labels on them? She realized why Mrs. Parr had steered her out of the room.

Stella rubbed her temples. She could feel a headache coming on. The old girl had taken her for a ride, hadn't she? The wholesaler jam now seemed to undermine the solidity of everything else. It was damned annoying when one couldn't trust one's sources. Stella felt irritable as she closed her notebook—but then she thought about the rum butter story and Jane Austen's teashop flirtation. She'd been spinning yarns too, hadn't she? Hell, was she as unreliable as Dorothy Parr? Was she as phoney as the wholesaler jam? Her whole book was constructed on appealingly packaged half-truths and for a moment its foundations seemed to tremble.

Chapter Thirty-three

Stella made a mental note that she must never again order spaghetti when trying to look professional. It wasn't that she was a novice fork twirler, but it was a challenge to appear scholarly while trying not to splatter tomato sauce on her blouse. How did the Italians manage it? But then they didn't have the constrictions of English table manners, did they? Stella resolved that spaghetti was a dish to be enjoyed privately or in the company of forgiving friends, and reflected that being English perhaps wasn't always beneficial for one's digestion.

"You know, the Normans brought pasta to England," she said. She was attempting to sound like she was on top of her subject and to divert attention away from her fork. "It goes that far back. There's a recipe for macaroni in the oldest English cookery manuscript. Mrs. Raffald has a good macaroni cheese with Parmesan, and she was fond of using vermicelli, but the first mention of spaghetti is in Eliza Acton's book. She's a fascinating woman and overdue a biography," Stella added. It never hurt to get these things in.

Mr. Williamson had ordered a breaded veal cutlet and

his plate was emptying considerably faster than Stella's. She supposed he was accustomed to business luncheons and had learned the perils of *salsa al pomodoro*. Her pasta was beginning to cool and coagulate into an uncooperative lump.

"I thought you handled the matter of outside influence well in your sample chapter." Mr. Williamson refilled her wineglass. He'd had a new set of teeth since Stella had seen him last. They were unnaturally large, startlingly white, and made a clacking sound as he talked. It was difficult not to stare at his teeth, but they seemed to be getting through the veal cutlet efficiently. "You introduced the story of the spice route while celebrating the essential Englishness of these recipes. That's what I hoped you might be able to achieve."

"I'm so glad," Stella said. So relieved, she might have added.

She had felt some trepidation about meeting Mr. Williamson today, and she'd looked for signs of disapproval or disappointment on his face as he'd stepped through the door of the restaurant. But then she'd seen the dazzle of his new teeth and knew that all would be well. He clearly hadn't detected the falsehoods, and it seemed that she'd got the tone right. Stella spiraled her spaghetti more confidently at that.

"If the text is all pitched at this level, it should do very well," he went on. "I shall be glad to report that to my colleagues. There were some who had concerns after *Mrs. Raffald*, who worried that this book might not have sufficient reach, but

I've always had confidence that you could deliver it. I'm heartened to know that my confidence wasn't misplaced."

"I'm so happy to hear that." The darling man. She could hug him. "I am grateful to have your support, Mr. Williamson."

"I have to say that I particularly chuckled at the Wordsworth anecdote. Just charming! Wherever did you find it?"

"It came to me in a letter from a Colonel Jenkins. I placed advertisements appealing for information in a number of newspapers and I've had some marvelous replies. People have been so generous in their responses. They've shared the most interesting stories."

"It's exactly the sort of thing I'd hoped you might uncover. So engaging, so fascinating, so deliciously English."

So embroidered, so twisted, so utterly fictional, Stella thought, but she grinned at him over her glass. "I have a delightful story about Jane Austen and Bath buns—and Robert Walpole and a lamprey pie!"

"Capital. There's going to be a lot of interest in this book, you know. We've already started putting the word out to reviewers and we're getting positive responses. You must start to give some consideration to what you'd like to write next. Let's be ambitious again. I can see this book giving you quite a following."

"Do you really?" He was saying all the right things.

"Incidentally, I've passed your sample chapter on to one of my senior colleagues. Have I ever introduced you to

Penelope Warner-Stewart? You might have heard of her husband, Geoffrey? We published his Wordsworth biography some years ago, but it's still regarded as a standard text, I believe. Anyway, I know that Penelope will be most interested in this delightful little snapshot of William and Dorothy's domestic life."

Stella stopped spinning her fork. She put it down and took a mouthful of wine. A serious Wordsworth scholar? Was this perilous? She had pictured her text being read by housewives, not academics. Would it be wise to forge a letter from Colonel Jenkins when she got home? But what address might she give him? And what if Geoffrey Warner-Stewart were to try to contact him ... This might become complicated.

Stella left the restaurant with a mixture of elation and anxiety. In some respects, it couldn't have gone any better—Mr. Williamson had been so encouraging—but the idea of him sharing the Wordsworth anecdote with an expert colleague had set off an alarm bell. An alarm bell which seemed to be sounding more loudly by the minute.

Chapter Thirty-four

Stella had spent the five hours on the train contemplating the potential consequences of her rum-butter recklessness, but as she drove home from the station, guilt added an extra flavor to her cocktail of concerns. Had her father been lonely for the past week? In deserting him for seven days had she neglected her daughterly duties? She imagined him spending long evenings with just a play on the wireless for company, eating his reheated dishes at the table alone, watching the clock until it was time for bed. She must push on with her work this week, must make space and time for it, but she'd bake him the coconut cake that he liked tomorrow and go to a special effort with the Sunday lunch.

As it turned out, she needn't have bothered worrying about him. She found him watering a new row of currant bushes in the back garden and whistling an obliquely risqué old music hall song. Patterns of begonias and petunias had also appeared and he seemed to be in an altogether cheerful mood.

"You've not been too lonely?" she asked.

"Not remotely! Your Mrs. Pendlebury made up her mind

that I needed looking after. She's rather spoiled me. To tell you the truth, I've had a thoroughly enjoyable week."

"Mrs. P called in? That was nice of her, wasn't it? I must telephone her and say thank you." Stella had actually paid Mrs. Pendlebury to call in once per day, but she didn't like to let on to her father that this was a formal arrangement.

"She's been a treasure." The sunlight highlighted the lines around his eyes, but the warmth of his smile prompted Stella to recall a younger version of his face. "She came over at eight every morning and insisted on cooking my breakfast. She popped back at lunchtimes, and even baked me a cake yesterday. She made me that coconut cake I like. You know, the one with the icing?"

"How kind of her." That really was above and beyond. Good old Mrs. Pendlebury, Stella thought. "She warmed up the casseroles that I left you?"

"For the first couple of days. But then she got me a piece of plaice on Friday, cooked liver and onions on Saturday and did a roast on Sunday."

"How entirely spoiled you've been!"

"We had dinner together last night. I cooked for her." There was suddenly something boyish and slightly embarrassed in his smile. "She's gone to such trouble for me, and I wanted to say thank you. It was only chops, you know my limits, but she seemed touched that I'd made the effort. She said it's years since a man asked her out to dinner and she couldn't recall that a chap had ever cooked for her before."

The phrase "out to dinner" had a hint of romantic

possibility about it, but this was only grilled lamb chops, wasn't it?

"That was very considerate of you."

"She said that too. I'm taking her out to tea on Thursday. You don't mind, do you?"

"No, of course, I don't mind. It's good you've made a friend."

He nodded, as if her words had confirmed something for him—but what? Stella was glad if he was happy, if he'd been well cared for in her absence, but was it quite nice that he'd been having *such* a jolly time with Mrs. Pendlebury? What would her mother think of that?

"Shall I put the kettle on?"

"There's some of that coconut cake in the tin. Try it. It's one of the best I've ever had."

Stella stood at the kitchen sink while she waited for the water to boil and watched her father tidying his tools away in the garden. New hanging baskets of fuchsias had also appeared, swaying slightly before the kitchen window now. Why did bedding plants suddenly seem to be in bloom everywhere and why had her father been humming as she'd walked away? She couldn't remember the last time she'd heard him hum. Had he had a nicer time with Mrs. Pendlebury than she'd had contemplating Michael and Cynthia's physicality, worrying about Mrs. Parr's credibility, and then interrogating her own relationship with the truth? What was it that her mother had written about cake and consequences?

*

Mrs. Pendlebury called in later that afternoon. Stella gave her the money that she owed her and a tin of Yardley talcum powder as a thank you. Mrs. Pendlebury told her about her father grilling chops and Stella observed the curious little smile on her face. It seemed to match the one that her father was presently wearing. And did she have lipstick on today? That was new, wasn't it? Standing in between the pair of them in the kitchen, and watching them exchanging those intriguing little looks, Stella felt like a bit of a gooseberry. Her mind skipped to an image of a basket of gooseberries and the sound of Freddie's voice rhyming John Donne in her ear. Her father couldn't possibly have whispered lines of poetry over the chops, could he?

As Mrs. Pendlebury was leaving, Stella noticed that she was wearing one of her mother's hats. It was a sweet little woven-straw hat stitched with raffia sunflowers. It had to be the same hat, didn't it? She supposed that her father must have decided to give it to Mrs. Pendlebury. It wouldn't have fitted Stella, and it had only been from Woolworth's, she recalled, but she felt oddly possessive of it as she watched Mrs. Pendlebury going down the path and opening the gate. Her father ought to have mentioned it to her, shouldn't he? What did it mean that he'd thought it appropriate to give Mrs. Pendlebury one of her mother's hats? This question troubled Stella.

Chapter Thirty-five

Mrs. Violet Birtley had responded to Stella's advertisement in the *Durham Chronicle*. She wrote that she was in possession of a recipe book written by her grandmother and suggested that Stella might be interested in her pan haggerty and singing hinnies. Stella had some qualms about leaving her father again so soon, but she couldn't resist the thought of the handed-down recipes and the musicality of the names.

Mrs. Birtley lived in a pit village to the east of Durham. Agnes Blenkinsop had written a hard-hitting piece for *Today's Woman* about challenging times in the coal-mining areas. She'd described despondent groups of men on street corners and scenes in soup kitchens for the unemployed. As she'd read it, Stella had wondered if Agnes had been trying to make a claim for journalistic worthiness and had leaned overly hard on the string section, but she realized now that it wasn't so. She passed boarded-up shops, pubs with their curtains drawn and long derelict-looking streets. She swerved around holes in the road and everywhere the paintwork seemed to be peeling. Everything about this place was broken down, crumbling and rusting; it didn't just seem depressed, there was a sense of a long-term abandonment, and she couldn't imagine how the corner shops might ever reopen. Men walked with their eyes down and hands in their pockets, just as Agnes had described, while children looked up and stared at her motor. Stella thought of the carefree chatter in London restaurants and the blithe prosperity of the square where Freddie lived. Could people really be wearing tennis flannels just a few hours' drive away? Getting heated over golf-club politics and worrying that their geraniums weren't going to put on a good show this summer? It might as well be a different country.

Stella knocked on the door of a terraced cottage. A widow in her sixties, Mrs. Birtley had bright green eyes, a wide, amused mouth and a singsong voice. She told Stella that she'd spent her working life in service, but had now retired, and held out hands that were twisted with arthritis.

Stella followed Mrs. Birtley through a dark, narrow passage and into a homely room. There was warmth coming from the range, a print of Queen Victoria over the mantelpiece and a lithograph Jesus looking down with tender, troubled eyes. Photographs of smiling children were pushed in between the coronation mugs and the pile of darning waiting on a chair suggested that three generations of a family perhaps lived here. The lace curtains were crisply white and the range was polished to a glossy black, but Stella couldn't help thinking back to being in Mrs. Parr's kitchen last week. Though she'd watched Dorothy Parr working hard, the loaded cake stands and the laughter of the holiday-makers seemed a long way from this place.

Mrs. Birtley boiled a kettle for tea and invited Stella to sit at the table. "You're from Yorkshire?" she asked.

"Yes, west of Halifax," Stella replied.

"You don't sound like it."

"Don't I? I've moved around a lot over the past few years." Though there was no judgment on Mrs. Birtley's face, Stella felt slightly guilty, slightly ashamed as she said it.

The tea was strong and Stella was glad of it. Mrs. Birtley opened a cake tin and offered her a slice of parkin. It was pleasantly bitter with treacle, but Stella found herself recalling Mrs. Parr's sugar-topped fruit pies and the spoonfuls of clotted cream.

Mrs. Birtley turned the pages of the recipe book while they drank tea and talked. Her mother and her grandmother before her had both been in service and three sets of handwriting followed on in this notebook. Stella liked the idea of recipes being passed on, that continuity, and the fact that some of the pages were splattered with batter and fat.

"We thought we had it hard," Mrs. Birtley said, "long days and always on our feet, but we didn't know how lucky we were."

"Do you honestly feel that?"

She explained that her son was presently unemployed, that he'd been laid off last year, and despite efforts to find work he presently had to draw the dole. "It doesn't do a man good," she said. "I see it on his face, more so every day. He walks miles, but there's no work going around here. He's always worked in the pit, like his father, and he's not trained to do anything else. It knocks a man's pride."

There was a mirror and a shaving razor by the side of the sink, which Stella supposed must belong to the son. What did he see as he looked into that glass? She pitied this man who must walk miles every day looking for something that might let him stand taller.

"I'm sorry," said Stella, but it felt like an inadequate response.

"Still, you're not here to hear me grumbling, are you?"

Mrs. Birtley pushed the notebook toward Stella. Turning the pages, she saw some recipes that were familiar, and others that were not. Pan haggerty wasn't dissimilar to a gratin dauphinoise (she could almost hear Freddie crowing that the English had got there first), but was fried in a pan in hot dripping. Singing hinnies were griddle cakes, it transpired, enriched with lard, flavored with currants and eaten spread with butter.

"They sizzle and sing on the girdle," Mrs. Birtley explained and smiled.

There was much use of potatoes in these recipes, Stella noticed, as she turned pages, lots of dumplings, leeks, dried peas and oats, and a wholesome sense of economy. These recipes suggested that the region had always been thrifty, but Stella heard pride, not complaint, in Mrs. Birtley's voice, a care and a particularity.

"I'd go back to work tomorrow, if I could," she said. "It's a rotten thing to watch your son struggling. It breaks a mother's heart. We have to be very careful with money at the moment, but it will get better," she said.

"I'm sure it will," Stella replied. The streets that she'd driven through had given her the impression of something already finished, a page in a history book turned, but she hoped it might not be so.

Mrs. Birtley encouraged her to copy out recipes and Stella told her that she'd credit her as the source. She thought about reaching for her purse and offering Mrs. Birtley something in exchange, but the polish on the fire brasses and the whiteness of the cloth on the mantel told her that such a gesture might not necessarily be welcome.

"It's a nice thing that you're doing," Mrs. Birtley said, as they parted at the door. "We shouldn't forget the old ways."

"No," Stella agreed.

She had a confusing mix of feelings as she drove back past the inactive pit head and the staring children on the street corner. Over the past year, she'd written several magazine articles on cheap, nourishing soups and how to stretch a shoulder of mutton through the week, but she hadn't realized that times were quite so hard up here. These people wouldn't care a hoot whether the food they ate was authentically English, Stella thought, where it came from and how it got here. These children just looked hungry. Nostalgia is a luxury for people with full bellies. It made Stella feel that what she was doing was decadent and irrelevant, but still she was glad that she'd seen this. Her book shouldn't be all clotted cream and oblivious Bath buns. This was the reality of England as much as that was. She perhaps wasn't being honest about everything, but she ought to acknowledge this truth.

Caroline Scott

Forgive me the liberty of writing to you on a matter which perhaps doesn't respond directly to your appeal, but you are interested in collecting information on the history of our diet, I believe, and I would contend that we live in history-making times. People don't expect places like Cheltenham to be touched by the current world depression in trade, but last winter the soup kitchen established by our branch of the Salvation Army provided 15,000 meals over three months. With the numbers of unemployed increasing, this winter is expected to produce yet more distress. Needless to say, we are now appealing for funds and would be grateful for your support. There is greater need than ever for real sympathy and charity at this time.

ROWLAND WALLACE, Cheltenham

It puzzles me why so many people presently oppose the distribution of food to the needy and hungry. Prolonged unemployment progressively undermines hope and pride, and thousands are now subsisting on tea and bread and margarine. I have observed that meat is seldom eaten more than once a week in these families, fresh milk is rarely on the table and vegetables, other than potatoes, have no part in this diet. It is not an answer to the fundamental problem, but a hot, nourishing meal in warm and friendly surroundings can offer some temporary respite to pockets and spirits, and isn't that worthwhile? I am happy to share a selection of economical, wholesome and tasty recipes that we're presently serving in our canteen and hope that you may find some use for them . . .

MARTHA MORRIS (Miss), Lincolnshire

*The weaving areas are now in a state of trade paralysis.
There are 22,000 cotton operatives in the Nelson district,
many now unemployed and others only partially employed.
With pits closing too, it feels as if the rhythm of industry is
slowing across the region—and when will it come back? The
Town Council here is providing free meals for necessitous
schoolchildren, a number of soup kitchens have opened,
and food parcels are being distributed. There is much quiet
suffering in the town, but also much unostentatious giving.
These things do not find their way into the columns of the
Press and any assistance would be appreciated.*

RUTH THOMAS (Mrs.), Nelson, Lancashire

*You are possibly aware of the Great National Hunger March,
planned for September. We wish to protest to the government
against the application of the Means Test and the general
conditions prevalent in the ranks of the unemployed. Parties
from every corner of the United Kingdom will converge
on London where we will present a petition of one million
signatures to the House of Commons. Destitution and
degradation are being experienced throughout the country and
action is needed. In my own county of Durham more than
ninety collieries have closed over the last few months, many
thousands of men have lost their employment, and there is
presently no prospect of the situation brightening. Donations
in support of the marchers and parcels of food, boots, socks and
blankets would be received with gratitude.*

GEORGE ROBINSON, Sunderland

Chapter Thirty-six

"I'm worried that I might get found out," she admitted to Freddie. Stella wanted him to keep his eyes on the road, but she did need to share her concerns with someone. Doubts had started whispering in her ears over the past month; they'd recently evolved wings too and had been trying them out inside her chest cavity this week.

"Get found out?" He grinned as he glanced across at her. "How serious you make it sound. How darlingly your brow creases! You've hardly been selling national secrets, have you?"

"But if it comes out that I've made things up, if I can't verify my sources, Mr. Williamson will lose his confidence in me."

"Oh, your face, Stella! It's a picture. How you fret over your Mr. Williamson's good opinion. But, sweet girl, what's the worst that can happen? No one is going to sue you, are they? You're not defaming anyone. And, at the end of the day, it's a nice book about food which will be read and enjoyed by housewives. That's your target market, isn't it? You're not aiming at academics, are you? I'm sure that if you were to put on a flattering blouse and your best smile, dear Mr. Williamson would forgive you for any little errors."

Would he? But Stella didn't want it to be like that. She wanted Mr. Williamson to respect her, to trust her, to esteem her. Was this how Freddie saw her? As someone who wrote nice little books for housewives? For all that he peppered his sentences with endearments, how insubstantial he made her work sound—and she felt slightly affronted on behalf of the housewives. (She heard their collective intake of breath and saw them giving Freddie a sideways look.) As he laughed now, and batted her concerns away, Stella wondered whether she had been foolish to trust his judgment. Freddie's opinions and suggestions were threaded all through her text. As Stella watched the hedgerows slipping by, she asked herself whether that might have been unwise.

"But I'll look unprofessional. I'd feel ashamed."

"Where has this defeatism come from? Where's your bravado today?" He frowned at her as he looked across. "You know that people who cower get trodden on."

But she was increasingly feeling that she had reasons to slump her shoulders. And bravado couldn't deflect justified accusations of dishonesty, could it?

Freddie had invited her down because his friend Edwin was hosting a dinner. Stella was curious to see Freddie's social circle and she had felt complimented that he wanted to introduce her to his friends. It also happened that he'd telephoned on the same morning that the invitation to

Michael and Cynthia's wedding had arrived. Stella had felt the need to have a brandy and a sit down after she'd opened the envelope. Seeing their embossed names above the word "Marriage" had almost certainly softened her up for Freddie's solicitations. The wedding was at the end of September, eight weeks away. Was it awful of her to hope that Cynthia might fall under an omnibus before then?

It had been a dove-colored morning when Stella had left home, a soft gray sky touched with pink at the horizon. It had brightened after the rain, though, and everything was edged with gold this afternoon, like the pages of a precious book. Mist clung on in hollows, and water was running at the side of the road, but the hedgerows glittered now, wood pigeons lifting from wheat fields, and the hills were burnished bronze. Stella breathed in a scent of fallen leaves and wood fires, and vaguely wished for a less complicated life in which she might simply sit and evaluate the light with a box of watercolors on her lap.

As they'd driven south toward Cirencester, they'd passed several properties that could have auditioned as backdrops for Jane Austen novels, but she was a little surprised to be passing between tall gate pillars now and then down a sweeping driveway. She saw fine old cedar trees, thickets of ancient rhododendrons and the glimmer of an ornamental lake in the distance. Stella imagined that there might well be a seashell grotto, a temple folly and a Chinese pagoda somewhere out there in the well-kempt green folds. There was a lot of clipped box hedging as they approached the house, sculpted shrubberies, statues of men in togas, stone stags and marble nymphs pursued by satyrs.

"Is the property terrifically old?"

"It looks early eighteenth-century, doesn't it? But it's not, actually. Edwin's grandfather was something in the Arts and Crafts movement." Freddie wafted a hand to indicate an imprecision around the something. "It's Queen Anne Revival, really, but it does have excellent parkland."

The house was the size of Halifax town hall. Its stone-work was rose-gold in the sunlight and a whole volume could have been written about its architectural whimsies. Baroque clouds rolled smoothly behind it, like wheeled-on stage props—in fact the whole prospect before her might have been a fanciful theatrical backcloth. Stella didn't know anyone who lived in a Queen Anne–style property (revived, or not) and who had liveried footmen on their front steps. She was half tempted to ask the man by the door for a ticket and to inquire as to the whereabouts of the café and gift shop. Three days ago she'd been stepping into Violet Birtley's two-up two-down. As she looked up at this house, at its great height of golden columns, pilasters and pediments, the contrast couldn't be greater.

The interior was all armorial shields, paintings of fox-hounds, worn brocade and boisterous spaniels. There was a smell of damp mackintoshes, antique dust and fusty dog beds. They took glasses of sherry from a tray and walked into a drawing room that had overfussy curtain arrangements, a lot of inlaid-marble tables and unsympathetic modern lighting. The elaborate plasterwork ceiling looked like a skillful effort with piped royal icing and Stella was tempted to say something about wedding cakes, but thought better of it, lest Freddie tell her women always said that. Young men in tweeds lounged untidily on tasseled Knole sofas, their faces lifting and turning toward them now.

"Freddie, you old rascal! How the devil are you?"

Freddie's friends were loud and confident. Several of them had been to the same minor public school, it transpired, and some joshing and horseplay ensued. They would have gone through all the verses of the school song had the excitable barking of the dogs not put a stop to it. They were all there with wives, apart from a chap in wire-rimmed spectacles, called Quentin, who said that he preferred the atmosphere of libraries. Given this particular selection of wives, Stella could sympathize. The women had expensive haircuts, satin sleeves, understated family diamonds, and seemed to be trying to score points off one another. Stella didn't warm to these women and their judgmental eyes, and so she'd found herself in a huddle with Freddie and his friends Aubrey and Anthony before dinner.

It was peculiar to listen to Freddie telling them about her book. Stella had felt belittled by him earlier—he'd made her feel trivial—but he seemed very keen to talk about her work now. He went on about food imports, security and national character, about pride and the morale of the working man. Stella recognized lines of her own text being quoted, but the slant that Freddie was putting on it didn't quite accord with her own conclusions.

"You know, you can buy Polish, Russian and Estonian bacon in grocers' shops in Cirencester now," Aubrey said. He had pale gray-blue eyes and the sort of complexion that her mother would have called "unfortunate." "Try to buy Wiltshire bacon, try to shop patriotically, and you can't! That's where it's all gone wrong. I mean, communist bacon!"

"Drive across this country and you'll see fields full of thistles, but you won't see any pigs," Anthony put in. "We ought to be getting the unemployed onto the fields. They'd be glad of it and it would build character. Once upon a time, Britain reared the finest livestock in the world and there was no meat superior. Of course, all the foreigners started their herds from British stocks. That's right, isn't it?"

"Well . . ." said Stella.

"It's time people started thinking about their food choices," Freddie said, "making patriotic decisions. Housewives buy imported tinned peas because that's convenient, but they could buy dried English peas for a fraction of the price and get far more nutrition from them. It's pure ignorance. No wonder our race is deteriorating. As the housewife picks up her French tin of peas and her can of pineapple from Malaya, she ought to be aware of the implications of her choices. That's why Stella's work is so valuable."

"Splendid stuff," said Aubrey, and put a hand out to squeeze Stella's arm.

She felt herself being congratulated, but couldn't help

thinking that if the woman of the house didn't have the time to boil dried peas, wasn't it a good thing that she had an option? And if tinned pineapple made her family happy, who had the right to deny them that? Who was she to tell people what they ought to be eating? Surely it was difficult enough to feed a family these days without patriotism being thrown into the mix?

Some of Aubrey's opinions made Stella's eyes widen, and she whispered as much to Freddie as they walked through to the dining room. Aubrey was hoping to stand as a parliamentary candidate, Freddie said, so he might be inclined to tub-thump, but his values were sound. It alarmed Stella that Freddie could defend Aubrey's views on the Means Test and Jewish financiers.

"He wouldn't say those things in public, would he?"

"Not in so many words, but it's what everyone thinks behind closed doors, isn't it?"

Not behind my doors, Stella thought. Did Freddie really believe that?

There was a hint of Masonic hall about the dining room. The highly patterned carpet, wallpaper and curtains were all competing for attention and the overall result was oppressive. Stella couldn't help beginning to mentally redecorate as she settled onto a dining chair upholstered in unyielding burgundy leather. This room might be so much nicer if it were lighter, and all those fringed damask drapes would definitely have to go. There were wax fruits under glass domes on the sideboard, paintings of anemic-looking women petting lambs, and the fireplace was like a tomb. The spaniels nudged and panted under the table. Altogether, it was a most unappetizing room, Stella felt.

She found herself seated between Aubrey's wife, Flora, and a former work colleague from Freddie's London days, called Crispin. Flora had a lot to say about various women who Stella had never met, and Crispin talked dryly about national reconstruction, sweated labor and industrial decay. Did they all have ambitions to be political candidates? Stella stifled a yawn. As she listened to Crispin boring on about the flight of gold and the folly of free trade, she caught Freddie's eye across the table and he winked.

Stella wasn't sure how to respond. Did the wink mean that he found these people tiresome and pompous too? But he was participating in those conversations, wasn't he? He was expressing the same views. It is enlightening to meet a person's friends, Stella considered, and this doesn't always show them to be the character we expect. In private, Freddie was funny and self-deprecating. He was cultured, knowledgable and charismatic. But what did it say about him that the friends he chose were so humourless and had opinions that made Stella feel distinctly uneasy?

The conversation moved to Russia, to communism, to public-sector wages, to youth organization and how the industrial situation was a nightmare, and then everyone put their hands up in despair. They all had views to share about the working man, and what the North needed, but Stella wondered how many of them had ever ventured beyond

Birmingham. Had they ever spoken to a mill-hand, a miner or a riveter? Could they find Sunderland on a map? There was something self-satisfied and hectoring in the way they spoke, she thought, and in their company Freddie assumed this personality too. They made him boorish, harder than the man who had rescued her in his furniture van, and even his voice seemed to have changed tonight. As Stella watched him across the table, she felt that she didn't actually like this version of Freddie much. For a man who was normally so charming, he was rendered strangely charmless by this company.

Flora, sitting to Stella's left, pushed her food around her plate and put very little of it into her mouth. She appeared to be trying to hide a slice of roast beef under a pile of runner beans now.

"I'm not a big eater," she said, evidently realizing that Stella had clocked the stealth with the beans. "I don't really like food, I'm afraid, apart from custard creams and pink wafer biscuits. I find having to think about meals for Aubrey and the children such a bore. It's tiresome when these things don't interest you, you know? Cook used to expect me to discuss the week's menus with her, but she's realized what a chore this is for me, and I leave it up to her now. I'm relieved not to have to do it, if I'm honest."

She gave Stella a slightly penetrating stare, which suggested there might be a subtext here, some confidence she'd like to share, but then Crispin had butted in and was talking about how hard it was to retain reliable servants.

Nobody remarked on the food while they ate, which Stella found rather odd—but then perhaps it was better not to overanalyze this particular dinner. After a nondescript bowl of Brown Windsor soup (she stirred in lots of pepper), they were served leather-hard roast beef, then a steamed jam pudding and custard. Though they ate off crested porcelain, and with weighty silver cutlery, it was like bad canteen food. It surprised Stella that no one commented on the fact that the vegetables had been boiled to the edge of their existence, that there was no seasoning in the mashed potato and that the custard tasted like the milk had scorched, but then they were all occupied making their competing speeches. Food seemed to be merely fuel for political arguments. It was all polemic and no pleasure.

"And another thing, why do I keep seeing Gorgonzola and Gruyère in our shops?" Edwin asked, as Stilton and port circulated. "What's wrong with Stilton? Every housewife in the land should resolve to buy British cheese and should insist on getting it."

"Hear, hear," said Freddie.

But not everyone could afford Stilton, could they? And foreign cheese wasn't to blame for the industrial situation, was it? Men weren't queuing outside Labour Exchanges because of Gorgonzola, were they? She poked at her rather dried-up piece of Stilton and would gladly have exchanged it for a nice slice of Gruyère. It tasted of crusty old gentlemen's clubs, baize-covered card tables and gout.

"We imported food because it was cheaper," said Aubrey

in a podium voice, "but then the outside world bought the products of our industry. The world has changed now, though. They're still happy to sell us cheap food, but they're not buying our exports any longer. Cheap food becomes dear food when it leaves millions of men unemployed."

"Germany is getting it right," Crispin said. "Their imports of wheat are a fraction of what they were. German people eat bread made from German grains now. They're pushing for self-sufficiency, while we let the world dump cheap wheat on us. We should be extending tariff walls here too."

"I read that the Nazis would like to ban women from smoking. They think they're unpatriotically risking the Fatherland's fertility," Stella said, exhaling smoke. "I'm afraid I wouldn't stand for being told that."

"It's just part of a bigger policy, a bigger ideology," said Freddie, as if that justified it. Stella decided it didn't and blew smoke in his direction.

She looked down to see a pug dog licking something off her shoe. It lifted its head, blinked eyes like shiny black marbles, and scratched at the pink satin bow that was tied around its neck. At this moment, Stella felt more tenderness and understanding for this plump, unpretty little dog than for any other soul in this room. She leaned down, fed it her piece of Stilton and untied the ridiculous ribbon from around its neck.

The conversation moved on to Mussolini, and Stella heard Freddie airing views on how a strong arm was needed. Mussolini was efficient, they all agreed, he had vision and drive, and there was no litter on the streets in Italy. Stella recalled Dilys calling Mussolini a thug. And Il Duce had a low opinion of women, didn't he? Hadn't he said that they were the inferior sex and should never be taken seriously? These weren't her people, Stella thought, as she listened to them talking. What was she doing here? These weren't her views. And yet had she written a book that justified their arguments?

"You work for women's magazines, don't you?" Crispin asked. He had a nasty little red moustache, which made Stella think about hog-bristle scrubbing brushes.

"I write the cookery column for *Today's Woman* magazine," she replied. "It's not an old-fashioned sponge cake and scouring-powder column. I'm writing for the modern woman and I'm interested in how changes in society, education and technology are impacting their lives." He didn't need to know that she wrote pieces on ways to keep lard fresh, tricks with tinned salmon, and how to be imaginative with root vegetables.

"Interesting," said Crispin. "It's useful to have female perspective and influence."

Influence? Did these men expect her to use that perceived influence on their behalf?

"My sister sometimes buys *Today's Woman*," said Flora, "but my father won't have it in the house. He says those sorts of magazines encourage notions that aren't quite ladylike."

Stella suspected that Flora's father might consider education to be unladylike too. He probably thought that young women ought to be out hunting, getting a nice healthy flush in their cheeks, not sitting in libraries and acquiring thick ankles. "It's exciting to learn that I'm writing for a subversive publication."

"We'd all like to see Freddie settling down," Flora went on, giving her an evaluating look. She had an elfin prettiness, with her wide eyes and retroussé nose, but a goblin malice occasionally seemed to sharpen her teeth. "It's about time that he got married and started a family. It seems so silly that he lives over that shop when he has a perfectly lovely house. He only goes there when he's shooting, but it would make a delightful family home. Has he shown it to you yet?"

"He hasn't."

"Oh, I'm sure he will. It's got excellent stables too. He rides marvelously, you know, and he's a fine fencer."

"Really?" Flora was giving Freddie an undisguised admiring look from across the table and Stella couldn't help wondering if she'd been one of his conquests too. He'd probably get a thrill out of sleeping with the wives of his friends.

"Freddie loves his home," Flora continued, still in the effusive tone. "He's always moving the furniture and pictures round. He adores doing that. Whenever we visit, he seems to have swapped it all around. He puts such a lot of thought into his furnishings. Men are so rarely like that, don't you find? Do you have an interest in antiques too?"

"I'm susceptible to the charms of Georgian jelly molds, but I don't have Freddie's expertise."

Stella suspected there would be no artificially antiqued furniture in Freddie's own home. She could visualize him fussing around with footstools and fencing trophies, plumping cushions and straightening pictures, and standing back to admire the effect. It would all be in self-consciously good taste. She would be curious to see the furnishings that he invested so much thought in, but as Flora's eyes toured her person, Stella felt as if she was being appraised as breeding stock. Had Freddie considered moving her into his delightful family home? Was tonight an audition for that role? Might she be expected to host dinners for these awful people there and give him a tribe of little Freddies? This vision wasn't a prospect that appealed, however exemplary his furnishings and sword play might be. Stella took a mouthful of wine and decided that there was much to recommend the life of a confirmed spinster.

"You needn't have booked the hotel," Freddie said, as they drove back. He looked toward her and she saw his eyes glinting. "That was very proper of you. I'd assumed we'd got past all of that."

"I'm tired," she said, "and I want to head off early tomorrow morning. The weeks seem to be racing by fast now and I'm under pressure to get the manuscript completed."

"You know what they say about all work and no play?"

Stella heard the challenge in his voice. Was he drunk? He was driving rather erratically. The headlights combed through trees, walls loomed suddenly out of the darkness and he stood on the brakes on bends. "I'm sorry, but I do need to be diligently dull."

"I thought we could perhaps go over to Oxford together for luncheon tomorrow. I know a place that does a top-hole roast. I was talking about our book with Edwin tonight and he had some excellent suggestions. We might go through them together tomorrow."

"*My* book!" Stella wanted to say, but managed to bite the words back. She didn't want any of Edwin's insights. She didn't want any more of Freddie's edits. She felt that she'd already had more than enough of that.

Stella let him kiss her in the doorway of the hotel, but as his hands began to probe under her jacket, she stepped back.

"What?" he said. "You haven't gone frigid on me, have you?"

He took a step toward her, grinned rather wolfishly, and began to kiss her neck.

"Please, Freddie. I've got a long journey back tomorrow and I just want to get some sleep."

"Oh, come on," he cajoled. She felt his breath in her ear. "I've introduced you to my friends tonight. That means something, doesn't it? I've told them that we're walking out together. I've had to sit looking at you from across that table all night and now I want to see a bit more."

"Walking out together?"

"Well, that's what this is, isn't it?" His hands were inside her jacket again and toying with the buttons of her blouse now. Did those words give him the right to do that?

"But we've never talked about that. We've not had that conversation."

He looked up from his campaign on her blouse buttons and laughed. "You make it sound as if we ought to have a debate about it! Surely my intentions have always been clear? You know I pranged that clutch business for you, don't you?"

She pulled back. "I'm sorry? I don't follow."

"I slipped Watkins some money. He could have done the job the next day. Your motor might have been fixed and back on the road within twenty-four hours, but I wanted to keep you here. I liked you, you see. I felt it straightaway. You amuse me, Stella, and it has to be said that you are tremendously easy on the eye. Aubrey said that to me tonight. You're just my sort."

She disentangled herself from his arms. "You paid the garage to slow the repairs down? To make a bigger job of it than it was? How could you do that?"

"Take it as a compliment, silly! That's what it was. Oh, don't look so outraged! It's all worked out well, hasn't it?" His lips tightened across his teeth, but the smile didn't reach his eyes.

"But I paid nearly eight pounds for those repairs! And then there was a week of hotel bills. It was a significant expense for me. You knew that!"

"I did try to persuade you to move over to the flat. If you'd been a little less prim, you might have saved yourself some money."

"Less prim?"

"Less conventional. Less concerned for your precious middle-class respectability." He said the word derisively. "Well, we got there eventually, didn't we? And I can't recall that you had any complaints." He took the lapels of her jacket in his hands.

"I can't believe you did that."

"What? Oh, come on! You're not going to be foolish about this, are you? I would never have told you if I thought you'd be oversensitive about it. But, hell, you look so serious suddenly! Come up to the flat and have a drink. It'll loosen you up. I didn't throw that money away, did I? Come on, Stella," he coaxed. "Be a sport."

"No, Freddie, I want to go in. I want to go to bed, *my own* bed."

He let go of her lapels then, his hands lowered to her wrists, and he looked her up and down. "You disappoint me," he said.

She wanted to say that he disappointed her too, but he was gripping her wrists tightly now and that hardness was back in his voice. She could smell the brandy on his breath and see something dangerous in his eyes. She didn't know whether he would let her go.

"Nobody likes a tease," he said. "Haven't I helped you? Haven't I been patient with you? There's a part of that bargain that you have to fullfil too."

"Freddie, *please.*"

"Don't be a silly bitch."

*

Stella didn't cry because it had hurt as Freddie gripped her arms, or because she'd felt pressured by him. They weren't tears of fear or pain. She cried for her own naivety, for the fact that she'd chosen to ignore the warning signs, for her carelessness, for her foolishness, for her battered, bruised pride.

Chapter Thirty-seven

Stella turned through the pages of the typescript. Phrases that she'd heard last night kept leaping out at her, but these weren't her words or her opinions, were they? She heard herself making statements about food security, about import quotas and tariffs, and these words might as well have been coming straight out of Freddie's mouth. She lit a cigarette and noticed the tremble in her hand.

Stella pushed the manuscript away. It wasn't like her to let herself be manipulated in this way. She'd always prided herself on being independent. She wasn't a pliable or gullible person, but somehow it seemed that Freddie's voice and views had worked their way into her head over the past few months, and now they were all over her pages. Why had she listened to him? How had she let that happen?

But then there were many things that she shouldn't have allowed to happen. Stella's mind kept taking her back to the words that Freddie had said last night. His altered tone of voice. How he'd been. What he'd done. She'd driven home very slowly and carefully, feeling alternately dazed and all too wide awake. It had taken her hours, and if her father hadn't been there, she might have sunk to the hall floor after she'd closed the door. She'd wanted him to put his arms around her and say that everything would be well, but instead she'd climbed the stairs and told him that she was longing for a bath. She'd seen the prints left on her skin by Freddie's fingers then, the bracelets of bruises around the tops of her arms, and her teeth had chattered as she'd scrubbed at herself with a loofah. Making eye contact with her reflection in the mirror afterward, she had felt like she'd shed a layer of self. But how many layers did a person have to lose?

Though she'd lit the range and put on one of her mother's jumpers, she was still shivering. She wanted to talk to her mother, to tell her all of it, and then to feel the grip of her hand and the reassurance of her voice. Stella could have wept like a child for her mother at this moment, for the absence of her when she needed her, but she made herself sit at the kitchen table and focus on what she had to do to rid her manuscript of Freddie's voice. She must do that now. As she'd scrubbed him from her skin, so too she needed to erase him from her pages.

It wasn't just that Freddie's political opinions had wound their way into her text, she was also aware of all the lies that she and him had concocted together. Where the facts didn't fit, they'd adjusted them. If there was no evidence to support a theory, they had simply made it up. They had laughed together as they had devised these stories. She realized now that it had merely been fun to Freddie. It was an amusement. She had been an amusement. But this was her career. She was risking her reputation and he had encouraged her to do that. How could she have trusted him? Stella felt angry with him this evening—fiercely, tremblingly angry—but more than that she was angry with herself. This shame, this self-recrimination, hurt more than the bruises. She stubbed her cigarette out. She couldn't let this book be published.

Stella turned through the typescript and now saw risks on every page. Every paragraph was set with traps that might snap and ensnare her. Could she salvage it? The sensible thing would be to go through the text and to delete every statement that she couldn't confidently verify. But that was a good portion of the manuscript, as much as a third of the text, and she had to deliver it by November. There wasn't enough time to do that, was there? Stella sat at the kitchen table with her head in her hands.

She made a pot of strong coffee, smoked another three cigarettes, and told herself that she needed to be practical. What were the odds of the letter writers she'd invented being exposed as frauds? She'd probably get away with that, she calculated. In all likelihood, no one would require her to produce sources to document the invented memories of farmers' wives and the recollections of made-up kitchen maids—these characters were sufficiently obscure—but she'd pushed it too far, hadn't she? She'd been foolish to invent stories about significant figures that academics spent their whole lives minutely researching. They were flights of fancy supported only by the flimsiest of hints and likelihoods. How had this ever seemed like an intelligent idea? Stella wished that she could wind back the clock six months and shake herself firmly by the shoulders.

She would start excising now, but the thought occurred that she'd already mentioned some of these stories to Mr. Williamson. She'd actually boasted about having secured these gems. Stella recalled how he'd nodded his head when they met in the restaurant, and talked of his faith in her being vindicated. If she was to back-pedal now, that faith would be undermined. But if she risked leaving these fabrications in and then was exposed after publication, wouldn't the embarrassment, the disappointment, be all the worse?

Could she seek her father's advice? Might Dilys understand? If she couldn't share it with her mother, she wanted to tell Michael—to tell him everything that had happened. She wanted to bury her head in his chest, feel his safe arms around her and to hear anger in his voice on her behalf. But their relationship would never be like that again, would it? Stella hugged her arms to her chest and rocked in her chair. She felt foolish this evening, embarrassed, vulnerable and overwhelmingly alone.

Chapter Thirty-eight

Dilys wasn't given to physical demonstrations; there was an aura about her that informed you that unsolicited intimacy might cause offense. One didn't trespass beyond Dilys' boundaries, they were to be respected, but she patted Stella's shoulder now and said, "There, there, my dear girl."

Stella really hadn't wanted to cry. As she'd stood on Dilys' doorstep, she'd bitten the inside of her mouth and taken a deep breath, but she found herself sitting on her sofa now, with a glass of sloe gin and Dilys' handkerchief in her hands.

"I am sorry. What must you think of me? What a perfect idiot."

"No, you mustn't apologize."

Dilys had been working in the back garden and was wearing a navy Guernsey, what appeared to be a pair of men's tweed trousers and mud-caked boots. The ensemble made her look capable and doughty. She might have been off to man a lifeboat or about to ascend Great Gable. There was something reassuring about Dilys' tweed knees.

"Do you want to tell me about it?" she asked.

"I seem to have been rather stupid," Stella said.

She'd come to regard Dilys as a friend over the past year, but they were friends who discussed work, politics, ethics, not messy, embarrassing personal feelings. Dilys had a certain enigmatic remoteness, and she was clearly more comfortable discussing Higher Things, so Stella felt like she was crossing a boundary now. Or tumbling downhill. Dilys would think her a fool, wouldn't she?

"An error of judgment?"

Stella nodded. "I've always considered myself to be a reasonably sensible person, and a good judge of character, but recent evidence suggests otherwise. My compass seems to have been demagnetized and I've been blundering around in some horrifically unwise directions." She looked up and saw Dilys' frown. "I can't imagine you've ever been so stupid as I've been recently."

Stella had formed the impression that Dilys had lived A Life prior to moving to Hatherstall. There were clues in her collection of antique corkscrews and in the lines around her eyes, but she rarely gave away more than hints of once-upon-a-time adventures and excesses. She habitually kept her conversation in the present tense, the eighteenth century, or the spiritual realm, and her tone was always practical and composed. So it surprised Stella as she seemed to shift gear now.

"Oh, don't you believe it! I made some hideous mistakes when I was younger. So terribly embarrassing when you think back. We all do, you know?" Dilys took her glasses off and polished them on her tweed knees. "I take it that the character you misjudged was a man?"

345

Stella dried her eyes, sat up and took a mouthful of sloe gin. "It was never anything serious; I wasn't expecting it to go anywhere, but I didn't think he was a bad man. It turns out that he is, though. He's really rather a rotter."

"I've encountered a few wolves in sheep's clothing in my time. Some frightful shits!" Dilys laughed and then cringed. She took out her cigarette case and offered it to Stella. "They disguise themselves well. You don't see it until they show their incisors and then it's generally too late."

Stella thought about Freddie's expensive white teeth and his mouth in a snarl of anger. She'd always known that he wasn't whiter-than-white—she'd made her mind up over the dinner that she didn't intend to see him again—but she hadn't expected him to turn into a wolf. He had frightened her then. There didn't seem to be a limit to what he might do.

"I think I might renounce men."

"I've long been of the opinion that men look better from a distance. Like the Cairngorms. I bet even Coleridge and Shelley were very trying up close. All that poetic melancholy and laudanum! I recall that Coleridge was terrifically fussy over the boiling of eggs." Dilys drew thoughtfully on her cigarette. "There's a lot to be said for the company of books and cats. They never keep you waiting, bore on about the finer rules of cricket or take more than you want to give."

Stella looked at Dilys. She hadn't told her what Freddie had done, but she saw a perceptiveness in her eyes. Dilys had occasionally mentioned the existence of a quondam husband (it had taken Stella by surprise the first time), referring to him in the same casual way that one might drop a childhood case of whooping cough into conversation. What had happened to him? Was she widowed, divorced or were they just estranged? There were no family photographs on display anywhere in this house, were there? And how old was she? She might be anything between thirty and fifty. It struck Stella then that she knew very little about Dilys, really. Or, that is to say, she knew a great deal about her opinions on commercial chicken farming and fascism, but hardly anything about her personal history. Should she have asked? Could she still ask?

"Why do we let men run countries and companies and families?"

"God knows, but it's about time it stopped. You love your father dearly, though, don't you? I see that."

"He's cast from an old-fashioned mold. They don't make them like that any longer."

"You're lucky." Dilys took the cigarette from her mouth and frowned at it. "Work can be a great healer, you know. Sometimes it's good to bury yourself in it. I've always found that it helps me to get my sense of perspective back."

Stella hesitated as to whether to tell Dilys that her sense of perspective had gone awry in her working life too, that everything seemed to be distorted and out of proportion on the pages she'd been writing, but perhaps she'd already embarrassed herself enough for one day?

"You're right, of course. I mean to give myself a good shake and then get on with it. I've got such a lot to do over the next couple of months."

"But if you want to talk, I'm here, you know? I've just signed up to help with the collection for the Unemployed Fund. They're expecting to be overwhelmed this winter. Isn't it awful? I've promised to write them a pamphlet of tips for thrifty living too. Perhaps you could help me with that? It goes with the territory of choosing writing as a career, doesn't it?"

Stella recalled Freddie talking about the unemployed needing to be weaned off charity, about lethargy and addiction to soup kitchens and doles. How had she sat and listened to that?

"I'd be glad to help, if I can."

"Have I ever told you that my father cut me off when I was nineteen?" Dilys relit her cigarette and breathed smoke out slowly. "He told me that if I was determined to be a bluestocking, I couldn't expect him to support that life. He didn't leave me a penny when he died; my brother inherited everything, but he's frittered it all away on racehorses and ill-advised investments. Money hasn't made him happy. He's terribly, pitifully sad. I feel very sorry for him, to be honest. Meanwhile, my threadbare bluestocking life has given me great satisfaction. I've traveled all over Europe for work, met painters, poets, prophets and revolutionaries, and I still sit down at my desk each morning with a feeling of exhilaration. I might have no savings, but I feel rich in experiences and fortunate for that. We're fortunate." She put a hand to Stella's arm. "When you look around at other people's lives, you realize that, don't you think?"

Stella recalled the faces of Freddie's friends around the dinner table two days ago and realized that she wouldn't want to be any of those people. Not for one moment would she trade her life for theirs. She didn't envy them their diamonds, their confidence or their social connections. She had friends, a father who loved her and, if she put some energy and application into her editing now, there could still be an exciting career ahead of her, couldn't there? How fortunate was that?

"You're absolutely right," she agreed.

Chapter Thirty-nine

Stella jumped as she heard the telephone ring. She'd been working at the kitchen table all morning and was absorbed in her deletions and insertions. Might it be Michael? As she picked up the receiver, she wanted to hear his voice. She almost dropped the phone when she heard Freddie speaking out of the Bakelite.

"I wondered if you might fancy getting together this weekend?" he said. His tone was bright and untroubled. "Would you be free?"

Stella wasn't sure what to say for a moment. She hadn't expected to hear from him again, and the shock of his voice now speaking here in her kitchen left her without words. She looked around at the familiar walls. His voice had seemed to change the lighting in the room. Could she just put the receiver down?

"Stella?" Freddie said. "Are you there?"

Wasn't he embarrassed about the way he'd behaved last week? Given the manner in which they'd parted, she'd assumed there'd be no further contact between them. But he was upbeat, amiable Freddie again now. She might just have imagined the grip of his hands on her arms and his hot, angry words in her ear. Had that meant nothing to him? Did he not feel ashamed? Could he simply have forgotten?

"There's a fete on in Cirencester and it might be a giggle. What do you think? I had dinner with Aubrey last night and he gave me a brilliant angle for your book. I really want to talk it over with you, and they do an excellent afternoon tea at The Feathers. You'd love it. They have three-tiered cake stands, heavenly scones and the most delicious little sandwiches. Oh, come on, tell me I can tempt you!"

His voice was so cheerful and light that Stella began asking herself if she might have been mistaken in her memory. Yes, she'd had quite a bit to drink that night. Could she have remembered it wrongly? Could she, in recollection, be making the scene into something uglier than it actually was? But she hadn't dreamed the bruises, had she?

"Stella?" he said. "Can you hear me? Is there a problem with the line?"

"No, Freddie. I can hear you perfectly well." Her own voice sounded flat. "I'm sorry, but I have a prior engagement this weekend."

"Let's get together next weekend, then. What do you say?" She could hear him smiling. "Surely you could drag yourself away from the tome for one day, couldn't you?"

"No, I don't think I could."

"You're not still being foolish about that garage business, are you? I've worried that you might. I wish I hadn't told you now. But I apologized, didn't I? I admitted it. Wasn't it better to be honest? You know I did it for all the best reasons."

He was accustomed to getting what he wanted, Stella thought, as she listened to the cajoling note in his voice. He was used to apologizing and being forgiven. Things would always fall into place for Freddie. It would always work out. Women would always fall into line. How many times had he done this before? She had an image of his hands holding her lapels and heard Dilys' voice saying "a frightful shit."

"Yes," she said. "But the fact that you admitted it and expected to be able to laugh it off rather sums matters up. I'm sorry, Freddie. I don't want to meet up again."

"But, Stella, that's ludicrous! That's stupidly oversensitive of you. I thought better of you than that. Haven't we been having fun together? Haven't I helped you? Stella—"

"Goodbye, Freddie."

Stella sat on the back step and tried to steady her breath. The matches had spilled out of the box as she'd attempted to light a cigarette. Sitting here, among the scattered matches, she knew she'd done the right thing, the sensible thing. She just wished she'd done it sooner.

"BONE SOUP"

[From the notebook of Elizabeth Douglas, 1920]

I felt slightly ashamed of myself for raising my voice in the queue at the grocer's. I felt embarrassed. But I'm not sorry that I said what I did. In fact, I now really rather regret that I didn't slap him.

He'd been standing behind me in the queue. I'd been conscious of him watching me and standing just an inch or two too close. When he'd started talking it was about the items in my shopping basket and, telling myself then that he was just being friendly, I'd turned to him and smiled. I should have known it wasn't harmless friendliness.

"What are you making your Charlie for his tea?" he'd asked.

I'd told him that I was planning to make my beef bone broth and he'd made a face at that.

"Poor old Charlie!" he'd said. "Bone soup? Are you hard up? What sort of a meal is that for a man after a day's graft? A man needs a piece of meat, woman! You know, I've always rather envied Charlie, but I'm having second thoughts if that's how you feed your husband."

I didn't like the way that he said it, the grin on his face or how his eyes looked me up and down. Who was he to question what I feed my family? I always put time, thought and care into my cooking, and while we might have to be careful about money at the moment, I feed them well. I don't see why I should listen to any man telling me how to feed my family, certainly not a man like Raymond Metcalf, who has never had to count the pennies in his pockets and make them stretch through the week.

When I got home I told Charlie about it, and how I'd replied—after all, I knew that it would get repeated back to him. I'd worried that he might be angry, what with Raymond now being on the council and a man of some influence, but he'd laughed. He kissed me and told me that he was proud of me for speaking up. He really is the best of men.

Of course, I didn't tell Charlie what Raymond had said next. He'd leaned in close to me, so close that I could smell the cigarettes on his breath, and had whispered into my ear that he knew of a way to put some extra money in my purse. He could make things easier for me, he'd said, we could come to a little arrangement, and Charlie need never know. I'd understood straightaway what he meant, I'd read it on his face, even before he put a hand on my waist. I was astonished and livid, and wanted to tell him what I thought of him and his little arrangements, but I turned my back instead. It took all my self-control not to speak.

The queue seemed to move forward so slowly then and all the while I could feel Raymond's breath on the back of my neck. A man shouldn't get away with making a remark like that to a woman, should he? It makes me angry that my daughter must grow up in a world where men may make insinuations like that and there's not a thing that a woman may do about it. It made me think that I must encourage Stella to stand up for herself, to be brave and determined and to speak her mind. I don't want her to ever feel humiliated, as I did today.

Councilor or not, I wish I'd slapped him.

Stella had gone to her mother's notebooks looking for the comfort of familiarity, but the passage that she'd read made her feel angry now. She found herself detesting this man who had humiliated her mother. Raymond Metcalf had been dead for years; she recalled the name and vaguely remembered her father reading an obituary from the evening paper, but she felt an urge to shout at his gravestone. With the sense of outrage and protectiveness that overwhelmed her, Stella understood how her mother would feel about what Freddie had done—and, yes, she had always encouraged her to stand up for herself and to know her own mind. How had she lost track of that? Stella resolved that she wouldn't let herself be manipulated again. She would never let herself experience this sense of shame again. She hated that her mother had known humiliation too.

Chapter Forty

Stella had heard the noise as she'd stepped through the front door. It was Mrs. Pendlebury, wasn't it? And was she *giggling*? That was the only word for it. It was a rather disconcerting sound. She'd never previously thought of Mrs. Pendlebury as a woman who might be capable of giggling. In the past, it had been hard enough to get a smile out of her. Whatever was going on in the front room?

Stella felt a mixture of embarrassment and irritation as she took her hat off in the hall. There'd been a lot of hushed voices speaking behind doors this week, and that had reminded her of a man's voice whispering suggestions into her mother's ear, but they'd been laughing too, hadn't they? This wasn't unsought attention, was it? What would her mother have to say about that? Was it proper? Was it nice? Stella wasn't certain, but she raised her voice to capital letters as she shouted "I'm home!" in the hallway now.

Her father's face appeared around the door. He looked flushed and his tie was awry.

"Did you have a productive morning in the library?" he asked. "Are you quite well? You look a bit stern and flustered."

Flustered? She could say the same to him. "I'm fine. I've just been concentrating. I've given myself a headache."

"Should I get you some aspirin? Can I make you a cup of tea?" He straightened his tie and seemed to gather himself. "I noticed that your light didn't go off until after midnight last night. Were you still up working?"

"I wanted to finish the chapter."

"You've always been overly conscientious," he said. "Oh, there was a telephone call from a Mr. Williamson about an hour ago. I wrote a message down. He's your editor, yes? He's rather brusque, isn't he? He asked if you'd call him back."

Hell's teeth. Was this it, then? Had he realized? Thoughts of improprieties were instantly eclipsed, all the air rushing out of Stella's chest and the pattern of the wallpaper blurring for a moment.

"Did he say what the matter was?"

"Only that it was urgent."

Possibilities tumbled through Stella's mind as she hung up her hat and coat. This insistence on urgency and the fact that her father had detected a brusque tone didn't bode well. There were so many things that Mr. Williamson might have cause to feel brusque about. Stella went through to the kitchen and shut the door on Mrs. Pendlebury's sounds of merriment.

"Miss Douglas, we need to talk," Mr. Williamson said. He did sound severe. "Some alarm bells have gone off here. Is there any chance that you could come into the office this week—and maybe bring your manuscript with you? I have some concerns, but I'm sure you'll be able to put my mind at rest."

Stella thought: he knows, doesn't he? And what could she say in her defense? It was one thing to exaggerate and elaborate a little, to lean the evidence slightly to support an argument, but that story was an outright fabrication. How could she have been so idiotic as to let Mr. Williamson read it? Why had she given him the blasted gingerbread chapter? But, then, any page of the manuscript might have been equally hazardous. There was a phrase she'd quoted there, "the gilt is off the gingerbread," an old saying, meaning that the truth will out. It sang in her head like a malign playground rhyme now.

"Of course," she agreed.

Stella poured herself a brandy for her nerves and leaned against the sink. She felt a little nauseous. She'd been half expecting a telephone call, but had kept telling herself she might get away with it. What had she been thinking in trying to get away with things? Mr. Williamson's tone had been noticeably different from the warm, approving voice that he'd used in the restaurant last month. It told her that she'd been found out. Only, there was so much more of it to come out. Mr. Williamson didn't know a fraction of it yet.

She'd agreed to travel down to London on the Friday and spent the next forty-eight hours working through the manuscript. Over the past week she'd already taken out the most flagrant fabrications and polemic, but going through the text again now, and imagining Mr. Williamson scanning through it, she saw just how much of it was still in there. Reading through her pages, she heard sweeping, unsubstantiated statements in Freddie's voice. It seemed to be tangled all through the text. Could she strip it out before she shared the typescript with Mr. Williamson? Was there time to start retyping all these pages? Or should she bolt the door and cut the telephone cable?

Chapter Forty-one

Stella had to wait in the reception while Mr. Williamson finished another meeting. She couldn't help wondering if her lack of professionalism might be the subject of that meeting. She felt like a schoolgirl who'd been caught copying another pupil's homework; it was as indefensible and embarrassing as that, but the outcome might be so much worse than a few strikes of the cane. Mr. Williamson had placed his trust in her and she didn't want to lose that.

Miss Salter, Mr. Williamson's secretary, finally called her through. She'd always been most friendly in the past, said that she'd enjoyed *Mrs. Raffald* and had complimented the color of Stella's nail varnish, but she seemed to be giving her a measuring look now. What did that look mean? Hell, did they all know that she'd been making things up?

"Miss Douglas, do sit down," Mr. Williamson said. "Thank you for coming in. I'm sorry to summon you here, but some concerns have arisen about your project."

It must be bad; he was straight to the point and speaking in that curt voice again. There was no tea, biscuits or small talk today. He hadn't even offered to take her coat and hat. But quite how bad was it? "Concerns?"

"Have you brought your manuscript with you?"

Must he see? Must he look now? Could she not ask for more time and present a new, clean version with all the suspect sections extracted? But Stella saw his raised eyebrows and realized that she couldn't back away.

"I've still got work to do," she said, trying to emphasize this, "references to check, information to validate. It's broadly there, but I've got to tighten it up now, make it all watertight. I have to admit that I'm embarrassed to show it to you at this stage."

Stella put the guilty sheaf of paper on the desk in between them and watched as Mr. Williamson pulled it toward him. She fought the urge to snatch it back. She had so much more to do than check references and validate facts, she thought, as he began to turn pages. The references didn't exist to check, and so many of the "facts" were outright fibs. No, not even that, that coy word of Freddie's didn't cover it—they were lies.

"Perhaps you know why I have concerns," Mr. Williamson began. He breathed on his spectacles and polished them with his handkerchief. The mood felt to intensify as he applied the full focus of his spectacles to her face. Stella hadn't previously noticed how piercingly blue his eyes were.

"I'm not absolutely certain." She wanted to take her eyes away from his, but she couldn't.

"I see." He nodded, but his expression suggested that his

patience was being stretched. "Well, I mentioned a colleague with an interest in Wordsworth, didn't I? I let Penelope Warner-Stewart read your chapter and she was interested in the Dorothy Wordsworth reference. As you may know, Geoffrey, her husband, wrote a biography some years ago. He's arguably the country's foremost Wordsworth scholar. He didn't recognize the anecdote, and so he made calls to several of his colleagues who research in the same field. When they all shrugged their shoulders, Geoffrey telephoned me. He actually laughed and asked me whether you'd made it up. Of course, I defended you, but it left me with a worry, because it's not like you, Miss Douglas. Not like you at all. You're normally so particular about your research, so committed to having everything shipshape. I don't think we've ever printed a book with quite so many footnotes as your *Mrs. Raffald*, and I said that to Geoffrey. I told him that I was confident you'd be able to pass the source on. Was I right to have confidence in your diligence? I've not made a fool of myself, have I? You wouldn't make a fool of me, would you, Miss Douglas?"

He flicked on through the pages and Stella watched the exaggerations and elaborations, the half-truths and the outright fabrications passing between his fingers. He was right; she was normally diligent, but for the past few months she had been careless. She couldn't pile all the blame for that on Freddie's shoulders. This was her error of judgment. She felt like the floor might be about to give way.

"I can't immediately bring that particular reference to mind. I'd have to go back and check my notes," she said.

"Of course." Mr. Williamson looked up from the type-script. "I don't mean to question your integrity, or to chastise you, Miss Douglas; however, it's a warning that you perhaps need to be careful. I am aware that we've put some pressure on you to make this one salable, but it does also need to stand up to scrutiny. You've always had such high standards in the past, and I'd like to think that hasn't changed. I don't want to have any more difficult telephone calls. Do you understand me?"

"I do. Could I perhaps ask for an extra month to comb through the text and make sure that I've pinned down every fact?"

He nodded. "I think we might be able to allow that. But rivets instead of pins, perhaps?"

Chapter Forty-two

"I'm in London," she said to Michael on the telephone. "I came down on the train first thing this morning. Could I possibly sleep on your sofa tonight?"

"Of course! You must have my room. But why didn't you tell me you were coming down? We could have made plans."

"It's a bit complicated to explain over the telephone. I don't suppose there's any chance you could escape for an hour at lunchtime, is there? I'm in need of a confessor and someone to tell me that it might all work out for the best."

"Actually, I could do with one of those myself—and a stiff drink. Could we make it a mutual sin-unburdening arrangement? Meet me in front of the market at midday, yes? I'll shuffle things and should be able to get away for a couple of hours."

Stella spotted Michael sitting on the steps when she turned the corner. He was dragging hard on a cigarette and looked rather pensive, but he smiled and raised a hand when he saw her. Stella knew she'd been an idiot, and was quite prepared to have Michael say that to her; however, she also needed to explain to someone why she'd done it.

He growled as he pulled her into a bear hug. Stella could happily have remained in that position for the next hour, just standing there, in the middle of Covent Garden, with the support of Michael's arms around her. His corduroy jacket had a familiar smell of kitchens and French cigarettes. She struggled not to cry when he pulled away and his kind, concerned eyes moved over her face.

"Stella? What's the matter? Are you quite well?" he asked. "You look awfully pale. Whatever has happened?"

Did she look ill? She felt a little queasy, all hot and cold, and thoughts were tumbling through her head at a hundred miles an hour.

"Can we go and get a drink?" she said.

They talked inconsequentially, of the weather and the architecture, as they walked through the market together, of autumn salads, quinces, medlars and damsons. Stella felt a sense that they were both stalling—what had Michael meant about sin-unburdening?—but she did need a glass in front of her before she could begin to talk of anything more consequential than cobnuts.

Michael put his hand up for the waiter, ordered wine and asked about the specials. Stella sat back in her seat and watched him. He was good with waiters, respectful but quietly authoritative, and the young man nodded in response to his questions. She thought of how Freddie had interrogated the poor waiter in Ely, and left the youth red-cheeked and stammering. It had been some odd power play and a demonstration for her benefit, she realized now. She looked at Michael and smiled.

"Right." He clinked the rim of his glass against hers. "Now, take deep breaths and spill it all out. Is it a crime, a misdemeanor or an indiscretion?"

"I've made a mess of my book," she said. She took a gulp of wine, breathed in, as he'd instructed, and then it all rushed out. "I've been making things up and now I've been found out. I was commissioned to produce a history, but I seem to have written something that's halfway between a political pamphlet and a work of fiction. I don't know what I was thinking. Really, I don't! Well, I clearly *wasn't* thinking. I've been so stupid, Michael, an absolute fool, and now I feel thoroughly ashamed of myself."

She was relieved that Michael didn't laugh, as Freddie had done—also relieved that he wasn't looking entirely horrified.

"That's not like you," he said slowly. "How has it happened?"

She'd spent the past week asking herself the same question. "I can't make excuses or blame anyone else. Not really. I felt under pressure to deliver a particular style of book, to make the facts fit, so I started being selective with the truth, but then it all got out of hand, and I've written something that I don't believe in, that I'm embarrassed to share. I've wasted so much time and effort and I don't know how to begin to put it right."

"I'm sure it can't be that bad." Michael was sounding sober and sensible. "You kept saying you had to apply a bit of gloss to this one."

"A bit of gloss is one thing, but I've been wholesale fibbing." That was Freddie's word, she remembered, and it wouldn't do. "No, not fibbing, fabricating. Lying." There, she'd said it.

"And what do you mean when you say you've been 'found out'?"

"Mr. Williamson has realized. I had to go into the office this morning and it was excruciating. Only, he doesn't know how bad it is yet. If he starts looking closer, he'll see that a large percentage of the manuscript is utter rubbish. I ought to have been more discerning, more professional, but I seem to have been inadvertently lobotomized at some point this summer."

Stella put her hands through her hair. She felt ashamed, but there was some relief in finally saying it out loud, and she was glad she'd told it to Michael. He was listening very carefully and it struck her how she'd become accustomed to Freddie's company. While Freddie never seemed to stop talking, rarely paused from sharing his opinions, Michael was encouraging her to speak and replying in calm, economical sentences. She was grateful to him for that.

"You can salvage it, though, can't you? They'll give you a chance to revise it, surely?"

"There's so much of it that needs revising, though."

"Perhaps you ought to try fiction next?" His expression was somewhere between a grimace and a grin. He dipped his chin and raised his eyebrows at her. "You might have a talent for it."

"Oh, don't!" Stella put her head on the tablecloth and groaned. She heard Michael's chair scrape back and he kneeled down at her side. "Darling, I was only teasing! I'm sorry. You'll put it right. You'll sort it out. You always do." He squeezed her hand and then nodded to the approaching waiter to refill her glass. "What say we get slightly tipsy and then we make a sober, sensible plan together?"

Stella sat up and blew her nose in his handkerchief. It smelled of soapflakes and of him. Dear Michael. She wished she'd told him sooner. Why hadn't she talked with him about this book? When she'd been writing *Mrs. Raffald*, they'd tried out recipes together and he'd made useful suggestions as he read through each chapter. All this wouldn't have happened if she'd been talking with Michael, she thought now. But then, he'd been getting on with his own life these past few months. And she had to let him do that, didn't she?

"I need to go through the pages slowly and carefully and mark up the sections that I can't defend. Lucien might have been right; there might be nothing but a pamphlet left when I've taken out all the parts that I've invented."

"How long have you got?"

"He's given me until Christmas."

"Get your head down, crack on with it, be methodical, and I bet it won't be that bad when you actually get into it. It won't be as awful as you think it is right now. I can read for you, as we did with the last one, if you'd like? I'd gladly do that. If I can help you, you will ask me, won't you?"

"Thank you."

The waiter placed plates of antipasti in front of them. Stella had no appetite, but Michael passed her the basket of bread and encouraged her to eat.

"Why did you feel under pressure? Can I ask that?"

Stella considered. "The specifics of the brief . . . and pride, I suppose. Everyone else seems to be working on such interesting projects and conspicuously thriving. That struck me when I came down to your engagement party; all the people we knew at college are so successful now, so fulfilled." So smug, so married, she could have added, but restrained herself. "I suppose I wanted to have something successful too, to have a book that people might take seriously. When I came to research it, it was all gravy and oatcakes, though. I had to polish it up then, I realized, to make it more inviting, more exciting, but I got carried about with my polishing. It's not easy to polish an oatcake, you know."

"Oh, Stella!" She saw sympathy in his smile. "You do realize what absolute rot people talk at parties, don't you? All that crowd from college wildly exaggerate their success. You know that. We all give each other the edited highlights. There's a substantial element of gravy and oatcakes to everyone's working life. And in their home lives too. That's what most of it is."

"Do you honestly think so?" Stella couldn't imagine that Cynthia's life contained much gravy and oatcakes. "My judgment seems to have gone off the rails these past few months. I've been making such stupid decisions. I don't know how I let that happen." She considered telling him about Freddie, but this wasn't the time or the place. "When did I become such an idiot, Michael?"

"I don't mean to sound competitive, but I'd hazard that my recent idiocy puts yours in the shade." He sat back in his chair and looked as though he wasn't quite sure where to go next with the conversation.

"I'm glad you've shaved the moustache off. I didn't like to say anything, but it didn't suit you. It made you look a bit caddish. Did Lucien tell you too?" He looked younger, healthier, more wholesome without it, but she still saw signs of tiredness around his eyes.

"It's not just the old soup-strainer that's gone." He straightened his cutlery as if this required some concentration. "The wedding is off . . . and everything else. I thought Lucien might have telephoned you, but evidently not. I have to say, he is crowing a bit. I've lost count of the number of times he's said 'I told you so.'"

"I'm sorry?" Stella put her knife and fork down. "Pardon? What? It's over with Cynthia?"

"Emphatically. Irrevocably. Slightly stingingly."

She resisted the urge to yelp delight, though it took some doing. His expression told her that wouldn't have been an appropriate response. "Michael, I'm so sorry! I had no idea. And I've sat here grumbling on about my work for the past half hour! Holy mackerel, I haven't stopped talking, have I? How are you?"

"Oh, you know, embarrassed, regretful, confused, all those adjectives that you've just been airing."

"But what happened? I thought it was full speed ahead toward the wedding? The last time I saw the pair of you, you were entangled in one another's limbs."

Michael topped up both of their glasses. "I did get rather entangled." He widened his eyes and then frowned. "But we've fought a lot as well. Cynthia can be difficult, unpredictable, impatient, not always as kind as she ought to be. We had a big falling out last weekend when she came into the restaurant and was extremely rude to one of the girls. She made poor Lydia cry. It's not the first time that I've seen Cynthia be like that. It's been building up; I've been having second thoughts for a while, if I'm honest, but that was the final nudge I needed."

"So you broke it off? How did she take that? Were there pyrotechnics?" Stella had a horrible image of Cynthia's red fingernails clawing. She couldn't see any scratch marks on him, but—

"I sat her down and began to explain how I felt, wording it as kindly and tactfully as I could, but then she realized where I was going and seemed to decide that she wanted to get there before me. She told me that she was bored of me anyway, and was only going ahead with the wedding because she'd already put a lot of work into the planning and the photographs would sell well."

"How awful for you." Stella reached across the table and took his hand. There was a scar where he'd burned himself. She touched it very gently with her fingertip and wondered how many other scars Cynthia might have left on him. She was sorry to have to take her hand away when the waiter returned to clear their plates.

"I should have seen it sooner," Michael went on. "I definitely should have ended it sooner. I knew I was with the wrong person—only, she's such a strong character, you know? It made me angry when she was horrid to you in the club that night. We had an almighty row about it the next day, but I ought to have said more at the time, and I've regretted that. I shouldn't have tolerated her being like that with you. Can you forgive me?"

"There's nothing to forgive you for." As she looked at Michael with his eyelashes cast down, Stella had to resist the urge to walk around the table and put her arms around him. "I recall that you defended me, and I was grateful for that."

"I have to say, you're being remarkably polite about her. I know you've never been keen, I've always known that, and I really ought to have given more thought as to why that was. Lucien wasn't polite. He absolutely let rip! If I had any lingering doubts, he jumped all over them."

She was glad to see him smile at last. "I can imagine! But how could Cynthia have said she was bored with you? What a horrid thing to say. There are lots of ways in which you are far more exciting and original than her crowd. You flambé foods quite unnecessarily, steal ashtrays from bars, and know the words to several rude songs." Stella could remember many times when they'd stayed out until dawn, incurred the headshakes of policemen, and been tutted at by people on the next table. She could have made a long list of all the ways in which Michael was far from boring, really quite the opposite, but told herself to put the brakes on.

"Thank you for your loyalty."

The waiter placed a platter of cured meats and a salad of artichokes between them. They were beautiful plates, worthy of a painting, but Stella felt distracted from the food.

"So, you see, your recent foolishness is minor compared with mine." Michael forked an artichoke and gave her a complicated smile. "What was it you said about being lobotomized? You might have had a slip of judgment, but my discernment has wandered off on a major diversion. Have you ever woken up and wondered if you've been under a spell?"

Stella thought about waking up next to Freddie. "Yes, as a matter of fact, I can empathize with that. Has there been something in the air this year?"

"I presently feel sufficiently embarrassed that I'd very much like to blame pixie dust."

She could see it on his face. "Let's agree to do that, then. How are you, though?"

"To be honest, I've had a stomach full of knots for the past couple of months, knowing that I had a decision to make, and I actually feel some sense of relief now."

"Are you sure it wasn't just bad indigestion?" She was glad when he grinned.

"I thought I might take a couple of weeks off come the spring and head over to France with my bicycle. I'd love to get out of London for a bit."

"Good for you. How nice that sounds."

"Come with me!" He brightened, as the idea seemed to unfold for him. "Yes, let's go together. Wouldn't that be fun? We can comfort ourselves with enormous platters of *fruits de mer* and blur out the embarrassing memories with cheap wine. I'd love that. More than anything. Oh, say you'll come with me!"

She pictured him cycling down Provençal roads, his hair all awry and his shirt fluttering in the breeze. She saw his face lit by the shifting, glittering, oyster-shell-colored light of a harbor. She so wanted to say "yes." "It's terrifically tempting, but I can't think beyond my deadline at the moment. Besides, I'm wobbly on a bicycle."

"Of course." He nodded. "I'll try to finish work early tonight, and then I reckon that we ought to sit on my sofa eating cheese-on-toast together, like we used to—but perhaps with the addition of a sorrow-drowning bottle of champagne? What do you say?"

"You did always have excellently sensible suggestions."

Stella resolved: from tomorrow she would work hard, be focused and ruthless with her edits, but tonight the idea of drinking herself into forgetfulness with Michael was very appealing.

"I've missed talking to you," he said, suddenly looking serious again. "I've wanted to telephone you, to tell you things, to ask your advice, but you didn't need to hear all my idiotic problems."

"I wish you had telephoned. I've missed speaking to you

too. To be honest, I suspected I'd lost you. I expected that we'd speak less and less."

"You did? Oh, Stella!" He reached out and threaded his fingers through hers. "It could never be like that. I'm sorry, my love, but I'm afraid you're lumbered with me for life."

Chapter Forty-three

Stella took a ruler and a red pencil and began to draw a line through all the most glaring falsehoods, the Wordsworth story, the Austen anecdote, the Walpole, the Dickens and the Brontës. She then started to delete all the made-up anecdotes from correspondents. As she squinted at the page, fact and fiction seemed to be blurring together. She hardly remembered now which stories and characters were real, and which she'd invented, but she rubbed her eyes and pushed on. Eight hours later, when she turned back through the pages, she saw that she'd erased a good quarter of the book.

She then went through it again, and put green asterisks in the margin where she'd deliberately excised the French chefs, the Portuguese traders and the Icelandic stockfish, the Flemish crop rotation systems and the Dutch plough. Freddie might have suggested those cuts, but she was the one who had actually taken them out. There were a lot of green asterisks and they made Stella feel ashamed. When she got to the end, and looked back through her marked-up typescript, it was like a battlefield. There wasn't a single page that wasn't scarred.

She had such a lot of work to do over the next two months and the house seemed to be full of ticking clocks suddenly. As she faced the task ahead, all that she would need to do to right her own wrongs, she felt like a tenderized escalope, all beaten into broken-down muscle. (Hadn't Lucien once predicted that Michael would feel like that? She sincerely hoped that he didn't.) But she drank a strong coffee and told herself not to be silly with similes. She'd have to approach it methodically and diligently, and work night and day. But she would make this right. She was determined.

Stella set up her typewriter and the gas heater in her bedroom, and explained to her father that she would need to put the hours in for the next ten weeks. He was understanding and encouraging, bringing her sandwiches at lunchtime, fueling her with regular cups of tea, and tiptoeing past the door. Mrs. Pendlebury came in, made his lunches, and took on some of the laundry. They went for walks together on mild evenings—Stella heard their voices going down the garden path—and listened to concerts on the wireless side by side. It eased Stella's conscience to know that he was companionably entertained, and freed from daughterly duties, she was able to work a long, disciplined day. The leaves on the apple tree beyond her window turned from green to brown and began to fall. There was a smell of coal fires in the mornings and she needed to put a cardigan around her shoulders in the evenings. Moth wings flickered against her window in the darkness, and she looked up from the pages to see her own pale reflection in the glass, only then noticing that midnight was long gone. But by the end of October, she could telephone Mr. Williamson and tell him that she was on track. To hear a more positive tone to his voice intensified Stella's resolve over the final weeks.

It took some time to eradicate Freddie's voice from the text. Stella kept hearing it there. How many of his words there had been, his opinions and his flights of fancy. The manuscript was perhaps slightly duller for these deletions, the opinions milder and the personages more minor, but better understated than precarious, Stella thought. She recovered Sally Lunn from her notebooks, the quotes from Escoffier, Francatelli and Carême, and the influence of all those nameless traders and immigrants who had disembarked at English ports with ingredients, recipes and know-how.

Reading through the correspondence she'd received in response to her newspaper appeals once again, Stella found these letters to be more useful than she'd first appreciated, and she managed to replace many of the fictional quotes with genuine testimonies. They weren't quite as bright, characterful and focused as the letters she'd invented; however, they were the real voices of people sharing their stories. These were often stories of hardship and making do, she saw now as she read them for a second time—but also heartfelt accounts of family, generosity and getting through together. Some of the letters moved her, as she read them again in her newly tenderized mood.

As well as the correspondence, Stella returned to the recipe book she'd picked up at the house sale, and to her mother's notebooks. She found a Lincolnshire stuffed chine, a Worcestershire jugged pigeon and Norfolk dumplings in Mrs. Fothergill's book, and her mother's handwriting filled several blanks. Having deleted made-up advice on pickled walnuts, salted beef and potted cheese, she discovered replacement recipes in her mother's books. Had these perhaps been at the back of her mind as she'd invented? It gave Stella a sense of satisfaction to write her mother's name and quote her words in the text. She was particularly gratified to find a recipe for "Westmorland Gingerbread' in her mother's handwriting. It was almost the same as the one she'd invented from Colonel Jenkins. Had she maybe baked this with her mother as a child?

The manuscript seemed to shout less now; it was less stridently flag-wavingly English. As Stella had reinstated the Spanish oranges, the Dutch salad gardens and the Jewish fried fish, the accent of the text had changed. Instead of a clipped BBC English, it now spoke with a hotchpotch voice. Stella felt it more authentic for that, though, and her confidence in it began to return. It might no longer have a lion's roar, but this was the story of a trading and a hospitable nation, turned outward, not inward. Perhaps the brass band wouldn't quite be playing the tune that Mr. Williamson had expected, all hope and glory; however, Stella felt that it was playing in the correct key now, and it wouldn't keep her awake at nights.

From her room Stella could hear the telephone ringing occasionally as she worked, but her father took messages and only relayed them to her if they were urgent. Freddie phoned again at the end of October and left a message asking her to return his call. It astonished Stella how thick-skinned he was—but then again, on other levels, that didn't surprise her at all. She had no intention of making contact with him. The bruises might have faded, but she wouldn't forget. Earlier that day, as she'd stood in front of her bookcase, her eye had stopped on the spine of the John Donne poems. With the thought of the inscription inside, she'd heard herself sigh. Whatever had happened to poor Phyllis? Had she eventually seen that side of Freddie too?

She and Michael were telephoning each other every couple of days. Stella posted pages down to him, and he returned them with useful suggestions and questions. She trusted his judgment and experience, knew he had no agenda and only her best interests at heart. Having his support and encouragement lightened the work, and he also passed on occasional insults from Lucien, which made her laugh.

Michael spoke of his regret at some of the things he'd done under Cynthia's spell, as he put it. He now realized that all the late nights had had an impact on his work, and he was trying to make that right, but he'd told his team that he was going to take a break in the spring. He talked to Stella of the route he was planning around France, the cathedrals and art galleries he meant to visit, the shellfish, the mush-rooms and the patisserie he intended to seek out. He'd asked her again if she would come with him, but she couldn't think beyond delivering the book. And then, when the book was finished, she'd still need to be there for her father, wouldn't she? Stella felt she had Michael back, though, his voice having returned to her life, and the routine of speaking with him somehow seemed to intensify the autumn colors and made her pause and notice the birdsong.

One thing they hadn't discussed again was her last night in London. They'd ended up finishing a bottle of cognac and had woken up slumped in each other's arms on his sofa. At one point during that evening of confessions and mutual consolation, he'd told her that he would always love her. There were parts of that night Stella couldn't now recall, but she remembered the instantly sobering shock of Michael saying those words. She had found herself going over them again in the weeks since, and asking herself what sort of love he had meant? And had it just been drink talking? She'd also asked herself what sort of love she wanted him to mean. But then, it was never mentioned again, and perhaps he'd forgotten that he'd ever said it. She wished she could find the courage to say more.

Stella stood at the open window and eased the ache from her shoulders. She lit a cigarette and leaned out. Leaves were blowing across the lawn and the garden was a November palette of umbers, ochres and touches of gold. Only the last chapter remained to revise and she felt that she knew where she was going with her conclusion. The end was finally in sight and her heart lifted with relief at that thought. She might make a wimberry pie tonight in celebration. Stella wondered, was this the final stage of catharsis? Was this what it felt like? How exhausting it must be to be Greek.

Caroline Scott

[From the notebook of Elizabeth Douglas, 1921]

I made wimberry pie because it's Stella's favorite and she's leaving for London tomorrow. We were together in the kitchen this afternoon, and I showed her how I always make it on my grandmother's old tin plate, how to paint the bottom layer of pastry with an egg white so that the juice doesn't come through, and how to put the sugar on top so that it makes a syrup but doesn't break up the fruit. As we worked together, we reminisced about going wimberry picking on the moors when she was a little girl, how we'd have purple fingers and purple tongues, and never really come home with enough fruit to make a pie.

It was precious to have that time together this afternoon, to share memories and to hear notes of excitement in her voice as she talked about the journey tomorrow, about the flat where she'll be boarding and what she's going to be learning in her classes at the college.

I told her how proud of her I am, how I couldn't be prouder, and how I want her to be ambitious and happy. I will hate working in the kitchen on my own tomorrow, but I'm excited for her and so pleased that she has the courage to pursue her dreams.

Though he still insists she'd be more sensible going to secretarial college in Leeds, I know that Charlie is proud of Stella too. He gave her an envelope of money that he'd been putting aside. I didn't know that he was going to do that. It touched me how they spoke together tonight.

I told her that we won't have wimberry pie again until she comes home. I'll buy a jar of the Polish bottled bilberries when she comes back in December. Charlie joked that she'll be too fancy for fruit pies when she next comes home, that she'll be far too sophisticated to want to eat off Grandmother Linton's old chipped tin plate.

"Yes, I shall want a champagne coupe not a tea cup, and I won't abide your elbows on the table, Father," she said.

My heart filled up as I watched them together and thought how her chair at the table will be empty tomorrow. I am going to miss my little girl terribly, but I am so very proud of the young woman she's becoming.

Chapter Forty-four

Her father knocked and came in with a cup of tea. "Fuel for the worker."

"That's kind of you. This book has been powered by tea. I'd have run aground long ago without it."

There was a coconut macaroon in the saucer too. Stella didn't recognize it, so she supposed it must be one of Mrs. Pendlebury's. She really was taking awfully good care of her father. Stella resolved that she must buy Mrs. Pendlebury a poinsettia this Christmas, or perhaps some nice embroidered handkerchiefs.

"I know you're busy, but would you have five minutes for a chat?" Her father was hovering in the doorway, stepping from foot to foot like a slightly nervous schoolboy.

"Of course!" Stella turned her chair. "Is something wrong? You look like you're about to make a pronouncement. Or lay an egg."

"Well," he said. "I am, sort of—the pronouncement, that is, not the egg."

Stella took a sip of her tea and sat back. Whatever was he taking so seriously? Did he have more radical plans for the vegetable plot? Did he want to rearrange the furniture in the front room again? "Go on," she said.

"I'm not quite sure how to say this, so I'm just going to blurt it out. Helena has asked me to move in with her and I've said 'Yes.'"

"Helena?" Who the heck was Helena?

"Mrs. Pendlebury. You must have noticed that we've become close over the past few months. You and I are crammed in here together, like sardines in a can; meanwhile, she's rattling around like a pea in a bucket. She's in a five-bedroom house on her own. You see that it makes sense, don't you?"

Stella was still trying to process his similes. She had noticed how they were together, how Mrs. Pendlebury was always fussing over his needs, and how he made her laugh, but she hadn't seen *this* coming.

"So you're proposing to leap out of my can and into her bucket?" Did that sound quite proper? "I thought things were starting to fall into place here, though? Yes, we're pushed for space, but we're getting into a routine, aren't we? I've been busy with the book for the past month—I know I've been preoccupied—but I'll have time for you once I've sent it off. I haven't neglected you, have I? You don't have to move out."

"It's not like that." He frowned. "Of course, you haven't neglected me."

"I feel like we've hardly given this arrangement a proper go yet. It was a bit of a shock when you first arrived, I'll admit that, but I've liked having you here. I've enjoyed cooking for you. I love having your company."

"But you've looked so unhappy over the past few months. I saw it on your face when I arrived. You actually looked slightly horrified, and I know I've disrupted your work and your social life. What's more, your mother wouldn't want you to be lumbered with me. I've realized that. She would have been furious with me for arriving here without having asked you first. I made a mistake."

Had she really looked horrified? "You didn't make a mistake. Oh, Daddy, don't say that! If I've looked unhappy it's because of this book, not because of you."

"You shouldn't be spending your evenings with an old man. You need your own space and your own time. I keep hearing your mother's voice telling me that—and she doesn't sound pleased with me!" He grimaced but it then turned into a smile. "I made an error of judgment and now it's time to put that right. Besides, I have feelings for Helena."

"*Feelings?*" It was strange to hear her father calling Mrs. Pendlebury Helena. It was rather a noble name, Stella thought. A Helena ought to chair charitable committees, take tea on a lawn, and holiday in smart Continental hotels. Stella would have put Mrs. P down as more of a Bertha than a Helena. Doughty was the adjective that best suited her. She moved through a room like a battleship. Her prow might well have been riveted by Harland & Wolff. What sort of feelings might her father have for Mrs. Pendlebury?

"There are different kinds of love, aren't there?" He

seemed to ponder the question. "My feelings for her aren't the same ones that I had for your mother, but then I'm not a lad of eighteen any longer. I shan't be getting moony over her, or writing her poems; however, I am very fond of her, if you must know. She makes me laugh and she cares that I'm happy. I love the way that her face changes entirely when she smiles, how she folds her hands in her lap when she's feeling self-conscious, and her habit of reaching out and touching my shoulder when she walks past my chair. Is that enough?"

Stella looked at her father and saw the sincerity on his face. She saw how he wanted her to believe him. But was it quite nice, quite respectful of her mother's memory? He shouldn't look at other women, should he? Noticing the qualities of their smiles? Wanting their fingers to stretch toward him?

"I shouldn't have left you on your own with Mrs. Pendlebury. I should have seen it coming. Did she seduce you?" Was that it? Had she used her feminine wiles? Shown him a bit of stocking? Did she have an agenda? Did Mrs. Pendlebury covet his ladderback chairs and his carved-oak settle?

"Seduce me? What, like Marlene Dietrich?" He widened his eyes and laughed. "Stella, have you not noticed that I'm on my way to sixty? And Helena's already there. Can you seriously see her as a seductress?"

"I don't know!" She held her hands up in surrender. "I don't know what to think. I keep hearing the two of you laughing together and it makes me feel confused. What would Mummy say?"

"'Good on you, Charlie?' She'd want me to have

companionship. I feel absolutely no doubt or guilt about that. She wouldn't disapprove and she certainly wouldn't give me the look that you're giving me now."

"I'm not giving you a look." Was she?

"Aren't you?" He sat down on the bed and seemed to think for a moment. "Don't imagine that I haven't considered your mother's feelings, but I need a little kindness. Most people do. I need to laugh and let go sometimes. If it was the other way around, if I'd died and left your mother behind, I'd want her to be happy. If she could have achieved that by being with another person, I wouldn't begrudge it. Not at all. I'm not replacing your mother with Helena, Stella. No one will ever replace your mother, but being with Helena makes me feel content and I might give her some comfort too. Is that so wrong?"

Stella couldn't quite square his need for Mrs. Pendlebury's kindness against the obvious grief that he'd felt on losing her mother. She remembered how her father had been twelve months ago, how emotionally fragile he'd seemed, how she'd worried about him being on his own. If he thought that he could be happy with Mrs. Pendlebury, she couldn't deny him that, could she? Wasn't it a positive thing that someone wanted to bake him coconut macaroons and touch his shoulder? Her mother wouldn't begrudge that, she realized. He was right. But in acknowledging this, Stella felt like she was being obliged to let something of her mother's memory go.

"I don't begrudge you happiness. Of course, I don't. It's just rather a shock. Do you mean to marry her?"

"At my age? What—me in a suit and her in a white dress?" His mouth curled up at the corners. "You are old-fashioned."

Was she? Perhaps these feelings weren't very *Today's Woman.* "So, when are you moving into Mrs. Pendlebury's love nest? You do know that people will talk, don't you?"

"Next week. I've asked Ted to come with the van again. And, frankly, I don't give a damn what gossips say."

Stella couldn't help but smile at that. He was a thigh slap and a vowel sound away from a Hollywood leading man for a moment. "You ought to buy furniture that's on castors, you know. All this moving around!"

"Helena has a comfortable home. She has fitted carpets throughout and an uncut moquette three-piece suite."

"Why does she do other people's cleaning if she lives in a five-bedroom house?" Stella had to ask. "Why doesn't she move into a smaller house and live on the proceeds?"

"Because it was her family home. And, besides, she finds it interesting to observe how people live."

Didn't she just? "I see."

"Don't look so sad."

Did she? Stella realized that she'd pictured a future in which she was caring for her father, and in many ways she'd wanted that. She felt somewhat rejected that he was choosing Mrs. Pendlebury's care over hers. "I can't help but feel that I've failed you."

"Don't be so daft, Stella. Of course, you haven't failed me. I'm grateful for how you've looked after me over the past few months, but you don't need me as a millstone round your neck. Get on with your young life. See friends. Travel. Pursue your ambitions. Be brave. That's what your mother always wanted you to do."

As her father's furniture had entered, so it now left again. How long had it been here? Was it only six months? Stella watched the linen press and armchairs exiting, and whatever he'd said, she couldn't help feeling that she'd failed. She knew she'd been too wrapped up in her book for the past six months. She'd spent her evenings at her typewriter when she ought to have been with him, talking to him, listening to him. If she hadn't gone away and left him with Mrs. Pendlebury, would this ever have happened?

Stella stood in the front room and looked around. It seemed rather empty now. Where there had been too much furniture and too much noise just hours ago, now there wasn't enough. She switched on the wireless and a voice began talking about life on a remote Hebridean farm. What would she do with all her empty hours and space after the book was done? Perhaps, as her father had suggested, it was time for her to make changes too.

"CHRISTMAS CAKE"
[From the notebook of Elizabeth Douglas, 1929]

The recipe below is my mother's Christmas cake. She wrote it out for me many years ago and I like the thought that my family is tasting the same flavors that my parents knew. It seems to bring us together.

Stella has come up from London for the weekend, so we made the Christmas cake together this afternoon. It was such a pleasure to have her in the kitchen with me again, to hear her talking about her London life, her writing and her friends, and we fell back into our old rhythm, working side by side as naturally and easily as we always did.

My mother also sometimes baked what she would call a Yule Cake, which was a recipe handed down from her grandmother. This was a bread dough, enriched with lard, eggs, sugar, currants, raisins, candied peel, nutmeg and allspice. It was what people ate in the days before Christmas cake, she told me, and in the olden times the dough would be formed into the shape of a baby, representing the new start that came with the new year. What will this new year bring?

It was considered unlucky to cut into the cake before Christmas Eve, I remember, but a little piece kept until the next year would bring good luck to the house. My grandfather would ceremoniously wrap the last slice in brown paper and hide it away at the back of the cutlery drawer. I remember looking at it sometimes as a child, but never daring to touch it. It was like some sort of holy relic. We had lots of little rituals and charms in those days. There was more magic in everyday life back then. It seems a pity that so much has already been forgotten.

I felt well today and Stella seemed so contented to be home that I couldn't bring myself to tell her about the appointment with Dr. Sinclair. I had fully intended to talk to her this weekend, but I didn't want to spoil the mood. I couldn't find the courage to say it and I whispered to Charlie not to speak of it then. He gave me a look, and told me that I'd have to let her know sometime soon. I've promised him that we'll have the conversation when Stella comes back up at Christmas.

I want it always to be like it was today. I want to think that we'll always be able to make the Christmas cake together. But how many more Christmases will we have? This illness is like a shadow at the corner of my eyes, it's there all the time now, ever present at the edges, but I don't want to see it yet. I'm not ready to acknowledge it. I know that when I tell Stella it will be real then, that it will change everything, dominate everything, and I refuse to let it take my normal life from me just yet. My mother would never even say the word "cancer" out loud. She'd have to mouth it, as if the mere sound of it might be contagious or bad luck. I have to trust in radium and surgeons now, I'm told, we're meant to be having cards-on-the-table conversations and making sensible plans in which calculations of luck should play no part. I know I ought to be facing up to those decisions and realities, but I'm struggling to say the word out loud too at the moment. I dread saying it to my daughter and filling her head with those terrible calculations.

Christmas is a time for remembering, for raising a glass to those who have gone, and for being appreciative of what we've got. Today I feel grateful that my mother took the time to write down her Christmas cake recipe and that I've been able to make it with my daughter this afternoon. In years to come, will Stella reach for this old recipe and remember us being in the kitchen together today? If she does, I hope she'll smile and recall the pleasure we had in cooking together.

Chapter Forty-five

"A present for you," Stella said, and put the parcel down on Dilys' kitchen table. "It's Christmas cake. I made my mother's recipe. Of course, I could easily have eaten the whole thing myself, but I'd be complaining about not being able to fasten my buttons in January, so really you're doing me a kindness."

Dilys put the palm of her hand to the brown-paper-wrapped parcel, as if it might contain something precious. "I can remember making Christmas cake with my mother, being allowed to stir the fruit in, tying a paper collar around the tin, and then the house smelling of cinnamon, allspice and cloves." She smiled fondly, a smile that Stella hadn't seen before. "Did you not want to give it to your father?"

"You haven't seen the way that Mrs. Pendlebury feeds him. I called over on Tuesday and I swear that every surface in her kitchen was covered with mince pies."

"Well, it will be a great treat for me. That was a very kind thought."

"It looks festive in here, like a house in a folktale." Dilys had wired ivy and holly branches to her beams, which gave the room an enchanted greenwood light. "I read your chapter on Yule traditions. Did you welcome the sylvan spirits into the house?"

"Of course. Be careful what you say. They're listening." There was a mischievous glint in Dilys' eye and Stella couldn't tell whether she was being serious.

"I wanted to say thank you for your assistance with the book too," she went on. "Talking with you helped me to pull it into shape. I appreciate that. Having your moral support over the past few months has made a great difference."

"It's a worthwhile book, really an achievement. It's valuable to have collected all that old knowledge and know-how. You should feel proud of it."

"Thank you." That was the first time that Dilys had ever complimented her writing. Stella found herself holding her chin a little higher. The company of the sylvan spirits seemed to put Dilys in a positive mood. She ought to invite them in more often.

"I had some good news myself this morning. A bookshop in Dewsbury has taken twenty copies of *More Ghosts and Folklore*." Dilys' fingers drummed the tabletop with pleasure and her turquoise earrings swung. "I had a long telephone conversation with the owner. Such an interesting and erudite man. It was most heartening. We should have a drink to celebrate."

Stella reached glasses down from the dresser while Dilys ventured into the further recesses of her pantry. Emerging with a bottle, she blew the dust away with some flourish, like a man returning from a cellar with a long laid-down Dom Perignon. It was an old Haig whiskey bottle, Stella recognized, but its present contents might have been dredged from the bottom of a rock pool.

"Raisin wine," Dilys said, pulling a cobweb from her hair. "There's brandy in it, and it's been in the bottle for three years, so it should have some oomph."

Though it looked thoroughly unsavory, it tasted like the distilled essence of Christmas, and by the time she'd taken a couple of sips Stella's cheeks were beginning to glow. It certainly had voltage. It could have powered a small hamlet. Even Dilys blinked. Noticing the date on the label of the bottle, Stella couldn't help thinking that her mother had been alive then. Her death still felt like an enormous fissure, a fault line in time, as if there might have been another great flood or an ice age in between that date and this, but she'd sensed her mother's presence at her side in the kitchen as she'd made the cake. She'd heard her voice as she read the recipe and she had smiled.

"Do you have plans for Christmas Day?" Stella asked. "I'm summoned chez Pendlebury, but she's bound to have over-catered and I'm sure they wouldn't mind pulling an extra chair up to the table. That is, if you don't already have other commitments?"

Dilys took a mouthful of her drink and coughed. "It's kind of you to think of me. I do appreciate the sentiment, but you'll forgive me if I play the pagan card, won't you? I'm not sure I could take Mrs. P's turkey extravaganza. There'll be cocktail sausages, Christmas medleys on the wireless and I'd be obliged to wear a hat out of a cracker, wouldn't I?"

How did Dilys mark her Yule? Stella supposed she'd be doing things with incense and herbs, drinking mead or hippocras, and reading poems about Odin. It did seem more exciting than sipping eggnog around the radiogram.

"Why didn't I think of paganism? Is it too late to convert now?"

Dilys' mouth kinked up at the corner. "The orgies aren't compulsory."

"Come and have a drink with me on Christmas Eve, then? I promise not to make you wear a paper hat."

"I'll bring one of the bottles that's lost its label and we can have a surprise."

"Wine roulette? How thrilling!"

A tabby cat leaped onto the table, skidding on the oilcloth and making Stella start. It eyed them both briefly before setting about its intimate toilette. Dilys barely seemed to register its presence.

"I can tell you all about my new book too then," she went on.

"Your new book?" Surely not *Even More Ghosts and Folklore of West Riding*?

"It's about folk medicines and the women who preserved the old knowledge. Thinking about your book and the traditional ways with herbs and hedgerow cures got me started on it. I've submitted it to the Pentagon and they've given the nod."

Stella suppressed a momentary image of druidic robes and sacrificial goats. "It sounds fascinating. I'd love to hear more about it."

"To new years and new projects!" said Dilys and raised her glass.

"To new starts and wise old women!"

Chapter Forty-six

There was a fairy-tale quality to the snow-covered garden. It wasn't white, Stella contemplated, but gold and rosy blue in the sunlight. It was the lightest wash of watercolor and the line of prints down the lawn (a blackbird? A thrush?) were marks in an oriental calligraphy. Snow creaked on the trees above and she breathed the icy air deep into her lungs. It felt clean and sharp-edged. The cold made her want to braise oxtails and steam a ginger pudding, and she would have time to do that this afternoon. She'd stoke up the range and enjoy the warmth of the kitchen, but first she meant to go to the churchyard. She pulled on her gloves and wound her scarf around her neck. The pristine snow crunched satisfyingly under her boots and her breath made a white cloud ahead of her.

She'd spoken to her father on the telephone last night and they'd made their arrangements for Christmas Day. It would be a strange day, Stella thought; it would be most peculiar not to be sitting at the table in the kitchen at the farm, but this was what her father wanted and she didn't feel that she had much choice. She was still finding it difficult to accustom herself to the idea of her father spending his evenings on Mrs. P's three-piece moquette suite. For her own part, she felt that it would be years before she stopped talking to her mother in her head (if she ever stopped at all) and experiencing a sharp stab of sadness several times a day as she remembered that, no, she wasn't there in the next room and never would be again. Was her father not still feeling that too? But he couldn't be, could he?

Stella followed a set of footprints under the lych-gate and down the path toward the graveyard, and then realized that she was walking in the prints of her father's boots. He'd taken the pots of faded chrysanthemums away and Stella could see from this distance that he was talking to the headstone. She watched him brushing snow from the grave and then touching the letters of her mother's name. One love doesn't end because another starts, Stella thought then; he'd said that to her a fortnight ago, but she'd found herself questioning his words. As she observed his tender attentions at the graveside, she felt that she could perhaps understand what he'd meant.

Stella sat on the bench and pulled her coat around her. Was he explaining to her mother about Mrs. Pendlebury? How she warmed his vests in front of the fire, smiled as she straightened his tie, and must always put a biscuit in his saucer? Her mother wouldn't object to that. She'd probably be amused, and Stella knew that she had no right to deny him those moments—after all, it's the small gestures of thoughtfulness that make life worth living. She ought to be grateful that Mrs. Pendlebury cared, Stella understood that, but still, there was something profoundly sad about the idea of a woman other than her mother performing those acts of kindness. Stella watched her father and her eyes watered over. She wiped the tears away as she saw him get to his feet and turn.

"It's bloody cold, eh?" he said, and put his arms around her. "But it's beautiful, isn't it? It's like a Christmas card. You know, this is the first time in decades that I've enjoyed snow."

Stella stood with her face in her father's winter coat and didn't want to move away. She breathed in his smell of pipe smoke, damp dogs and peppermints.

"Are you feeling sad, petal?" he asked, as he pulled back.

"I can't come here and not feel sad," she said.

"Of course. I miss her too, you know. I miss her every moment of the day. I always will. She's a big hole in my chest and I will feel that until I breathe my last breath."

"I know that."

"Are you telling her that Michael's coming up?"

"I might."

"You should. She'd be pleased. She always liked him." He nodded. "Come over early on Christmas morning, eh? Don't be on your own."

"I finished it," Stella said to the gravestone. "I took the parcel to the post office yesterday. I didn't think that I'd ever get there, but I did. I know you've been helping me with that."

She must wait for Mr. Williamson's verdict now, but Stella felt she'd made the best job of it that she could have done.

Whatever happened next, she was satisfied with it. There was nothing there now that made her conscience smart. When Mrs. Denshaw had put the parcel on the scales in the post office, she'd called it a weighty tome, and Stella had even felt a little flush of pride then.

"Michael is coming up on Boxing Day. He's going to stay until the new year. He's taken a week off from the restaurant."

It had surprised Stella when he'd asked. She couldn't remember when he'd last taken time off at Christmas, but he'd said that the past year had made him reevaluate his priorities. They were going to cook together, drink mulled wine and Rhum Saint-James cocktails, and he'd warned her that he was determined to talk her into coming to France with him in the spring.

"He says it's time we went on an adventure together. Those were his words." Stella smiled as she said it, remembering the resolution she'd heard in his voice. Could she go now? She wasn't obliged to be here any longer, was she?

"Mrs. P has knitted Daddy a jumper for Christmas, but he's put on so much weight recently, it might need letting out. You'd laugh to see how she feeds him and fusses. Honestly, he's getting quite spoiled! He does seem happy, though—and that's as it should be, isn't it? I'm sorry that I ever thought you might object."

Stella arranged the branches of holly on the grave. Under the snow, the churchyard was like a woodblock print, and the red of the berries and the glossy green leaves seemed to intensify in color. Her mother had always dressed the fireplace in the kitchen for Christmas, Stella remembered, taking care and pleasure in arranging the fir branches, the clove-studded oranges and the candles. Stella hadn't decorated the cottage, hadn't felt inclined to before today, but perhaps she might do it before Michael arrived.

"I'm going to be brave," she said. "Like you always wanted me to be." She would have given anything to hear a reply. "Happy Christmas. I miss you so much, Mummy."

The comfort of the familiar constellations

(from "How the English Eat")

Over the course of writing this book I've discovered that trying to define a nation's cuisine is as tricky as attempting to summarize its culture or its language. Every time that I've been tempted to write "This is how we do it in England," I immediately seem to have happened upon someone at the next farm or in the next butcher's shop who is doing it a different way. We are inclined to follow our own personal rules and tastes, and our recipe writers have never been prescriptive. While the cookbooks of some other countries are precise, substitutions and approximations aren't frowned upon here. We're quite happy to shrug and swap raisins for currants, if that's what we happen to have in our cupboard, an orange for a lemon, a chicken for a rabbit, a saucepan for a frying pan, and I suppose that attitude stimulates inventiveness. (But rule-breaking and multifariousness aren't good for a writer who is striving to discern patterns and draw tidy conclusions.)

One of the privileges of researching a book of this kind is the opportunity to travel, and I have seen different versions of England over the past year—the England of new red-brick bungalows and modern white-tiled factories and the coal-blackened terraces of Industrial Revolution England. I've visited timeless cathedral-city England, the landscapes of Wordsworth and Jane Austen, recognizable still, and the England of village greens and fleeces and orchards full of shiny apples. I've seen silenced shipyards, rusting cranes and queues outside Labour Exchanges, and the England of lidos, motor cafés and nightclubs, all presently coexisting, and I've been struck by what a land of contrasts and contradictions this is. As much as I have asked myself "What is English food?," I have pondered, "Where—and what—is England?" A land of contrasts (and it always has been, I suspect) creates a food of contrasts. English food is elaborate and simple, conservative and adventurous, regionalized and international.

Our history is a tale of immigration, invasion, colonizing and trade, and our food reflects that. Many familiar flavors turn out not to be wholly English on closer inspection. But does that mean these ingredients and recipes should be omitted from a book about how the English eat? Isn't that akin to excluding words with a foreign origin from the dictionary? We would be left with a very narrow vocabulary and an extremely short bill of fare. These dishes may be mongrels, but they're our mongrels. We have bred them, cared for them, and occasionally neglected them, but they've picked up something of our habits and temperament.

While it has been thrilling to look at the food of the elite—those eye-arresting tables bedecked with roasted peacocks, astonishing pies and trembling turrets of gilded flummery—these were the dishes of a tiny (if conspicuous) minority. The food of the mass of the people is about simple sustenance, resourcefulness and economy, using every bit of the beast and eking out what we have, navigating a way through the rhythm of the seasons and the hazards of each harvest. I've been mindful of that over the past year as we've seen newspaper headlines about hunger marches and official inquiries into the nation's nutrition. At a time when many know hardship again, perhaps it's no bad thing to be reminded of our ancestral inventiveness with the cheaper cuts of meat, our thrifty ways with pulses, oatmeal and leftovers, our nourishing broths, hotpots and dumplings, and the dozens of different puddings that we seem to be capable of creating with a handful of currants.

Our modern food is full of echoes that we don't always hear. It's shot through with forgotten memories. But look closer, and it tells a story of continuity and disruptions, of families gathered together and of separation. The philosopher gastronome Jean Anthelme Brillat-Savarin wrote, "The discovery of a new dish does more for human happiness than the discovery of a new star," and it's true that there will always be excitement in discovering new flavors, but there's comfort in returning to the familiar. Working on this book, I've remembered and cooked my mother's and my grandmothers' recipes, some of them dishes that I haven't tasted for decades. I've found consolation and reassurance in those flavors and the memories they evoke.

Food makes a connection between people. It's a way of showing love and care, but it's also about caring for ourselves, nourishing ourselves both physically and emotionally. I hope that you will find memories of your own family in this book, that you will be inspired to cook faintly recalled dishes from your own childhood, and that you will find joy in sharing them with the next generation.

STELLA DOUGLAS, December 1932

Chapter Forty-seven

London
April 1933

Stella looked up at the building. It was cold for April and there was a glitter of frost on the curled lips and clawed feet of the gargoyles. She'd come down in her mother's Astrakhan coat and had been glad of its warmth on the train. Underneath, she was wearing the green velvet dress that Michael had bought her, and it was a bit too light for the weather, but it made her feel like a dignified *femme de lettres* and she'd developed a notion that it brought her luck.

Stella felt that she might need luck this morning. Mr. Williamson had sent one of his cryptically concise missives—another summons for a "little chat'—and she had no idea what to expect today. The edits had been light and he'd said all the right things, but hadn't that been the case with *Mrs. Raffald* too? Stella knew he'd have the first reviews and sales figures in today. She looked quizzically up at the gargoyles. Their stone faces told her nothing.

Mr. Williamson was on the telephone when they reached

the door of his office. Miss Salter took Stella's hat and coat—at least she got to take her hat off this time—and Mr. Williamson gestured for her to sit in the chair facing his across the desk. He was frowning at the telephone receiver.

"And what's the prognosis from the lawyers?" he asked his interlocutor. He leaned his head back, put a hand through his hair, and Stella heard him sigh. "It shouldn't have been allowed to get to this stage," he went on. "It's dashed annoying. I really am most displeased that she's put us in this position."

Stella strained to hear the voice on the other end of the telephone line. There was a clipped male tone, but she couldn't pick any words out. Ye gods and little fishes! She'd taken everything controversial out of her text, hadn't she? Had something slipped past her? Something that might have *consequences*? She found herself mentally turning through the pages of her typescript, trying to shine a light on the slip of judgment that could require the urgent intervention of legal minds.

"I'm disappointed," Mr. Williamson continued. "It was substandard work. You can tell them my feelings on the subject."

That fluttering sensation was in Stella's chest again. She thought of birds' wings beating against the bars of cages. She would be upset to disappoint Mr. Williamson, but just how much worse might this be? The word disappointed also brought back a memory of Freddie's voice. She fumbled with the straps of her handbag on her lap and considered sprinting for the door.

"Can I bring you some tea?" Miss Salter whispered.

Stella contemplated asking for a large brandy instead, maybe with a cyanide tablet on the side, but then Mr. Williamson was shaking his head at Miss Salter. So it was one of those days when she wasn't deemed worthy of tea.

"Listen, I'm going to have to ring off now. Miss Douglas is here. Yes, I'll tell her. Please do get on to the lawyers straightaway, though. We need to close this thing down before it escalates."

Escalates! Stella's hands were sweating and the swirls in the Turkey carpet were starting to swim. But then Mr. Williamson had put the receiver down and he was leaning toward her with an unfathomable expression on his face.

"Well," he said.

Well, what? Stella wanted to reply. Damn it, couldn't he get to the point? "Yes?"

"Stella, I'm glad you could come into the office. I thought it best that we have this conversation face-to-face."

It was the first time he'd ever used her Christian name, but . . . what conversation? Just how bad was it? "I couldn't help overhearing. I take it there's a problem?"

"What? *That?* Oh, you didn't think . . . Good Lord, no!" He put his hands up and laughed. He laughed rather heartily. "We've got an actress spilling secrets in her autobiography and writs are popping up like mushrooms after autumn rain."

The held breath finally left Stella's chest. She could have slumped her head on the desk. "I have to admit that I've never been more glad of an indiscreet actress!"

Mr. Williamson showed his dazzling white dentures. It was a beautiful sight. "I know it's a little early in the day, but I say we forgo the tea, what?" He turned to Miss Salter. "We'll have that bottle of champagne now, I think. And have we got any of those special ginger biscuits?"

Michael was waiting for her, as arranged, by the entrance to the Underground station. When Stella saw him she couldn't help but run toward him and put her arms around him.

"So what happened?" he said, pulling back. "Tell me! I've been having kittens for you. I've had several litters over the past hour. Was it good or bad news?"

"The very best—the reviews are universally lovely, sales are better than expected, and he took me out to lunch at Chez Maxime. We had *turbot meunière* and profiteroles and talked about my next book."

"But that's brilliant! That's wonderful! I couldn't be more proud of you."

He lifted her into the air and spun her around. It was rather exciting—no man had ever done that to her before—and as she looked at Michael's face she could see how genuinely delighted he was. He was very handsome when he was being ardent, and his enthusiasm made her news all the sweeter.

"Thrilling though this is, you'd better put me down. I don't want to see my profiteroles again and you mustn't do yourself an injury before you've helped me move house. There will be a lot of heavy boxes to lift."

He laughed. "It's good to know where I stand."

"Absolutely! Let's have these things established from the start."

She'd told Mr. Williamson that she was planning to move back to London shortly and was presently looking for a flat with her young man. He'd begun to offer his congratulations on her engagement, and had blinked his eyes when she'd stopped him. It wasn't so shocking, though, was it? People wouldn't speculate about her reputation and whisper about them "living in sin," would they? No, their friends wouldn't give a hoot, she was sure, and even her father was living in open concubinage these days. (She really didn't want to contemplate what sins he and Mrs. P might be sampling.) Moreover, she and Michael weren't exactly rushing things, were they? Yes, they had only been walking out together since Christmas, but she knew Michael's hat size and glove size, how he liked his toast buttered, his opinions on marmalade and modern poetry, and the words that he murmured in his sleep. One can't know a person better than that, and they had both admitted that they'd been experiencing complicated feelings for one another for over a decade. That was hardly fast work, was it? As they'd talked between Christmas and New Year, Michael had admitted that Cynthia had strode into his life just as he'd reached the conclusion that the woman he cared for most in the world didn't feel the same way about him. They had briefly debated whether they might take wedding vows that incorporated words about outmoded institutions, subjugation and brood mares, but had agreed that they'd rather have a new sofa than a wedding ceremony, for now, and that seemed like an indisputably sensible decision to Stella.

Michael stopped to buy a bunch of violets from the woman on the corner and put his arm around her as they walked on. She glanced at him, at his handsome-as-a-fresco profile, and breathed in the blue-purple scent of the petals. If she were a character in a novel, the sun would probably break through the clouds at this moment, Stella thought, but the pearl-gray sky over the rooftops of Bloomsbury had its own beauty.

"Did you have any luck with the lettings agency?" she asked.

"Actually, yes—possibly," he hesitated. "I've found something interesting. It's rather more than just a flat, it's a bit more complicated than that. How would you feel about taking a leap of faith together?"

Chapter Forty-eight

France
June 1933

Stella saw fields of maize and tobacco from the train window. Shadows slanted away from poplar trees, sheep huddled together in the lee of walls and heat was beginning to shimmer. She sketched the rolling clouds, the lines of vineyards and the fresh new green of the oak trees. She noted the colors of ochre and terra-cotta, the cattle flicking their tails, and the sudden dazzle of light on limestone.

"You've started drawing again?" Michael asked.

"I seem to have fallen back into the habit." Stella closed her notebook and looked up at him. "I've been thinking that I might start painting again when this book is done. I keep feeling an urge to get back to it. It's been itching at my fingers for the past year."

He smiled. "I'd be so happy if you did. You've always undervalued your talent. I've been telling you for years that you ought to have more confidence."

He had said that, hadn't he? "I do listen to you sometimes. It might take a while, but it eventually gets through."

Stella had drawn him as she'd watched him sleeping earlier. It had been warm for the past week; the sun had streaked his hair lighter and there were new freckles on his cheekbones. She'd felt such tenderness as she'd studied and recorded each line and freckle on his face. She saw the flash of turquoise in his up-close eyes now, the color of a jay's wing feather, and wanted to put it down on paper so that she might precisely remember this moment.

"What brought that decision on? Have you been thinking about your mother?" He wound his fingers through hers.

"Yes, that's part of it, I suppose." Stella had told him that she'd found sketches in her mother's notebooks and how that had given a new weight to the words that she'd often repeated about courage. She'd decided that she would frame those sketches and hang them above the desk in her new study—and perhaps that room might be her studio too? Her paints and brushes had been boxed up for almost ten years, but she felt an excitement at the thought of unpacking them there. "I might paint something for the restaurant—if you'd like that?"

"I'd love it."

They'd signed the lease on the new restaurant the day before they'd left London. For the next two months they would be traveling, and while she was researching her book, Michael was working out menus. The restaurant only had a dozen tables, and he was going to keep the menu simple, but this was theirs, their new dream to share. They were aiming for Périgord today, and an *auberge* that served an *omelette aux cèpes*, duck confit and a prune and Armagnac tart. They would taste walnut oil and truffles this week, he'd promised, sweet chestnuts and saffron, and a dozen cheeses the names of which Stella didn't recognize. Life felt to be a great adventure at the moment and there seemed to be so much to discover.

"Did I tell you that Lucien wants to bring a guest for the opening night?"

"Oh, really?" She heard the smile in Michael's voice.

"He asked if he might bring some chap called Philip with him. I got the impression that he's quite keen to show him off. Apparently, they're in amour."

Stella laughed at that, though the word, pronounced in Lucien's accent, brought back an image of Cynthia. She and Michael were both working on suppressing images of Cynthia.

"That's lovely. I'm so pleased for him. Is he finally over you, then?"

"Me?" Michael frowned. "Whatever do you mean by that?"

"You really don't know?" She looked at him and saw that he was in earnest. "Michael, do you need an eye test? Lucien has been in love with you for years. Oh dear, perhaps I shouldn't have told you that? Is it going to be awkward now? But I seriously can't believe you've never noticed!"

"Are you teasing?"

It was endearing how he colored. "You have plenty of other virtues, but you're not the most observant person, are you?"

"Evidently not."

The new restaurant was on the corner of a pretty residential street in Bloomsbury and the flat above it would be their home. Her father had shed a tear as he'd helped them carry the boxes out to the van. He'd also smiled, though, and said "About bloody time." Her inheritance from the farm, and Mrs. P's commitment to feeding her father macaroons, was making this new project possible. He'd told her how much that pleased him and she'd seen it confirmed in his smile.

They'd unloaded the van and carried everything up to the flat, but they'd had tickets for the boat-train that afternoon, and there'd been no time to begin unpacking. Michael had wound the gramophone before they left, though, Josephine Baker's voice crackling out, and they'd danced arm in arm around the boxes. He'd sung "Nothing but blue skies from now on" into her ear. It had taken Stella back to a day when her father had cried in the kitchen at the farm, and then to an image of her parents as a young couple dancing together up on the moor. She'd given Michael a dubious look as he'd strained to hit the high note, but as a cerulean-blue sky stretched ahead now, she felt a new sense of acceptance and of optimism.

"Do you know that the ancient Greeks believed a praying mantis could help lost travelers find their way home? You just have to keep on walking in the direction that it's pointing. I read that last week."

"I'm sorry?" Michael turned to her. "Where did that fact come from? Is it meant to be pertinent?"

Stella shrugged. "Not especially."

"That's the second time this week you've told me a praying-mantis fact. Is this what our life together will be like? Am I going to spend the next fifty years trying to piece together seemingly random fragments of obscure information?"

"Very possibly. Do you think you'll be able to cope with that?"

He kissed her. "For the remainder of this lifetime at least."

Stella leaned back against his shoulder and watched the fields of golden cattle passing by, the distant red rooftops and the wooded hills. A woman on a station platform looked astonishingly like her mother for a second. Stella saw her touch her hat and smile.

HOW THE FRENCH EAT
by Stella Douglas

A tour around France by charcuterie, patis-serie, brasserie and auberge.

From the best-selling author of
HOW THE ENGLISH EAT
(and *The Marvelous Mrs. Raffald*).

To be published by Fleet, Everard
& Frobisher in March 1934.

Acknowledgments

This novel was inspired by reading Florence White's *Good Things in England*, and my greatest debt is to her. Aged sixty-nine at the time of her book's publication in 1932, Florence had had a long working life as a governess, a housemistress, a shopkeeper, a cook-housekeeper, and latterly was probably the first female freelance food journalist. By the 1920s she'd developed a conviction that English food was in peril; traveling through the country she recognized that the ancient rural traditions of home cooking, preserving, foraging and growing locally were dying out. In an effort to reverse this trend, she founded the English Folk Cookery Association in 1928. In her own words, this was "a learned society formed originally for purposes of research, with the firm intention of restoring and maintaining England's former high standard of cookery." After an unpromising start, the press began to take an interest in the EFCA, the menus of its monthly dinners being widely reported, and the society would go on to publish a *Good Food Register*, detailing establishments where authentic cooking could be sampled, and to operate a catering school. "It was delightful to see how everyone was interested when once the veneer of fashion for foreign cookery and

Acknowledgments

modern fads was chipped," Florence wrote. Through news-paper advertisements and a series of radio broadcasts, she also appealed to the public to submit their own recipes to her. She had over a thousand responses, and extracts from these letters are reproduced in *Good Things in England*. They speak not just of cooking traditions, but of wider customs, culture, values and folk memory, and, as such, they provide a unique insight into English domestic lives. On its publication, *Good Things in England* was instantly hailed as "a classic." It has influenced many food writers over the years, remains in print and if you would like to try any of the recipes mentioned in this novel I would urge you to seek out a copy. Florence White was an exceptional woman—a resolute campaigner, a dogged worker, and her championing of simple cookery using locally grown, seasonal ingredients is very much in line with modern culinary trends. She also had a sense of humor and an appreci-ation of the absurd. I hope she wouldn't be offended by Stella.

Books don't make it from manuscript to printed page without allies and assistance. As ever, I am grateful to my agent, Teresa Chris—for saying "yes" to this idea and then for gently reminding me that I was meant to be writing a novel, not a cookery book. I also owe huge thanks to my editors, Clare Hey and Ariana Sinclair, for responding so positively to my first draft, and for investing time and care to guide the text into this final shape. I feel tremendously lucky to be able to work with the brilliant teams at Simon & Schuster and William Morrow. (Please note that Stella's experience of publishing is *entirely* fictional!)

About the Author

Caroline Scott completed a PhD in History and has an interest in the lives of women in the interwar period. Her family tree is full of cooks and she financed the writing of her first novel by working in kitchens.

Caroline is originally from Lancashire, but now lives in southwest France.